Praise for *T*

The Gold Rose is a work of fiction in the historical fiction and interpersonal drama subgenres. It is suitable for the general adult reading audience owing to some very mild language and delicately handled scenes of wartime violence, and was penned by author Jodi Lea Stewart. In this thrilling historical adventure with action, murder mystery, and romance, we follow the tale of the titular organization, which has performed its duties as a covert rescue agency since the early 1940s. Agent Charlotte Hunt-Basse has two targets to save, both of whom were hidden and given extremely unusual childhood experiences. During the civil war of the Communist takeover of China, these two souls will find their skills coming into their own just when it counts.

I love unusual mystery dramas, especially those that feature non-Western history and culture, and author Jodi Lea Stewart pitches this historical piece perfectly to make it inclusive and respectful at the same time as being exotic and exciting. I was absolutely fascinated by the upbringing of both Pinkie and Babe, whose converging and twisting plot lines are individually fascinating. The key to the author's success is in bringing them together in the wider storyline under Charlotte's charge, and this makes for some really thrilling conclusions later in the book which are well worth waiting for. I was on the edge of my seat throughout, and would heartily recommend *The Gold Rose* for fans of atmospheric historical tales and well-penned, well-plotted mysteries that will have you grinning from ear to ear when all is finally revealed.

~ *K.C. Finn for Readers' Favorite*

"Taking readers back in time and around the world, Jodi Lea Stewart's *The Gold Rose* delivers another page-turner full of her signature heart, soul, and adventure. Get ready to be drawn in and carried away as the characters deal with love, loss, and the search for something more. A truly satisfying read."

~ *Cyrus Webb, Media Personality/Top 100 Amazon Reviewer*

"Hold onto your hat... this ride is gonna be fast, furious, and exciting! That's what I'd tell anyone wanting a review of the new Jodi Lea Stewart bestseller, *The Gold Rose.* An international secret organization, war, intrigue, bravery, and passion mixed with history make *The Gold Rose* a book hard to put down. Following the lives, souls, and fortunes of Pinkie, Babe, and Charlotte makes this story a keeper."

~ *Wayne Edgin, Communication Expert, Action-Shooting Competitor, Extremely Avid Reader*

THE GOLD ROSE

The Gold Rose

By
Jodi Lea Stewart

Names, characters, businesses, places, events, and incidents are either the products of the author's imagination or used in a fictitious manner. Any resemblance to actual persons, living or dead, or actual events, is purely coincidental.

Published 2023 by Progressive Rising Phoenix Press, LLC
www.progressiverisingphoenix.com

ISBN: 978-1-958640-31-9

Printed in the U.S.A.
1st Printing

Edited by: Chris Eboch

Cover and Interior Artwork: "Set of Gold, Shining Roses on a Black Background," BigStock Photo ID: 318342841, Copyright: Blackmoon979, Used With Permission.

Chinese Brush-Art Rose and Characters by Bob Schmitt. Used With Permission.

Cover Design by William Speir and Kalpart
Visit: www.kalpart.com

Interior Design by William Speir
Visit: http://www.williamspeir.com

Books By
JODI LEA STEWART
Published By
PROGRESSIVE RISING PHOENIX PRESS

TRIUMPH, a Novel of the Human Spirit

SILKI, THE GIRL OF MANY SCARVES SERIES:
Summer of the Ancient
Canyon of Doom
Valley of Shadows

BLACKBERRY ROAD

THE ACCIDENTAL ROAD

THE GOLD ROSE

Table Of Contents

Our basic needs as humans are quite simple…

we need someone to care about

what we do,

what we think,

what we say, and

where we are.

To the few and the wonderfully brave

who cared, especially my dearest Mark…

Thank you.

One of the most thrilling aspects of life is not knowing when it will end. It's a box of mazes, an electrifying game of chance—

frightening and beguiling at the same time.

When will come the final breath,

the coup de grâce?

Providence alone has the answer.

Hence, venture not to hinder me before that appointed time.

- ROSE tenet number three

PROLOGUE

Shadowy impressions are all I have of my two years of life before my new mama found me on a dirt road in Texas. Whisked away in a pickup truck bound for Mexico, I settled into my life only to be taken to Argentina by an aging *Romni* hoping to capitalize on my fair looks to feed her coffers. I was tossed about as flotsam in the sea before making it back to America. Let me ask… what is survival of every calamity worth when you are finally *saved*, but your savior turns out to be worse than all the others? All that I went through before I was ten years old was nothing compared to what came next — *Pinkie*

Life was danger and death during the Japanese invasion and ensuing civil war in China. Though my parents left me when I was a young child to go into hiding in 1942, my nature compelled me to see everything through rose-colored glasses. Only after I witnessed firsthand the tragic consequences of hatred and power while hiding behind a *píngfēng* screen did my attitude change. The brutality of life pushed me into silence, and later, into seeking remedy from people weak in mind or character. The long hours of gut-wrenching, secret practice of the art of *Yǒng Chūn* became my life. Now… come and get me. I'll be waiting — *Babe*

I limped back to the street shaking with cold and anger. Thank God, and I truly mean that, I saw a blurry neon sign on a building not too far in the distance. If I hadn't been so livid about what transpired in that alley, I might have worried about making my way down a dark, snowy street in a deserted part of town. My exposed toes were deadly cold the whole time, but let me say, my soul was charged and ready for a fight. You just don't cross me like that. Not anymore — *Charlotte*

1
Midnight at the Bus Station

Bangor, Maine
1958

Charlotte

I didn't drown in the South China Sea holding Babe's rooster in the air, but nearly. A year later, Pinkie and I scarcely escaped cutthroat thugs chasing us down a slum street in Los Angeles. It's all part of my job. It's not unusual for me to be praised, cursed, hugged, stomped, chased, or flung through the air in the course of fulfilling my professional duties. Dancing on tables, bribing hotel personnel, flirting with criminals, and playing daredevil with death more times than I care to admit are *fait partie de la routine.*

Having engaged in the epicenter of every human exertion and sentiment for more than a decade, why, then, do I presently find myself so distraught from simply being pushed from an idling car and having a shoe flung in my face?

I'm still piecing it together, but I'm quite sure it revolves around my rarely-given trust being so callously mishandled. Having a presumed friend and colleague turn on me as savagely as a rabid dog earlier this evening seems to have triggered a certain psychological shockwave most likely linked to my, let me say… less-than-perfect childhood. Little more than half an hour ago, I sat splattered on my derriere in a cold alleyway, broadsided by a man I have been on assignment with, one with whom I spent a wonderful three hours this very night at a company *fête* at the Bangor House reception hall.

I'm surprised to see my hands shaking. I automatically revert to ROSE *Recovery number two*—the protocol we are trained to follow after any episode evoking high emotion.

Deep, slow breaths. Concentrate on your surroundings. Remember your purpose.

I do a few quick inhalations and exhalations, then take long, slow breaths as I sit expressionless on a plastic chair placed solitarily against the wall. My nylon-stockinged feet are resting on top of what's left of my open-toe high heels. Judging from the stinging in my toes, I believe they were close to frostbite by the time I entered this small rustic bus station on the ground floor of a downtown Bangor building.

Casing the room slowly, I allow all five senses to take over. A small huddle of hollow-eyed street people sitting on the floor is excitedly comparing their goods from a day in the streets. My quick perusal shows necks of whisky bottles jutting from tattered cloth bags, half-eaten foods wrapped in crinkled foil—most likely rummaged from restaurant trashcans—and yards of dirty yarn masquerading as skull caps and scarves. How those poor souls avoid freezing to death in this cold-winter city, I do not pretend to know.

A station security guard emerges from a door and flushes them outside. He imperiously holds the door open as the mismatched crew marches outside like naughty children. When the last one is through the door, he steps partially outside and peers into the night sky. Tumbling ice crystals shine as nocturnal jewels in the light escaping from the doorway—cotton-wrapped bullets pelting the snow and forming a crust of ice over the streets and sidewalks.

The guard shakes his head and beckons the group back inside, lecturing them with extended finger to stay put and not bother, that is, beg from, anyone in the station. The relief on their blotchy, weathered faces matches his mock austerity.

Flattened garland scotch taped across the ticket windows and a hand-painted *X-mas Greetings!* on the outside doors show a brave attempt to bring holiday spirit into the mostly deserted station. The cream-colored walls sport a long metal cutout of a loping greyhound. Crinkled posters thumbtacked to the walls portray buses traveling on highways passing through redwood forests and beside sparkly seashores.

I'm calming down. I settle back a few more inches in the chair and continue perusing the room. A young couple sits tight-lipped and straight on the end of a Naugahyde sofa on the opposite side of the room. She is dressed simply in saddle shoes with thick knee-high stockings, a plain shift dress too thin for winter, and a sweater stretched crooked by a hundred washings. Her coat is draped over the back of the bench. A modestly wrapped Christmas box sits on her lap. Judging from her expression and straight neck, along with the man's restless shuffling and terse glances in her direction, it's easy to see they're in the middle of a quarrel.

A fleshy man in a cheap wrinkled suit and loosened tie, who only minutes ago exuded bored resignation and nervous hand clasping, pulls out a white handkerchief and wipes it across his forehead. He isn't all right; anyone can see that. Everything about him, especially his tattered briefcase and out-of-season Panama hat, screams *weary salesman.* In my peripheral vision, I covertly watch him fumble with the folded newspaper on the bench beside him. He works at it until part of a page rips off, uses it to vigorously fan his face. He exudes a loud sigh, more like a grunt, and, between his spread legs, drops his face toward the tiled floor. His hat falls off, and he leaves it there.

Lord to goodness, is he about to have a heart attack?

Sensing my stare, he raises his head and looks at me. In his eyes is a look of surrender. The lines on his face bear a striking resemblance to a Bristol-paper charcoal etching of an old man I saw in the Louvre Museum in Paris a few years ago. What lot in life has this man traveling by bus in such obvious disappointment, as well as in scruffy shoes? Perhaps he was hired to sell French copper cookware to the shantytown wives? Frustration that deep might prompt the ruination of anyone.

It hits me with a peculiar, half-jaunty air that I, CeeCee Jones, fit in well with this midnight-at-the-bus-station crowd with my disheveled hair and blood-caked lower lip. I'm a mess right now, and I find that rather memorable. At least it covers up the expensiveness of my clothes—clothes I wore to our celebration tonight. I re-cinch my street-length camel coat, dirty spots and all, and dab my raw lip with a handkerchief. No fresh blood.

My feet are swelling. Shoving my toes back into the narrow strip of see-through plastic across the toe box isn't possible now. That means I'll have to walk across the room to the ticket counter in bare-footed hosiery with additional runs humming up and down my legs with every step. On the side of my left foot, I notice an unattractive hole. A hot flush invades my cheeks.

Honestly, can I be more of a dichotomy?

I'll dive into a waterway with alligators if I have to, though I did that only once. I'll tenderly coerce a ship captain with promises I'll never keep or pretend to be a dizzy chorus girl, but walking barefoot in public with disgraceful hosiery insults my Southern roots and pushes me to the edge of vulnerability—an emotion I refuse to entertain.

You have no choice.

I sigh abjectly and head toward the ticket counter. I feel the salesman's crimson-rimmed eyes follow me as I pass. I admit one of my objectives is putting distance between us before he collapses. I simply cannot get involved right now. Haven't I been through enough tonight? Still, I feel the old twinges of guilt.

Guilt was my constant companion for most of my younger life, and one of the strongest catalysts to seeking the life I now live. Frankly, I don't regret my history with it. It has proven to be a good and gracious commodity… gracious for me, and good for the ones I *replant,* as Harry Wáng loves to label our processes. As a matter of fact, my rushing to answer the guilt-laden *siren of distress* only certain people allow themselves to hear is how I met my two favorite *assignments,* Pinkie and Babe.

2
Racing to the Border

San Antonio, Texas
1941

The day's business routine and erratic weather patterns held no hint that evening would find Clint Cullen Sutton barreling down the highway with Cruz and Angelina. Driving southward out of the city, Clint sits rod-straight with a death grip on the steering wheel. Outside, the sky presents an enticing sunset kaleidoscope of coral, gold, and blue, along with a wedge of angry gray in the southwest, but Clint sees only the road ahead of his wheels. It's taking all his strength to keep his inner man at bay. If he were to open the floodgate, he, too, might commit murder.

Without anyone's permission, San Antonio's weather on this mid-November day started out cool and refreshing with no breeze. Clint, president and heir apparent of the Canyon Coyote Oil Company, cruised through the day completing menial tasks and extinguishing brushfires with his usual perturbed mindset. With his father, owner and CEO of the company, intentionally and perpetually missing-in-action, Clint expects and deals with the daily clutter of his position. It brings him no joy.

Temperatures rose to the mid-seventies by early afternoon. Winds charged in from the south bringing the thermometer to a high of eighty-five degrees with scattered showers and a touch of humidity by late afternoon, high temperature for south Texas this late in the year. Weather patterns, usually of great interest to Clint, matter not a smidgen right now. What matters is sitting next to him in the seat of his pickup.

"I'll come get y'all when this blows over," he says. Stay put in Laredo, on the other side, of course, in Nuevo Laredo, and I'll head back your way soon as this mess is cleared up. Lay low, 'cause you never know how friendly those border federales are with the guys right across the line. Deputies, I'm talking about. I wouldn't put it past that woman to offer a ridiculously high bounty for turning you in. Why not? Her future out of the gas chamber demands it."

"But you're an eyewitness to what really happened, aren't you, Clint?" Cruz asks.

"You bet, and it's my word against hers. They'll have all of Texas to tangle with if they believe that little rattlesnake over a Sutton." He sighs. "Look, I just want y'all safe so I can square this up without worrying about you."

Angelina, sitting between Clint and Cruz, leans against Clint's arm and kisses the gold cross hanging from the chain of her necklace. Her sniff garners Clint's full attention. Wet eyes meeting his in the darkening cab make him desire slamming on the brakes, taking her in his arms, and never letting her go. The reality of his current fate causes a muscle to pulsate under his left eye.

The truth is, he's in love with Angelina and has been since the three of them—she, her brother Cruz, and he, now all clandestinely racing to the Mexican border—were playmates in the family's other home in Midland, Texas—*Casa de Rosas.* Those were the good days when life still made sense.

The pickup swings abruptly into the left lane as if pushed by an unseen hand. Clint overreacts, whips the wheel to the right, hits the unpaved shoulder. Dirt showers the front of the pickup. He brakes and turns the wheel to the left. The truck skids back onto the paved road, wobbles, and finally rights itself.

"Dios mío, Clint! *Qué pasó?"* Cruz says.

"Wind." He rolls down the window. Gusts blow his Stetson onto the dashboard. Angelina retrieves it and holds it in her lap. He rolls up the window with one hand, fights to keep the vehicle on the road with the other. "Dang," he mumbles. "Feels like forty to fifty miles an hour out there." Two large tumbleweeds blow across the highway. Angelina gasps as Clint plows through them. He grins. "Hey, you know me and my pickup are meaner than a wad of weeds, don't you?" Her hand circles his arm. Lord, how he wants to protect her, hold her, make her his woman.

"Will this high wind cause a tornado this late in the year?" she asks.

"Well, let's just say it's happened before, Lina. We sure don't want to tangle with one of those things, do we? Hail, either. I don't want my new truck all dented up, that's for sure. I saw some green in the sky this afternoon, so who knows if it'll blow over or what." He shakes his head. "Texas weather."

Angelina bends toward the floorboard to check the cords on the cloth bundles she furiously packed for herself and her brother with Clint hurrying them along with terrifying urgency. They rushed out of *Casa de las Magnolias,* Clint's family home in San Antonio, and into his pickup without any explanations. Clint filled them in as soon as they headed down the highway. Angelina gasped when she heard they were supposed to be guilty of murder. Cruz was deadly quiet as he listened.

They hadn't lived anywhere other than in the care of Clint's family since they were babies, twin toddlers who captured Mrs. Sutton's heart from the first day of their parents' employment. She insisted they call her *Tia* Maybelle, and she saw to it they lacked for nothing, including education, music, and horses.

Angelina sighs. "You know you are taking us to a foreign country, don't you, Clint? Cruz and I… we do not belong in Mexico. Who is our family? Only you. What happened to *Mama y Papi* when they went there to visit their own parents when Cruz and me were young? They never came back. Maybe that will happen to us, too."

"Aw, Lina, Nuevo Laredo's different. Lots of folks go there all the time from New Orleans, Texas, back East, all over. It's not so foreign feeling like some of the places down there. I'll get this stuff straightened out and be right back to get you. I want to talk to Daddy as soon as possible and tell him what happened before that *loca gringa* fills his ears with a bunch of malarky. Lord knows she's got plenty of Canyon Coyote Oil money to peddle her lies locally."

"But I do not know what to do in this different place. I only want to take care of *Casa de las Magnolias* and… and you, Clint."

The knife twisting in his chest is painful. It doesn't have to be light inside the pickup cab for Clint to see Angelina's tears. He feels them in his heart.

3
A Bump in the Road

Backroads of South Texas
1941

Pinkie

Clint exits the paved highway and turns the pickup onto a narrow dirt road with weeds cluttering the middle stretch. His tires rolling over the first set of ruts causes all three passengers to bounce around the cab. "The law might be looking for us by now," he says by way of explanation. "Backroads are safer."

"Why did you go and buy this kind of truck, Clint? No one else has a truck with, uh… the paint, what did you call it?" Angelina says.

"Chevrolet calls it ruby-maroon. Hey, now, you went crazy for it when I first drove up in front of the house. You jumped in for a ride before I could whistle, remember?"

"*Sí,* I did, but we weren't outlaws running from sheriffs like now."

"We aren't outlaws. Stop worrying, hon. We'll be okay. I know all the shortcuts and backroads to get us to the border."

"Those clouds open up, we might get stuck in this soft dirt, my brother," Cruz says.

"Got a few timbers in the back for the tires if we need them."

"You got a jug of water for the radiator?"

"Always."

Only the sound of the pickup navigating the rough road fills the pickup as the occupants drop into their own thoughts. Clint periodically rolls down his window checking the velocity of the wind. They pass barbed-wire fences and reflected cow and wild-animal eyes staring like lit-up marbles from the darkness. Live oak trees and weedy shrubs two-step with the wind on either side of the road.

"Stop!" Angelina and Cruz yell in unison.

Clint sees the little bundle inside the wheel rut the same time they do. He brakes hard, sending the truck's backend into a shimmy.

"*Dios, ayúdanos!*" Angelina screams.

Clint turns the wheel in a hard left, clutch and brake pedals to the floor, stops with the right front tire even with the bump in the road. The wood in the backend thumps into the bulkhead. Clint groans as his chest bangs against the steering wheel. Cruz's right forearm slams into the edge of the dashboard; his left arm pins his sister to the seat. A panting silence fills the cab.

"Let me out!" Angelina cries. Cruz fumbles for the door handle as Angelina scrambles across his lap.

"Hold on, *hermana loca*… aghhh!" His torso falls sideways out of the cab. Angelina climbs over him, is waylaid by the heavy wind when she tries to stand. Holding onto the truck, she squats and duck-walks to a small child whose rump is in the air, face buried on tiny arms. Clint backs up and repositions his headlights to light up the area. Angelina kneels in the road beside a little girl in diapers, not a baby—maybe two years old? She touches the matted blond curls. The toddler is wearing a soiled white summer dress, drooping diaper, and scuffed high-top white shoes with socks slightly showing above the rims. She raises her head, looks at Angelina, drops her head back onto her arms. Angelina motions for help. Both men hurry to her side.

"A baby girl?" Clint yells, trying to be heard above the wind. Angelina nods and scoops her into her arms. Cruz comes from behind and lifts them to a standing position. He keeps his arm around his sister as they fight wind going to the passenger side with Clint following close behind. They place the girl on the seat and crowd in close to observe her. "Get that flashlight out of the glovebox, Cruz," Clint says. Cruz finds it, shines it on the child.

"Bebé, can you talk?" Angelina asks softly. "Where is your mama, honey?" The girl's clear blue eyes are open, blinking, but she stares past them. "So many scratches," Angelina says, rubbing her hand over the girl's legs and arms.

"Poor little outfit is scared out of her wits. I'm mighty glad something else didn't find her out here before we did, if you know what I mean. What the hell you suppose happened?"

"Clint, no cussing in front of the baby," Angelina says.

"How did a little *niña* like this wander off alone?" Cruz says. "Lina, put her on your lap. Let's go see what's going on. Has to be a search party out here somewhere. We'll just have to take our chances with the law."

"No one out here knows us. We'll return her and slip off slick as a whistle," Clint says.

Angelina nods, presses her cheek against the little girl's face. "Poor baby," she whispers. "I will save you." The girl latches onto Angelina's neck and buries her face in her long hair.

"Mama," she whimpers in a barely perceptible voice as if she has learned to exist unobtrusively.

'Shh, shh, shh, *mi pequeña adoración.* I won't leave you." Angelina settles into the middle of the seat holding the child tightly against her. Clint and Cruz exchange glances. Angelina is already saying *my?* The truth is, Angelina has mothered everything from limping lizards to broken-winged birds ever since she was knee-high to a cicada. The trouble is, she never wants to let them go once she *heals* them.

Around a bend, they see an old pickup with the driver's front wheel suspended over the bar ditch on the side of the road. Clint rolls to a stop. "Well, here's our answer. An accident. Probably some unconscious folks here. This little thing got spooked and took off. Hey, you checking out that old relic of a truck, Cruz?"

"Sí, one of those Ford Model-A pickups. Look at the wood rails in the back, Clint. Maybe we should put some on your truck."

"Nah, I'm a rancher, not a farmer. Sure a beat-up thing, isn't it? I haven't seen one of those jobbers around in a long time. Look how the spare tire hangs there on the driver's side behind the front fender. You can barely see it from this angle."

"Yeah, you know, I saw one like that when—

¡Ay, caramba! Are you guys crazy?" Angelina snaps. "Stop talking about stupid old trucks. Look…" she says, pointing, "… someone in a cowboy hat is leaning over the steering wheel. He must be hurt."

"Still got that flashlight handy, Cruz?" Clint asks.

"Yep."

Clint cuts the engine. The men exit rapidly from either side. A sudden onset of uneasiness leans Clint back inside the cab. "Stay put, hon," he says.

They move awkwardly toward the rusty Ford fighting against winds that have slowed but not stopped. Cruz shines the light on the truck and waves a hand in the air as a greeting. He moves the beam to the wheel balancing over the gap of the ditch, spies a shoulder protruding in the air. "Clint, someone's in the bar ditch!"

They hurry to crouch beside a woman lying on her side. "Ma'am? Miss, uh, are you awake? Can you hear me?" Clint asks. He raises the woman's limp hand, lets it fall, touches her face. He draws back. "Um… feel her neck, buddy."

Cruz touches her neck, then cradles her face with his hand. Both men recognize the early stages of rigor mortis. "Good God, she's dead," Cruz mutters, arching backward and crossing himself.

"Yeah. I'd say a few hours now. Bring that light a little closer. Look at the bruises and cuts all over her face and arms. Good lord, man, what kind of a one-truck wreck does this kind of damage? Is the front window busted out on the pickup?"

Cruz glances over his shoulder at the vehicle. "No."

They stand, turn simultaneously, weaving a little in the wind, which, miraculously, has settled into a more rational speed. The end of a pistol is pointed at them through the open window. Four hands raise in the air. Clint takes a forward step.

"Don't come any closer." The man has a slight slur, but his tone is unmistakable.

"Hey, you got it all wrong, mister. We're here to help. Your, uh, this lady needs a doctor. How's about we get y'all to the next town—"

"Shut up!"

"Senor, let us assist you. You had a bad wreck, and this woman in the ditch needs, uh… she needs help. We found your little girl down the road. She's awful scared." Cruz says, nodding toward Clint's pickup.

Keeping his eyes and pistol on them, the man lifts a liquor bottle, takes a long swig, sets the bottle back in the floorboard. He wipes his mouth on his sleeve.

Clint says, "Mister, that little girl we found, she's real tore up—"

"Keep her. Hell don't need no little girls."

He aims the gun at his temple and shoots.

4
I Will Call Her Pinkie

Backroads of South Texas
1941

Slowly, almost reverently, the pickup rolls past the bloody scene of death. Angelina shakes with suppressed sobs, eventually quieting into occasional sniffs. The rutted country road takes them closer to the Mexican border, but their minds remain locked on the tragedy behind them. The storm turns east, bypassing them. Clint breaks the uneasy silence. "Man, I sure didn't expect anything like that. By the looks of it, I'm thinkin' that *hombre* might have beat that woman near to death before his truck ran off the road. Never saw so many bruises and cuts on a body. Bless her heart! Wonder how she wound up in the ditch?"

"Maybe trying to get away?" Cruz says.

Clint groans. "Bad business."

"Do we dare go to the law?"

"I don't think so, Cruz. Might cause too many problems."

"And questions."

"We can't afford to get in the middle of a mess like that. Dammmn… that man just out and out wiped the two of them off the face of the earth. You suppose they're this little girl's parents? Kind of have to be, right?"

"That woman in the ditch had the blond hair like *la niña,*" Cruz says.

"I saw that. A beautiful woman at one time. Yessir, probably this one's mama."

"That man… in the truck, he-he made this little girl an o-r-p-h-a-n," Angelina says in a shaky voice, spelling the last word.

"I don't think she knows that word yet," Clint whispers.

Angelina presses the toddler tighter into her chest. "Maybe not, but she must never know this terrible thing that happened tonight. Never."

"She's asleep, Lina," Cruz says, tilting his head to stare into the small face resting on Angelina's shoulder.

"I will make her forget all her troubles. She will laugh and be happy. Wait and see."

Both men stare at her. Cruz says, "Oh no, no, no, Lina, we're not keeping her. We don't know what's ahead for us, and a *bebé* in diapers is, well, no, we can't."

"Honey, he's right. Be sensible, now. That's a little baby you're fixing to take across the border. What will you tell folks? Besides, she's bound to have some grandparents or other kin who'll be worried sick. Let's figure out a way to get her in the authorities' hands without us getting caught up in it."

"Authorities? That means questions. Sheriffs. What if they blame us for killing her parents? That makes three people they will say we murdered. We're all she has. I feel it in my heart. What made us be driving on this old road tonight?"

The men are silent.

"A miracle, that's what. She needed us, and we came to her. Besides, *Dios me escuchó.*"

Cruz angles his body to glare at his sister. "Oh, I see. God heard you. Heard you what… going crazy?" Cruz says.

"Shh, Cruz, you'll wake her. I have been praying since we left home. Don't you understand we are losing everything? We lost our parents. Only *Dios* knows what happened to them. We lost *Tia* Maybelle to the grave, *Senor* Sutton to his broken heart, and now our own Clint. He is our only family, and we may never see him again. *Dios me escuchó!*" She sobs aloud, then breaks into a non-stop stream of Spanish.

Both men speak the language, but this is something else, broken sentences passionately delivered. They have learned over the years it is best to leave her alone at such times. It's hardest on Clint, who wants desperately to refute her dire predictions for the future.

Switching to English, she says, "I will keep her, Clint. You must please pretend to be my husband, and this is our baby. Her light eyes and hair are from you. It's what we can say if anyone gets nosy."

Cruz leans forward, head in hands. *"Ella es terca coma una mula!"*

"Maybe. At least I'm not *el tonto."*

"I'm stupid? You're the one who never listens to reason, Lina."

"And you—"

"Hey, how's about taking it down a notch or two?" Clint says. "Now's not the time for one of y'all's knock-down-drag-out squabbles. Angelina, listen, there's a little town with a filling station coming up in a few miles. They have a public telephone booth outside. I know folks all over south Texas who'd be happy to give us a hand—you know, find out if this baby girl has more family back there. They'd treat her like she was their own. That's reasonable, isn't it?"

"No, she doesn't have nobody. I swear it, Clint, It's true in my heart."

"It's true in her heart, Clint. *Ai-yi-yi,"* Cruz mumbles, shaking his head.

"I will clean her up at that filling station," Angelina says.

"How?" Cruz asks.

"Rip up one of my blouses. I don't mind."

"Lina, you're about to make things about a hundred times harder than they have to be. You know that, right?"

"Yes, Clint." She starts to hum, stops, says, "I will name her Daniella... Daniella Izabella Francisca Angelina Serrano after our grandmother, our mama, and me, but I will call her *Pinkie.* Did you see? She's so creamy-pink with yellow hair, see-through crystal eyes like blue jewels. Just like a doll in a fancy store."

Clint sighs noisily. "I will allow this on one condition, Angelina, and I mean it. You can't keep her forever. As soon as I get the truth out there about tonight and we head back home, we're searching for her family. This isn't for keeps. You understand?"

"Yes, Clint."

"I'm dead serious. It isn't right any other way."

"Don't worry, *mi cariño.* I understand."

Clint would gladly give this woman the moon on a gilded platter, but a baby they found in the road? Doesn't she know this isn't the same as keeping a horned toad in a box after she finds it with a leg missing? The only part he likes is Angelina wanting him to pretend to be her husband, even if it is a ruse. One day, it won't be.

He lets out a long draw of air and wonders how in the Sam Hill he wound up seeing three dead people in the same day.

5
Nothing is Certain

Galveston, Texas
Yúnnán Shěng, China
1937

Babe

Two historic events that affect Bernadette Beatrice Wayne's life for many years happen in July 1937. On her second birthday, she is rescued by a good Samaritan stranger from a near drowning when she precociously breaks free from her mother's grip and runs straight into Galveston Bay. On that same date, the Japanese Imperial Army exchanges shots with Chinese troops at the Marco Polo Bridge in Bēipíng, leading to full-scale warfare and the invasion of China's mainland by Japan.

When Mrs. Olivia Alma Wayne delivered all six pounds, seven ounces, of her baby girl in her hometown of Galveston in 1935 while on pregnancy leave from her work with the China Inland Mission, CIM, she promptly nicknamed her daughter "Baby Beatrice." After the near-drowning incident, her mother, ever edgy concerning her unusually active toddler, calls her simply "Babe" to shorten the time it takes to shout her name and save her from the brink of peril… or so Olivia explains to anyone asking.

Babe is the second, and last, child born to Edgar and Olivia Wayne. Leaving China during the final trimester of her pregnancy,

Olivia, as well as her five-year-old son, have not seen Mr. Wayne in more than two years. With CIM funds dwindling, Olivia takes a job as a telephone operator to supplement her monies. She is ironclad-set on returning with both children regardless of the tumultuous war rumors filtering back to her, or her husband's subtle hints for her to stay in Texas.

Her Texas family calls Olivia irrational for returning to Asia with two small children during dangerous times, but she calmly answers she is *called by God to return to her husband and to bring the Truth to the neediest of the Chinese, for God did not call her for only the good times, but for all times.*

And, that was that.

Seven months later, Olivia, true to her personal commitment, returns to China via subterfuge with Babe and Eddie in hand to rejoin her husband. Edgar in no regard expected Olivia. He repeatedly instructed her in veiled hints to stay where she was, though he was not specific in letters that could be, and usually were, intercepted.

When she arrives on foot with several peasants assisting with the children and her luggage, he is angry. He lightly hugs her, then turns aside to look for the first time into the dark, lively eyes of his young daughter. Her eyes, hair, and skin tone are so like his late mother's, it gives him a start.

He tosses Eddie into the air three times amid howls of laughter from the boy. Afterward, he sends the children off with their housekeeper-nanny, Méi-Mèi, to have a private talk with Olivia in the humble bedroom of his quarters. His face clouds up as soon as they are alone. "Olivia, I am not happy… not happy at all with this rash decision. You may be a rock in the Kingdom of God, but you are a foolish woman on this earth."

Stung by her husband's rebuke, she replies, "But I can be helpful in assisting refugees, Edgar, and whatever else is needed. I am called to serve. I have my purpose from Above as you have yours."

"That I do not disagree with, but you deliberately ignored my pleas. You are the only person I know of who would bribe passage *into*, instead of *out of*, a country in the midst of a terrible invasion. I am shocked, to say the least."

"But we are safe here, aren't we? The supervisors must think so."

"The Japanese have left the Westerners alone so far, but what about tomorrow, and the next day, and—"

"Therefore, do not be anxious about tomorrow. Sufficient for the day is its own trouble," Olivia quotes.

Edgar frowns at her. "Do not throw Matthew 6:34 at me when you purposely ignored Ephesians 5:22. You certainly did not submit to my wishes and keep yourself and the children out of harm's way, Olivia."

Olivia sits down on the bed and turns a tearful face to her husband. "We have been apart for more than two years. I missed you so terribly, Edgar, don't you know that? I felt I could not continue in the midst of such loneliness. You know I have never been strong without you. And-and my family… so many doubters and naysayers."

Her tears bring her husband to her side. He lifts her by her hands off the bed and wraps his arms around her. "And I missed you, darling. I understand your commitment to this mission. I really do, but the children—"

"Are they not safe here? I thought—"

"Truthfully, I'm wholly uneasy about it. Many of our colleagues have already sent their children away to the CIM school for foreign missionary children in Chefoo in Shāndōng for safekeeping. Such a tedious journey it is!"

Olivia gasps. "They did?"

"Yes, dear."

"You told me no such news in your letters."

"We have been warned that our letters are being opened and read. It's dangerous to write anything but the lightest patter in them. There are many things I left out of those letters and my telephone calls."

"I-I'm sorry, Edgar. I had no idea things had changed this drastically. You're right. I am a foolish woman."

He sighs. "We'll do the best we can, dear, but I think we should send Eddie off to that school in Chefoo. It's a rough journey, but it may be necessary."

"But he is still five."

"He begins first grade next year. That's the primary age to attend."

"What about Babe?"

"We shall see. Nothing is certain at this time."

6
Foolish Man!

Bangor, Maine
1958

Charlotte

Where is that ticket clerk? I waltzed shoeless across the room with the grace of a knock-kneed giraffe, and he's nowhere in sight. There's no denying I am still a Texas girl when it comes to public protocol.

I hadn't planned for my forthcoming journey to take place on a bus, but it's quite appropriate, now that I think about it. Imagine me returning to my home town of Fort Worth, Texas, in a public bus! I was never allowed to ride one in all my eighteen years at home. The irony of it makes me laugh. I've come so very far to end up this low, and I'm absurdly proud of it.

Of course, the situation placing me in this bus station in the middle of the night certainly wasn't enjoyable. The low moral fiber of some people in this world—Dolion, for example—never fails to astound me. Truly, I hope that never changes. If ever I stop being shocked, I'm afraid it will mean I have lost my faith in humanity.

What I resent terribly, even though to do so now is purely retrospective nonsense, is that Dolion sliced through the heel strap of one of my high heels before throwing it in my face. Obviously, that was an extra jab at me for what I had revealed to him of my past. I assume it helped assuage his male ego to insult me in a personal way.

Why the extra animosity? My fault. I foolishly revealed my real family name a little while before his attack. I can count on a few fingers how many times I've done that in the last ten years, which only demonstrates how safe I felt in the car with a man I trusted. Worse than revealing my full name, I had earlier shared some of the dark side of my childhood with him. I never do that, and it's disturbing how he wielded it as a weapon against me as soon as he didn't get his way.

Before our altercation, Dolion and I spent the evening in an elaborately decorated reception hall with our associates. Our agency is publicly known as *ROSE International,* but privately, of course, it is known by its real name, *The Gold Rose*—a grand name, but one we rarely say aloud. We insiders simply refer to it as *ROSE*, which is not an acronym, but a quick reference tag only.

Our gala was a dress-up affair toasting our recent successes. Understandably, we always have many agents who cannot attend the yearly extravaganza due to assignments or, regrettably, injuries. This year, at least a hundred and twenty-five of us with American roots were there. Added to that were more than fifty of our foreign affiliates. All three founders attended this time, which created an extra celebratory mood as we exchanged hair-raising stories, dined like royalty, and compared projected agendas to see who might be paired together for assignments in the future and who might attend the next quarterly meeting in Nassau this coming April.

As usual, our annual festivity was first-class in every detail. It was held at the Bangor Hotel on the corner of Main and Union Streets in downtown Bangor, Maine, which some locals call the Queen City. It was thrilling to learn some of the other Bangor Hotel guests of the past included Teddy Roosevelt, Ulysses S. Grant, Bette Davis, Duke Ellington, Gene Autry, John Phillip Sousa, and many others.

Sid Caesar, a comedian I had the privilege of seeing one other time, entertained us during the second phase of our cocktail hour and was brought back to make us laugh during our dessert. The most humorous part was his thinking we are a group of horticulturists involved in solving world hunger problems, and he geared many of his jokes to that end. That's what we deem a success due to our completely underground nature, and it's always a wonderful private joke among us.

The singer of a beautiful recording, *Hawaiian Wedding Song,* happened to be staying in the hotel. When he heard our boisterous revelry in the reception hall, he asked if he could sing a song with our orchestra, which is, naturally, privately screened. One song became four songs, and they lulled me into such a tranquil mood, it made the later experience with Dolion that much more appalling.

Several men, including Harry Wáng, the supreme *ROSE* founder and my personal mentor, offered to drive me to the train depot after the evening concluded. I chose Dolion. Who wouldn't have? Smart and engaging, he was a delightful table companion all evening. I looked forward to prolonging our time together on the drive to the depot. Of course, he has been with *ROSE* a rather short time versus my decade, but that made no difference to me at the time.

Our lively banter and good-natured laughter continued in his car. My two glasses of port wine with the crème brûlée had filled me with a pleasant giddiness as we ventured through the snowy city in cheerful holiday moods. Driving along streets usually avoided at night—which I asked him about, and he waved my question aside—he quite suddenly pulled into an alleyway. It was partially lit by the garishly yellow and green lights of a closed greasy spoon facing the street. He cut the engine and turned toward me.

"What is it, car trouble?"

He chuckled. "No, this is man trouble. Come here, baby. I need some of you."

Can you believe I laughed? He had been so amusing all evening, I thought this was more of his playfulness. If he had merely wanted a kiss or two, I would gladly have acquiesced, had even thought about it during our third dinner course when he took me on a breathtaking *hike* through Athens, the heart of the ancient world, to "see" the Acropolis as he saw it every time he was there.

Dolion, by the way, is very attractive with gray eyes that carry a hint of blue, classical features, a wavy mop of dark-brown hair… all accompanied by a charming Greek accent. Literally, he almost had me swooning, a rare occurrence, which made his lusty, sophomoric lunge at me in the car all the more shocking. What really angered me was that he didn't care if I was or wasn't open to his overt advances. My polite protests and gentle reprimands didn't faze him.

As I became more ardent in my protests, a strange gleam entered his eyes. It still gives me a shiver, and I can only explain it like this… picture a repressed jealousy taking over a beautiful set of eyes and turning them coldly sarcastic. I think part of the reason was because of who I really am—that is, Charlotte Catherine Hunt-Basse, though all but a very few know me by my alias CeeCee Jones.

From that look in his eyes and the ensuing insults, it became obvious Dolion was turning my rejection of intimacy into an issue of class snobbery. He accused me of refusing him on the grounds that I thought I was better than he with my wealthy background compared to his deprived one. It wasn't true, not at all, and I denied it, but it soon became apparent I was going to have to physically defend myself.

By implementing the *xiǎo niàn tóu* and *biāo zhǐ* martial-arts moves Babe taught me, I blocked his attempts to unzip my dress. Anger and surprise glittered in his eyes as he stared at me afterward. A thought in the back of my mind that perhaps he had imbibed far more alcohol than I realized made me try to reason with him one more time. I smiled and acted as if his behavior had been a mistake, a joke we could laugh off. His reaction was to jump on me like a crazed schoolboy, brutally crushing my mouth with his and tearing at my clothes. When I screamed at him to stop, he slapped me.

Foolish man! I had no choice but to show him who was in control, and it certainly wasn't him. I have too much of Pinkie and Babe's verve in my craw nowadays to put up with brutality of any kind. I inwardly sighed and met the challenge. After a few of Babe's *Yǒng Chūn* chain punches, and by using the principle she taught me of relaxed force versus strength, Dolion was soon sporting that familiar frantic fear in his eyes I am beginning to love far too much. For my part, I got a bloodied lower lip from a flailing elbow before I actually initiated action with the flurry punches Babe uses to warm up in practice sessions. Those punches always scare the living daylights out of an attacker.

I hate to admit this, but I have to fight an urge not to laugh when I see the astonishment on the face of someone who has stepped over the line as I begin my fist flutters to his chest and jaw. The fact that I didn't know how to use this excellent type of self-protection earlier in my career makes it that much sweeter now.

Unfortunately, I didn't get a chance to use any *Pinkie tactics* on Dolion, and now, considering my total revulsion of him, I sorely regret it. Pinkie, the little darling, takes the art of eviscerating people with a few choice words to a whole new level. Babe likes to claim Pinkie can cut a tree down from twenty feet with her acrid tongue, and isn't that something quite formidable to be known for?

Personally, I find it fascinating.

7
Crazy Gringa

Backroads of South Texas
1941

Wearing a miniature makeshift dress constructed from a ripped blouse, Pinkie settles into the grooves of Angelina's lap inside the truck. "This little angel seemed so… I don't know, confused when I cleaned her up. No matter what I said, she only stared at me and blinked her eyes," Angelina says.

"Sounds like shock," Clint says.

"I made her a thick diaper from strips of material and safety-pinned the sides. I think it will hold for a little while."

"That's good thinking, sister," Cruz says.

"It's a ways before we get there. Why don't y'all try to catch a few winks if you can," Clint says, alternately looking at them and the road. Cruz places his hat upside down on his lap, folds his hands and uses them as a pillow against the side window. Angelina sighs contentedly and leans her head on Clint. The familiar yearning surges through him right on schedule. Her rhythmic breathing soon signals she is asleep.

Thoughts brawl through Clint's head as he drives. What kind of day has this turned into? It started out normal enough. He adjourned his meeting with the Canyon Coyote Oil Board of Directors at the San Antonio First River Bank early and craved solitude to finish double checking the month's accounting statements and to make a few calls.

His father is the majority stock holder of the company, and he, as the only heir in the family, owns the majority of the minority stocks. It creates a lot of daily busy work for him while his dad recklessly tramps all over the world as a late-in-life Romeo.

He enjoys conducting his business affairs—whether a solitary duty, as is needed when going over figures, or an actual meeting—from the small antique desk in his home library. The thick-carpeted room is quaintly rich with books, memories, and artifacts his mother and he collected when he was a boy. In that room, his world feels reasonable again.

His work area of choice is nothing at all like his father's imposing office across the marble-tiled entry hall. That room, with its massive furniture and Western works of art, was a world Clint dearly loved to visit, upon invitation from his father, as a youngster. His father encouraged him to talk about whatever was on his mind back then, and he often shared insights of his own with his son. Nowadays, his father refuses to discuss, or even see, what dangles right in front of his nose.

Grant Byron Sutton stopped some time ago paying attention to anything on the home front, whether it involves his much younger second wife, Darla, his son Clint, or the day-to-day workings of Canyon Coyote Oil. Darla is a volatile powder keg Grant encountered in Las Vegas on a booze-saturated weekend. For reasons beyond anyone's understanding, Grant had his driver rush him and Darla off to Elkton, Maryland, to tie the knot. Within weeks, he deposited Darla at their San Antonio home, took off for *Casa de Roses* near the oil rigs in Midland, and has been habitually absent ever since.

That was two years ago. Before international restrictions tightened from the war raging in Europe, Grant was keenly interested in world travel, often taking along his new secretary—a blond stunner with more curves than a mountain road, or so Austin Brenshaw, their business manager, curtly informed Clint.

It turns out Grant has a knack for stirring up woman troubles wherever he goes. Clint regularly gets laconic phone calls from Brenshaw asking for permission to pay off this woman, or that husband, or someone who believes they can prove they are entitled to financial retribution because of Grant's reckless abandon.

Beady-eyed, stiff-statured Brenshaw, Grant's personal broom for sweeping up all his dirt, also happens to be the first one to remind Clint of his responsibility to represent Canyon Coyote Oil Company with austere respectability. The irony of it keeps Clint half-cocked and ready to fire every day of his life.

Darla grew increasingly and shamelessly more brazen with her affairs until she made no attempt at all to hide them. Nor did she hide her daily alcohol guzzling or brash, unsuccessful plays for Cruz. Why his father refuses to divorce her baffles Clint, but he believes it can be chalked up to the chauvinistic idiocy he witnesses far too often in the older set—their "wink-wink" habit of keeping a *feisty* girlfriend on the side. The ones who participate in this *good 'ol boy* mentality of the South wear it as a badge of pride… proof of their virile masculinity.

On the other hand, Clint marrying Angelina would tarnish their business reputation beyond repair because of her Mexican nationality? The absurdity of it infuriates him, keeps him a hair away from doing something rash, something like marrying her in the next five minutes and telling them all to go to hell.

Clint brought up the subject of Darla's escalating and embarrassing behavior when Grant came to San Antonio six months ago. His father puffed angry cigar-smoke clouds in the air and gruffly maneuvered the subject back to the business at hand. Twice. He never stays in the same bedroom with Darla, but he was, as usual, pleasantly cordial to her—not a bit of reproach or reprimand.

He seems to care not a whit about the low morals of the woman carrying their Sutton name, but, to Clint's disgust, he blew a gasket when Clint hinted, half-jokingly, he had thought about one day marrying Angelina. He dropped it lightly into his father's lap, but the heated reaction from his father almost caused them to go to blows. It was the last time they had spoken to one another other than concise, strictly business-related phone calls.

"Mama!" Pinkie screams, startling everyone in the truck.

"Wha-what's going on?" Cruz asks sleepily.

"Shh, shh, baby. I am here," Angelina sooths, rocking back and forth.

"Poor little critter," Clint says.

As everyone settles back into sleep, Clint watches the road in a mood vacillating between anger and regret as he hashes out how the day went sideways. As usual, it started with Darla, and it came out of nowhere. Coming home from downtown San Antonio this afternoon, he noticed the grayish-green tinge in the sky. With the possibility of rain or hail, he parked his new pickup in one of the five enclosed garages and strode to the horse barn and corrals, his favorite place on the ranch. He perched on the rails outside the circular enclosure and watched Cruz working Gallo, their newest horse.

Cruz waved, then hoisted a saddle blanket in front of Gallo's face. Gallo stood still. He threw the blanket on the ground in front of the horse. A slight jiggle from the animal. Cruz turned and walked away. Gallo considered the blanket, then stepped over it and followed. Cruz stopped. Gallo stopped and nuzzled his shoulder. Cruz turned to praise the horse, rubbing his hands down his forehead and onto his legs. He sauntered over to Clint with Gallo a few steps behind.

"Good going, brother. That's not even the same horse we brought home two weeks ago," Clint said.

"Sure isn't. Smart as a whip, too."

"Impressive conformation. Love how he moves."

"Tomorrow, I'm riding him. I'll know more about his movements from there, his gait when we trot and gallop. I think this might be a good one for your new cutting horse, *mi hermano.*"

"That's mighty fine, Cruz. Poor 'ol Chester's pretty stiff in the legs lately."

"But the best in his day, *sí?*"

"Good gosh, yes. He's going to retire in style, you can count on that. I'm thinking of building him a special stall with all the luxuries of the St. Anthony Hotel. You know, air conditioning. Lights going off and on when we close the door. Heated. Maybe a sauna."

"Nothing but the best for our Chester," he said, laughing along with Clint. He nodded toward Gallo. "This one… he has a keen eye already. Tomorrow we'll know more."

"Very good. Well, I got to go see a man about a horse. I'll check on that sister of yours while I'm at it."

"Pull her hair for me," Cruz said, grinning. He saluted, turned his attention back to Gallo.

Clint entered the house through the kitchen to pause and watch Angelina knead dough for the yeast rolls Darla demanded be served with dinner three times a week. Darla seldom ate one herself, nor did she formally have a specific dinner hour or even show up most of the time, but she always conjured up extra duties to make Angelina's housekeeping and cooking chores as tedious as possible.

Angelina's smile did to Clint what it always did, lit him up like a hundred candles. After teasing her by swiping and eating a hunk of dough and whipping her apron off to tie to a chair, something he had been doing since they were kids, he departed with a wide grin that faded immediately out of her sight.

Working at his desk in the library, he heard his father's silver Cadillac V16 come to a quick, gravelly stop under the *porte-cochère*. Just last year, Grant wouldn't let anyone near that car, but as the months passed, he didn't seem to care when Darla took it over or who accompanied her when she did. Everything his dad's wife did was irresponsible, and the way she maneuvered that expensive car was no exception.

The sound of the heavy front doors banging open sent Clint leaning back in his chair. He watched Darla dash up the stairs, white boa feathers flying around her like a molting bird. Close behind was her current paramour, Rafael, a low-titled Spaniard who made a habit of courting bored married women free to spend large sums of careless money. Angry accusations and cursing from both of them shattered the quiet Clint had been savoring. They stopped to yell at one another at the top of the stairs, entered Darla's upstairs bedroom, slammed the door.

Clint rose from his chair and stopped just inside the French doors of the library. Obviously drinking heavily, the couple hadn't noticed the small, green-tinted light gleaming from his desk. Loud obscenities, furniture skidding across the floor, the crash of a decanter shattering against a wall caused Clint to cross the room to the bottom of the stairs. He paused, listened to their muffled voices and the sounds of a scuffle.

"Darla, no! *Ella no significa nada! Por favor!* She is only a friend!" Raphael shouted. More thumping noises, curses, then a long groan—a groan so odd, it prompted Clint to take the stairs two at a time. Darla's bedroom door flung open. She staggered across the landing and dropped to her knees, one arm outstretched toward him. Blood splatters covered her clothes.

Through the open door, Clint saw Rafael sprawled on his back on the bedroom floor. Hesitantly, he stepped inside. Raphael stared open-eyed at the ceiling. Blood ran freely from his neck and midriff, soaking into the luxurious white carpet. Clint exited the room fighting nausea. He grasped the handrail and stared incredulously at Darla.

"Clint, my dear Clint. Thank God you've come home. Rafael… he-he's been… been murdered. Stabbed. I-I just got home and found him on the floor. Dead. A corpse. A corpse in my own bedroom!" She let out a scream that, to Clint, seemed surely stolen from hell's own choir.

She wiped her bloody hands down the front of her dress and crumpled over sideways. She raised back up with alcohol-glazed eyes, intertwined her fingers in the spindles of the railing. "Oh," she moaned, her head dropping to her chest. "If only I had come home sooner, maybe I could have saved that poor, sweet man from this horrible death." She rose to her feet with *a* vacant, *deer in the headlight's* expression.

Speaking in a singsong cadence, she addressed the space above his head. "Poor Cruz. Poor, sensitive Cruz. He did this, you know. Always so jealous of me being with Rafael. Staring at him all the time with an evil eye. I should have warned Rafael to stay away until I got those two shipped back to where they belong. Angelina… she-she's the one who put it in her brother's head to do this ungodly thing. Of course, she did." Her face contorted angrily. "She hates me! Sashaying around my house like she's the queen bee. Thinks she so beautiful with that long hair and innocent face. Ha! She had bug eyes for Rafael, don't think she didn't. Cheap little Jezebel!" Darla broke into momentary sobs that drained away as quickly as they came.

Every nerve in Clint's body wanted to throw Darla over the balcony, but her tirade of theatrical lies offended his mind into a stupor. She was creating and stepping into her own fantasy of innocence. All this ran through Clint's mind like liquid mercury as he moved aside for her to swish down the staircase. His eyes fixed on the red smears on her white chiffon dress, then moved to the circles of blood surrounding the rhinestones in her shoe straps.

She paused inside the wide doorway downstairs with a disengaged expression. "Those horrid Mexicans. You don't know the many times I told Grant to get rid of them. You'd think they were his own kids. I'm-I'm going for the sheriff, Clint. My beautiful Rafael has been ravaged by savages, and they won't get away with it." Her voice rose to an unnatural pitch. "Come with me, dear son?"

Clint stared at her, unable to mouth any words. She melted out of the house like a ghost in a bloody dress, not bothering to close the doors. If he had witnessed the murder of Julius Caesar, he couldn't have been more shell shocked. He realized he was grasping the handrail to the point of pain. He rubbed his free hand roughly over his face.

Darla had lots of money to dangle under the nose of any greedy fool ready to jump into her pool of lies. How long would it take for her to drive into town to the sheriff's office and back with the law? How much weight would her fake story carry? Would they believe her because she's married to a Sutton?

"Get your head on, boy!" he had commanded himself aloud as he ran down the stairs to save Angelina and Cruz.

Crazy *Gringa!*

She had managed to ruin everyone's life in one drunken afternoon. He knew one truth… never would that sad excuse of a woman get away with blaming his friends for the murder of her no-good lover boy.

8
Think Like a Bandito

Nuevo Laredo, Mexico
1941

Clint turns off the dirt road onto a paved highway. Angelina stirs beside him. He looks down at her and the sleeping child she intends to call Pinkie. Why doesn't he go ahead and marry her and tell the world to jump off a cliff? He snorts. His mother's final minutes of life is why. That blasted promise he made is the neck-tightening cord he can't break. Her words, and the truth of them, changed his life.

"Son, I would be a fool not to have noticed how you look at Angelina. I love her and Cruz, too, but you and I are different from the world. I beg you to consider the whole picture. Don't let the bigotry of the world turn you away from reason. The facts are, you cannot have a Mexican wife while your father is still in charge of Canyon Coyote Oil."

He started to protest, to shout at the injustice of it, but his mother lay white as a sheet, skin and bones, as fragile as a teardrop. He held his tongue.

"He might disown you, darlin'. He's old-fashioned and unreasonable about such matters. When he passes the gauntlet legally making you the majority stockholder and sole voice of the company, then do as you wish. In fact, I encourage you to slap every convention in the face once you have absolute power. In the meantime, you mustn't let the inheritance my father slaved so hard to leave me be squandered on

your unbridled desires as a young man. The company must be passed to you or I shall never rest in my grave. Promise me you'll wait. Please, promise me, son."

Nineteen years old and full of anguish, he eased his mother's fevered mind by promising what she asked, sealed it with a kiss on her forehead, and watched her fade within the hour into a death coma. That quick promise, and the fact that she was right about his father, have scissored his soul into ribbons these past five years. It isn't fair. The double standard he witnesses in his father and most of his colleagues in one way, or a thousand ways, lies bitter in his spirit. He grits his teeth. *Damn the bigoted blowhards who shut you down if you don't play by their asinine rules. One of these days, I'll show them where they can stick those rules.*

He tosses around the idea of stopping to phone his father to give him the truthful version before Darla has a chance to pack his ears with her lies. Can he trust his father? A few miles later, he makes up his mind he'll drive to Midland to tell his old man in person after Angelina and Cruz are safe across the border because, no… he does not trust his father.

A simple move of Clint's shoulder awakens Angelina. She leans forward, cradling the back of Pinkie's head as she does so. "Where are we?"

"Somewhere between hither and yon, sleepyhead."

"Are we in Mexico?" Cruz asks, seeing lights outside the window.

"Sure are, little brother."

"But… no stopping? No questions for how long we are staying or where we are going?"

"While Lina fixed up the little girl at that filling station and you were arm wrestling that soda pop machine, I gave a buddy of mine a call. He lit a few torches, greased the wheels. He's one of the good ones. I didn't want any official descriptions of us or this pickup floating around down here."

"You crossed the big bridge over the Rio Grande and didn't wake me up?" Angelina says.

"I'm not sure a shotgun blast would've woke you two up." He chuckles. "Don't worry, honey. You'll see that bridge nice and clear in the rear-view mirror when I fetch you two out of here."

"What time is it?" she asks, yawning.

"Getting on to about eleven. Those backroads kept us off the highways, but they're what you call the shore-nuff long way around."

"When did we get back on the main highway?" Cruz asks.

"Oh, about twenty miles back yonder. Luckily, I didn't see any county cars on the last stretch. Anyways, we're safe now."

"What do we do now?"

"Head for the hotel to get y'all some shuteye. I'll take you to the one my folks and I used to stay in when we came down here for the bullfights."

"Tell us some stories from those times, Clint," Angelina says.

"Now?"

"Yes, please. They make me feel happy."

"Well, okay. Those were some good times back then. Mama and Daddy always had supper at the Cadillac Bar before we caught the train to Mexico City the next morning. I've told y'all about it. It's that restaurant-bar where they got Pancho Villa's saddle."

"I remember some photographs of you on that saddle," Cruz says.

"Yep, ol' Pancho. Now there's a man of many sides. A hero to many, and an outlaw to others. Kind of like us. Anyways, Mama and Daddy were good friends of the owner of the Cadillac Bar. Let's see… oh yeah, Mr. Bessan. Nice guy. Always made the waiter bring Mama a special Ramos Gin Fizz as soon as she sat down. He remembered things like that about his customers. Made everyone crazy about him."

"*Tia* Maybelle didn't drink the alcohol drinks," Angelina says.

"Except for those famous Gin Fizzes, hon."

"Your mama shopped a lot on those trips."

"Uh-huh. Deutsch's curio shop on Calle Guerrero."

"She bought me this cross necklace there."

"Oh yeah, I'd forgotten that. Daddy said once that place started selling perfume and baubles, he 'bout had to pry Mama out of there with a stick. Only those gin drinks and Mr. Bessan's chicken *envueltos* did the trick." Clint chuckles at the memory.

Cruz rolls the window down, sticks his hand out. "Bet it gets plenty warm down here in the summer."

"Yeah, pretty close to the weather in San Antone, only hotter."

"Ugh."

"Yeah, but not quite as humid."

"Bueno."

"Please, Clint, get us to a toilet," Angelina pleads.

"Oh, yeah, uh, bet that's right. Okay, I think the street we want is up ahead. I haven't been down here for a spell, but I'm pretty sure I have it right. Tomorrow early, we'll get you some real lodgings. Something like a cute little hacienda they rent out to tourists for a week or so. I'll have to head back home right away. Remember, there's still a dead man upstairs at our house."

The silence following Clint's words is thick. The thought of Raphael's murder and a crazy woman pointing to them as the murderers is sobering.

"Shoot-fire, I need some coffee, Clint," Cruz says. "What are we supposed to do down here while we wait? You know I can't sit around some hotel like a damn… uh, like some soft city dude."

"Believe me, Cruz, I know how restless you are when you're not sitting a horse or winking at the ladies. That's something I want to talk to Mr. Bessan about. I'll give him a call tomorrow if I don't get the right responses when I see Daddy. You know, in case it looks like y'all might be down here a few weeks.

"You'll like Mr. Bessan. He came to Nuevo Laredo from New Orleans way back in the twenties. He knows everyone, so I'm thinking he may have a job or two, or know someone who does, for y'all. Short term. Something to keep you busy while I see Darla locked up for murder."

"Um, Clint, I think we should re-think some of this," Cruz says.

"What do you mean?"

"I understand how much you regard this man, this Mister, uh…"

"Bessan."

"Yes, Señor Bessan, but me and Lina got to be careful till Darla is arrested. From what you say, people from San Antone and everywhere know this nice man. They eat and drink at his restaurant. Sometime, I think, someone might talk about the terrible killing at the Sutton outfit and how the Mexican workers took off for Mexico since they're the murderers. Maybe they will hang a drawing or photo of us in the bars and hotels with a reward."

"Dios, Cruz, I'm not used to thinking like a *bandido* instead of a *turista.* Staying at a hotel so close to the border with all the upper crust and the Texas visitors and all that… well, you're right. Guess we'd better give this another hard think."

"I don't like the way she looked at Pinkie, that Madam Rosie lady. She gives me a bad feeling. Something in her eyes," Angelina says. She places Pinkie on one of the two small beds in the room and covers her with a full skirt she pulls from her bundle. She plops belly first onto the other bed. "Who wears all those rings? And her earrings are bigger than-than Texas grapefruits. Did you see—"

"Stop complaining, Lina. She's only the owner of this place. We'll never see her. The important thing is we're safe here, especially since she thinks Clint is *tu esposo.* Big 'ol strong guy like that doesn't look like someone to tangle with. Me neither, for that matter."

"But, is Clint here? Our Clint? No! He's gone, and we are alone in a foreign land and staying in this ugly place."

"It's not ugly, just a little old. Safest thing to do, stay here in a boarding house away from the border with all the *turistas,* especially with Thanksgiving in a few days. You heard Clint. Texans flock down here for all the holidays. You're spoiled, *mi hermana.* Not everywhere can be as beautiful as *Casa de las Magnolias* and *Casa de Rosas.* It's good for you to see some of the other side of life. Maybe suffer a little."

She sits up in the bed ready to quarrel with her brother, but she can't. She bows her head and weeps into her open hands. "I feel so sad. I won't be home to fix the turkey and tortillas and dressing and pecan pies *Tia Maybelle* taught me to make for Clint for Thanksgiving."

Pinkie awakens and sits up, looks at the two strangers, begins to cry. It's the first time she seems fully awake and aware since they found her on the road.

"Oh, *pobresita*, I am sorry to wake you like this. Selfish, selfish me. Here, I have for you to eat a little corn cake while I cook for you delicious food on our tiny stove." She rolls her eyes at Cruz. "Our stove that is smaller than a flour tortilla. I will make you fat and happy, *mi pequeña princesa.* Yes, you are my little princess."

Pinkie stares at Angelina with eyes filling with tears. Her chin quivers. Angelina wraps her in her arms.

"I'll be in my room, Lina."

"Wait. I must make a list for *el mercado* on the corner."

"We already bought enough for a few days."

"No, I need more for my skinny little Pinkie. Clothes, too."

9
A Big Load of Horse Manure

San Antonio. Texas
1941

Clint drives into San Antonio with the rising sun annoying his right eye through the side window, but that doesn't compare to the overall irritation closing in on him. A hot shower and a pot of coffee are to be his only indulgences before driving the three hundred miles to Midland to talk to his father. He sighs loudly and massages his forehead. What he wouldn't give for a few hours of good shuteye.

The familiar sound of his tires crossing over the cattleguard off the main road is comforting. It's an old sound, one he's heard all his life. He drives the curvy, magnolia-lined road to the house wondering how home is going to feel without Angelina and Cruz there and with a murdered man upstairs. His thoughts dissipate at the sight greeting him, not the least of which is his father's Cadillac parked in the wide driveway—the deep-green beauty loaded with every special accessory money can buy.

Inside the *porte-cochère* is an ambulance containing, Clint presumes, the body of Raphael. The sheriff's car, a Texas Ranger pickup, three horses tied to the hitching post outside the corrals, and men in Levi's and cowboy hats fill the driveway and grounds like hungry picnickers searching for fried chicken and potato salad.

Clint's face flushes hot. Raphael's murder is an open and shut case!

Darla simply killed a no-account during a drunken lover's quarrel. He assumes the muddle of men on his property are searching for Cruz and Angelina, which has to mean the sheriff believed *la gringa loca.* He parks and strides quickly toward the house with a gut full of mad.

Grant Sutton and Sheriff Jeff Kearney step outside, obviously having been notified of Clint's arrival. Clint steps up the shallow front steps of the entry porch and stops even with the pillars. Removes his hat.

"Son," Grant says evenly.

"Daddy," Clint answers, echoing his father's tone. They shake hands stiffly.

"Let's go inside."

"Look, I can clear this mess up right now—"

"Clint, please step into my office."

Clint swallows a crescendo of resentment. It took his insane wife committing murder in their own home to merit his father's presence? The three men walk side by side through the open entry door. Clint is surprised to see a whole swarm of women in black dresses and white aprons scrubbing the stairs, the landing, and, by the looks of the open door upstairs, Darla's bedroom.

Sheriff Kearney stops as father and son enter Grant's office. Grant closes the door, sits down on a corner of the massive desk. "It's good to see you, Clint. Have a seat."

Clint sits on the edge of the overstuffed leather chair, legs spread, hat in hand. "Look here, Daddy, I was downstairs when Darla killed that cheap Casanova, and—"

"Stop," Grant says, raising a hand.

"What do you mean? I need to tell you—"

"It doesn't matter."

"What doesn't matter, the truth?"

"What you saw or heard."

"What the... of course it matters!"

"Clint, I've handled it."

Clint stands to his feet. "Yeah, I'll bet. Just like you handle everything else, right? In case you have any doubts, Cruz and Angelina had nothing to do with this. Nothing!"

"Of course, they didn't. I know they're innocent. I assume you carried them down to Mexico?"

Exhaustion and anger form a wad of hard clay in Clint's stomach. He releases a sarcastic snort. "We might talk about their whereabouts later. Right now, you better tell me what the hell you're talking about."

Grant nods. "I'm talking about the deceased, for one thing. Raphael Hernandez De León was a flashy little rat on the run from officials in Columbia, Spain, and Mexico. Wanted for murder in one or two of those places, for extortion and burglary in the others. Long history. I got to give Darla some credit; she sure knew how to scoop from the bottom of the barrel. Wonder what that says about me?" He chuckles, low, as if it's not funny even to himself. Clint's hard glare causes him to clear his throat.

"Um, well, it seems they got bored with getting boozed up and making goo-goo eyes at each other, so Darla started helping the little buzzard concoct schemes to separate wealthy ladies from their jewelry and funds. All those cruises they took? They planned them according to ship-guest logs. How they got their hands on those, I don't rightly know. Darla paid someone off, is what I figure. All the law outside poking their noses everywhere? They're looking for an estimated hundred thousand dollars' worth of confiscated jewels, money, and other things those two swindled over the past eighteen months. Detectives have been working on this case for a few months. So far, haven't found any foreign accounts or hiding places, so they're taking the opportunity to search here."

"Hell's bells! And you never thought to tell me any of this?"

"You've had your hands full, Clint, and, I'd like to say, you're doing a mighty fine job of keeping this company in the black. I haven't been, well, you know—"

"Save it. We're not hollering down an empty well here. Let's keep this on the business at hand."

Grant sighs wearily. "Yeah, well, I'm still going to tell you you're the only reason the whole company hasn't folded."

The acrimonious lump rising in Clint's craw is suffocating. He swallows hard. "How'd you find all this out anyhow?"

"I was contacted by a detective agency from back East about three weeks ago. Seems a Mrs. Eleanor Groot, a wealthy widow and heir to some cosmetic company—don't remember the name right off—anyways, she suspected the pair of lifting her diamond necklace from her hotel room in Chicago and contacted the authorities.

"See, she met them on a cruise some other time before the incident. Some of her emerald jewelry went missing from her cabin on the ship, but she didn't suspect Darla and Raphael at that time. When the pair turned up in Chicago acting like old friends, the woman went out for a night on the town with them. That night, while they were dining and dancing, Raphael excused himself for the good part of an hour. They were with a group, so his leaving for a short time didn't arouse suspicions. Later, when Mrs. Groot returned to her hotel room, the necklace was gone. The villains, of course, had already fled town. Turns out, she's one of twenty-odd women with similar complaints. All roads led to Raphael and Darla, which, naturally, led to me and Canyon Coyote Oil."

Clint is silent.

"'Course, the Nazis dancing up a hell-storm in Europe put a big damper on their international travels, so they focused on targets closer to home. Some right here in San Antonio. It didn't take long for local authorities to get suspicious. They started building a case and cooperating with outside detectives and lawmen."

"You mean, Sheriff Kearney knew from the onset she was tossing him a big load of horse manure when she said Cruz killed Raphael?"

"Good lord, yes. They already had the goods on both of them, about to make an arrest when she breezed in there covered in lover boy's blood and ranting that her Mexican help murdered her, uh… *friend,* Raphael." Grant chuckles. "She right quick found herself in the clinker."

"What did they charge her with?"

"Suspicion of murder, theft, and a sundry of other crimes. Looks like her free-wheeling days are over."

Clint stands, blows out a noisy gaff of air. "Well, that's that. None of this would have happened if… oh, never mind. After I rest up an hour or two, I'm going back for Lina and Cruz."

Grant touches his arm. "Hold up, son. Here's where it gets a little tricky."

10
You're in the Army Now

San Antonio, Texas
1941

Clint's eyes narrow. "Now, listen here, if you think I'm leaving them down there, you have another think coming. This is their home. It's where they belong, and, furthermore, Daddy, Angelina and I are—"

"Naw, it's nothing like that. Truth is, the sheriff had my car Darla's been driving searched top to bottom. Seems she had some paperwork in the backseat that's about to change your direction for a while, son. Apparently, a list was published in the newspaper, but my guess is you never saw it."

"Newspapers? Ha! I've barely had time to spit with our end-of-the-year figures to double check and all those meetings with government reps about the future of oil, toluene, and gasoline. All kinds of meetings are set up in Dallas and several other cities next month with the oil industry tycoons and that fella President Roosevelt put in charge. What's his name? Ickes something. Harold Ickes. That's it. He's apparently implementing all new policies going forward for oil producers, large and small."

"I understand. You've had to bear the brunt of my, er, restlessness since your mama passed, and I'm sorry about that. I-I'll be coming back on board while you're gone, I can promise you that. As a matter of fact—"

"What do you mean while I'm gone?"

"It looks like a draft board representative came out here and delivered your orders and paperwork to someone. I'm thinking it had to be Darla because Angelina would have made sure you knew about it. Probably delivered sometime when Darla was getting in the car and she just threw them in the backseat and forgot about them. Didn't care about nothing or nobody, that little gal." Grant steps behind his desk, moves a stack of mail to the side, picks up a small pile of paperwork. "Here you go, son."

Clint reads a minute, looks up with disbelief on his face. "My name was picked from the national lottery? I'm drafted? Damn, I can't do that. I'm too involved right here. Who's going to run the business? You say you're back on board, and I'm supposed to believe—"

"Put your mind at ease, Clint. Don't worry about Canyon Coyote Oil. The way things are headed, we're about to prosper beyond our wildest dreams. I'll be right here keeping the home fires burning. You just make sure you do come back home, you hear me?"

Clint drops into the leather armchair, hands entwined between his legs. "Dammit, this puts a hitch in everything. We're not at war, so why a lottery draft?"

"The way I understand it is we had a pitiful army a few years back, and it made us weak. Certainly not a good position to be in with the whole world fighting like bearcats. Last year, they started the draft back up with one-year terms. The war keeps heating up in Europe and Asia, and some say Britain can't sustain without help. Roosevelt reacted by asking Congress to extend the term of military duty from twelve to thirty months. He got his way, as of a few months ago. August, I believe."

"You mean I'll be in for a few years?"

"Maybe. This year, lots of those ol' boys who went in with that one-year promise have been threatening to desert once their year is up, so that's blowing around, too. The winds of war are turning into tornadoes around the whole globe, as you well know. I'll say this… it sure has affected our bottom line in a positive way. I saw that by the ledger on your desk in the library."

Clint exhales loud and long, reads something on the paper on his lap, looks up with wide eyes. "It says here I'm supposed to be at Camp Bowie in Brownwood at seven in the morning! Good gosh, I'd better get back on the road right now to fetch Lina and Cruz."

"How long since you slept, Clint?"

"I don't know. A day or two."

"I'll send someone to get them first thing in the morning. You should rest up before you start that army hitch. Can't go in all tired out. I'll call Norman Dustwin and have him rev up that little Cessna Airmaster of his. It'll fly you into Brownwood in a couple of hours. Tomorrow, you fly out early, say, four in the morning. I'll have you a car waiting at the airstrip in Brownwood, and you can report to duty in plenty of time. It'll be mighty different for you, that's for sure. Make me a few notes tonight, won't you? I need to catch up on the state of the company and what that Board of Directors is up to."

Clint looks at the floor, swallows the anger threatening to gush out in a flood of verbal accusations. What good would it do now? Maybe his father is serious about stepping back in as CEO of Canyon Coyote. Marrying Darla was obviously his stupidest move, but everything else he's put his hand to these past five years stacks up pretty proud alongside it. Clint holds his tongue, but enjoys his private promise to himself that he'll marry Angelina on his first leave. *If the old man doesn't like it, he can stick it where the sun don't shine.*

"Who you sending to bring our family back home?" he asks.

"Family?"

"Cruz and Angelina."

"Oh, yes, uh, I thought I'd send Bubba."

"Bubba? Why him?"

"Who better than my trusty driver?"

"Where is he? I didn't see him when I drove up."

"He's taking care of some business for me in Austin. Making a delivery or two. Be back late today. I'll send him first thing tomorrow."

"Listen…" Clint stares a hole in his father. "… I want your word on this."

"On what?

"I want your word Cruz and Angelina will never be implicated in any way in the murder of Raphael."

"They won't be. The sheriff knows Darla did it. Believe me, her charms of persuasion went *adios* a long time ago."

"But I have your word?"

"Of course."

Clint rakes his fingers through his hair, puts his hat back on. "I'll write a letter to them explaining everything. Be sure Bubba understands how to approach them so they don't think they're being hornswoggled. I'll write down directions to the boarding house where they're at. I'd call them, but that landlady there said her phone was on the blink. No phones in the rooms, of course."

Grant nods. "No worries, son. None at all."

11
Not at this Time

Nuevo Laredo, Mexico
1941

Bubba is a massive man with a baby face belying his foreboding ability to protect Grant Sutton from every kind of danger. His job as driver isn't half the story. His true employment is grinding down the jaws of jealous boyfriends and husbands and fighting his way out of barrooms and hotels. A bodyguard becomes an inevitability for a man worth two hundred or so million dollars, especially when that man has an obsession for partying with young women of dubious character and those with matrimonial ties. Bubba has muscled his way in and out of some of the most expensive, and some of the cheapest, establishments in several states, as well as in many foreign countries… all to keep his employer alive and in one piece.

Right now, half of Bubba's new assignment happens to be walking down a Nuevo Laredo street. His Tom Mix hat partially conceals his face, but Bubba easily recognizes Cruz Serrano by his confident gait. Something in a man's walk shows off the kind of grit he has with animals. Cruz's natural ease with horses, and his mostly unaware effect on womenfolk around him, is something Bubba admires more than he's ever let on.

Bubba is parked across the street and one building down from Madam Rosie's boarding house in a pickup with a Mexican newspaper in front of his face. He was given two assignments. One, make sure Clint told the truth about Cruz and Angelina's whereabouts, and two, drive straight back to San Antonio without them seeing him.

"You don't leave Mexico until you're sure they're at that boarding house. I need to know for certain," Grant ordered.

"They'll recognize any of your vehicles, boss."

"That's right. That's why you're borrowing Ted Sliger's pickup, the beat-up one he uses for deer hunting. I've called him. He's expecting you."

"You don't want me to give them Clint's letter or bring them back home?"

Grant looks down at his Ostridge-skin boots. "Not at this time, Bubba."

12
Thrown from the Car

Bangor, Maine
1958

Charlotte

I don't care two shakes about my mussed hair, the mud on my camel coat, or my bloody lip, but bare feet and dirty stockings with wide runs up the legs still feel as improper as a woman wearing her girdle outside her dress. In my part of the country, a lady follows a certain protocol in public.

I sit down to wait for a ticket clerk to return as prudently as a publicly barefoot woman can sit on a hard bench. I've cased the room, evaluated the people in it, checked to see if the public telephone is working—it isn't—and there's nothing for me to do but allow a landslide of thoughts to keep my mind occupied.

I think back to the moment I released Dolion after extracting a promise he would cease and desist trying to seduce me. As soon as I let go, he croaked for me to get out of his car. His voice was as scratchy as an old toad, and of course it would be after my jab to his vocal cords. In my gentlest voice, I said, "Dolion, it's night, and it's snowing. This is December in Bangor, Maine. Won't you please be a gentleman and drive me to the train depot? I won't be any trouble to you."

I swear, his eyes changed again, and I realized at that moment I was dealing with someone *off,* someone not mentally sound. I forced a smile and softly said, "Listen, I'm sorry about our little differences this evening. Truly I am. I promise I'm forgetting about the whole thing right this instant. It's already gone, actually. Not a sliver of it do I recall. You know, Dolion, odds are high that we'll work a case together again in the future. Do you suppose we'll ever go back to Cuba with Harry as we did in your beginning internship a year ago?"

Of course, I was hedging because nothing in this world would make me accept an assignment in which I was alone with this man again. In fact, when I get through explaining this evening to the powers that be, Dolion will find himself unemployed and unable to prove anything he ever spouts about *ROSE* or me. That's how it is, amen, and it will be done.

He was quiet for a few moments after my little spiel, simply rubbed his throat. I was beginning to hope he was returning to normal. I was looking at him, smiling nicely, when another squall blew across his face.

"CeeCee, get the hell out of my car now!" he bellowed so ferociously it felt like live embers blowing in my face. I jumped out of my skin, it was so loud.

"Goodness, there's no need to swear at me."

"Get out!"

Oh, it was fast, just a blink of an eye, how he reached across my lap, pulled the door latch, and pushed it open with a hard thrust. My heart was thumping against my chest. I forced a smile, lame though it was, but I still disbelieved his intention was to actually throw me out of his car in the middle of the night. I used my most soothing voice, the kind you use with a person teetering on a ledge. "Dolion, listen, please. You're a good man. We're friends, aren't we? Can't we—"

I never finished that sentence because he violently pushed me out the door into a pile of dirty slush collecting in an asphalt gash. My left shoe strap… the one that goes around the heel to hold a fancy party high heel on a lady's foot… well, that strap caught on something. I'm not sure what it was, but it was a protrusion inside the car-door frame, most likely a bolt.

As soon as he realized my predicament, that is, of my being partially attached to his car, Dolion pulled the shoe off my foot, reached under his seat for a knife—which gave me a start, let me tell you—and cut the ankle strap in two as if he were cutting a length of rope. I was taken back by the eccentricity of such an act, and I instinctively knew it was because I'd shared with him what my childhood caretaker used to do to my shoes.

He threw the mangled shoe straight at my face. I dodged. His car rolled forward, almost taking my leg with it. I pulled it out, somersaulted sideways, and barely missed collision with the open car door swinging loose. That lunatic pulled the car forward, then backed up fast with his red brake lights shining in my face. I rolled out of the way and watched in shock as he drove over my discarded shoe, pulled up, and ran over it again before backing all the way out to the street. Indeed, Dolion was the quintessential Dr. Jekyll, pleasant and amusing, then turning into the evil Mr. Hyde when spurned.

The repercussions of my job have left me in some pretty odd places. This time, my personal rebuff of a man's inappropriate desire left me in an alley full of haphazardly placed trash cans and one pitiful cat staring mournfully big-eyed from a small cardboard box. It was shivering so desperately, it reminded me of some of the *unfortunates* I have traveled around the globe to rescue, especially Pinkie that terrifying time in California. I removed my warm neck scarf and tucked it around the skinny little creature. I know, I know… that was probably stupid considering my predicament, but I couldn't resist. The cat stopped shivering and started purring, making me smile despite my situation.

I limped back to the street shaking with cold and anger. Thank God, and I truly mean that, I saw a blurry neon sign on a building not too far in the distance. If I hadn't been so livid about what transpired in that alley, I might have worried about making my way down a dark, snowy street in a deserted part of town. My exposed toes were deadly cold the whole time, but, let me say, my soul was charged and ready for a fight. You just don't mess with me like that. Not anymore.

Finally, the ticket clerk is back behind the counter. I find out the bus to Boston and Cleveland won't arrive until tomorrow morning, and that, of course, is all to be determined by the weather conditions throughout the night. I guess I look crestfallen because the clerk smiles at me in a fatherly way. His gold glasses with square lenses reflect the silhouette of my messy hair.

"The benches aren't too awful bad for beddin' down, Miss. Get one of those with the plastic seats on 'em. It'll give you a little cushioning, don't you know? If you don't mind, would you kindly stay over on this side…" he nods his head to his left "…away from our, uh, street folks a'beddin' down over to there by that wall? I'll be keepin' an eye on you myself, and that's a promise. Would you care to use some of our station blankets? I have a stack of 'em in the back all washed up nice by my missus."

I show my gratitude by accepting two blankets and giving him a genuinely warm southern-girl smile. I hunt for a spot to recline for the long hours ahead and notice the ailing salesman is now fully reclined on the bench. One of his legs stretches the length of the seat, the other one counterbalances his weight in a ninety-degree angle to the floor. I tiptoe closer. He's breathing rhythmically and almost appears to be smiling in his sleep.

He survived.

But, then, haven't we all?

13
Vulnerable

Yúnnán Shěng, China
1941

Babe

Draped over the only settee in their small quarters, Olivia is in swoon position with one hand loosely holding a piece of paper and the back of her other hand resting on her forehead. Edgar paces into the tiny kitchen and back, circles the settee, repeats the pattern.

"Edgar, what are we going to do?"

"We are going to get our boy from the school in Chefoo and leave for the states, that's what. We'll resume our missionary work in the future, perhaps in a different country not so prone to upheaval."

"We won't ever return to China?"

Edgar drops to the floor, crosses his legs. "Frankly, I don't know the answer to that question. If it isn't the Japanese invasion of this country, it's the Communists fighting the Nationalists, the *Guómíndǎng*. Always there is war here. So much death and sorrow. Neighbors turning against one another for money or food. It-it's risky conditions in this part of the world, especially for we who have children."

Olivia shakes her head. "The awful stories I hear!"

"Dear, you mustn't—"

"Water and hot chilis forced up the nose for being a hero to his own countrymen, for protecting his children or neighbors? Yes, that is but one of the hundreds of tortures being inflicted on these poor people, Edgar. From some of the other stories Bǎoyīn heard from her other family members in that puppet state, the Empire of Manchuria, chilis up the nose is a church social. Never have I heard of such cruelties. Do you know about the garrote death, husband?"

Olivia ignores her husband's raised-hand protest. "It's ghastly. A rope is placed around a prisoner's neck and slowly, ever so slowly, tightened until the poor thing dies an agonizing and torturous death. Then, there is the terrible starvation. Forced to give all their rice to the invaders, the railroad coolies and all the physical laborers are having to eat acorn meal and sorghum. Can you imagine eating only that and then carrying dreadfully heavy loads from dawn until dusk? Unbearable stomach pains, malnutrition, turning into skeletons." Her voice shakes as she says the last words.

"Olivia, stop this."

"I-I believe we are in God's hands, but this attack on…what is it called?"

"Pearl Harbor."

"Yes, Pearl Harbor in Hawaii. Oh, it makes me feel so vulnerable, so worried for our children. I can't believe they had the nerve to attack a U.S. military base. Lisbeth Karlsson said in our meeting this morning that all Americans and all Westerners are now labeled enemy aliens to the Japanese. That places us in dreadful danger, Edgar."

"I know, my dear, I know."

Olivia waves the paper in her hand in the air. "This memorandum all but shouts that each one of us must prayerfully consider our own future plans. No suggestions or orders are overtly stated, but we can read between the lines. The Gromwells intend to stay in China in one of the CIM stations in a southwest region they hope remains unoccupied, and they feel that is God's plan for them.

"Mikael Sweeney said the armies are interning missionaries faster than anyone predicted, and many could lose their lives. This station we are presently in is not a bit safe, he said." Olivia stares at the ceiling and wipes away tears. "Oh, this is terrible, Edgar. What in the world can we do?"

"I've already told you. We will get our son, and all of us will return to Texas. The journey to get Eddie may be extremely difficult, sometimes barely possible, but we must make it."

"Yes, oh, yes. Eddie, my love, we are coming for you," she says, dabbing at her eyes. "Thank God for Bǎoyīn, Edgar."

"Yes, and Ena."

"How did Bǎoyīn become such good friends with a Japanese woman?"

"The way I understand it, both women believe in humanitarianism first, race and creed second. That's the way it should be. Their concern for others caused their lives to intersect. Bǎoyīn is a marvel. She has traveled all over China working with missionary organizations. There are other underground groups besides Bǎoyīn and Ena's operation, but they all work to rescue people from heinous fates."

Olivia sits up from her reclining position. "Is our United States truly involved in a world war now?"

"I'm afraid so."

Six-year-old Babe runs into the house through the partially open door with Méi-Mèi close behind her. "Mama, Mama, Méi-Mèi is a dragon! She is going to breathe fire and turn me into cinders!" she giggles, thudding belly first against the settee's upholstered edge. Her cheeks are rosy; her dark eyes flash with excitement.

"Méi-Mèi is only teasing, darling. There are no real dragons, right, Méi-Mèi?" Olivia's tone holds a reprimand toward the girl as she and Edgar do not allow tales or superstitions around the children.

Méi-Mèi looks down as Olivia stands to her feet. She places a hand on the young woman's shoulder. "That's fine, dear. Now, please take Babe for a stroll so Mr. Wayne and I may finalize our plans. It's chilly out, so Babe shouldn't be running so hard and become flushed."

"Hǎo de tàitài" Méi-Mèi says.

She watches the pair walk away hand-in-hand. "Edgar, isn't it sweet how Méi-Mèi says *yes, auntie* to me when I give her a task? Such a darling girl she is." She cranes her neck to watch them as they disappear down the slope of the hill toward the stream.

"What are you looking at, Olivia?"

"The girls. I can't get over how our Babe looks almost Asian with her dark bob of hair, unusual skin tone, and those beautiful dark eyes. It's ironic, I believe. Watching the two of them, one might think they were sisters."

"Her skin is tanned from the sun, dear. She would sleep outside if we would let her, even in winter. You know she refuses to keep a coat on, so she, uh, gets darker toned than us. You, my sweet, are alabaster." He leans forward and kisses her hand. "Babe especially fits in now that Bǎoyīn cut her hair last night in a genuine Chinese style." He watches his wife. "You don't mind, do you?"

Olivia shakes her head, a rare glint of humor in her eyes. "Not at all. I thought it would look adorable, and I was right."

"The Chinese girls in some regions dare not let their hair grow below their earlobes. Not even half an inch. Japanese rules."

"Ugh, I've heard. Why, it's so un-feminine for a girl's hair to be so short, especially when these girls have such glorious hair. I still say our Babe looks almost Chinese, Edgar. I can't get over it."

Edgar clears his throat, licks his lips. "Actually, it astonishes me how much she favors my mother. Her dark eyes are exactly like hers."

"She looks French then?"

"Um… yes, I would say so."

Edgar scrambles to explain Babe's different looks every time the subject arises. What he never confesses is that his mother was a French *Gitan,* a gypsy who fell in love with an English soldier during the first world war. Because of a universally negative and unfair stigma often attached to *Roma,* he never tells of his mother's true ancestry, not even to his wife.

"How I wish I had met your mother, Edgar. She sounds so colorful. When you describe her happy dancing, her way with tambourines, and her wonderful skill in training birds and dogs, I so wish the children and I had been given the opportunity to know her."

Edgar smiles. "As do I, my dear. Now, about our journey… it will be fraught with challenges, perhaps the most difficult endeavor of our lives. You must be courageous. Will our packing take long?"

Olivia frowns. "I don't think so. But, Edgar, you do believe Eddie is safe at his school right now, don't you?"

He sighs. "We have prayed day and night for him and about the tedious journey we face. We must move forward in faith." He glances nervously around the room. "Um, my sweet… how soon did you say we can we be packed for departure?"

14
The Underground

Wéifāng, Shāndōng Province, China
1942

Attempting to attract no more attention than the dull color of the dirty streets, a group clothed in plain layers over loose, gray pants walks down a street in Wéifāng, sometimes hesitantly, other times quickly. On their heads are *kasa* in the traditional Japanese style, hats difficult to attain but assuring a slight degree more safety on the dangerous journey to Wéifāng. The man and one woman in the group keep their heads down and their stained faces as discreetly covered as possible.

Two other women maintain constant humble expressions, not shielding their faces. Each of them holds the hand of one small girl dressed in the demure, colorless clothes of Chinese peasant children. The young girl smiles and greets everyone she passes. One of the women holding the girl's hand bends down and whispers in her ear.

"But I wish to talk to every person, Bǎoyīn! I like to make them smile." Babe says, breaking into a loud song.

They increase their pace, are soon noticed by a pair of soldiers lingering to smoke cigarettes outside a shop. "Hey there, stop!" one shouts in Japanese, and all four adults halt in their tracks. Ena reaches quickly into her sack, retrieves a package, and breaks apart from them to speak to the soldiers in her own language.

The rest of them stay back appearing to be busy with the child, chins on chests, especially Olivia and Edgar. Ena exchanges conversation, laughs a little, bows a lot, then hands the men a brown paper package wrapped in string. The men open the package and instantly begin devouring the delicious pastries. Oh, how hard-pressed the group was to obtain and abstain from, first, the ingredients, and then the result of Bǎoyīn's eggy custard tarts with flaky lard crusts, the last ones she made during this journey.

Thinking of the pastry's subtle sweetness of winter melon and lotus bean filled with shaved coconut and sweetened roast pork makes their mouths water almost to the point of pain. Not one bite have they had of the coveted sweets, nor of the ones Bǎoyīn prepared previously in safety houses on this journey. The purpose of the sweets has been bribery and distraction, assisting them in getting the Americans to safety before it is even an issue. This is the last package of pastries to have aided them thusly.

Bǎoyīn's attractiveness, even in her late thirties, has been played down in wrinkled, loose clothing, covered hair, soiled cheeks, and a hat tilted so that it covers much of her face. Intermarriage and relations between Japanese men and local Chinese women have been encouraged during the occupation, but single and married Chinese women are sometimes confiscated to serve as *comfort women* for the troops. Age and marital status of a female are of no significance to the army. The lust of human misappropriation never sleeps, and this group is keenly aware of it.

Ena returns and hastens them down the street as would a mother hen protecting her chicks from the dangers of nightfall. After turning down three more streets, each one narrower and filthier than the last, they reach their destination, a series of beehive-like hovels sprawled and hoisted up two levels on grayed lumber over dirt butting up to a hill of mostly rock. Tattered fabric drapes separate family units or groups.

These are the temporary slum lodgings of the laborers working on a nearby bridge. The workers are allowed to live with some of their family members provided each member also works on the bridge project from before the first light of day until after dark. It's unusual, and strangely generous, considering the horrendous conditions most of the laborers and railroad coolies have endured on recent projects throughout China.

Bǎoyīn instructs Olivia and Edgar to be silent, keep their chins on their chests, and look no one full in the face. Everyone is suspect. Money, food, and favors are always waiting for tale bearers who turn in their own family members, neighbors, or strangers for anything slightly suspected as worrisome or illegal. No children under ten are allowed in the slum other than for momentary visits. That makes gregarious Babe an extra worry to everyone.

Bǎoyīn and Ena lift one curtain after another, walking through as they politely bow and smile at each person they encounter and trusting the rest of their group is following behind them. They see mostly Chinese men malnourished into skeletons with sunken eyes and sallow skin stretching over protruding bones, a few empty-eyed women, and many other bedraggled workers indistinguishable by race or gender.

Outside an exceedingly worn tapestry suspended from poles attached to the rock wall, Ena looks around. When she is certain no one sees, she slips behind the tapestry and motions for the others to follow her into a niche carved into the bottom of the tall boulder. Inside are five people, no children. By gesture, Ena tells Edgar and Olivia to sit along the edge of a dilapidated rug in the center of the alcove.

"You uncover face now. Here friends," Ena says. She and Bǎoyīn break into conversations with different ones who steal glances at the Wayne's, smiling or dipping their heads slightly when their eyes meet.

"This is remarkable," Edgar whispers to Olivia. "This brave assembly cares not of one's ethnic race or religion, but only of being kind to their fellow human beings. I feel as if we are witnessing a touch of heaven in the midst of a hellish time."

She squeezes his hand. "I am grateful for them, and for the kind people we've met since leaving our residence. How did this secretive system originate, Edgar?"

"It's the heartbeat creation of Bǎoyīn and Ena. For the last three years, one Chinese woman and one Japanese woman joined with others of like mind and assisted Westerners, Chinese families, Japanese sympathizers, missionaries, Koreans, or anyone else, to escape tyranny.

"But, Edgar, thousands of civilians are being tortured, raped, killed. I shall never be able to erase from my mind the things we have witnessed on this journey."

"I know. Insufferable tragedy, but, Olivia, do not forget that we are to celebrate *even the one that is saved.* Keep your mind on the good and not the bad."

She nods, wipes uninvited tears from her eyes. Edgar taps Bǎoyīn on the arm. "Is it possible that we may get Eddie from the Chefoo school tomorrow?" Bǎoyīn rolls her eyes toward Ena, says something to her. Ena turns toward the couple looking grim but resolute.

"I sorry. No good news," she says. "Chefoo school full with Japanese soldier now."

Olivia gasps. Edgar puts his arm around her. Babe picks that moment to circle around to her father's back and wrap her arms around his neck. She begins singing *Jesus Loves Me* in Mandarin, *"Yēsū ài wǒ wǒ zhīdào..."* bringing a smile to all the faces in the alcove.

"Mother, uh, can you…?" Edgar says, pointing at the little arms around his neck. Olivia stands and pulls Babe off Edgar. She howls in protest. Bǎoyīn gives her a cube of sugar and plops her down next to her. She sucks on it, smiles happily.

"Japanese come to school day after Hawaii bomb. Bring Shinto priest. Do ceremony. Teachers, children, no leave now. Say *everyting…* furniture… people… belong to great emperor of Japan," Ena says.

"What? They say our children belong to the Japanese emperor? Not my Eddie!" Olivia cries.

"Worse *ting...* soldier put foreign people in prison now. Need hide. Not go Chefoo. You go my brother's house. Little one stay with Bǎoyīn. We hide good."

15
Goodbye, My Darling

Wèifāng, Shāndōng, China
1942

Olivia kisses her precocious, angelic-when-sleeping daughter one last time. She smooths her thick, dark hair, newly cut last night into a blunt style scarcely covering the top of her ears. She pulls the two thin blankets up and tucks them under Babe's chin. Her tears fall torrentially in the pre-dawn light as she backs away, her eyes sealed on the sleeping child.

"Goodbye, my darling," she whispers, a sob punctuating her words.

Edgar places a finger on his lips and shakes his head. His eyes turn toward the commotion on the other side of the tapestry as workers exit the hovels reporting for work before morning's light. Olivia takes a deep breath, nods, and turns to hug Bǎoyīn. The two women shake with silent sobs. Olivia breaks away, blows her nose noiselessly in a handkerchief she stuffs into a pocket, picks up a wide-mouthed bucket of scrap metal with both hands. She staggers with the weight. Edgar puts a hand on her sleeve. He removes several hunks of metal from her bucket and puts them into two buckets attached to a yoke.

Ena and Bǎoyīn lift the bamboo yoke balancing two buckets of scavenged, rusty iron pieces onto Edgar's shoulders. Ena hoists an enormous bundle of sticks onto her back, picks up the last bucket of bolts and screws, and moves toward the tapestry. Bǎoyīn whispers, *"Shàngdì yǔ nǐ tóng zài."* Her words are echoed by some of the others now roused from their sleep.

"God bless you, too, dear Bǎoyīn, and all of you," Edgar says.

Theirs has been a bitterly cold, sleepless night after dining on much-appreciated soy sauce-soaked turnips. What lies ahead for the couple is the grueling chore of hiding in plain sight as they accompany Ena to her brother's home near the Yunmen mountains.

Their faces are freshly stained, their clothes loose and gruesomely smeared with dirt, a detailed story memorized for anyone questioning them. The most troublesome detail is Olivia's blue eyes. If stopped, she must endure, with a degree of pain attached, an herb quickly rubbed into them and the lie that she has a most contagious eye disease.

Ena assured them her brother, Hiroshi, is sympathetic to the missionaries and will hide them until they find a way back to the United States. It is understood Edgar and Olivia will not leave China without their children, so their stay with Hiroshi is presumably a long one. They have no other choice, as it is reported that safe conditions for foreigners in China are declining by the hour.

As Babe slumbered, her fate was sealed. Hard decisions were made. Olivia tried again and again to rationalize taking her with them to the mountains, but everyone in the alcove rejected the idea. They all agreed the child would cause unwanted attention with her happy ways and songs and would surely arouse suspicions from the soldiers.

It was also determined her parents must depart while Babe slumbered to avoid chaos and crying. Everything about the high-spirited child presents challenges in risky times, but bribing her with sugar cubes and a fake promise of joining her parents right away seemed the only reasonable bait for getting Babe to Húnán Province with Bǎoyīn once Edgar and Olivia are gone.

Olivia hesitates, stares again at the slender lump underneath the blanket, then follows the others as they step into the now empty area beyond the tapestry.

"God will be with her every moment, Edgar whispers to his wife, not at all certain if *God's Will* portends his little family will ever be reunited on this earth.

16
All Things Work Together

The mountains, Shāndōng, China
1943

Sunlight filters through the bare tree branches creating a web-shaped mosaic on the round tabletop in the tiny *yuànzi,* the courtyard. To keep her bones from aching, Olivia sits on a pillow on the marble slab of a bench placed in a way to allow access to part of the table. She is wrapped in a coat, scarves, and a blanket. She tilts the lid of her blue-orchid *gàiwān* slightly to hold back the loose tea leaves and takes a sip. Her hands shake.

"My sweet… um, do be careful. That is the last one from our set of four *Qing Hua* lidded bowls from the Taylors."

"Oh, yes, of course." She sets the *gàiwān* down. "Edgar, I fear the cold here in our abandonment has seeped into my very marrow. If we were not opposed to it altogether, I would sip some of Hiroshi's *sake.* He says it does wonders for heating the bones." Her small laugh reveals she is joking. Edgar feels no need for even the slightest husbandly admonishment. To be truthful, if not for Olivia, he, too, might partake of the rice wine to ward off the relentless cold of winter in these northern mountains.

"Shall we go in then, my dear?" he says, placing his book on his lap and yawning. "Hiroshi's mama-san will surely share the *kàng* in the kitchen long enough for us to warm ourselves. It shouldn't be too dangerous if we go back to our room after a few minutes."

"Though I crave the warmth of the *kàng*, please, let us tarry outside a bit longer. I become so weary inside, especially in our small room. How the walls suffocate me! They grasp at my throat like bloody fingers, tormenting my…" The anxious glint shining from Edgar's eyes stops Olivia's outburst. She clears her throat. "Let us merely say this brief interlude in the courtyard always helps my lonely soul believe there will be a better day. I believe it has literally saved me this past year—this little space outside with its changing seasons, the free, sweet birds, the sky, nature. Even the cold is not entirely unwelcome, if you know what I mean."

"I do." Edgar allows himself to relax, takes a moment to weigh his next words. "We must keep our minds fixed on celestial things and never lose hope, Olivia." He pauses to let his words sink in. "And… I have good news to share with you."

"Good news? Oh, please tell me, Edgar!"

He smiles. "The rumors have become too many to ignore that the Japanese soldiers are taking over the Chefoo school to convert it entirely to a military base. Thus, the children and teachers will be transferred soon to the Weihsien Internment Camp in Wéifāng. This change of events brings a sprig of hope to us, darling."

Olivia stares at her husband. "Hope? Did you say *hope,* Edgar?" She tilts her head back and laughs—a disconcerting, slightly delirious sound. She fixes Edgar with a stare, her chin trembling. "It means only that our Eddie will be a real prisoner in a real prison. Think of it! What shall he eat? Is he being cared for right now? Will they torture him? Has he been tortured already? And-and what of my baby girl? What if she is…" Her weeping rises quickly from a soft sob to a wail.

"Olivia!" Edgar's extra-firm tone instantly quells her crying. She looks at her husband, eyes dripping, body quivering.

"Hush now! Think of Hiroshi! We must not put him in danger after his kindnesses to us. Be encouraged. Babe is with Bǎoyīn and her family. She is a worthy, capable woman, and this blasted upheaval cannot go on forever. Remember, there are encouraging signs that the

Guómíndǎng are scoring victories in some areas."

"It's not enough… not enough." She weeps quietly into her open hands.

Edgar rises to comfort her. The past year of fear, hiding, and constant worry about the children have taken an unusually drastic toll on his fragile wife. Some of her recent behavior has been worrisome.

"Listen to me now. If you will promise to be very much in control of yourself, and I know you can be if you try really hard, I have something special planned."

"Oh, Edgar, what-what can be special here?"

He crouches beside her and takes her hands in his. "We shall disguise ourselves and venture back to Wéifāng to watch the children as they are transferred to their new location. The date this is to occur has been leaked. Everyone is whispering about it. I have already made arrangements through Hiroshi and Ena to take us there in a wagon so we do not have to walk so far on foot. That will be less dangerous and will provide an easier way to remain camouflaged."

Olivia stares dully at him, as if her mind can't soak in his words.

"Take heart, dear wife. We most likely will catch a glimpse of our son. Our eyes can feast upon him if only from a dis—"

Bells tinkle from the street just outside the *yuànzi*. Over the high wall, a policeman announces, "Checking registrations! Checking registrations!"

Edgar and Olivia fly into action gathering their things and making a quick dash through the private door from the *yuànzi* into their tiny bedroom. They open the secret door leading into Hiroshi's aged mother's room, dash through the room, and turn into a short hallway ending at a small room stacked with fuel.

Hiroshi motions for them to hurry as he directs them by gesture into the fuel room. They sit flush against the wall with their legs drawn up under their chins. Hiroshi covers them completely with bundles of dried sorghum. He touches the toe of Edgar's shoe. Edgar pulls his foot in a few more inches. He throws more dried sorghum on them, rushes to close the door to the room, then saunters slowly and smilingly into the main room with Old Mother. There he will offer hot green tea and Japanese *hanami dango* or Chinese *dàngāo*, depending on the season, to the officials in the region who announce their arrival at certain places in exchange for tea, delicacies, women, or a showering of gifts from the civilians.

These "blind police" in the region are usually Chinese, some are mixed, a few are Japanese who may or may not be secret sympathizers. Basically, they are the ones who care little about rounding up people or of war policies, but care very much about satiating their appetites.

Hiroshi moved to the newly occupied land of China to express outward patriotism. It was all for show. The real reason were the threats that he would lose his warehouses and his shipping business in Japan if he did not participate in a relocation program. His prosperity puts him in good stead with officials, making him doubly likely to shower gifts on any policeman or official who makes an *announced* visit.

Under the dried sorghum, Olivia's body quakes so violently, Edgar worries the stalks might fall away and expose them. He grasps her hand and silently prays for his wife to regain her sound mind before it is too late.

The crowds are lined up thick along the road in Wéifāng waiting for the procession to pass by. Olivia, wearing special darkened glasses that deem she is blind in order to hide her blue eyes, stands her ground, along with Edgar and Ena on either side of her. The crowd heaves them forward, seeking to gain advantage over the front-liners. Those in the coveted front-line positions relentlessly push back to hold their positions.

Olivia's heart is pounding. She has promised with her hand on the Bible to stay in control of herself when and if they spy Eddie among the children and teachers marching to the internment camp that day.

"Here they come! *Tāmen láile!*" a woman shouts, and the crowd gathers life, moving and breathing in a wave as the first of the two hundred teachers, children, and old people come into view. As they near, their pitiful gauntness is blatantly apparent. Each person carries at least one tiny bundle which, most likely, contains the sum total of all they own in the world. Armed soldiers position themselves in front of the crowd punching, slapping, or delivering rifle-butt blows to anyone venturing too near the road.

Nearer, nearer the procession comes, and the air is shockingly… obtusely… filled with songs—songs of hope and redemption. The crowd falls mute.

My Lord in Heaven, never have I seen such blessed optimism in the face of such wretched oppression, Edgar thinks, staring at the line of emaciated children and adults.

The crowd watches in strange awe as the procession moves along the road. The prisoners have been nearly starved to death, wear frayed, soiled clothing, look to have both dirty hair and bodies, carry rampant sores and insect bites on their skin, and yet… the light of hope and fortitude on their faces creates a heavenly aura around them that defies logic.

Olivia stiffens beside Edgar. He glances at her, but cannot tell where she is focusing her sight because of the dark glasses. He tries to follow her gaze, and finally, within twenty feet, he spies Eddie. He is standing tall, all disheveled eleven years of him, singing with sweet abandonment. The look on his face is indescribable, a mature acceptance and resolve that, matching that of the other youngsters, is a marvel of the highest order.

Edgar's eyes consume every detail of his son, his heart delighting in the closeness of him. Like a flash of lightening piercing his spirit, a fearful premonition shoots through him… and it is not wrong. Olivia abruptly drops to the ground, breaking his and Ena's hold on her arms. She rolls past the soldier standing in front of them, and, in a heartbeat, stands and breaks into a run.

"Eddie, my Eddie! Eddie Wayne! My baby! Mama is here! Mama is here! Eddie Wayne!" she screams.

She is within a few feet of her son when a shot rings out. Edgar knows with a sickening surge the bullet has hit his wife. He roughly shakes off Ena's arms pulling him back and races to Olivia. He falls to the ground ignoring the cane blows on his head and back. Eddie is somehow there, and Olivia, whose body is now in an ever-growing puddle of blood, smiles weakly but jubilantly at her son. She rests her palm on his face and motions for him and Edgar to lean in close. It is almost impossible with hands pulling at them from everywhere, but, miraculously, they manage to do so.

"I couldn't bear another day apart. Promise me… promise me you'll find my baby girl." Edgar nods vigorously, feels the crack of a bamboo cane on his scalp. Olivia places Eddie's hand in Edgar's hand. Her hoarse voice is barely audible over the soldiers' screaming commands. "You see, my loves? All things do work together for good after all."

Her eyes widen as if in fear, then transform into peaceful serenity before closing. Soldiers jerk Edgar and Eddie from her side, and the last breath leaving Olivia's body heaves the chilling rattle of death into the air.

17
No Gypsies

Nuevo Laredo, Mexico
1944

Pinkie

Angelina sits on the tufted stool in front of her dressing table studying her image in the mirror. The Brazilian rosewood surround of the mirror is intricately carved and matches the ornate dressing table below it. White, magenta, and pink paper roses wrapped with tape and wire are interlaced into the wood cut-outs in the surround. A see-though shawl of pale mauve covers the lampshade of a hand-painted lamp on the tabletop.

She fluffs her dark hair and smooths silky strands down each side of her face and onto her bare shoulders. She smiles at her reflection. She is beautiful. All the men who have fallen in love with her the last three years have told her so. They lavish her with gifts, Nicolás especially. In her other life in Texas, she neither dreamed of, nor wanted, that kind of male attention—only Clint's. The fleeting thought of him makes her wince. She can never understand why he abandoned her.

Bottles of perfume are arranged neatly in a circle on a silver tray beside the lamp. Behind the dressing table and mirror are yards of pale sheers crisscrossing the window and dropping to the floor. Angelina sprays her wrists and neck with perfume, covers her full lips with red lipstick. She presses them together and blots them on a handkerchief.

A framed poster of the renowned bullfighter, Manolete, standing elegant and poised, is on the adjacent wall in the bedroom. In the lower corner, it is signed, *Para Angelina, la mujer más bella del mundo.* Manolete has told her many times she is one of the great beauties of the world. Beside the poster is a framed black and white photo of the famous singer, Toña la Negra, with a personal message, *Sigue cantando, pequeño ruiseñor.*

Yes… keep singing, little nightingale.

"Mama, are you to be very late again tonight?" five-year-old Pinkie asks. She is sitting underneath the dressing table, knees drawn up, her back against the wall as close to Angelina's feet as she can get.

"Um, not too late, *mi niña pequeña,* but you will be asleep."

"When can we go to the bullfights again? You said the handsome Spanish *matador* gives you free tickets."

"But you don't like the bullfights."

"Because the poor little bull is hurting when they stick him. I wish he would run away and never come back. I like to go so I can be with you all day, Mama, and for the candy pineapple rings."

"Come here, my darling." Pinkie scrambles off the floor and into the waiting arms. After a tight squeeze, Angelina scoots her off her lap and turns back to the mirror to finish her makeup.

"Is Carmen coming to watch me tonight?"

"Mm-huh."

"May I go play with Cita later? *Por favor?"*

"No, I told you, Pinkie. You must not play with the gypsy children."

"But they have so much fun. They play games in the street until late at night. Their *casita* across the road has lots of people coming in and coming out. If I listen through our kitchen window, I hear music and laughing. I wish I could play with Cita, Mama."

"No. I hear stories that, um, well, you know… I have told you before. You must never go there to play. *¿Entiendes?"*

"Yes, I understand, Mama, but Cita comes all the time to ask for me to play. Can she play with me here in our house?"

"No."

"But you let Carmen come and watch me, and she's *gitana.*"

"No, she isn't. Why do you say that?"

"She can't make tortillas."

"Everyone can make tortillas in Mexico."

"Not Carmen. She cooks things I don't know."

"It is good to try new foods."

"She smokes lots of cigarettes when you aren't here and makes me cough."

"I'll speak to her. She is supposed to smoke only in the courtyard."

"She plays too much with her cards and not with me."

Angelina's eyebrows raise. She pivots to face Pinkie. "She does the cards?"

"She says I have a bad future coming. What does it mean… a bad future?"

Angelina shoots from her chair, passes from the bedroom through a small sitting room. "Stay here," she tells her little blond shadow. She steps outside into a garden surrounded by a high rock wall covered in ivy and fragrant with hyacinths, roses, and hydrangeas carefully tended by her elderly landlady. She follows the stepping stones to a narrow blue door with an iron grate on the exterior. Two clay pots, wider at the top than the bottom, grace the backdoor of *Señora* Lupe's *casa.* Curly clusters of red cockscombs grow brightly from the larger pot, habanero plants in the other.

"Señora Lupe!" Angelina yells, knocking on the door. No answer. She bangs harder. "I must talk with you. Open the door, *por favor!"* She continues to assault the door until it opens. A tiny woman with gray hair pulled into a tight bun appears behind the iron grating.

"What is so urgent, *mi cariño?* Is there an earthquake? Perhaps a volcano?"

"I thought you were sleeping."

"El diablo can't sleep through your knocking. Are you going to the club to do your singing tonight?"

"Soon. *Señora* Lupe, it's Carmen… you promised she wasn't *gitana,* but Pinkie told me she does the cards. What do you say about this?"

"I say we all enjoy to hear the cards speak to us. It doesn't make us gypsies. Oh, *cariño, la mayoría de las gitanas son buenas.*"

Angelina taps her foot. She doesn't agree with *Señora* Lupe that most of the gypsies are good people, but she wishes to remain respectful. "Now that I consider it, I am certain Carmen is *gitana.* Pinkie says she can't make tortillas. Who in Mexico cannot make a tortilla? All you know of her is she was kind to you at the market, yes?"

"*Sí,* she helped me carry my vegetables and *carne* home two times. A good woman. And she is nice with Pinkie. I hear them laughing and playing in the garden. Why such concern? I am friends with the *gitano* families in this neighborhood. They are nice. No trouble."

Angelina shakes her head. "No, no, no. I won't have my baby around those people. Who knows what they might do? I hear they will do anything to get money." She sighs, looks agitated. "Never mind. I shall stay home and forget the club. *!Ai-y-yi!* Such an important night—the most important night of my life." She rolls her pretty eyes wistfully to the side and assumes a pouty look. "Tomorrow, I shall ask Nicolás to send me someone else to watch Pinkie, but tonight… yes, everything in my life is a catastrophe."

She puts a hand to her forehead, closes her eyes. "My one opportunity. The only one I shall ever have in this lifetime… ruined." She waits for a reaction for a few seconds before turning away mumbling a continuous stream of indecipherable words.

She is five small, measured steps closer to the backdoor of hers and Pinkie's *casita* when *Señora* Lupe calls out, "*Mi cariña,* do not concern yourself. I will watch *la niña pequeña* for you. You must attend your important night. Bring her to me."

Angelina stops in her tracks, smiles, trots back to the elderly lady. Only a little does she feel guilty for her manipulation. "*Mi querida mujer,* ¡*Gracias!* My baby is no trouble. She has no more of the nightmares like before. She will be an angel for you. Now I shall not miss my chance for a better life for us. Yes, you are a dear woman!"

The old woman soaks in the accolades with a warm smile. "Is *el Presidente* Camacho coming to see you?"

"Oh no," Angelina laughs. "Not the president. Someone else is coming to the club to hear me sing tonight, *un hombre importante.* A close friend of Jorge Negrete, the film star. You know who he is, of course."

The old woman shakes her head.

"He's the actor in the film, *Ay, Jalisco… no te rajas!* Do you know of it?"

Again, the woman shakes her head.

Angelina laughs. "I must take you to a film, *mi madre!* The man coming tonight hires all the singers for the big plaza shows in Mexico City, even for the bullfights. Nicolás says all of this man's friends and connections are in the films or entertainment business. Oh, I hope he likes my singing. What am I saying? He will love my singing!"

Angelina's joy is infectious. The old woman clasps her hands together, grins widely. The gaps from her few missing teeth only make her seem more precious to Angelina. She motions for *Señora* Lupe to open the iron grating. Angelina hugs her warmly, kisses her on each cheek.

"I will send Pinkie here in a short time with her baby doll and her *ropa de dormir.* I'll be home at midnight to get her. Oh, no, I left my red lipstick on your cheeks, *mi madre.*"

"No importante, mi cariña," the old woman says, her eyes sparkling.

"Can I trouble you to make supper for Pinkie, too? She eats like a little bird. I will pay you extra."

"No need, no need. I prepare too much food, Angelina, the same as when *mi familia grande* was here with me. Pinkie will love my *arroz con pollo* and my fresh tortillas. My *frijoles* are delicious today with the pork fat and chilis and onions."

"Ay, my mouth is getting jealous," Angelina says, smiling. "I will call and leave a message for Carmen not to come anymore."

She blows a kiss to the old lady and hurries back to her own door, never guessing this is the last time she will ever see *Señora* Lupe.

18
Room 109

Nuevo Laredo, Mexico
1944

The dull bulb suspended over the scarred table casts shades of dinginess on everything inside the stuffy room. An overflowing ashtray and stale coffee in half-drained cups add to the pall of Room 109. Angelina occupies a wooden chair scooted close to the table, her head bowed, a handkerchief pressed against her mouth.

"*Señora,* please, let us hope for the best. We will be looking for the woman and the child all night and as long as necessary. How far can they go? We shall find them." Officer Ramirez's words offer Angelina no relief.

"We must go over the facts one more time, *por favor.* First, allow me to call some of your family, *señora.* You should not be alone at such a trying time."

"Pinkie is all the family I have," she answers, voice quivering.

The official is overcome with pity for the ravishing young woman who previously told him she is a widow. "No *mama y papi* to call? No sisters or brothers? Perhaps a *tio* or *abuela?*"

"No uncle. No grandmother. My only brother is in California working the vineyards with the *Braceros.* I haven't seen him for two years. He may be working for the railroad now, but I don't know."

"And your husband *está muerto, señora?*"

"No, he-he isn't really dead."

"Just a little dead?"

"He might as well be. He forgot about us. He left us here three years ago and never came back." She presses a cross from her necklace to her wet cheek. Uncertain if she and Cruz are still wanted for murder in Texas, she adds, "We were going to return to, uh, I mean, go back to, um… California, but—"

"Is your husband *gringo*… I mean *norteamericano?*"

"Yes."

The official frowns. It figures. What man with any sanity would abandon *this* woman? She is as gorgeous as a movie star he saw in the *norteamericanas* films when he was staying in Laredo, Texas, with the other half of his family. *What is her name—the amazing actress with the dark hair, full red lips, and emerald eyes?*

"Excuse me, please. Have you been in any movies? You are so, uh… so very attractive like a film star."

Angelina raises her head and looks full at him. He can't tell if the contemptuous glare in her wet eyes is because he is flirting with her, or something else. The truth is her face reflects inner disgust at her own folly for going to the dinner club last night. If she had stayed home, her precious Pinkie would not have been left in the care of *Señora* Lupe, who is now, incredibly… dead.

Her silence, the expression on her face after his professionally inappropriate question, and her undeniable beauty, make the police officer uncomfortably hot in the closed room.

Deja de ser un idiota! he scolds himself.

He clears his throat and assumes his most officious demeanor. "*Muy bien.* We shall go over the facts, and then I will have Esteban drive you home. Every small detail you remember may lead to a clue we find useful. Do you wish for a glass of water or some of my scorched coffee, *señora?* I am happy to have fresh coffee made for you if you desire it." She shakes her head. "Let us proceed then. When you got home from *Club de Fantasía,* what time was it?"

"Ten minutes after midnight."

"And who—?"

"I already told your attendant a boy was there. He was waiting inside the front courtyard, sitting cross-legged on the sidewalk. He wore a white shirt and light-colored pants. Baggy pants with a red and yellow sash in the loops. A scarf around his neck, uh, a red bandana. His hair was brown. Is that enough detail for you?"

Her voice is rich with sarcasm, a fact Officer Ramirez chalks up to his earlier comment about her looks.

"Um, yes. Did you ever see this boy before?"

"If I did, I don't remember."

"Did you previously know he lives across the street from where you live?"

"No, I never paid attention."

"What did he say?"

"He said *Señora* Lupe was gravely ill with her heart. He told me she and Pinkie were driven to the hospital."

"Did he tell you who drove them to the hospital?"

"Yes, he said his family did. The ones who live across the street."

"Did you know he meant the *gitanos*, the gypsies?"

"I figured it out."

"Do you know these *gitanos?"*

"Of course not. They live across from *Señora* Lupe. Some of them live there all the time, but they have many visitors. Cars come. Cars go. I never met them, and I don't let Pinkie play with their *niños."*

"I see," Officer Ramirez says. "What did the boy say to you next?"

"He said his uncle would be pleased to drive me to the hospital."

"Did his uncle drive you to the hospital?"

"You already know I was driven here to the police station instead of the hospital. Enough questions, sir! The gypsies have stolen my daughter, and we sit in this room wasting time. I-I must find my baby!" She rises and aims for the sole door in Room 109. Officer Ramirez steps between her and it.

"Please calm yourself. My whole force is searching the town for the mysterious woman who said she would take your little girl to *el baño.* We must consider every detail in order to put the pieces together. Please, *señora,* sit down."

Angelina sits on the edge of the chair, cries quietly with her shoulders shaking, "I'll take a glass of water now, if you don't mind," she says softly, not looking up. The officer opens the door, gives an order to someone. In a few minutes, a young officer comes in with a full glass of water, sets it on the table. Angelina raises it with a shaking hand. She takes a bird-sized sip, puts the glass down, picks it up and drains the glass.

Officer Ramirez sits down in the chair across from her, crosses his legs. "The family that drove *Señora* Lupe and your girl to the hospital are, as you say, *gitanos*. The Bangó's. Please put your mind to ease concerning them. They have lived here in Nuevo Laredo the last few years. They traveled to Mexico from many other places to escape persecution. Perhaps you know of what is occurring *en Europa* to the Jews?

Angelina nods, "Everyone hears those rumors."

"Did you also know it is the same for the *gitanos?* Imprisonment, work camps, sterilization, even death, I am told."

The startled look in her wet eyes make her all the more stunning to him. He knows he could get lost forever in those luminous pools.

"Yes, yes, the situation is very bad. The Bangó's... they escaped before it was too late. From Hungary, I believe, but I do not remember exactly. Many of our *gitano* immigrants come from Croatia, others escape to here from Germany and Poland. Many countries. I know this family personally. In fact, they are good Catholics who go to mass. The woman who took your girl is not associated with this family."

"How do you know?"

"Because they told me. They have no reason to lie about this incident, *Señora* Sutton."

"It's Serrano."

"Perdóneme?"

"My name is Serrano, not Sutton."

"I see." He makes a notation on paper. *The mystery surrounding this woman makes me loco,* he thinks. "Very well, *Señora* Serrano, the Bangó's, they live here. They work here. Their children grow and go to schools here. *Se sienten terrible por este incidente.* They are out looking everywhere, along with my officers. They have recruited their friends and family to assist us. I believe they will uncover something for us to investigate."

"Why did they trust a stranger with my child?" A sob follows her words. She again presses the handkerchief to her mouth.

Officer Ramirez frowns. "The facts are strange, it is true. When the Bangó's took *Señora* Lupe and, uh, I'm sorry… I see on this statement the long, proper name of your daughter, but did you not call her something else?"

"Pinkie."

"Ah, yes, Pinkie. *Rosado.* When they took her and the old woman to the hospital, there was *mucho angustia* because the *señora* was in great pain. You see, she is… was… very special to this family. The children call her *Abuela* Lupe. They tell me she always takes them fresh flowers from her garden and shares her delicious *comida* with them. She is… I mean, was, considered family.

"When they were informed by the doctors *la señora* had died, they lost control. It was at that precise time a stylishly dressed middle-aged woman kindly offered to take your daughter, uh, Pinkie, to the ladies' bathroom. They thought she was assisting to keep the little one from their worst time of grief. *Gitanos,* you know, are very passionate people, *similar a los Mexicanos.* There was a great deal of weeping and teeth grinding and striking of the floor with their hands while they absorbed this sad news. Very sad."

Officer Ramirez scoots the open folder over to Angelina. "It says here no one of the Bangó family remembers seeing this woman before she approached them tonight, but her accent may have been Croatian. She was *gitana,* they believe, but not someone they are acquainted with. All they know is when they went to locate your daughter in the bathroom, she was gone."

Upon hearing the words, *she was gone,* Angelina moans, drops her head to the table and sobs. Observing her, Officer Ramirez remembers which actress the woman in his interrogation room looks like. Gene Tierney—the most beautiful actress in *norteamerica.* Only the eye color is different. He gulps. If he were not married to a saintly woman, he would fall in love with Angelina Serrano.

Perhaps he will anyway.

19
Make Your Own Luck

Driving south through Mexico
1944

It's not the first time Rosario Ivana Banović, also known as Madam Rosie, has cleverly *borrowed* a product to drum up business. The last time, it was a dancing monkey she *accidently* took from a traveling band of performers. Was it her fault the monkey got out of his cage and followed her one day simply because she dropped a few crumbs from her lunch sack?

The monkey was an impressive attraction for a time, drawing people like ants to spilled sugar and making her a lot of money. One day, with no warning, the monkey began screeching and misbehaving in front of paying onlookers. When she tried to control him, he bit her on the neck and ran away. She wouldn't waste money posting a reward for such a disobedient animal, so, as usual, she moved on to the next opportunity.

A woman alone in the world must make her own luck, and that is exactly what she continues to do. With no children of her own, she is owed something to assure her coffers stay plentiful as she ages. There is a war going on around the world, and she is in her fifties—two aspects that point to her deserving a measure of good luck, even if she must create it herself. This time, her *luck* has lavish blond curls and crystal-blue eyes. She is an unusual beauty one does not see often.

Given the right training, the girl is the perfect ploy to entice customers to have their fortunes told and to warm them up to buy her trinkets and tonics. She predicts the child will one day beguile everyone with her charm and beauty. Such an asset! Later, who knows? She will marry the man Madam Rosie finds suitable, one with many resources, and they will take care of her in her last years.

Fortune caused this "chance meeting" between them to happen a second time. She first saw her three years ago. She was but a few years old when she came with the handsome Texas cowboy and the two Latinos, one claiming to be the child's mama, the other her uncle. The brother and sister rented two of her rooms for a month before they moved out. The Texas man never returned. Strange. Was he really the child's father as they claimed? The child resembled him a little, so maybe.

Of course, there was the cowboy's thick letter arriving in the mail at the boardinghouse about a week after he left Nuevo Laredo. Madam Rosie had mostly intended to give it to the lady or her brother, but it was mislaid. She guesses it slipped behind the tall wood and tile sideboard in the hallway of the quarters she occupied as owner of the boarding house. It didn't worry her that it got lost. Nothing about anyone but herself ever did. So much for all of that. The past is invisible, and the future awaits with greedy arms.

She studies the girl sitting in the seat beside her. She must handle this *piece of fortune* very carefully as she slips her out of town. Should the girl become hysterical or make a scene, it would attract unwanted attention. Speaking in her most pleasant maternal voice, Madam Rosie coos, "I know you must be thirsty, dear girl. We must stop for only a moment at my boardinghouse. I shall go inside and bring you a cool Coca-Cola. Do you like soda pop?" Pinkie, hesitant at first, nods. She relaxes enough to tell the woman her name is Pinkie and that she's five years old.

Pinkie? A most terrible name. I will deal with this later. She shall have an exotic name, one more fitting for our business, the woman thinks.

Her nephew Luka parks the car outside the boardinghouse. Keeping up her pleasant tone, Madam Rosie says, "I must take these medicines inside to a sick lady, dear. I will return shortly with your special drink, uh, Pinkie. We must make haste and go to meet your mama, yes?"

As she walks toward the car after her errand is completed, she first smiles at Pinkie in the backseat, then leans down and asks Luka through the rolled-down window to help her loosen the cords on one of her boxes in the car trunk.

"What are you doing?" he asks, watching with furrowed brow outside the car as his aunt pours ground powder from a small envelope into the girl's beverage, making it bubble up. He already asked her repeatedly in the car why the girl was with her when she came out of the hospital, only to be shushed and ordered in low tones to keep quiet.

Madam Rosie puts the envelope back in the box with the other roots, herbs, and powders. "Tighten the cords on the box, Luka."

"I asked you something, *tetka.*"

"You are so nosy! Must I have all the brains in this family? We are in Mexico, Luka, and, as it is in Argentina, we may be stopped while we are driving or walking. Anytime. Anywhere. The child must be quiet and no trouble while we leave town in case we are inspected."

"What's the difference if we are stopped? My papers are in order. Who is this little girl? You never mentioned a child was to travel with us. I heard you telling her we are taking her to her mama? What mama? What are you getting us into?"

"Gledaj svoja posla, nećače."

"No, I will not mind my own business."

"I'm doing her a favor. Do not worry. She is nearly an orphan."

"How is anyone *nearly an orphan?*"

She waves a dismissive hand at him. "Stop irritating me. You are my nephew, not my superior. I know what I am doing."

When Pinkie falls asleep from the gypsy's potion, Madam Rosie pushes her into the contour of the seat and folds her hands in her lap. "Ah, now she is resting. That is what we say to anyone who asks." She looks up to see Luka scowling at her in the rearview mirror. "Stop giving me evil looks, Luka. Your papa told you to help me, not magistrate what I do. He knows I can make us money in difficult times. Are these not difficult times with war everywhere?"

Luka continues to glare at her in the mirror. Madam Rosie sighs noisily. The upcoming journey will be unduly tiresome if she must continually explain her behavior to her nephew. He has no right to question her. She decides to put him in his place.

"Luka, when Ivan and I left Croatia, we first traveled to Spain. You already know this. That is where he met your mother. I tried to tell him she was the wrong woman, an outsider." She snorts, "He wouldn't listen. Later, I told him his wife should never leave Spain. She wasn't strong. She was tied to her family. I told him, but Ivan was stubborn. He wanted to live where many of our tribe were settling in Argentina, so he closed his ears to the truth. What happened? His beautiful, weak wife agreed to leave Spain with him, and then… she died as I told him she would.

"Do you remember how you behaved, Luka?" She sighs noisily. "I'll tell you in case your memory is dull. You were ten years old, and for months, you acted like a sniffling baby crying for your mama. You still had your papa and me, but it didn't matter. Of course, we all know you inherited your weak character from your mother."

Luka grips the steering wheel until it hurts. If he were to comment back to her, it would come out as an angry lion's roar. Throwing his aunt out of the car seems a pleasurable thought at the moment.

How dare she degrade my mother like this? She was a saint—gentle, loving, and intelligent.

"Finally, your papa learned to respect my *eye* into the future. Now, you listen to me… we *Machwaya* live in many different places in our lifetimes, as have our ancestors. It doesn't matter. Only two things matter. Never become entangled with outsiders, and never throw away our venerable traditions. Our traditions are where we live, not one country or another. So… tell me, what does tradition say right now, Luka?" After a brief interlude, she says, "It says you are bound by our hallowed traditions to obey your papa and to do what your aunt tells you to do. Do you understand?"

Oh, yes, he understands. He is once again the victim of an elder pulling rank with the long-standing whip of *tradition.* The traditions of his people are so strong, they are choking the younger generations. Fierce. Rigid. Unconventional, and formidably real. He says nothing, stares down the road. He resentfully recalls his father's excitement when he learned his sister was coming back to Argentina.

"Don't you see what a gift from the Virgin Mary this is? At last, my prayers are paying off. Her ways are unusual, I admit, but she has the magic to make much money. She can see the future, Luka," Papa said.

"Then why does she need an escort to accompany her to Argentina from Mexico? She sounds capable of doing whatever she wants," Luka had replied.

"She needs an escort because she is selling the boarding house she inherited from a lover. Think of the money she will have with her! We have not seen such money, my son. We must make sure she is not robbed on her long journey back to us. I release this whole responsibility to you, Luka."

Luka had waited for the conversation capper. His father always found a way to bring a certain phrase into every lecture. He didn't have to wait long.

"You see, when you bring my sister home safely, you are being courageous. You are also bringing money to us so we can live happily. Yes, *Hrabrost i novac.*"

Loosely translated, it means *courage and money.*

"Of course, you must not forget about my leg," Papa had said.

Who can forget about Papa's leg? The injury at the metal factory changed his father's life, as well as his. It stopped Papa's dancing at the festivals and filled him with fear for the future. It made him constantly worry about having enough money to live.

In the end, Luka conceded. After all, tradition says a son does what his father asks. Add to that Papa's thinly veiled threat to keep Luka's life savings if he didn't concede, and it was a sealed deal.

In the backseat, Madam Rosie is busy concocting stories to tell her people about this pale, lovely girl. She studies her as she sleeps. She looks nothing like Madam Rosie or any of her kin. What if she snitches that she is stolen? In the way beautiful people are believed more than plain or ugly ones, she would most likely be granted credibility.

That could be trouble. Bringing trouble to a *Roma* tribe can get her shunned, a terrible fate for a woman alone, especially one on the down-side of youth. Her face lights up with an idea. She will say this is the daughter of two of her boarders who were like a son and daughter to her. They had no other family and, alas, perished in a terrible accident. She was appointed guardian over their only child. The girl's made-up stories are from grief. She will lie that the girl tells wild stories about her life to flush away her misery. Her brother can back up her story because he will believe it with all his heart.

What of Luka?

He will do as he is told.

20
A Stubborn Girl

Driving south through Mexico
1944

Stops and starts through the small villages traveling toward Monterrey awaken Pinkie. She opens her eyes and stares at the torn flaps of upholstery on the car ceiling. A picture of a man holding something in his hand with a small cross on top of the object is tacked over some of the ripped material. She sits up straight in the seat, glances side to side, stares again at the picture.

Madam Rosie follows the girl's gaze. "See, that is my Sacred Heart of Jesus. He will watch over us and keep us safe. I never travel without this holy picture near me. Luka fixed it for us in the car."

"Where is my mama?"

"We are traveling to your mama. Remember, I told you she had to leave and go to another town. She asked us to take you there to meet her. We must travel for several days, even on a boat, and there your mama will be waiting for you."

"You didn't say it would take so long."

"I think I did. You forgot."

"Why did she leave without me?"

"Someone in your family became ill. She left *muy rápidamente.*"

"Who is ill, my Uncle Cruz? He is in California. Are we going to California?"

"No, we are going to another place."

"I don't have other uncles."

"This uncle you never heard of."

"No. Uncle Cruz is my only uncle," Pinkie says, her voice wobbly.

"Child, you are making my bones ache. Be still, please."

Pinkie scoots as far away from the stranger as she can in the narrow backseat. Her mama never leaves her except to go to work or when she eats supper with a friend. Never for very long. Why did she leave her now? She watches out the side window, determined not to let anyone see her cry.

Madam Rosie digs into a cloth bag by her feet. "Are you hungry, Pinkie? We have traveled for many hours and shall eat *carne y papas y tortillas* when we come to a good eating town. For now, I have for you *el mazapán* from de la Rosa. It's very delicious. Eat some."

Pinkie looks down at the wrapped confection Madam Rosie places in her lap. She is angry at everything, the rings on the woman's fingers and the multiple earrings in her ears—even the ugly, torn upholstery on the ceiling of the car. The terrible memory of *Señora* Lupe clutching her chest and screaming, and the strange-tasting Coca-Cola this stranger gave her which has left a bitter taste in her mouth, make her feel even more short-tempered.

Oddly, she wishes she could say something mean to this woman beside her. She has never wanted to say mean words to anyone before, but, right now, they are a weight on her tongue. She bites the inside of her jaw and flicks the candy onto the floorboard with her finger. Fixing the woman with a scowl, she says, "I don't want your candy."

This… Madam Rosie had not expected. She has been kind to this obviously spoiled little girl, and she doesn't deserve rudeness in return.

"I see that you are a stubborn girl. All right, we shall see. Yes, we shall see." She retrieves the candy from the floorboard. "Now you will not have any of my delicious peanut candy, not a morsel. You can be hungry while I eat it." Pinkie's defiant glare is so powerful, Madam Rosie pivots toward the window. She smacks her lips excessively, hoping to perturb the child into being sorry for her stubbornness. "Umm, so delicious." She smiles, but, truthfully, the child's obstinacy is disturbing.

She looks so angelic, but obviously, there is more to her than meets the eye.

Strength and beauty both, huh? Very well, her resistance can be controlled with training and discipline. Eventually, they will work in my favor. What an opportunity is this child!

The woman stumbled upon this *opportunity* when she was picking up medicine at the hospital for her sickly boarder—a wealthy widow hooked on numerous medications. Madam Rosie knew the widow would tip her generously for doing this favor, her last deed as the former owner of the boardinghouse. She already had her belongings packed into the old car being driven by her nephew and was ready to step into the car when the woman called down from the window asking for help. All the regular businesses were closed at that late hour, the time Madam Rosie preordained to slink out of town. She knew the late-night hospital *farmacéutico* well and that he, for the right price, had medicines for sale at all hours.

Walking down the corridor from the pharmacy she happened upon a room teeming with the Bangó family. She knew of this *gitano* family, but not personally. She knew enough about them to know her *gitano* roots are nothing like the Bangó's. Not only are they Hungarian, but they also assimilated into the Mexican culture as easily as fleas invading a mongrel dog. Assimilation of that degree is unheard of in her own tribe.

As Madam Rosie watched them through the glass partition outside the room, it was apparent the Bangó's were lost in anguish. It was also obvious they had forgotten a little girl sitting by the wall with tears streaming down her face. The child sat very straight in a turquoise-colored lobby chair wearing a meticulously ironed yellow and white dress with a satin ribbon sewn around the hem of the skirt, white anklets, and shiny white shoes. Something about her struck a familiar chord. Squinting, Madam Rosie studied her. Was it possible? Could she really be the fair-haired two-year-old who stayed at her boarding house three years ago with her mama and uncle? Why was she at the hospital with this *gitano* family?

A plan shaped quickly in the cunning woman's mind. How easily she slipped off her excessive jewelry to drop into her purse and transformed into a kindly matron wishing only to assist the grieving family by escorting the girl from the room. Instead of taking her to be refreshed, she simply walked the girl outside and into her waiting car, leaving the Bangó family in the midst of grieving the loss of *Señora* Lupe.

Because of her clever conniving, her purse now bulges with money from the sale of the boardinghouse *and* the generous gratuity from the grateful widow begging for medicines. Now, she has both money and a new *product* to brighten her future. She will start training the child slowly. She can picture it now—a deep blue sign painted with luminous stars and moons advertising the madam's readings. An attractive, smiling child beckoning customers to come inside. Irresistible! She sighs contentedly, leans forward.

"Luka, I hear funny noises. Will this car take us all the way to Mexico City?"

"I hope so."

"You hope so?"

"Well, it's a hand-constructed car, *tetka.* It can't even be named with so many different parts from different cars. Maybe the carburetor is wrapped in tape. Remember, you told me to buy a very cheap one for the first part of our trip." He shrugs. "Any moment, these wobbly wheels might fly off. I pray the motor doesn't drop into the road. That would be a problem."

Madam Rosie squawks, "*O moj Bože!* Why did I trust you?" She crosses herself, takes a deep breath. She doesn't see the slow smile spreading across Luka's face. He watches in the mirror as his aunt frets. She kisses two fingers and raises them toward the Jesus and his sacred heart picture. She reclines her head on the seat and closes her eyes, blotting out her present concerns with daydreams of speaking her beloved native language every day again and of selecting her new wagon.

If she has to rent a little space to do her fortunetelling and sell elixirs, so be it. She will still purchase her own small wagon to stay ready for the road, even if she settles down in her brother's home in Buenos Aires for a time. *Always be ready to follow the road* can be her motto once more.

An eccentric elderly man with no family is the reason she was in Nuevo Laredo for nearly five years—the longest time she was ever in one place. The man loved to visit her on the edge of town to hear his fortune and to flirt with her. Whether their relationship was more than a flirtation, no one but she will ever know. The facts are that he bequeathed his boardinghouse to her when he died. She moved into the owner's quarters right away and, for a time, became a semi-legitimate resident of a Mexican border town.

As more Croatian *Machwaya* left Mexico and returned to Argentina or migrated to *norteamerica,* an old familiar longing returned. She yearned to be on the move again, to die in her old age *on the road to somewhere else* just as her ancestors have been doing for centuries. Though it is true her tribe allows themselves to take root in the culture of countless countries, they never fully lose their travel fever. In time, they always move on.

Recently, that travel fever hit her hard. It exacerbated when certain nosy officials in Nuevo Laredo started breathing down her neck regarding a few of her side business deals. Too bad for them. Making money is what she does, and it is none of their business how she does it. How would they like to be an aging woman alone in the world?

She settles back into the seat. At last, her head tilts forward onto her chest. Her snoring draws Pinkie's attention. She stares at her, feels a stinging in her hands. She opens them. Her fingernails have bloodied her palms.

21
Of All Human Dramas

Bangor, Maine
1958

Charlotte

No matter how or why I travel, I never let circumstances overcome my commitment to being *well turned out,* as they call it in the South. Looking our best is what it boils down to. Fulfilling my duties around the globe often means I'm wearing faded blue jeans and tucked-in man shirts, but I am never without well-applied lipstick and my Maybelline mascara.

Right now, I pull out my purse mirror and check my face. It's still there, and it's looking tired. I can't sleep. It's not the Naugahyde-covered bench I'm occupying, my memories of past rescues, or the disgraceful state of my stockings and shoes keeping me awake. Heavens, I've slept in perfect contentment on a slab of ancient Mayan limestone in the jungle and in a smelly dinghy beside a bucket of fish heads in San Diego. Once, I was so weary on an assignment in Iran—which I still prefer to call Persia—I fell asleep on the swaying, humped back of a camel. Now *that*... was an experience.

No, my lack of sleep isn't due to my location. It's coming from a plethora of things, not the least of which is excitement about my *ROSE* assignment in Rome this coming January. I've always wanted to go to Italy, have thoroughly studied Italian, and have a vague idea of planning a reunion with the girls there sometime next year.

Another reason for my restlessness is the strangeness of my returning to my hometown of Fort Worth after so many years. I have something big planned that I intend to ask my father to finance. I'm paid extremely well for what I do, but the project I have in mind is bigger than my very nice salary. The thought of confronting him gives me a hint of anxiety, but I know I'll have the right amount of courage when I need it. I always do.

Perhaps if I trace the water stain on the ceiling with my eyes for another hundred times, I'll get sleepy. A mental picture of chopping my way through the Amazon jungle with a plastic toy sword makes me laugh out loud, and a man raises his head from slumber and frowns at me. Now, I'm more awake than ever.

They lowered the lights a few hours ago, but I still see that stain on the ceiling. Most travelers delayed by weather are bedded down one way or another. Not much going on at three in the morning with no buses arriving, no doors opening or closing. I yearn to call Harry Wáng and tell him about Dolion just to hear his reactions. His angry screeching in Mandarin Chinese would soothe me as much as a sedative, but I can't contact him with a broken public telephone.

I stretch my legs out in front of me all the way. It's not very ladylike, but no one is looking at this hour. I think about how I shared with Dolion only a fraction of my childhood victimization at the hands of a malevolent nanny, Miss Wraith. I don't know why I deviated from all the fun and frolic we were having to share such a private part of my background. It must have been the combination of the elegant dinner with all those delectable courses, the picture slides, awards, the lighthearted fun with people I respect that put me so at ease. Or… was it because I had been developing a crush on Dolion? Goodness, what a thought! He is terribly handsome and charming, but inside, I found out he's Frankenstein's monster.

Lesson learned that *outer looks in no way define the inner person.*

He was so warmly sympathetic when I told him how Miss Wraith treated me when my daddy traveled, how she slapped me in the face only a few times, but how it was painful enough to make me quick to obey her anytime she raised that left eyebrow of hers almost to her hairline.

Later, she controlled me through humiliation and shame of Daddy's wealth, his position in society, our beautiful home, and mostly, of the opportunities that lay before me as I grew up—opportunities, she pointed out continually, that neither she, nor any of her siblings, would ever have. It created constant guilt inside me, which, as I mentioned earlier, was one of my main motivations in joining *ROSE*.

Like Dolion, Miss Wraith had two distinct personalities—one she put forth for my father, the household staff, and outsiders—and another one she showed to me. I became almost a recluse in those years, tiptoeing through my days to stay on her good side. When I think about Miss Wraith now, I picture her as a snake curling around my feet, spitting and hissing that I should be ashamed for everything I was born into, and for anything my father bought me.

One of her favorite ways to torment me was by mutilating my pretty shoes. Awfully odd, isn't it? It all started with my early, extraordinary love of shoes. Daddy thought that peculiarity of mine was adorable, and he brought me beautiful shoes from everywhere he traveled in the states or abroad. How Miss Wraith clapped her hands with *faux* joy when he handed me a new box of shoes tied with a taffeta or a satin ribbon! She cooed over me to his delight, further exemplifying, in his mind, how much his employee loved his little girl—his only child.

When he left on a trip again, she used a razor to cut gashes in the sides of my new shoes, slit the straps, pulled off any pretty adornments, or purposely left them outside in the weather to dry up and curl. I can still remember the concern and pity on my father's face when she took my ruined shoes to show him what I had done to them in his absence.

What *I* had done? I tried endlessly to convince him of the truth, even with her looking on and knowing the consequences I would suffer later. But, you see, the artificial tears of compassion she shed in front of him for "his darling Charlotte and her mixed-up mind" outweighed my river of anguished tears every time.

I still resent his spectacularly blind eye to the truth, and, at the same time, I'm grateful for the entire spectrum of those early experiences. They shot me into the adult world with an over-developed sense of guilt, which, when properly channeled, has the potential of becoming a burning desire to see justice fulfilled. That sense of justice can fuel a passion to help the downtrodden rise and overcome, for them to *triumph over adversity*, which, I believe, is the most beautiful of all human dramas.

22
The Silver-Masked Saint

Mexico City, Mexico
1944

Pinkie

Luka looks in the smudged mirror and ruffles his hair. He dips a finger into a jar, rubs his palms together, and slicks them openly over his hair. He combs part of it forward, then makes a straight part on the right side with the edge of a comb. He gathers his longer hair into a band at the back of his neck, pats a slight wave into the top, then turns his head back and forth smiling at his image.

"Your hair is long when you don't pull it back, Luka," Pinkie says.

"Shh, Goldie. We don't want to wake her up," he whispers, pointing at Madam Rosie curled into an S on a slender motel bed. Her head rests on her bent arm, her mouth open and drooling, her eyes partially rolled back in her head. Her snoring has taken on a life of its own.

Beside the bed is a polished stump of wood holding a bent horseshoe lamp and an empty chipped pottery ashtray. A nearly empty bottle of José Cuervo tequila, hunks of dry, squeezed limes, empty 7-Up cans, and a turned-over glass are on the floor beside the stump table. Leaning against the wall is the picture of Jesus holding his heart in his hand. The edges look more tattered than before.

"Luka, you forgot again. My name is Pinkie, not Goldie," Pinkie whispers.

"Really? I wonder why I keep forgetting that? Let's get out of here before she sees what we're up to. We don't want to be late, do we?"

"I guess not. Why is she sleeping so long? It's not time for bed yet."

Luka smiles. "When we arrived this afternoon, you were dozing in the backseat. I didn't want to bother you, so I walked to the little market and bought my aunt a new kind of tonic, a beverage. It's called tequila."

"Did you drink the tonic, too?"

"She thinks I did."

They tiptoe out of the motel room and quietly close the door. Luka puts the key in and locks the door. Pinkie is quickly diving into his heart. He hesitates to tease her because his aunt frowns at him every time.

"I'll race you!" he says.

Pinkie hesitates, then takes off in a run toward the old car. He trots slowly, letting her win. "How did you get so fast, Miss Yellow?" he asks, sliding in behind the steering wheel. She closes the passenger door and looks at him. For the first time, the barest hint of a smile plays around her mouth.

"I'm Pinkie, not Miss Yellow."

"Oh, that's right. Sorry. Maybe after I eat some food, I'll get a better memory."

Over bowls of beans and spicy chili prepared from local chilies and served with a basket of warmed tortillas, Luka excitedly explains they have been invited to see an off-night fight between two unknown Mexican wrestlers. The invitation came from his distant cousin, Arturo, who is part of the ever-growing *Machwaya* population in Mexico City. He was a close ally in planning Luka's journey from Nuevo Laredo through Mexico with their aunt. Arturo will meet them tonight at the gym to make sure they are allowed to see the fights.

"The most wonderful part of this event is seeing *El Santo Enmascarado de Plata,* the Silver-Masked Saint—the greatest *luchador* of all time! He will be there to coach both amateur fighters before the public show, um… Reddie," he says.

"Reddie?"

"Um, yes, isn't your name like the color red?"

Pinkie rolls her eyes. "You know it isn't, Luka. It's Pinkie. Is the man with the silver mask going to wrestle, too?"

"No, unfortunately, *El Santo* is recovering from a serious auto accident he had this year. Arturo says he will do tag wrestling soon, but for now, he's assisting some of the new wrestlers while he gets well from his injuries. It's like a penance he's doing for Jesus saving him in that wreck. Arturo says he never did this before, but he's paying God back."

"Paying God? Does God want *pesos?*"

"It's different than paying with *pesos,* little one. You'll understand when you are older. You know, one time, *El Santo* battled eight men on the same night and won. Right here in Mexico City. He was the double champion in two weight classes for almost a year. Seeing him tonight is very, very special."

"Is it good?"

"Is what good?"

"Being a double champion?"

"Oh, yes, in *lucha libre,* that is excellent, Blue-Blue."

"I'm not Blue-Blue!"

He relishes the happy grin spreading across her face. He slaps his forehead and covers his face with his hand. When he takes it away, he's smiling.

All eyes are transfixed on the man in the silver clothes and mask as he enters a small gymnasium featuring an elevated wrestling ring in the center. Escorted by a man on each side, the masked man walks with a slight limp. Pinkie, a little scared of the costume, scoots closer to Luka. *El Santo* steps up the stairs to the ring and grasps the ropes. When he somersaults robustly into the ring, Pinkie sits straight up with one hand over her mouth.

El Santo poses with his hands on his hips, his cape blowing slightly from the heavy fan above the ring. The small group in the gym collectively gasps at the sight of the famous *luchador* in full regalia exhibiting his dramatic showmanship.

"¿Dónde están las vaquitas recién nacidas?" he shouts.

As two muscular young men dressed in body-hugging shorts bound from their seats and somersault into the ring, Pinkie whispers to Luka, "Why did he call them newborn calves?"

"Because they are amateurs. It means they are not very good fighters yet."

"But what is a newborn *calve?"*

Luka laughs. "Calf, not calve. It's a little cow just born. A *becerro."*

"Oh."

The men stand in respect with their chins on their chests not looking at *El Santo.* He barks a command at them, and they fall to the floor on all fours. *El Santo* jumps up on their backs, one foot on each man. He rocks back and forth, bends to speak to one, then the other. He moves over and stands on one man only. Then the other. He jumps off, slips through the ropes, and yells, *"Muéstrame!"*

The men somersault across the ring, through the ropes, and jump to the floor. People move aside as they run from one end of the room to the other, touching the wall on each side, then repeating. One is consistently ahead of the other. *El Santo* studies their conformation and style from their feet to their heads. He bends his head sideways as though he is cracking his neck, then peers for a long moment into the group of onlookers.

"Was the silver man looking at me?" Pinkie asks.

"I don't think so."

"Why won't he take his mask off so we can see his face?"

"Oh, no, *Niña Verde. El Santo Enmascarado de Plata* never takes off his mask."

"How does he eat and drink?"

"He removes his mask when no one is around."

"Is he very ugly?"

Luka laughs. "No, I don't believe so. It is for mystique, you know?"

"What is mystique?"

"Charm. Something that makes you irresistible."

"Hmm, okay. Anyway, my name is Pinkie."

"Huh?"

"You called me Green Girl, *Niña Verde*, a while ago."

"Did I?"

Their conversation is interrupted by *El Santo's* loud orders to the men. They return to the ring and instantly spring at each another. They throw one another from one set of ropes to the other, leap into the air, and jump on top of each other, grunting and shouting all the while. In a short time, the slower runner is on the floor of the ring with the other man's knee in his chest.

El Santo yells, "*¡Párenle!*"

At his command to stop, the wrestlers freeze in position. The Saint slips through the ropes, kneels down and speaks directly in the ear of the wrestler on the floor. He talks a long time, then stands up. He raises both arms as though he has won a serious championship, then somersaults out of the ring through the ropes. Before stepping off the platform, he briefly points at Luka and Pinkie and nods.

He is joined by his two escorts, and the trio leaves the room to thunderous applause from the coaches, managers, and the lucky few onlookers who had connections in order to gain entry to the exhibition. Clapping and whistling the loudest are the two young *luchadores* who received treasured advice from the greatest *luchador* in Mexico.

"Can you believe this, Luka? The king of all wrestlers!" Arturo says, jumping up from his seat and slapping Luka on the back. "Do not ever forget! Today… this day… we had the privilege of seeing the great *El Santo Enmascarado de Plata!*"

"*Si,* Arturo, and I shall never forget that today… this day… I and my little *amiga* here received a special message from this great man."

"*Que?*" Arturo says.

"*No importante,* Arturo. There are times when destiny points straight into a man's soul."

Arturo stares at Luka until his attention is drawn back to the announcer saying the two wrestlers will have a match in fifteen minutes. The room is filling quickly with boisterous fans of amateur *lucha libre*.

Pinkie tugs on Luka's sleeve. "Why did the silver man point at us?"

"Ah, you saw it too. It is because he knows we have a destiny we must fulfill."

"What is a destiny?"

Before Luka answers, she leans into his arm as the two amateur *luchadores* appear in full costume with frightening masks. The wrestler who was the slowest runner and who was taken down first in the practice maneuvers wins every round.

"You see," Luka says on the drive back to the motel, "*El Santo* is wise. His advice made the lesser man become the better man. I, too, am making important renovations in my mind."

"What do you mean?"

"I mean, we will take *El Santo's* advice, Pinkie. Wait and see. Our futures are in our own hands. Remember that in the days ahead."

"I only want to see my mama."

23
José Cuervo

Driving south through Mexico
1944

Pinkie looks up once in a while to see Luka smiling at her in the rearview mirror. They share the secret of seeing the silver masked man, and it makes this day better than the nine days before it.

She promised Luka never to tell Madam Rosie where they went, but she can't wait to tell her mama all about the famous *luchador* who pointed at her and Luka. Before her mama gets to hear any exciting news, though, Pinkie will scold her for letting this strange woman take charge of her. Madam Rosie says she has known Pinkie and her mama since they first moved to Mexico when Pinkie was two years old, but Pinkie isn't sure it's the truth.

They are driving a different car, a better one, or so Arturo promised this morning when he brought it to the motel. The same picture of Jesus with his heart out of his body is tacked onto the ceiling, but, this time, there are no rips in the ceiling upholstery. Madam Rosie is sitting up front, her head resting on the back of the seat. She periodically pats her forehead and cheeks with a dampened handkerchief. She says her head is pounding, and her stomach is not good, not good at all. Luka shakes his head and gives her a sympathetic tsk ever so often.

"What did you do last night while I, uh, rested, Pinkie?" she asks from up front.

"I read the *Pepín* and *Paquín* comics Luka bought me. I'm going to enter a contest in one of the comic books. You have to draw a new cartoon person.

"You like to draw?" Luka asks.

"Uh-huh. I'm going to draw a man in a cape with a blue costume and a mask. A very scary mask."

Luka grins at her in the mirror.

"You read comics all evening? Your eyes are going to fall out," Madam Rosie says.

"Not all evening. We ate supper across the street at *La Cocina de Chilis.*"

"Don't talk of food," Madam Rosie says with a groan. She rocks her body slightly with her hands pressed to her temples.

Luka looks at his aunt. "What's that, *moja tetka?* You say you want food? Very well, we shall stop at a café in the next village and eat chili," he says.

"Chili? No, please, don't mention it."

"The chili we had last night was so greasy and good. Lots of gristle pieces. They looked like frog eyes floating in the red grease. *Muy delicioso!*"

"O moj Bože, Luka, shut up!"

"All right, no greasy chili for you. You can eat something else. I think oily corn tortillas dipped in the melted white cheese with lots of hot peppers on top will taste good to you. Pinkie and I can eat the chili with the red grease floating on top. If they have some, would you like to eat the fish with some of the scales still clinging to the sides? So fresh! I love the fish eyes to remain almost raw. They crunch when you—"

"Stop the car!"

Luka pulls over. Madam Rosie bolts from her seat and slams the door behind her. She turns away, retching.

"What's wrong with her?" Pinkie asks. "Luka, why are you laughing? Tears, too. What does it mean?"

Luka slaps the dashboard and keeps laughing. When Madam Rosie turns around, he looks solemn. She gags, bends to vomit again. He laughs aloud.

"Luka, if I vomit, will you laugh at me, too?"

"Never, *La Niña Morada.*"

"But, you… hey, you called me Purple Girl."

"Zaboga, I must be more careful."

"What language are you speaking now?"

"Croatian."

"I never heard of it. How many languages can you speak?"

"Four or five. I pick them up very quickly."

"I only speak two. What was that word you used… zap, uh, zabo—"

"Zaboga. It means, uh, let's see… *Dios mio* or maybe *ai-yi-yi."*

The car door opens. An ashen Madam Rosie drops into the seat. She digs another handkerchief from her purse to mop the sweat from her forehead. "I need something to drink," she whispers hoarsely.

"Of course, *tetka!* I have more José Cuervo in the trunk. I'll get it for you. Do you want a full glass or only half a glass?"

"Aghh!" Madam Rosie cries, opening the door and hanging her head out to dry heave. She closes the door gently and lays her head back on the seat. "My head is so painful. I-I must have a Coca-Cola, Luka. Get me one. Please. I'm very ill."

"I shall hurry." Luka starts the car and pulls onto the road so quickly they all lurch forward. Pinkie notices he's turning the steering wheel hard to the right and left and taking curves in the road where none are. They swing side to side.

"Luka… Luka, what kind of driving is this?" Madam Rosie cries, holding the handkerchief over her mouth.

"I'm so sorry, my dear aunt. I am having trouble with this steering wheel. Arturo should have informed me of this problem. I'll keep working on it. I think it needs a lot of exercise, you know? Too tight. Say, you don't look so good, *tetka.* I should hurry more."

He speeds down the road, puts on the brakes. Pinkie almost hits her head on the back of the front seat. "What was that in the road, an armadillo? Oh, I guess it's nothing. Merely shadows." He starts again, gently, but constantly moving the wheel back and forth. They stop three more times for Madam Rosie to get in and out of the car. When they reach the next settlement, Madam Rosie says she will choke Luka to death if he does not find her a bed and a Coca-Cola.

24
Daniella Izabella Francisca Angelina Serrano

Toluca, Mexico
1944

Nailed to a stake beside the road is a hand-painted sign with the words, "EL MOTTIL." They drive past it less than a quarter of a mile and find themselves out of town. They turn around and drive back to the only lodging available in the miniscule settlement in which Madam Rosie demands they stop. Next to a small, weathered adobe house with chips in the exterior, the "motel" room is a separate building constructed of horizontal gray boards. Inside the room are two cots barely lifted off the floor—each with an old feather pillow and a natty blanket—a chair, a small table, and a brown-stained sink with a cloudy mirror above it. Their toilet is a stinky, fly-infested outhouse twenty feet away. Chickens roam freely outside scratching the dirt and clucking.

Luka says Pinkie and his aunt can have the cots, and he will sleep in the chair, a maroon, threadbare lounger of good proportion sporting saggy cushions. He buys his aunt two warm Coca-Colas from the motel owner, leaving one capped for later. She downs the open one and sinks into one of the cots.

"Bring me a receptacle, Luka," she says weakly.

"What kind of a receptacle?"

"To vomit in."

Luka locates an old jar by the corroded sink, hand wipes the network of webs covering the exterior, blows inside. A puff of dust swirls into his face. He sneezes and takes the jar to his aunt. "This is all we have," he says.

She raises up, eyes the jar, and falls backward. *"Moj život je gotov,"* she mumbles. Luka places the jar on the floor close to her limp arm hanging off the cot.

"What did she say, Luka?" Pinkie asks.

"She says her life is over."

"Is she dying?"

"No, she only thinks she is."

He walks over and wiggles Madam Rosie's foot.

"Wha-what do you want?"

"I know what you need, *mi tia*—soup! Everyone needs soup when they are sick. Papa always says so. I shall drive to the next town and bring you back some *mole de panza.* Arturo tells me it's a tasty Mexican soup made with cow stomach and red chili-peppers. What do you say?"

"I say… get out!"

"Get out? Now?"

"Yes, and bring me my Jesus from the car. Put it where I can see it."

Luka smiles and beckons Pinkie to follow him outside. He removes the picture from the ceiling of the car and takes it inside while Pinkie settles into the passenger seat up front. When he returns, she asks, "Why does she love that picture so much? The Jesus in it looks like a girl with only a small beard. I've seen many better Jesuses."

Luka laughs. "I agree with you. *Tetka* thinks it's more sacred since it is like the most famous one by the painter Batoni a long, long time ago."

"How long ago?"

"I don't know, maybe in the 1700s."

"Is that a long time from now?"

"Well, this is 1944, so it's more than two hundred years ago."

Pinkie gasps. "And Madam Rosie owns it?"

"No, she owns a replica. A copy of it. I promise, if that original painting was anywhere she could get her hands on it, it would be hers."

"Why?"

"Because that's how she is."

"Luka?"

"Yes?"

"I don't like that motel room."

He sighs. "I know. *Tetka*'s probably getting bedbugs in that nasty place. I tried to warn her, so it's her own fault."

"Bed bugs? I don't like bugs."

"Don't worry. I'll shoot them."

"Shoot them?"

"Sure, with a rubber band." He laughs. Pinkie doesn't.

"I'll give you a blanket and let you sleep in the backseat of the car tonight, okay?"

"The blanket in that room looked dirty."

"I know. We'll use the ones we brought with us."

"But I'll be afraid outside in the car by myself."

"I'll sleep under the steering wheel."

"Sitting up?"

"Of course. I like it."

"Where are we going now?"

"Toluca."

"Is that a town?"

"Uh-huh."

"What's there?"

"Everything. It's where we were going to spend the night if my aunt hadn't changed our plans. I have a great desire to see the flamenco dancers at the Cactus Cantina. Arturo's friend, Bruno, told me about them. He says they are beautiful, and some of them are from Spain. We have to find *La Plaza de los Mártires.* The cantina is located two streets behind it on the north side."

"Why is it called Square of the Martyrs?"

"Because a hundred people died in that plaza. Mexicans who

wanted to be free from Spanish rule. They are the martyrs."

"Why did they want to be free?"

"Everyone wants to be free from oppression, even the kind that comes from within their own family."

She wrinkles her nose. "What kind of dancers are we going to see?"

"Flamenco.

"What's that?"

"A beautiful dance from Spain. It's melodious. Passionate! Most people don't know the real Flamenco dancers are Andalusian *gitanos* mostly from southern Spain. I, too, know a little of the Flamenco dancing."

"Are you really a *gitano,* Luka?"

"Yes, I am, *Señorita Naranja.* My father's family is from Croatia and Serbia, but *Roma* have migrated to everywhere in the world. Let me see." He lifts his fingers off the steering wheel to designate the countries. "India, France, Turkey, Egypt, Hungary, Albania, Spain, Germany, Scotland, Russia, Chile, Greece… everywhere."

"What is *Roma?"*

"A name that means *Gitanos, Roms, Machwaya, Calé,* Travellers, *Sinti, Cigán, Gitans, Cigány,* Wanderers, *Tsiganes, Zigeuner,* and lots of other names."

"Why do they have so many names?"

"Because they are all different and came from different countries. They have different traditions and beliefs."

"Why do you remember all those names but you do not remember my name is not Orange."

"Que?"

"You called me *Señorita Naranja.* a while ago."

Luka taps his palm on the steering wheel. "Oh no! Again?" Okay, let me think. Hmm." He nods, then raises a hand in the air. "I think I got it now. Your name is Pinkie! I remembered!"

"Yes!" She giggles. "Do you want to know the rest of my name, Luka?"

"Is it Pinkie, *la niña azul?"*

"Pinkie, the blue girl? No!"

"Is it Pinkie, *la niña rosita encantadora?*"

"The delightful pink girl? No!"

Her smile kills him. It's so innocent, and he never saw a hint of it until yesterday.

"My whole name is Daniella Izabella Francisca Angelina Serrano."

"That's a big name. Why are you called Pinkie?"

"My mama says because I looked like a doll you buy in a fancy store when I was a baby. She said my skin was pink and creamy, and I had yellow hair and blue eyes like a doll."

"Ah, yes, I can understand her reasoning."

She settles into the seat beside him. "You're my first *gitano* friend, Luka. My mama won't let me play with Cita where I live because she is *gitana.* I always want to, but Mama is scared to let me."

"Scared?"

"Uh-huh. She said gypsies steal children."

25
The Truth of History

Toluca, Mexico
1944

Pinkie's words nail Luka's stomach to his spine. Of course, he knows *Roma* who operate as does his aunt are the main reason all *Roms* get blamed for every bad thing that happens wherever they go. A wave of shame washes over him. He strikes the steering wheel with his flat hand.

"Que paso?" Pinkie asks.

"Oh, a-a bug. A fly. I was swatting a fly."

She looks confused. "Where is it now?"

"In fly-heaven, of course," he says, forcing a smile. She smiles back, then resumes her stare out the side window.

It's Papa's fault. The bricks of this terrible deed are Papa's insecurity about money and tetka's mercenary heart. Old-fashioned traditions of obeying without question are the mortar between the bricks. Why didn't I stand up to my father? I know Papa wasn't really serious about keeping my money if I didn't do as he asked. It was a foolish threat he didn't mean. At twenty, am I not my own man?

"Luka, I forgot to drink some water at our motel room. I'm thirsty."

"We will drink nothing that comes from that sink. We'll be in Toluca very soon."

Pinkie yawns, and Luka tumbles back into dark reflections of the dishonest minorities who muddy the waters and cause all *Romani* to be distrusted, spit upon, run from town to town, country to country. Such has been the agonizing truth of history for centuries.

He side-glances at the little girl who calls him her friend. She has already been stolen from her home by his terrible aunt, but what kind of future awaits her in Argentina?

His Croatian kin in Mexico filled his ears with news that Hitler was having all the *Sinti,* the German *Romani,* named *enemies of the Third Reich.* He said they have been rounded up from Bavaria, Bohemia, Austria, Poland, France, and, of course, Germany. They are locked up in work camps, worked almost to death, sterilized so they can bear no more children, starved. Many die from disease and injury or are murdered for no reason. Women are raped, children often exterminated, especially the babies. Arturo's father, Jakov, said they are used in experiments the same as the Jews.

"If you do not fit their perfect mold of a human, it is over," Jakov said, using a finger to draw a line across his throat. "Thank God we are safe in Mexico! Many Croatians have died in Europe, Luka. You and your papa should wake up. Leave Argentina and come here! I don't understand Rosario going back to Argentina when the Nazis use it as their second home. Pay attention to the tragedies of the *Romani* in Europe!"

Jakov's anguish and the stories he told Luka were shocking. Luka had not heard such news in Buenos Aires. There, Hitler, and the Nazis in general, are held, at least clandestinely, in high regard despite the rumors filtering in through non-German immigrants. Are the periodic arrests by the Perón government of so-called enemy agents really only puppet maneuvers and not legitimate *enemy cleansing?* Who are they appeasing with their fake arrests?

Whispered rumors that Hitler is rescuing his beloved country of Germany and is a great and courageous hero to his people are prevalent, even in the newspapers. *Good Christians, those Germans…* is a mantra proclaimed in one manner or another in Argentina. Christianity, especially Catholicism, is highly esteemed by Argentinians. The falsehood that Nazis are Christians is propaganda spewed by a fawning government, Jakov insisted.

What is the truth? Good Christians do not torture or exterminate people. What will happen if the underlying Nazi influence causes the Argentine powers to despise *Romani* as they do in other countries?

Luka sighs noisily, his mind uneasy.

"What's wrong, Luka?"

"I-I, uh, nothing."

"You look mad."

He forces a smile. "No, no. I'm only thinking how hungry I am. Are you hungry?"

"My stomach is growling."

"Let's eat before we go see the dancers." He smiles. "Pinkie, I am half Croatian *Machwaya* and half Spaniard. My mama, bless her memory, was a beautiful woman from a good Spanish family who fell in love with a handsome *gitano* man—my papa. When you see the dancers, you may see someone who looks a little like my mama."

26
La Cantina de Cactus

Toluca, Mexico
1944

A big man wearing a white shirt with puffed-out sleeves, black trousers, and a multi-colored, woven sash underneath his overhanging belly blocks the doorway of *La Cantina de Cactus.* He looks as out of place as a bull in an orchestra pit. Guitar music seeps around the small space between him and the door frame. A scar across his lip, his doleful eyes, and his annoyed expression make Pinkie take a step behind Luka.

"*No se permiten niños,*" he informs them in a gruff voice.

"No children? *Por qué no, Señor?*"

"*Los niños causan distracciones.*"

"Oh, no, *Señor,*" Luka says, in perfect Spanish. "*Esta niña es más callada que una monja. ¡Lo prometo.* She will not cause any distractions." Luka drops coins into the man's hand. The man looks at his hand and back up at Luka. Luka digs in his pocket and takes out paper money. He places several bills in the large palm.

"*No levantarse ni caminar,*" he says directly to Pinkie with a scowl. "*A las bailarinas de flamenco no les gusta.*" He reaches behind himself to a standing hat rack and brings out a crushed straw sombrero. He extends it toward Pinkie. She shrinks back. The man glares at Luka. "*No se permiten niñas ni mujeres en las cantinas mexicanas. Ella lleva pantalones. Si usa el sombrero, parecerá un niño. Siéntese en el rincón oscuro y mantenga la boca cerrada."*

Luka takes the hat from the man and bends down to Pinkie. "If you don't put it on, we can't go in and see the dancers. You have to look like a boy. He says no women or girls allowed in Mexican cantinas."

"I heard him myself, Luka. Why didn't he say that before he took your money?" She steps forward, scowling at the big man. Luka drops the hat on her head, straightens it.

"Okay, Pedro, *mi hijo*, let's go see the dancers," he says, winking.

The big man turns, walks down a short, narrow hallway inlaid with intricately decorated tile on each side and bright green paint the last two feet to the ceiling. The hallway opens to a large room. On the far wall facing the hallway are shelves of liquor bottles reaching several feet to the sides and at least ten feet high. Three men dressed in white shirts, black string ties, and full-length, white aprons are drying glasses with small towels and serving drinks at the massive bar.

On the long wall on the right side is a mural of three women dancers, the bottoms of their long dresses swirling, their legs showing, smiles lighting their faces. On the left wall, a mural of men from the waist up playing guitars, a town painted behind them, a sunset behind the buildings, and saguaro cacti placed intermittently throughout the scene.

Two round tables on the far left of the room are filled with men playing cards. A large stage with a semi-circle front fills the far right-hand corner of the oblong structure. A man on a stool in the middle of the stage is strumming a guitar and singing. Behind him stands a group of musicians. One holds a *Guitarrón Mexicano,* two have violins, one has a *vihuela.* All are dressed in typical *charro* with tight black pants, short jackets, and scarves tied at their necks. Stringed lights of red, white, and green create a colorful grid above the room.

The room has a festive air with male customers laughing, drinking, and eating at the tables and bar. The big man points to what looks like darkness. Luka raises both hands as if to say, *"Que?"* The big man frowns, then heads in the direction he is pointing. In the dark shadows of the room is a niche with a lone round table about a foot and a half in diameter covered in tanned leather. From the tabletop, crisscrossed leather on a wood frame drops to the floor. The big man points to the two matching chairs.

"Mantén a la niña aquí," he says, and walks away.

"He's a mean man," Pinkie says.

"He acts like we know nothing," Luka says, nodding. "I'd like to punch him in his fat stomach. Just a few times to teach him some manners, you know?"

"He said no standing because the dancers don't like it. He says no women are allowed. No girls. He said for us to sit down and shut up our mouths. He's a mean, ugly man."

"I agree. I bet he cannot dance even a jig, *el cerdo grande.* He does not know what a flamenco dancer wants or does not want. I must be *loco* bringing you in this place."

"But I love it here, Luka." She rotates her arm in a circle. "I have never seen a room like this. Or dancers. Wait until I tell my mama!"

Her words are an iron claw raking across Luka's insides. He traces his finger over the rim of a wide-mouth jar holding a small lit candle inside. Why is he such a coward? If he were a brave man, he would get in the car right now and drive Pinkie back to Nuevo Laredo. Could he bear the shame of disrespecting his older relative by abandoning her? He sighs. Tomorrow, he will call Papa. Papa will surely be angry at this terrible thing his sister has done, and he will order her to find a way to send the girl back home. Tradition says a woman bends to the authority of a man over her, and Papa has authority over his sister. Let them obey their own traditions for a change.

Alas, what if Papa—being a different man since his accident—laughs and calls this another *interesting business arrangement* devised by his sister? Then… his father is not the great man Luka believes him to be. He will no longer deserve or receive his son's respect. If that happens, Luka promises himself, he will take the child back home and not care about elders, traditions, or anything else. He looks at Pinkie. Her eyes reflecting the light of the candle are full of childish wonder as she gazes around the room.

"Stay here, Pinkie. I'll bring us something refreshing." He returns carrying a round tray holding two glasses with ice pieces inside, two bottles of Coca-Cola, and a plate of broken *totopos* sprinkled with sugar and cinnamon.

The musician sings a soulful ballad of a young woman who cannot marry the man she loves because of family decisions for her life. She feels alone and unhappy. She is contemplating running away from her family and her town. Only dancing can consume her deep sorrow.

"It's a sad song," Pinkie whispers to Luka. He nods, doesn't break his stare at the stage. When the song is over, the singer moves to the back of the stage with the other men. A man assists a woman as she emerges from a curtain and climbs the steps to the stage. He deftly unhooks and dramatically swirls off a long emerald cape that had been fastened across her chest. He leaves as the dancer strikes a pose in the center of the stage under the spotlight, one arm across the small of her back, the other in the air, her head bowed.

Her shiny green dress flares at the bottom with many layers. Her dark hair is pulled back, and a wine-red flower with crystals on the petals secures it to the back of her neck. She lifts with one hand her sparkling skirt to above her knees and begins tapping a slow rhythm with her black shoes. Her face is fixed to one spot as she turns, her back straight.

She uses both hands to lift and hold her skirt up on each side. The music begins. Her body moves gracefully sideways as she lets the skirt slowly drop. Her hands move up, down—undulating, twirling. She bends backward, comes back up to pause momentarily in a pose. Her tapping resumes as the music increases in tempo.

"She is dancing out the ballad the man was singing to us, Pinkie. The slow part at the beginning represented her aching heart for her lover. This fast part will show her frustration because she is not allowed to make up her own mind," Luka explains, leaning into Pinkie.

The dancer flings her hands several times into an arch over her head, claps them, then extends one hand toward a girl who runs up the stage steps to give her something. The musicians stop playing. The girl fades quickly off the stage. The musicians play a slow melody. The dancer quickly flicks the object, and a black sequined fan opens dramatically as her body glides to the side.

Pinkie gasps. "Did you see, Luka? Did you see her beautiful fan?"

Luka says, "Yes, little one. I think I am in love."

"What?"

He laughs. "Just a joke."

The music builds. The music spills out a frantic tempo as the dancer yells, her feet moving rapidly. One musician claps, the others furiously work the strings on their instruments. With one last shout, she finishes her dance by throwing the fan in the air, turns quickly in a circle to catch the fan. Her final pose is her face pointing upward with her neck in a straight line. One hand holds the fan in front of her face, the other arm is arched in the air. The audience claps passionately.

"She's decided to run away with her lover! She will defy the traditions of her family!" Luka says, rising from his chair and clapping. "Another message to me, Pinkie. First *El Santo* and now the lovely flamenco dancer."

"Luka, the mean man said not to stand up."

"He won't see us in this dark corner." He sits down, then pops back up. "Stay here, little one. I shall return shortly."

Before she can ask him where he's going, Luka darts to the wall on the right and follows it. The dancer descends the stairs and goes behind the curtain. Luka steps behind her as close as a shadow.

"Luka," Pinkie whispers, fear clutching at her stomach. With Luka gone, the room is too large, too full of strangers. Why did he go behind the curtain? She nibbles a *totopo,* puts it down. The mean man passes close by and peers in her direction. She gasps. Will he notice Luka is gone?

The onstage singer sings another lively song, and, afterward, he and the other musicians walk toward the steps. The girl who earlier brought the fan to the dancer runs up the steps and tells them something. They back up. The spotlight comes back on. The same lady dancer comes through the curtain arm-in-arm with a man dressed in black pants, black waistcoat with glittery buttons, and a green scarf tied around his neck. The ends dangle in front of him almost to his waist.

They ascend the steps, and the lady tells a musician something in his ear. The musicians begin to strum. She steps out of the spotlight as the male dancer slowly taps a rhythm with his back turned to the audience. He slow-claps in time with the music and steps backward. His shoes tap as he continues to step backward with his hands up, down, rotating at the wrists. He pivots rapidly in a full circle, hair flying.

Pinkie stands up worrying that Luka will miss the other flamenco dancer. She gazes at the curtain where he disappeared. The room is quiet as the male dancer poses. The music begins again, then accelerates. He swivels quickly right, then quickly left. Suddenly, his feet are moving so fast, Pinkie can barely keep up with them. His hands clap and coil and turn. His long hair twirls wildly. He stops and extends a hand to the lady dancer who was clapping in time from the sidelines. She walks slowly, gracefully toward him, castanets clicking in her raised hands. She turns her back and steps backward. Click, click. Tap, tap. They meet. He turns his face to the audience.

Pinkie gasps. Luka!

They move separately, meet, match arm and body movements until, at the end of the dance, they are entwined—two trees encircling one another to become one tree. The crowd whistles and claps profusely. The couple bows and steps gingerly down the steps from the stage. Luka kisses the woman's hand for everyone to see before they disappear behind the curtain.

Will Luka come back for her? Pinkie considers running toward the curtain. She takes two uncertain steps, sees the mean man bending down to talk to someone at a nearby table. She freezes, goes back to her chair with a locked stare on the curtains.

At last, Luka exits the curtain. He stays in the shadows close to the wall as he returns to their table in his original clothes, hair coifed neatly. He sits down fanning his face with a hand.

"Did you see me, Pinkie? Oh, what joy that dance brought me! It made my troubles lighter, you know? Is it okay if I have some of your Coca-Cola? Dancing makes me so thirsty. What is it, little one?"

"I-I, oh, nothing."

"Did you not enjoy to see me dance?"

"I didn't know where you were. I wanted to go find you, but the mean man was too near. Why didn't you tell me you were a dancer?"

"I think I did."

"Why didn't you say you were going to dance with the woman?"

"To surprise you! Also, I didn't know if Adriana would allow it. She's the dancer you saw both times. She's the boss of the other dancers."

"Why did she let you?"

Luka chuckles. "You are too young to understand, Pinkie, but I'm considered *un hombre encantador*. He winks. Besides, Adriana is a Spanish *gitana*. Once I told her of my father's dancing, and of my Spanish mother, she wanted to propose!"

"She what?"

"She wants to marry me!" He laughs. "I'm only teasing, but she did ask me to stay until after her performances. Begged me. I told her we had to go."

"You didn't tell her *we*, did you?"

"Of course not. No children are allowed in here, especially girls. He pops a large hunk of *totopo* in his mouth, swigs down the last of Pinkie's drink. "Ah, dancing. It is almost as good for your soul as religion, but now, we must go," he says, checking his watch and standing. "Stay close to my side as we leave so no one makes a problem. Make sure your sombrero is pulled down on your forehead, uh… Pedro.

Pinkie follows closely. She is angry but doesn't understand why. Maybe she doesn't like sharing Luka with pretty flamenco dancers.

27
Don't Be a Tourist

Near Toluca, Mexico
1944

An annoyed face greets the pair as they come through the ill-fitting door of the dreary motel room. She occupies the lone chair with a low table placed in front of it. Tarot cards are lined up in rows touching each other on top of the table. Her head is covered in pin curls fastened with bobby pins and with a scarf circling the edges of her hairline. Luka and Pinkie stand as frozen as two thieves exposed under a police spotlight.

"Where have you been, Luka? Did you think I would sleep until tomorrow? Do you think you can traipse off anywhere you wish for half the night?"

"It's not that late, and yes, I did. You were very ill. I expected you to sleep for many hours."

"I did sleep for many hours, and you were gone when I woke up. No note or letter. What was I to think?"

"We didn't want to bother you, and we were hungry. Nothing is here in this little village, so we drove to Toluca to find food. It isn't far."

"And you brought nothing back for your aunt, did you? Thank the stars I had dried fruit and *carne seca* in my bag." She eyes him suspiciously. "You were gone a long time. Too long to only eat."

"We looked at landscapes, too. We saw a cathedral and museum in *la Plaza de los Mártires.* Did you know—"

"Are you a tourist? Driving takes gasoline. Gasoline costs money. Don't forget it is my money paying for this trip, and that does not allow for you to be a tourist!"

Luka quells the rising tide of anger in his throat. How badly he wants to scream at her, tell her he does not respect her, inform her that he is taking Pinkie back to her mama, express his disgust of what she is doing. *Wait until you talk to Papa* reverberates inside his head. He wipes a hand across his mouth and fakes a smile. "You are right, my dear aunt. How could I forget that money is everything?"

"*Los turistas están locos.* You are not a tourist!"

"Yes, very *loco,* those tourists. Maybe the most *loco* of all people in the world."

Madam Rosie studies his face, finds only a benign expression on it. "I smell smoke. Have you taken up smoking cigarettes? Do you think I will pay for them?"

"Of course not, but the tourists, you know, they smoke all the time, and it makes us smell of their smoke."

"They smoke in the cathedrals and museums?"

"Isn't it terrible? No respect, those tourists."

She snorts, waves her hand in a gesture of dismissal, squints as she peers at Pinkie. "Where did you get that ridiculous hat, Pinkie?"

Pinkie grabs the floppy sombrero off her head. "I-I…"

Luka laughs. "It's a funny story. You see, in the restaurant…" and he lapses into a tale that never happened.

"Well, throw it away. It looks like this room. We are going to get bedbugs in this dump. Why did you bring us here, Luka?"

"Why did I…? Don't you remember you made me stop here instead of driving us to Toluca?"

"Nonsense," she says quietly, then lapses into mumbling in her native Croatian language as she gathers the tarot cards into a small wooden box. "Go to sleep. We leave for, uh, what is the name of that town?"

"Chilpancingo."

"Yes, we leave for there early tomorrow. Then, Acapulco. We must be in Acapulco in two days, Luka. Our boat is waiting."

"Boat?" Pinkie asks.

"I told you already we have a long journey and part of it is in a boat," Madam Rosie says.

"Where does the boat take us?"

"If we are very lucky, to Chile first. Maybe it will be Peru instead. Then Argentina. Now, go to bed. So many questions hurt my bones late at night."

"I asked only two."

"Too many."

Pinkie folds her arms. "Why did my mama leave me with you?"

Madam Rosie sighs noisily. "I told you."

For the second time tonight, Pinkie is angry. She glances at Luka. The sympathy on his face changes her anger into trepidation. Something isn't right. She takes off her shoes and picks up the folded blanket from the end of the unused cot. She crawls under it and turns away. Her tears drip onto the yellowed pillow ticking.

"Pinkie, do you wish to sleep in the backseat of the car as we talked about?" Luka says gently.

Madam Rosie croaks, "What? Sleep in the—" The look Luka sends in her direction silences her.

"No gracias," Pinkie whispers.

"I can get you a blanket from the car. You don't have to use that ugly one," Luka says.

"It's all right. Good night, Luka."

"Good night, Pinkie."

Madam Rosie's eyes narrow as she glances from her nephew to the little form curled underneath the blanket on the cot.

28
Cross-Double-Cross

Chilpancingo, Mexico
Acapulco, Mexico
1944

Supper in the café the next evening in Chilpancingo is quiet. Madam Rosie steals covert glances at Luka and Pinkie. Luka excuses himself twice to use the pay phone in the booth outside the café *to call Papa and tell him how successfully we have made the journey so far,* he explains to his aunt. Each time, he returns with the news that Argentina is impossible these days to reach by telephone. He and his aunt watch each other carefully, smiling coyly when their eyes meet.

Madam Rosie leaves Pinkie drawing a masked man with a cape and Luka reading a magazine in their motel room and goes to the lobby. She has a conversation with the motel manager and uses the pay phone. Luka follows her the second time to see if he can guess what she is up to. He sees her gesturing with her free hand as she talks inside the phone booth, but he can't get close enough to hear her conversation. He goes back to their room unseen by his aunt.

"Tomorrow is *Día de Muertos,"* she announces on her return. "As you know, Day of the Dead is a big deal in Mexico. The manager says we cannot drive a car through Acapulco because the streets will be flooded with parades and revelers. He says the ship dock is many blocks from any of the places we can drive a car, Luka."

"What time do we meet the ship's aide tomorrow afternoon?

"Two."

"It won't be difficult. Acapulco is not far from this town. Arturo gave me a number to call for two men to bring a cart to carry our things to the dock. Carts are the best transportation during this time, he said. I'll go call them later and have them meet us at noon."

"What is the name of the market where we are to leave the car for that man, uh, what's his name?"

"José Padilla, and we leave our car for him at *la Mercado de los Ranchos.*

"Ah, yes. Very well." She smiles at her nephew, and he can't help but wonder what lies behind it. She proclaims she has one more call to make.

"What is so important for all these calls?"

"I have many arrangements to make. Do you wish to sleep next to rotting shrimp and fish guts, or do you want suitable accommodations on that leaky boat we board tomorrow?"

"Rotting fish guts? Leaky boat?"

"The only boats available are old boats barely seaworthy. The governments steal all the others to fight in the war. We're going to Peru on a fishing boat, or perhaps several boats. We have to switch them if one starts sinking. *Tko zna? Možda se utopimo.*"

"Really? You say you believe we may drown? Why should we get on such a boat?"

She shrugs. "Is life for cowards?"

Her words anger him. *No, nor is it for thieves,* he thinks.

He is careful not to reveal in his face that his secret strategy does not put him or Pinkie on that leaky boat, or any other. His plan is to covertly tell Pinkie to remain in the car at the market tomorrow until he tells her to get out. He will supervise his hired men as they load his aunt's bags and boxes onto their cart and tell them to leave his bag and the small suitcase they bought for Pinkie with her few new clothes in the car. As soon as *tetka* is settled on the cart seat and her things are loaded, he will quietly slip behind the wheel of the car and drive away. His aunt can protest all she wants, he doesn't care. Pinkie is going home.

All day he has tried to call Papa to discuss with him his aunt's travesty, but the telephone lines were down. One time, his papa answered, but his voice was quickly drowned out by static. Such are the problems with the telephones since the terrible earthquake in San Juan in January.

After much soul-searching, Luka decided it doesn't matter what Papa says. What his greedy aunt is doing is not acceptable. The Silver-Masked Saint and the dance of the woman last night prove Luka must be his own man and do what is proper. Will his father disown him for abandoning his aunt? Perhaps, but Luka cares more for Pinkie's life at this point than anything else.

Día de Muertos decorations and people in garish costumes flood the roads into Acapulco. Outside the *Mercado de los Ranchos,* two men and a mule-drawn cart with massive wooden wheels are smiling and waiting for them to arrive. Wood spikes holding fake human skulls protrude from each corner of the square wagon bed on the back of the cart, and crepe paper skeletons are affixed to the sideboards. One man wears a black shirt with skeleton bones painted in white. Just when they finish loading Madam Rosie's things into the cart, a car drives into the market's parking area and stops even with their car. Two men step out. One nods at Madam Rosie. Luka looks back and forth at the men and his aunt.

"*¿Quiénes son estos otros hombres, tetka?* We don't need these men to help us."

She doesn't answer.

The men go into action as if they know exactly what to do. One steps to the trunk, looks inside, grabs the last two remaining pieces, tosses them into the cart alongside Madam Rosie's things.

"Hey, wait for my orders!" Luka barks. He glances at the mule-pulled cart, trying to think of a reason for removing his and Pinkie's travel bags from it. His aunt watches from the sidelines, hands on her hips. The man who handled the remaining bags gets back into the car he and his companion came in and stares straight ahead, hands on the steering wheel.

Luka sees his aunt nod toward the car Luka has been driving. The second man quickly opens the front door, leans the seat forward, and pulls Pinkie out by her arm. She screams. Luka's protests die in his throat as the man pushes her out of the way, climbs in the front seat, and drives away in their car! The other car follows, leaving Luka staring with his mouth open. It all happened so fast, so *unnaturally* fast.

Luka hurries to put an arm around Pinkie, who is silently crying and rubbing her arm. He turns an angry face toward his aunt. "What is the meaning of this? Did you see how rough he handled Pinkie? Why did those strangers drive off with our car? *Señor* Padilla has been hired to return the car to Mexico City. He will be here soon, and there is no car for him to take."

She shrugs. "Are you complaining because I hired more workers for you? See how simple and fast it was?" She steps onto the wooden stair behind the mule and hoists herself onto the seat. "The crowd is increasing, Luka. We must hurry and get to the dock. Lift the girl up here and let us be on our way."

Her victorious smirk infuriates Luka. The crafty crone beat him at his own game!

He stares as the cart rolls forward with his aunt and Pinkie on the seat, all their belongings piled in the back. He sees plainly that the woman he has always called *tetka* is a tricky cobra beguiling her prey before striking.

29
Day of the Dead and the Deceived

Acapulco, Mexico
1944

Pinkie holds onto the rough-board seat in the cart as the wooden wheels roll over wads of crepe paper, paper hats, and discarded food trash. The cart owners walk one on each side of the mule. They are hemmed in on all sides by people dressed as dead people. A throng of people holding high in the air an enormous replica of a human skeleton lying on its back, its grotesque head flopping backward, crowd in close to the men and mule. The blackened eyes of the skeleton stare at Pinkie, but she doesn't care. She is desperate to keep her eyes on Luka behind the cart, but he is often delayed by the masses of people celebrating *Día de Muertos.*

Pretty ladies in festive, low-cut dresses, shiny hair cascading down their backs, wear frightening white and black masks or have their faces painted in black and white. Black noses. Black eye sockets. Sometimes, there are black beards drawn on the ladies' chins. Red, bloody scars are painted on their chests and arms. Never has Pinkie seen women dressed like this, but she has heard of it.

She learned about *Día de Muertos* in school. Her teachers encouraged the students to make *esqueleto* drawings and masks. On a special day right before the holiday, the teachers brought treats of sugary candy formed into tiny human *calaveras.* One time, her very first teacher brought in *pan de muerto,* a sweet, baked bread, for them to taste.

Mama explained to her it was an important celebration to the Mexican people in which they believe the line between the world we live in and the world the dead people live in is erased for one day only in November. She said the people invite the ghosts of their dead relatives to drink, dance, and play music with them. They light candles and offer stacks of fruits and tortillas on the *alteras* in their homes or along the roadsides.

"Why don't we do that, mama? Don't you wish to drink and dance with your *mama y papi* on the day of dead people?"

"*No, mi dulzura,* we believe a different way."

"Why?"

"Because different people have different beliefs."

"What is ours?"

"We believe we die and go to Heaven and stay put. Maybe we play with puppies or ponies until everyone else gets there."

"No dead-people ghosts can come back to see us?"

Mama laughed. "We'll see them another time, but I believe they will look pretty, not dead."

"Can we go see the parades even if we don't get to see our dead relatives?"

"I don't think so. It might scare you."

Now, here Pinkie is in the middle of a Day of the Dead parade as it meanders westward on a street leading to the ocean. She isn't scared of the masked ladies, the men in their painted faces and top coats, the ghouls, ghosts, or skeletons, but she is frightened to death of losing sight of Luka in the crowd. She pivots in her seat constantly looking for him. He watches for her, as well, waving when they catch sight of one another.

A cart heaped with yellow and orange marigolds and fuzzy magenta cockscombs pulls up beside them. Pinkie is aghast at the sight of all the beautiful flowers heaped together. Among the flowers are crosses made of sticks with red painted names on them. When she finally breaks her stare, she turns to look for Luka, stretching her neck in all directions. Where is he? An arm waves at her from several feet behind the cart. At last, Luka emerges from the crowd still waving his arm. He staggers forward, grinning.

She waves back, sees two men ease in behind him. Pinkie recognizes them as the men who parked near their car at the market earlier, one of whom pulled her out of the car by her arm. They walk behind Luka, but he doesn't notice. She waves big at him, points, wishes he would turn around and see them. He waves back. He is still smiling at her as they throw a burlap sack over his head. He kicks and squirms as they pull him out of the crowd. All three disappear down a narrow alley between an open fish market and a curio shop.

30
Blue Zebra Shells

Acapulco, Mexico
1944

"Please, please make them stop the cart, Madam Rosie!" Pinkie begs. "We have to save Luka from those bad men. They were hurting him!" Madam Rosie seems not to hear her. Pinkie shakes the woman's arm, pulls on her dress, but she looks straight ahead, paying no attention to the girl's pleas. Pinkie sobs, wiping her face on her arm. She considers the distance from the cart to the ground, glances at the woman beside her. She jumps. Firm arms grab her and pull her back onto the seat.

"I hate you! I hate you!" she shouts, struggling against the woman's grip. She glares at Madam Rosie with tearful contempt. "Luka… Luka," she sobs.

The cart turns down a side street, and the *Día de Muertos* crowd thins, eventually stopping. Skulls, flowers, and offerings are plentifully grouped on each side of the street. Children play in the streets with balls and sticks. Their laughter makes Pinkie cry harder. The road dips, rises, and suddenly, like a blanket of sparkling blue diamonds, the ocean spreads out before them. Pinkie momentarily pauses. It's the most beautiful sight she has ever seen, but, without Luka… without her mama, how can she love it?

Madam Rosie lets go of Pinkie and steps down. A man is waiting for her. They talk, and he points first to a large boat gently swaying in the harbor, then waves an arm toward a rowboat containing four men waiting by the shore. Madam Rosie digs into her purse and pulls out a bag to hand to the man. He looks inside, moves his hand around the contents, nods and leaves.

Madam Rosie stands below the hysterical child with her hands on her hips. "See that big boat rocking in the sea? That is our boat—a shrimp boat that used to be a sardine boat. It's old, but it is good enough to get us somewhere."

Pinkie grabs hold of the seat boards with both hands, yells for Luka.

"Get down, child. Those sailors won't wait all day for us."

Pinkie turns her head away and screams.

"What is the matter with you? Luka will be on the next boat to meet us in one of the ports. Didn't he tell you?" Madam Rosie says.

"I don't believe you! I hate you!"

"Hate me, no matter, but we are getting on that boat."

"I want my mama!"

"Then come with me. She is waiting in Argentina as I told you so many times already."

Pinkie stomps her feet and screams again.

The men who own the cart stare in bewilderment. The sailors waiting in the small rowboat grasp their heads. This is the height of the shrimp season, and their livelihood depends on its success. They will put down anchor with their fresh catch every few days, exhausted, sun whipped, and operating on little sleep. Must they also contend with this racket as they do so?

"The shrimp will swim to cold waters to get away from those females!" a sailor says.

"I wish I brought cotton to stuff my ears." another says.

"Use fish guts." says another.

¡Mala suerte! Bad luck! We are headed for disaster!" still another of the four sailors says. "It is always bad luck to have women on a commercial ship. *Muy malo."*

They can only guess their captain, the old salty dog, had his pockets lined good and thick to agree to such madness as bringing a woman and a girl on their southbound shrimping expedition. The whole crew, those already aboard and those in the rowboat, will be squeezed tighter than sardines, skinny ones, to make a private room for the intruders to occupy.

Wear trousers at all times. No peeing off the top of the boat when the women are on deck. No swearing, no liquor, no talk of loose women and what you will do with them when we drop anchor, the captain declared at the time of the disclosure. One of the sailors was so incensed at the new rules, he lunged at the captain. His insubordination nearly got him grounded, but the others vouched so passionately for him, the captain reconsidered.

Madam Rosie beckons to the men waiting in the boat, oars in hand.

"What does she want now, a private *camilla* to carry that spoiled brat to our boat?" grumbles one of the sailors. A sailor climbs out and makes his way to the attractive woman he guesses to be in her fifties. Perhaps she will be his girlfriend as they troll for the shrimp. They converse, and Madam Rosie drops a few coins in his hand. He moves toward the howling girl, not quite sure how to accomplish what the woman asks of him.

"Uh… *ola?"* he says. Pinkie kicks a foot at him, continues crying. He looks back at Madam Rosie. Her scowl and head bob convince him to try again. "Uh, *niña,* I, uh, c*omo…* no *mas* crying. I give to you these," he says in broken English, filling up an interlude as Pinkie coughs from throat strain. He reaches into his pocket and brings out three small, vividly striped navy-blue and white shells. *"Conchas de cebra, de* Australia. *¿Las quieres?"* Pinkie turns away but can't resist turning back to peek at the exotic shells in the man's hand.

"Zebra shells?" she asks in a soft voice.

He nods, smiling excitedly. *"Si, si, niña."*

Pinkie studies his face with teary eyes, eyes so sad they tug at the man's heart. The eyes looking back at her are the color of golden syrup. Kind eyes. Pinkie takes in a shuddering breath and lets it out as a sigh.

"Mi name *es Miguel,"* he says, extending his open palm with the shells to her. She hesitates, then takes the shells from his hand. He

offers his now empty hand to her. In a few moments, she allows him to assist her stepping off the cart. The sailors in the rowboat cheer. Madam Rosie steps forward to reach for Pinkie's hand. Pinkie recoils, runs to catch up with Miguel as he proudly strides down the dock to the hurrahs of his boatmates.

31
A Cursed Journey

At sea
1944

It comes slowly, the realization that Luka isn't going to be waiting for them. Not ever. After traveling in two more sea-ravished boats, three storms at sea—the most terrifying one near the *Gulf of Tehuantepec*—endless vomiting with seasickness, Pinkie knows from experience she can't believe anything Madam Rosie says. At each new port, she has craned her neck and strained her eyes to see Luka. He is never there. Madam Rosie continues saying he will be at the next one, and the next one. Now, Pinkie doesn't believe her mama is waiting for her in Argentina. Each disappointment seals off more of her heart.

The sailor, Miguel, was her only friend on the first boat, and he taught her, when she wasn't seasick, how to play Chinese checkers and dominoes. It helped having Miguel for a friend, but she cried every night for her mama and Luka.

Miguel was shocked to learn Pinkie spoke Spanish even better than English. She asked him why it surprised him, and he said she looked too pale to speak such good Spanish and be from Mexico. Perhaps she was from Spain? When she told him her mama lived in Nuevo Laredo, Mexico, and that Madam Rosie says her mama is waiting for her in Argentina but she never saw the woman before she walked her out of a hospital one night, Miguel grew suspicious. He went to the captain, and the captain threatened to ground him at the next port if he caused any trouble. Miguel needed pesos and a job so his sisters and brothers and all their children could survive. He kept his mouth shut.

Pinkie found it hard to sleep, lost her appetite. Her sadness escalated when Miguel avoided her more often, and it was worse when she had to say goodbye to him. In the middle of a rough night on yet another boat, the sea tossing them fitfully in every direction, Pinkie comes down with a high fever. Delirious, she thinks Madam Rosie is her mama. Glassy eyed, dreamlike, she puts her arms out to the woman, weeping with joy. When Madam Rosie comes closer, she screams and falls back onto her pillow.

She won't eat or drink. On the third day, Madam Rosie forces water down her throat, threatening to slap her until she drinks. "You can't die now, not after all the trouble you've caused me," she says. She puts water-soaked handkerchiefs on Pinkie's head to bring down her fever, but there is always a fight if the girl comes to herself.

Their journey on the shrimp trawlers concludes at the Gulf of Panama. Pinkie is carried by *camilla* aboard a dirty sardine fishing boat stinking of mildew and fish parts and manned by a coarse-talking crew in filthy clothes. This part of the voyage causes Madam Rosie to throw up continually. When her head is not in a bucket or hung over the side of the boat, she profoundly curses the sea, Luka, the vessel, and anything and anyone else she can think of.

Pinkie, a fortunate victim of sick-sleep, sleeps all day and night in a small tent the two share below deck, luckily missing the days in the worst boat of their travels. When they arrive in Peru, the journey continues in rickety buses, in the back of a truck with many other people, and in a caravan of people with mules and llamas. Pinkie awakens from her fevered sleep to each new scene in terror, then thankfully, slides back into the dark comfort of slumber.

Madam Rosie consults the *gitana* healers and spiritualists they encounter to verify the child's future. She has made up her mind if they tell her the girl will die, she will abandon her, merely walk out and leave her wherever they happen to be. If they say she will live but never fully recover, she will sell her to a family to be of assistance in tending their babies and cleaning the family's latrine pans. No prognosticator says either, so Madam Rosie hangs onto the possibility of training the attractive child to drum up business once they reach their destination.

Everything is a fog to Pinkie, including the warm broth her abductor tries to force her to sip every morning. She refuses, but Madam Rosie is relentless, giving the girl no choice with her badgering, waking her every time her eyes close.

"You are trouble, a bad omen. You have brought a curse upon my bones. I should sell you to a traveling carnival. I need peace in my older years. Already you have cost me a fortune. What was I thinking by kindly offering to take you to your mother? When will you get up and be well? Shall I continue to suffer like this?"

To make the woman stop pestering her, Pinkie at last takes the cup and drinks it each time it is offered.

"Perhaps you will fatten up again. Right now, you are ugly skin and bones. *Lijepo, ali užasno.* Do you know what that means in my Croatian language? It means you are pretty, but you are awful!"

Pinkie listens without responding to the woman spew her vile talk. The hateful broth she forces her to drink causes her to recover, and for that, Pinkie is bitter. She doesn't want to get better.

"Tomorrow, we shall be in Argentina, thank God. Aghh, what a cursed journey, this. You and Luka are the roots of all my troubles. Wait until I tell his father. The disrespect! And you… so sick and vomiting. I spent money and more money to have you hauled around like a bundle of limp clothes. One month it was supposed to take, but, look, it took more than two months—almost three! Half my fortune spent on this cursed journey because of you."

Pinkie is perched on a narrow bed staring at a tree outside their motel window. She turns a spiteful face to Madam Rosie hoping to taunt her, but the woman is lost in her own rant. Pinkie turns her whole body toward the window. She reaches for the knitted bolso Luka bought her in a shop in Mexico City and shakes the tiny blue and white zebra shells Miguel gave her into her hand. She holds them and watches two brown birds chatter and hop along a tree branch.

She places the side of her face on her bent knees and concentrates on a special place in her mind that has Mama, Luka, birds, and pretty flowers. Madam Rosie can never come there. Never.

32
Possibilities and Impossibilities

Bangor, Maine
1958

Charlotte

It's four o'clock in the morning, and the bedraggled salesman is sitting up sipping a cup of hot coffee the ticket agent made for us a few minutes ago. Obviously, he has slept his anxiety away. I'm thinking his sleeping on bus station benches and drinking before-the-sun coffee is quite normal for him. The bickering couple made up from their quarrel. Her head rests on his shoulder, and his head leans on her hair as they slumber the night away.

My night of insomnia continues. A few people trudging into the station at all hours have at least given me something to contemplate as I play a personal game of guessing their occupations and fates. I decide everyone in here surely has at least two or more stories that others would find impossible to believe. It happens that I have harvested so many impossible stories, I want to someday write a book titled, *The Probability of Possible Impossibilities,* or something along that order.

What are the odds that I would be where I was one particular day in 1947 when a very unique person briefly addressed a community meeting I attended for extra credit for my senior-year civics class? Very low odds I think, considering that Miss Wraith, who, by now, had elevated herself into *star status* in my father's eyes, rarely agreed to let me go anywhere outside of school or church. Almost eighteen, and I was still treated like a wayward child requiring constant vigilance.

"I'm only protecting her because of her special type of anger and her severe lack of self-control," she told my father with those big eyes of hers brimming with pseudo-concern when I complained I was not allowed to go anywhere with my friends or to attend off-campus functions. "We wouldn't want the state to get involved in her case, would we, John? You know where that would lead, and neither one of us could bear them taking our girl away from us."

As usual, her dramatic entreaties and eyelash fluttering won him over. I never understood why he always took her side over mine until one day when I was fifteen. That's when I discovered Miss Wraith had become far more to my father than his daughter's nanny and companion. When I caught them in an intimate embrace in our home library, they broke apart quickly, twittering with embarrassment, hemming and hawing that she had something in her eye that he was helping to remove. Of course, only a fool would believe that. I don't know when their affair began, but the effect it had on manipulating my father's gullibility hardens my heart toward him even now.

Possibilities and impossibilities—life is over-flowing with them, as demonstrated by that one unusual moment in time away from *my keeper*. It changed everything. It continues to astound me that a special speaker a decade ago, given only a few minutes to talk at that public meeting, would shower my soul with possibilities and, thus, change my impossibly terrible life forevermore.

The speaker was Harry Wáng. He was, at that time, in his mid-twenties, of Chinese descent, lived in San Francisco, and had recently, he said, returned from a trip to Hong Kong. His English was impeccable and delivered with a wonderful, clear accent. I was thrilled from the start. He first told us he was a survivor of the Japanese invasion of China. That alone ignited my dull life with visions of intrigue and mystery. Looking back, and thinking of the other participants' reactions at that gathering, I don't believe his few words penetrated anyone's spirit as they did mine.

The overall subject of the meeting was *Compassion,* and actually, it was aimed at *commercial compassion* in a world recovering from World War II. It was about sharing discoveries and inventions that inevitably result from conflicts—startling innovations that lead to sweeps of upgraded modernization of weaponry, medicine, and technology.

Mr. Wáng didn't fit that criterion exactly. He spoke a mere five minutes about the importance of farming and gardening as a worldwide concern in view of famine and want. It was interesting, especially since he said his organization was called *ROSE International.* Soon after his very brief speech on food, famine, bees, and produce, he launched into opening one's mind to the… here is that word again… *possibilities* of organized, even commercialized, compassion for the downtrodden. He kept his words airy and vague, but they flowed into my spirit like warm nectar.

I was dying to ask him questions after the meeting adjourned. The line waiting to talk to him was only two-deep, and I was the second of the two. I shook his hand and, in a lowered voice, asked one question, D*id I perceive that you have an international operation of mercy?* He studied my face for what seemed like a long time, then he broke into a broad smile.

"So, you are the rose I am picking today?" he said.

"Excuse me?"

"The world has many roses. If we are not their gardeners, then whom shall be?"

He handed me a small card, and his eyes moved on to a person who walked up behind me. I was a little surprised being dismissed so quickly when I still had many burning questions tickling my tongue. I moved aside glancing at the card in my hand. It was black with a single gold rose embossed on the top and a phone number on the back.

33
Behind the Píngfēng Screen

Zhijiang, Húnán Province, China
1945

Babe

Word comes that guerilla soldiers are marching into the village this April day, and Bǎoyīn sends for her married daughter, LíngLíng, to come stay at her house all day. "I have a bad feeling," she tells her when she arrives. Her daughter nods. Her mother is very intuitive. For years, she has been a key target for imprisonment, or worse, considering her constant *illegal activities* aiding missionaries and many others to escape and hide from the invaders.

Lately, with the American B-29s appearing more often in the sky, the Japanese soldiers have become crueler than usual. More looting. More beatings. More rationing of food. More enviable rewards for spies who tattle on their neighbors and families. The invaders' insecurity about the forthcoming war results manifests daily in forced marches to their shrines to make the Chinese people pray for Japan's worldwide victory.

Bǎoyīn calls Babe inside from playing in the gate of their *jiā.* She mutters slight reprimands for Babe's mussed hair and the dust on her pants. Bǎoyīn smooths the child's hair, kneels and slaps at her clothes with her hands.

"You are impossible to stay clean. Just like my nephew Hālǐ. He played in the dirt, climbed trees, hung upside down. Foolishness. A terrible boy."

Babe sees through Bǎoyīn's façade, grabs her around the neck in a tight hug. Bǎoyīn hides her smile and gives her a fistful of precious dried corn to feed to the three ducks and four chickens they manage to own by giving all but two of their daily eggs to the soldiers.

A neighbor brought three newly-hatched Silkie chicks to them a week ago after the mother hen met the ill-fated honor of providing supper for the soldiers. The fuzzy, yellow chicks with black feet and black eyes were quickly adopted by a maternal female duck and now follow her around inside their pen in the *yuànzi*. Bǎoyīn has delayed getting official permission to raise the chicks. She knows when she applies for it, she will have to give away another piece of family jade or a fancy comb to cinch the deal, and that would be getting off easy. She wouldn't bother keeping them at all if not for Babe's delight over them.

"After I feed them corn, can I play with the little chicks if I am very careful?" she asks.

Bǎoyīn rolls her eyes. "*Tiáopí* child! Do not get your clothes dirty again. Save for going on adventure."

"Adventure?" She claps her hands. "With you, *Bǎo Māma?*

"With LíngLíng."

Babe's eyes roll toward the young woman across the room. They smile at one another before Babe skips out the narrow back way to the courtyard. Bǎoyīn watches through the open door while the child pets and feeds the fowl, then darts around the courtyard in her usual carefree way. Zhēn Gāng, Bǎoyīn's husband, many years her senior, rises from his favorite chair in the far end of the room. He senses his wife's unsettled emotions and puts a hand on her shoulder.

"*Nǐ sǐ wǒ huó*... every day, you walk the line between life and death with joy. Why this mood today?"

"Husband, I sense darkness all around. For reasons I do not understand, I fear this is the last day I shall see this child who is such a delight to me. She has become as precious to me as our own nephew Hālǐ. How empty for him was my heart before this one came to live with us."

Zhēn Gāng knows his wife is weary. She has toiled tirelessly and at great risk with her Japanese friend Ena and other sympathizers to assist the Westerners, missionaries, and other unfortunates in China to escape death and internment. Hidden cavities and tunnels under their *fángzi*—masterfully perfected over the years—were built to hide or transport first one family or person, then another, before secreting them out of China or moving them to another safe house.

Though she must always hide her beauty under hats, dirty face smudges, and loose clothing, his wife has evolved into a shrewd negotiator with everyone, including the invaders, in fulfilling her soul's purpose of aiding the helpless and oppressed.

Nonetheless, he has to agree with his wife… today feels different.

If Bǎoyīn were not so embedded in her new beliefs, Zhēn Gāng would encourage her to look on the bright side. The number ten, along with the numbers six and eight, all symbolize good luck. Ten means perfection, and is not Babe ten—a fortunate age? What's more, the child prefers the color red over any other color, and red is the color of happiness. Are those not lucky signs? Of course, Bǎoyīn would scold him half the day and *forget* to make his tea if he expressed such beliefs now.

LíngLíng steps behind her parents and watches Babe take one of the Silkie chicks and place it gently under her chin. "*Māma,* how shall we know if the soldiers are coming here today?"

"Lǎo Yáng will watch and listen in the village. They always stop at his inn to steal his beer and food. If he suspects they are coming, he will send the pigeon. His grandson may run here, too. If something unfortunate happens, you and Babe must leave from the side of the *yuànzi,* through the northwest tunnel into the forest. Stay in *Shénmì* cave until I get word to you. If you do not hear from me in one day and one night, remember the plan, LíngLíng… remember the plan."

LíngLíng knows well her mother's plans and wishes. The three years Babe has been her mother's ward have been fashioned with hidings and different schemes to keep dozens of people hidden, not the least of which is this little daughter of missionaries Edgar and Olivia Wayne. Babe's outgoing personality has caused extra challenges, but in the process of trials, LíngLíng has come to love her and think of her as *mèi mèi*—her little sister.

Even more precautions have been necessary for the child because she is not Asian. In the warm weather, and sometimes in the cold, they let her stay outside to keep her skin a rich tone. Her love of the outdoors, especially the forest, makes that easy to accomplish. Her thick, dark hair is cut to regulation length to please their adversaries, and they make her speak entirely in the Chinese language, ignoring her when she first came and spoke English or the French language her father was teaching her. It has been a good plan, for if one knows nothing to the contrary, Babe passes for at least part-Chinese, and she sounds precisely the same as a native speaker.

Who is watching FēiFēi?" Bǎoyīn asks, her eyes still locked on Babe outside.

"P*ópo.* Under the pretense I needed medical advice. I told her I may be pregnant and I wanted to be checked by a doctor. She was elated. Now, she'll keep FēiFēi for as long as I need her to without complaining. I know I'm not pregnant, but it is her day and night wish for me to have another child. Ugh, *Māma,* three or more times a day she gives me herbs, leaves, roots, and bark to eat and drink to make me fertile. She always criticizes me and accuses me of refusing to give her another grandchild because I am selfish. She insists the next child must also be a boy. She is never satisfied with anything I do."

"You are still calling her *pópo* after being married so long?"

"I will never call her *māma.*"

Bǎoyīn nods. Friction and cruelty from a mother-in-law toward a daughter-in-law are normal and traditional. Nothing to worry about. When LíngLíng is a mother-in-law, if she is so inclined, she may act the same way without it bringing dishonor.

Bǎoyīn pulls a decorative tin from the cupboard, opens it, sniffs above the opening. "I will make us tea with what leaves we have left. Not many." She puts her hand on her heart and sighs, closes her eyes to pray, then busies herself preparing the brew.

"LíngLíng… Zhēn Gāng, how I wish we would hear some international news. Perhaps the Americans and Allies are defeating our enemies. If they—"

"Tàitài! Tàitài!" Lǎo Yáng's grandson appears in the gateway panting. He bends forward to catch his breath. "The soldiers! *Yěyè* heard them when they were drinking beer. They say they have proof you and Zhēn Gāng are traitors… sympathizers! An American who stayed here with you was captured. They beat and tortured him. He told them everything. The soldiers are two houses down the road!"

Bǎoyīn sends LíngLíng to scoop up Babe from the *yuànzi* and bring her inside. The small messenger is pushed back out the front door with instructions to dawdle and run his stick along the ground as would a carefree youngster headed home for a meal. Bǎoyīn rushes to the sleeping room to retrieve the ugly box of Babe's clothes. The box, not the clothes, means everything.

"Remember my instructions, LíngLíng, and do not forget to protect Babe's box," she tells her daughter. LíngLíng nods, presses her mother's hand. Before she and Babe can return to the courtyard and escape the prearranged way, they hear heavy footsteps approaching. Bǎoyīn frantically points to the corner of the room. "Use the drop, LíngLíng! Remember… us… always!"

Babe and LíngLíng are scarcely concealed behind the black-enameled wood and paper *píngfēng* screen when soldiers file through the gate shouting and cursing. LíngLíng pants in fear hearing the bellowed accusations, cups and vases shattering against walls, her father's expensive redwood chair splintering. Bǎoyīn's appeals for explanations are answered with slaps. LíngLíng toils with shaking hands to loosen the drop cord on the trap door disguised as part of the pounded-earth foundation of the house. The trap door swings down. She lowers Babe's box carefully into the dirt cavity and turns to get Babe. The child is staring through one of the tiny rips in the paper along the frame's inner edge. Unable to resist, the young woman finds another rip to look through.

Bǎoyīn is on her knees. Her hair has loosened from the hard slaps to her face. It is spread like a beautiful fan on her shoulders—beauty in the midst of chaos. Her lips are swollen and bleeding, her face drenched in tears. Still, she peers at the men towering above her with gentle eyes. Questions are asked about the people she has illegally helped to escape. She lowers her chin and remains silent. A soldier to her left shouts obscenities, walks behind her, kicks her in the back. She cries out, slumps to the side. He kicks her again and again. LíngLíng clamps a hand over her mouth to keep from screaming.

"No, stop! She is innocent! *Wǒ shì pàntú!* I am the traitor!" Zhēn Gāng shouts. He breaks free from the man loosely restraining him and drapes his frail body over his wife. A soldier grabs his shoulders and throws him across the room. He rises, grabs a curved sword off the wall, and shrieks as he rushes toward the soldiers. He is seized from behind by a heavy-built soldier. The soldier's hand is swift as he stabs Zhēn Gāng in the neck, then slides the sharp knife along the curvature of the old man's throat. Zhēn Gāng stares ahead with widened, confused eyes, then drops to the floor inside a fast-spreading pool of blood.

Bǎoyīn screams. She tries to crawl to her husband. She is pushed to the floor by a boot in the small of her back. The same man grabs her by her hair and pulls her to her feet. Her hands are quickly bound behind her. LíngLíng can no longer see her mother inside the huddle of soldiers surrounding her. They march her from the humble home that has been a refuge for the hopeless these past years. Soldiers canvassing the courtyard and outside shed enter the room and scan every inch of the house with devouring eyes.

"Ah, see the *píngfēng* painted with birds and trees? My fiancé will love it for a souvenir," a soldier says. He steps toward them.

Stars and flashes burst like fireworks in LíngLíng's peripheral vision. She grabs Babe around her waist and jumps into the dirt hole below the floor line. She soundlessly refits the trap door in seconds, willing herself to stop quaking. She pushes and pulls the girl and the box through the dark crawl space and into one of the tunnels leading into the forest.

Inside the *Shénmì* cave, Babe pulls a tiny chick from her pocket.

34
Surrender

Shí Niú, Shuāngfēng, Húnán Province, China
1945

LíngLíng's brow furrows as she watches the child whispering to her chick. Babe is drawn into a ball by the window in the Liú's *jiā,* the preordained refuge. Where they are and where Babe is going next were all part of Bǎoyīn's intricate plans in case of dire circumstances.

The family they fled to knew immediately what to do when the terrified pair arrived at their door. As soon as LíngLíng said *Tomorrow will be a joyful day,* the woman of the house loudly proclaimed for any nearby ears, "Ah, so you have arrived, my nieces! Come in! You must stay here after so long a journey. I am saddened to hear of the unfortunate accident in the fields. Your poor parents! See how soiled you are! Come in! Come in!"

They were literally pulled inside and escorted without words to a bathing house in the courtyard. They silently sat on the floor while water was heated for their baths. Babe took the chick from her pocket and let it roam inside a circle she created with her arms. LíngLíng was grateful the tiny fowl hadn't peeped when they were hiding behind the *píngfēng.* Neither it nor Babe made a sound while the atrocities were committed on LíngLíng's parents.

They were bathed, hair scrubbed, helped into swaddling towels, and taken to a bedroom where clothes were laid out on a carved canopy bed taking up a third of the room. A young servant brought them tea and hot noodles which neither girl touched. Not until the next morning did LíngLíng explain, away from Babe, the tragedies she had witnessed. Tears and grief flowed from the young woman and her hosts, the Liú's—a kindly, prosperous couple in their mid-years who own department stores in town.

In the weeks since they arrived at the Liú's home, Babe's only sounds have been murmurings to her chicken. She looks past anyone addressing her with no expression on her face. LíngLíng saves her private grief for the loss of her parents away from the youngster and worries Babe's young mind may have become addled from what she witnessed. She has, after all, lost two mothers—the missionary, Mrs. Olivia Wayne, who is somewhere in hiding, and, now, *Bǎo Māma.*

Soon after their arrival, word was sent to LíngLíng's mother-in-law's house that her daughter-in-law has been detained by the Japanese as a temporary clerk, is safe, and that she asks they tell her son FēiFēi she will be home soon. Missing her son makes her cry, but she does not miss her husband or his bossy mother. When LíngLíng goes back to them, Babe will begin a new life in a different family. That breaks her heart, but fate has won over love. Her husband's mother despises females, including her own daughter-in-law. It isn't fair to make Babe suffer as she does. She has no choice but to carry out her mother's emergency strategies and pray that the rumors of a Japanese retreat are true.

Cryptic notes are passed along the secret underground explaining the recent misfortune and the need for Babe's new family to prepare. When Bǎoyīn scouted for a new family to take Babe in case of dire circumstances, she found the Chén family. Bǎoyīn presented two important requirements before acceptance as Babe's foster family. First, they had to swear on Bǎoyīn's secret Bible pages they would do everything to help Babe reunite with her family when the occupation ended. Secondly, they had to promise to treat her as kindly as they did their own children as they grew up.

The Chéns readily agreed, though they put no value on Bǎoyīn's religious theories or the Bible pages she treated so preciously. What they cared about was the loneliness of their empty house with only them and the husband's father, Jìnhǎi, living there. Their youngest son was killed in combat, and the other son fled to Hong Kong with his family. The prosperous family's earnestness and the quiet of their *jiā* convinced Bǎoyīn they would welcome a smart, lively youngster to brighten their days until the occupation was over. Of course, Bǎoyīn's greatest heart's desire was that Babe be with her until the war ended.

On a humid August day, shocking news comes like an unexpected whirlwind as a neighbor pounds on the door of the Liú's *jiā*. "An announcement! An announcement is coming on the radio!" the woman calls excitedly. "We hear it is good news! Please let us hear it on your radio set!" Lined up behind the neighbor is her eager family and several other people from the community. When the door is opened, they rush through the house and collect in the Liú's *yuànzi*. Upon instruction, a servant props the doors to the courtyard open and turns the radio up for them to hear that the Japanese emperor has surrendered.

The bulletin causes a tidal wave of reactions to wash over the listeners; ripples of both joy and panic to the Liú's and LíngLíng. Will the occupiers reek more havoc before they leave? Who is in charge now? Will civilian's movements be free or restricted? Why are they hearing shouts of jubilation along with screams of terror in the streets? LíngLíng perceives her time away from her husband and son will soon be over, but not before Babe is settled into her new life.

The excitement is too much for the troop of invading listeners in the courtyard. They charge noisily through the Liú's house and into the streets. The quiet of the family inside the house contrasts sharply with the racket outside. Later, they learn of the vigilante retributions paid back to many Japanese soldiers, cruel teachers, and dishonest merchants at the hands of the formerly oppressed.

"This news means I will soon be going home to my son. We must make sure Babe is with her new family right away. I must know she is safe," LíngLíng says, wringing her hands.

"We agree," said Liú Línà. "I will send a messenger immediately."

The sealed answer from the Chéns doesn't arrive for a few weeks and contains a shocking requirement. They are overjoyed the child is coming soon, but she must come disguised as a boy. In fact, she has no permission to come to them as a girl. No more information is given to explain such an outlandish request.

"What is this?" LíngLíng asks her hosts, waving the message in the air with eyes flashing. They shake their heads and motion toward the courtyard away from the servants. As usual, since the occupation ended, it is noisy outside the walls of the courtyard. They sit quietly on the benches under the willow trees. Each time one person catches another's eye, there is a shrug of the shoulders or a dip of the head.

Liú Línà calls a servant girl and instructs her to fetch their trusted messenger, Hǘ Làing. Twenty-one years old, he has shown himself talented in remaining friendly with all sides. He has learned the art of finagling and bribing to get information, or anything else, and has proven to be completely trustworthy.

"Hǘ Làing..." Liú Línà says when he is seated in the courtyard drinking a cup of their best green tea, "... will you go back to the Chéns and ask an explanation of why they require this young girl to be disguised as a boy? We do not understand."

He continues sipping his tea a few moments before answering. "I think I have the answer, Liú Línà," he says.

"Please... inform us."

"The reason is the Soviet Red Army."

"What have the Russians to do with this matter?" LíngLíng asks.

"Unfortunately, our *liberators* are not the heroes we wished they would be. There are numerous stories and rumors throughout the land of them raping women, and sometimes... young girls. Pretty ones have it worse, but not even the homeliest females are safe from those brutes," he says.

"But are the Russians not in Manchuria, very far away from us and the Chéns?" Liú xiānshēng asks.

"Yes, that is so. You must consider that some people are easy victims of rumors. If the Chéns are refusing responsibility for a girl, it means they are afraid. As we know, fear can cause reasonable people to be unreasonable. I would not rely on a change of heart from them."

Liú Línà breaks the long silence following Hǘ Làing's words. "Then, the child will stay with us as our niece. Everyone knows already she is a girl. It isn't necessary for her to pretend to be a boy here."

"Liú Línà, how do we know if the Soviets will come to our province or how safe any of us will be as time passes?" LíngLíng asks.

Hǘ Làing nods in agreement. "No one knows what to expect. Presently, they are chasing away the Japanese invaders and opening schools, but they are also dismantling our factories and refineries and shipping the equipment back to the Soviet Union. They are a strange people—hungry like vultures for everything Chinese. They want our watches, our clocks, our building materials, our jewelry, our silks, our females." He drains the *gàiwǎn* and sets it on top of a short parapet running perpendicular to the benches under the trees.

Liú xiānshēng shakes his fist in the air. He stands up, bends backward to stretch his back, begins to pace. "Is it the Communists or the *Guómíndǎng* who will restore honor to China? Harmony in China is nothing but an illusion. Why are the Chinese people forever the slaves of warlords and invaders? Why are we the victims of continual civil wars? We have no country of our own. Where is the *ānníng*, the peace and harmony?" he asks. He sits back down.

There are no answers, and the group remains under the flowing trees in silence. Hearts are heavy. Minds are scrambling to conceive of ways to camouflage Babe as a boy.

"Perhaps her prolonged silence will work in our favor," LíngLíng says. Every head nods.

35
Liberty!

Wéixiàn Prison Camp, Wéifāng, China
August 17, 1945

After two years of imprisonment, Edgar Wayne and his son Eddie are underweight and hollow-eyed, but they dare to be hopeful on this August day in the Wéixiàn prison camp. Rumors have shot through the camp of impending liberty and of the Japanese emperor's possible surrender. Can the rumors be true?

Better to keep a firm grip on one's emotions, Edgar believes. The tragic death of his wife and the uncertainty of knowing if his little girl has survived, in addition to the horrible, scarce food, and the unsanitary conditions in the prison—conditions such as squatting over a foul, fly and maggot infested hole, or using a toilet with no water to flush it, and never any toilet paper—have left Edgar not as steady physically, nor as emblazoned emotionally, with his previous desire to save the world.

"Son, when we are blessed to leave this place… when that most joyous event occurs… we shall find your sister and return to Texas posthaste," Edgar declares over their breakfast of boiled eggplant, half-dollar-sized portions of dubious meat, and coffee that has been re-boiled countless times.

"Daddy, will I still have to eat those terrible powdered eggshells when we go home?"

"No, not at all, son. Right now, let us be grateful they're keeping you and the other children from getting rickets in this, uh, this hellish hole. Thank the Lord we have managed to have any eggs at all."

"Thank the farmers. They smuggle them in to us.

"You know I don't discuss the black market here, Eddie."

"I know, Dad, but David says Chinese farmers have been smuggling food over the walls ever since we got here. It's true, isn't it? And, those latrine cleaners, the Zhāngs, didn't they…?"

At Edgar's raised hand, Eddie stops talking. Edgar closes his eyes and wipes the sweat from his brow. Early morning, and he's already covered in perspiration from the insufferable humid Wéifāng climate. He opens his eyes to look pointedly at his son. "It's true, son, but it's important to stay in ignorance of these things while we are here."

"I'm thirteen, Dad, not a baby. My friends talk about them all the time. I already know about the Zhāngs, how the father was caught and tortured. Robert said he saw him when they took him out of the compound. He was covered in blood, and parts of his skin was hanging down in strips."

"Oh, dear God," Edgar mumbles. "My boy, how I wish I could have saved you from these horrors."

"I'm all right, Dad. David says the farmers sneak in more than food."

Edgar nods. "They get news and messages to us. That's how we know the tide is turning in this God-forsaken war."

"I don't see how they do it with the barbed wire and electrified wires everywhere. The soldiers in the guard towers shoot at a mouse if it moves, and those guard dogs can smell trouble a mile away."

"It's miraculous, son." Sensing a teachable moment, Edgar sits up straighter and peers into his son's eyes. "You will find in this life that where there is a will, and if it is virtuous and right, there will somehow always be a way, especially when you rely on the One who watches over us night and day."

Eddie's smile in response to his father's encouraging words is beautiful to his father, but the decay of Eddie's teeth makes Edgar desire fighting their captors with his bare hands. Perhaps if they are liberated soon, Eddie's teeth can be saved before it is too late.

"How will we find my sister when we leave?" Eddie asks, holding his nose and poking the last morsel of meat into his mouth.

"Oh, my, the memory of her is a heartache to me every day. I regret deeply that I did not appreciate that sweet bundle of joy when I had her with me. Babe was… heaven on earth. So full of life and vitality. Did I tell you she laughed and sang all the time, Eddie?"

"Yes, Dad."

Edgar rubs his eyes, leaves them closed as he speaks. "I should have spent more time with her." His voice breaks. He clears his throat and manages a tight smile. "I choose to believe if we travel back to Húnán Province where Bǎoyīn lives, we will find them all waiting for us. Hopefully, by the grace of God, Bǎoyīn's family has survived the atrocities of the occupation."

"What if they aren't there?"

"Then we will not rest until we find our little girl."

Edgar pushes the small make-shift plate of tainted meat in front of Eddie. Any meat at all is a rare occurrence and is always in different stages of rotting. Usually mule or horse meat, it originates from an army slaughterhouse and is brought to the prison by train. Unrefrigerated, uncovered, the unidentified meat is sometimes so far gone it is folly to even attempt cooking it in one of the camp's only two frying pans or stewing it in one of the compounds only two copper pots.

He bows his head to silently pray for Eddie, Babe, and all the prisoners whom he has come to respect so greatly—the incarcerated teachers especially. Eddie and the other children have received actual schooling the past three years thanks to the teachers. Already, three groups of students have graduated. They enforce good manners and respect, telling the children to sit up straight, not to wipe their noses on their sleeves, never to talk with food in their mouths, and so on.

Edgar jumped in to help them as soon as he arrived, beaten and bruised though he was from the canes and rifle butts as he knelt in the road alongside his dying wife. The satisfaction of aiding the children took his mind off his tragic loss.

Inspired by the teachers, the other adults formed a committee to keep church and medical treatment ongoing. They set up an entertainment committee for putting on plays and ballets. Girl Scouts and Boy Scouts groups continue. The children earn badges for collecting bedbugs and swatting flies or making coal out of coal dust. Incredibly, the general mood in the camp, despite ghastly conditions, has remained a positive one, and that alone has been irritating to their captors.

After his imprisonment, Edgar didn't see his son for two months. One day, unexpectedly, the two of them were given permission to reside together. The prayers of his fellow prisoners are what caused this miracle, Edgar believes and proclaims.

Finished with his morning prayer, Edgar raises his head and smiles at Eddie.

"Push your armband up, Dad, before you get in trouble again."

Edgar looks at the white band with the large, black "A" designating he is an American. It continually falls lower on his arm as his body grows leaner from lack of nourishment and the physical toil required every day of all adults and children as young as four and five. Each nationality is marked with a letter on their armbands. Edgar isn't sure, but he thinks there are almost two thousand people total in the compound. Americans, British, and Canadians mostly, but many others from Australia, Sweden, Norway, and other regions. It seems China was on the world agenda as a place in need of care.

The older and younger Wayne separate after breakfast to attend to their jobs of manual labor. On the second roll call of the daily three, they are in different parts of the prison. Edgar notices a severe decrease in the number of Japanese soldiers as the day progresses. Later that afternoon, when the heat and humidity border on suffocating and the soldiers seem to have vanished, the drone of an airplane above the camp sends prisoners scrambling to the windows.

They spot a B24 Bomber circling above them dropping lower with each sweep. As it gets closer, a large American star is noticeable on the side. A panel on the bottom of the plane opens and seven parachutes drift downward like billowing angels. Cheers and shouts fill the hallways and yards. Bedraggled people of all ages and sizes sprint or limp to the prison gates to welcome their liberators.

36
Watching from the Rafters

Shí Niú, Shuāngfēng, Húnán Province, China
1946

Babe

Babe doesn't understand the Chén's discussions about the National Revolutionary Army led by General Chiang Kaishek having connected for a time with the Communist guerrilla army under Máo Zédōng or that the two leaders attempted and failed to reach any mutual agreements in their negotiations after the occupation.

"They are throwing us back into civil war like before the Japanese invaders came. How can they agree on how China should be managed? Two heads cannot share one body. How many years must our people suffer?" Chén Jìnhǎi says as they eat breakfast this morning. He pounds the table one time with his fist as his daughter-in-law DānDān, his son Chén Lì, and Babe watch him.

As usual, Babe observes this passionate tirade with neutral eyes. She doesn't understand these words, especially the emotions with which they are stated. After LíngLíng left her in this different house with strangers five weeks ago, she knows the only thing safe to care about is Noodle, her pet rooster.

She didn't cry when LíngLíng hugged and kissed her repeatedly before she left her there, crying bitterly during their goodbye. LíngLíng once again reminded Babe of their *special secret,* something she had been drilling into her for months.

In her final goodbye, and in the privacy of Babe's new bedroom, LíngLíng said, "If you are in dire circumstances or if something happens to the Chéns, use the abacus codes painted on the bottom of your box of clothing. Each row has only the number of beads painted on it that indicate the numbers you are to use. One is a telephone number here in China. It's a store, but the people who answer are part of us. They will help you.

"The other abacus has a telegram wire number to use if you are in Hong Kong. You will need help doing this, Babe, if you are still young. It doesn't matter who answers the telephone or who calls you or wires you back or whatever instructions you receive. If it is on the phone, and they say, 'How can I help you on this joyful day?' you say something special. Do you remember the special message you are to say to them?

Babe stared at the floor in silence.

"You say, 'Tomorrow will be a joyful day.' You know this already. I've told you repeatedly these past weeks. After you say this special message, someone will ask you where you are. You must tell them the name of the town or village and anything else they ask you. If you send a telegram, you will likewise use the secret message. You know where on the bottom of the box to find the coded address for the telegram, as well as the name of the person to contact. Please give me a sign you understand."

Babe's chin stayed on her chest.

"Oh, please, little sister, hear me! Our *Bǎo Māma* loved you and wanted you to be safe. I want the same!" She took hold of Babe's hand. "She planned this for you for many years because you are so special to us. You are my *mèi mèi*." Babe's silence was a heartbreak to LíngLíng. She sobbed into her free hand. Rising from the bed, she felt the slightest pressure from Babe's hand.

"Oh, my sweet girl! Now, I can leave with faith that you will survive. You are forever in my heart, Babe, or shall I say… Bójǖn?"

No answer. LíngLíng kissed her again, hugged her tight, and departed, turning once to look at her for the last time. Babe's emotions were safely tucked into a remote crevice in her heart—that special place where only Noodle is allowed to enter.

Her precious Noodle is now a white ball of fluff with thin protrusions jutting from his fluffy crest. Chen Jìnhǎi, the grandfather of the new family, held him and announced he might become a rooster but too early to know on a chicken of that breed. Babe already knows Noodle is a rooster, but she doesn't know why she knows it. It doesn't matter what Noodle is, only that he never leaves her. Never. He is the only living creature she speaks to or listens to. She doesn't answer anyone in the new family when they talk to her, especially since they lie and tell her she is now a boy with a new name of Bójǖn.

Babe sleeps in her own carved wooden bed in a room previously belonging to the youngest son. Noodle stays in a basket or in her arms. She is given many tidbits by the family for him to eat. When the dirt warms more, she will go outside and find bugs and worms for him. Most of the time, she sits alone humming or whispering to him so he is not afraid.

The days grow warmer as Spring approaches. This afternoon, while the family drinks tea and partakes of a bowl of peanuts and a plate of dried plums, Babe takes her cup and sits as usual by herself across the room. Jìnhǎi says, "The old men were talking at the marketplace this morning. I heard more rumors that if the Communists take us over, they will not allow citizens to keep their land and businesses. Chún Róng told me the family records of our ancestors will be burned if not hidden."

"*Fùqīn,* those are only rumors. I hear good things about the Communists. They care about everyone. They will be fair," Chén Lì, his son, says.

"Lies! Wáng Wèi and Chún Róng say if Máo succeeds, he will stop our *wǔshù!*"

"Maybe that's because *wǔshù* is associated with the monks and temples," DānDān says. "The Communists don't participate in religion."

Jìnhǎi nods. "That is part of it, but there is a prevalent falsehood that *wǔshù* is a rich man's pastime. Rubbish! It is a sacred art passed down through the generations. It cares nothing of your wealth or lack of it, only that you are honorable and disciplined enough to understand it and practice it. If this disgraceful regime takes over, *wǔshù* will be abolished, and eventually, so will the ones who teach or practice it. That is the gossip I heard over the bamboo shoots this morning at the market. I believe they are true, and they make me sad."

"But our *wǔshù* has survived many generations in this family, *Fùqīn,"* Chén Lì says.

Jìnhǎi folds his arms over his red silk *chángpào* and stares at his son. Chén Lì lowers his eyes. He knows Chinese families keep their style of martial arts a secret and pass it down only to their worthy sons and other chosen relatives. Chén Lì, Jìnhǎi's only son, had no interest in *Tàolù* or *Sànshǒu,* nor did Chén Lì's first son. Only the youngest Chén son followed his grandfather's path with the patience and intelligence to learn the revered and complex fighting arts belonging to the Chén family. Now, he is dead at the hands of the Japanese invaders.

"Fùqīn, I-I will make you a secret place to practice your *Yǒng Chūn.* In my heart, I know you will not find peace if you must stop doing what you most love," Chén Lì says. His father looks up from his tea with surprise, a fresh light shining in his eyes.

Babe watches Jìnhǎi prepare to go outside. Rain has fallen in the night, polishing all the foliage around the Chen's *jiā.* She slips quietly to the peg holding her own light jacket above her outdoor shoes and pretends to stare out the window.

"I am going for a walk in the forest looking for where the good mushrooms will grow as the weather warms more," Jìnhǎi announces loudly. "Perhaps I will take a longer walk afterward or walk to the market."

The code. It means Jìnhǎi walks into the forest a short way and doubles back to the *yuànzi* from the north side that has flat stones and boards placed along the ground. No footprints showing in the mud or wet foliage make the secret place safer. He will climb the stairs inside the stable where the family's livestock is kept and step behind the tall haystack. A door that looks not like a door must be pressed in three certain spots, acting as a "key" to unlock it. Inside, Jìnhăi goes to another secret door and presses it five times to make it open. Behind it is the wood-man dummy, his *mù rén zhuāng*. He wrestles it into the open space.

Day after day, Babe follows or beats Jìnhăi to his hideaway. She thinks he never sees her waiting for him inside the barn, nor sees her creep quietly into the room after pressing the door three times. She thinks her climbing the second set of stairs in the back of the secret room to watch him from the rafters is completely unknown to him. In truth, Jìnhăi's keen eye and highly-trained instincts knew of her first step on the first day she followed him. Babe's stool she carries to reach the high spots on the locked outer door is a clue someone of her tender years would not think to hide.

He is curious about this girl who communicates only with a chicken and who, for her safety in unsettled times, must pretend to be a boy. Her snooping to watch his *wŭshù* thrills him, for she has not missed a single day of observation since Chén Lì finished the secret room. Jìnhăi has long held the art of *Yŏng Chūn* is more conformed to a woman's structure and mindset than to that of a man. Ancient history of the art hints that a woman designed it, taught it to another woman, and it blossomed forth from there.

Intrigued with the possibilities that may lie ahead if the child continues her inquisitiveness, Jìnhăi performs his practice movements ever slower and, recently, has begun calling them out as he practices. He names the moves, explains them, shows the right and wrong approaches, even talks of the philosophy behind them. In all of his years of personal practice and teaching his grandson the beauty of *wŭshù*, he has never felt any more excitement than he does now. He can barely suppress his delight as the little girl watching and listening moves further down the rafters each day to get a better view of his movements below.

37
Rage

San Antonio, Texas
1946

Cruz mentally kicks himself in the pants for not waiting until after midnight to slip into *Casa des Magnolias* to wring Clint's neck. His legs feel like dead logs. A cramp in his shoulder makes him wince. He carefully rotates it a few turns. How long has he been crouching in this body-hugging larder… half his life?

The ornery little mustang he was grappling with on the Wyoming ranch a few weeks ago left him with an injured shoulder and a broken rib or two. He can't seem to resist the spirit of the wild mustangs, especially since they respond to him so quickly.

He watches through the door louvres a man spreading plaster and a woman affixing dark-blue and white tiles to a half-wall in the kitchen. They earlier finished tiling an intricate arc design framing the large cooking area. Now, they're working on the adjacent wall.

If he'd only waited. He started to, planned to, while he and his pickup were hiding in a clump of mesquites out by the cattleguard off the paved highway. He grew impatient with his windows rolled down and the lyrics of the katydids and crickets drifting inside. Too peaceful a sound for the revenge wrestling through his mind.

The singular thought of making Clint pay for his wrongdoing and its awful consequences occupied his mind while he jogged swiftly through the trees, across the driveway, and up the shallow steps to the front door. He slipped soundlessly through doors he knew were never locked and was about to climb the stairs to Clint's bedroom when he heard racket and voices coming through the back door. He dashed to the kitchen and into the larder just as the pair came in with tools, bucket, tarp, and tiles. It was ten o'clock. What kind of workers does Clint hire these days that they tile a kitchen so late at night?

It's past midnight now, and the one redeeming thought about this screw-up is he knows Clint never stays up too late. It'll be to his advantage to catch him off guard. He shifts slightly. A can of tomatoes tumbles off a shelf barely missing his head. It rolls off his shoulder bone and hits the floor. He watches through the slats on the door as both workers look in his direction.

"*Senor* Clint's cat?" the woman says.

"*Gato loco,*" the man mutters, turning back to his work. He spreads a layer of plaster and waits, tool in the air. The woman stares at the larder door.

"*Juanita, ¡dáte prisa! ¡Quiero ir a la cama!*"

"*Si, si, si,*" she says, turning quickly to place a tile on the wet adhesive.

The man's impatience to finish so he can go to bed would have been humorous to Cruz if he didn't have violence on his mind. A shadow crosses the bottom of the larder door, stops. Slight rustling sounds. Whiskers press between the slats. A paw slides under the door and lies still. The furry leg pushes in further, swipes back and forth, turns upside down. With a cowboy's lack of house-cat experience, Cruz presses his thumb on the cat's foot pad hoping to dissuade him from continuing his attention-drawing antics. Sharp claws instantly dig into his flesh.

¡Maldita sea! he cusses silently. He frees himself, grasps his bleeding thumb.

The woman rises from the floor.

"*¿Adónde vas?*" the man asks.

"*Para conseguir* a broom. *El gato* has a mouse!"

"*Nita, no.* Only three tiles more. *¡Terminamos!*"

The man's annoyance holds the woman at bay. She helps him clean up the drips, roll up the tarp spread below the wall, and carry the materials out of the kitchen. Cruz attempts to stand, fails, tries again. He exits his recent place of confinement and limps on deadened legs to the living room. He squats awkwardly behind a stuffed chair and watches as the woman, just as he expected, enters through the kitchen door and retrieves a broom from the cleaning closet. She flings open the larder door and peers inside. In a minute or so, she bends to pick up the fallen can and puts it back on the shelf. She shakes her head, wonders how the mouse managed to escape the larder.

Watching her are the ones who know the truth… Cruz and a sleek orange tabby with green eyes.

In the darkened bedroom, Cruz gazes at the outline in the bed of the man he grew up with, someone as close as a brother, his best friend. He sits down in one of the upholstered chairs across the room and stretches out his cramping legs. His sides ache, his shoulder burns, and he hasn't slept the last couple of days. The gentle sound of the clock ticking on the fireplace mantle brings memories of younger years when he and Clint played battlefield soldiers and rodeo *vaqueros* in this very room. Despite his intentions, his eyes close.

He awakens some hours later with a start and with a personal rebuke on his tongue. He came here to fulfill a mission to restore his family honor, not fiddle around taking a damn snooze. He stands, winces from pain as he stretches, forces himself to concentrate on his sister to provide the angry fuel needed to accomplish his goal. He swallows hard.

"Get up, Clint. Get up so I can beat you into a bloody stain on the floor," he says, not too loud, and yet, the man in the bed is instantly awake and sitting up.

"Wh-what?"

"Eres un pedazo de caca que no vale nada."

"Cruz? You're calling me a piece of worthless poop? My God, is it really you, *mi hermano?"*

"Don't call me your brother! Get out of bed and fight me. I can promise you this… one of us won't see the sun come up this morning."

"Huh? What the…? Where's Angelina?"

Cruz snorts angrily. "Do not… do not even say her name, you coward. You-you dirty snot from a pig's snout."

The covers are thrown aside. Clint swings his legs to the floor. "What the hell, Cruz? Have you—"

"Shut up, you steaming pile of cow crap. The only sound you get to make is begging me to stop beating you while I make you pay."

"For what?"

"For what? You dare ask me *for what?"* He throat growls. "Stand up now, Clint, or I'll…I'll attack you where you sit!"

Clint stands up quickly, wavers a little. "Good lord, Cruz. You drunk?"

Cruz lets out a roar, charges. The men fall on the bed grappling and grunting. They roll off the end with Cruz on top of Clint. He clamps his hands around Clint's throat. Clint rams an elbow into the side of Cruz's jaw, flips him over and punches him in the face, then his side. Cruz yelps, then counter punches Clint's chest and belly. They scramble to their feet. Clint, sensing Cruz's weak shoulder, grabs his arm and bends it backward as Cruz kicks him in the stomach. Both men cry out in pain.

Clint swivels one way; Cruz in the opposite direction. Cruz grabs his shoulder, his face a mask of pain. Clint bends at the waist, his breath coming in short gasps and his palms flat against his thighs. He turns on a lamp beside the bed.

"Dammit, Cruz, you're lucky I just got out of the hospital or I'd finish tearing your head clean off your body. You know you can't beat me in a fight, you big idiot."

"You've never won."

"I've never lost, either. Hell's bells, you go *loco* or something since the war? What do you mean showing up here calling me a worthless piece of—"

"You're bleeding through those bandages."

"Yeah, you probably messed up my stiches, *tonto.* I just had my umpteenth surgery since being discharged."

"You were injured?"

Clint snorts. "Shoot, I reckon. Concussion. Had my leg almost ripped off, shrapnel everywhere. They had to take out one of my kidneys. I just got home from the last surgery two days ago."

"Shrapnel? You were in the war?"

"You dadgum right I was. You know that. Whatcha got, a pee-ant's memory these days?" Clint peels off his pajama bottoms, picks up his Levi's from the back of a chair, shakes them out. He groans as he slowly sticks one leg in, then the other, pulls them up and zips them. "Oh, that just ain't fun right now. You might have punched me right back into the hospital."

Cruz stares at all the scars on Clint's torso.

Clint selects a dark-blue western shirt from his closet, pulls off the paper wrapping from the dry cleaners, puts it on with his back to Cruz. "This one probably won't show the blood as bad. Anyway, I've been worried sick about y'all. I tried calling that boarding house in Nuevo Laredo a million times. I think it must be vacant or something. Ever since I flew in from Virginia after getting the green light to travel again, I've been trying to recover enough to get down there myself. You know how many letters I wrote you two? Why didn't you answer any of them or call us? Our telephone number hasn't changed."

"Letters? Ha! Quit lying, Clint."

Clint stares at Cruz as if he's a stranger. "What in blue-blazes makes you think I'd lie about something like that, Cruz? I sent my first letter with Bubba the next day after I left you two down in Mexico. Told you how I had to fly out for the army camp in Brownwood. I got damned drafted and only found out when I got home from Nuevo Laredo. Didn't get any choice in the matter. Had one night here before flying out early the next morning to report for duty.

"Bubba said he handed my letter over to you personally the next day. Said y'all wanted to stay down there a day or two since Angelina was feeling poorly—had the *turista* from something she ate. Daddy said when Bubba went back down there to carry you back, you'd left the boarding house and no one knew where you went.

"That's bull crap! We never saw Bubba, and we got no letters."

Clint sits down in the chair. "But, he, uh, they said… okay, how about the big 'ol letter I sent from Camp Bowie? I mailed it to the boarding house a few days after I left. No answer from y'all. I started sending letters whenever I could. Some, I just flat out mailed to general delivery, and I don't even know if they have general delivery in Mexico.

"I sent a bunch to Daddy to get them to you. He said he had Bubba leave them at the police station and other places down there when he was inquiring about your whereabouts. Said he never got a word or a call from you, and you know I didn't. I told Daddy to hire an investigator to find you, and he did and the investigator said you must have left Mexico because there was no sign of you anywhere. I was so dadgummed worried. I think that's how I got injured the last time, fretting about you and Angelina."

Cruz's face registers shock. "Good lord, Clint. I, uh, well… are-are we still wanted for murdering Darla's boyfriend?"

"God, no. That was cleared up the first day. Don't you read the newspapers, brother? Oh, I guess it wouldn't be in a Mexican newspaper. Anyways, everyone knew she did it. That little hussy's long gone."

"Where?"

"Prison. Goree State Farm for Women down in Huntsville."

Cruz sits gingerly on the edge of the rumpled bed holding his side. "I-I don't know what to think. All this time and we… we could have come back home." He bends to wipe the top of his boot. Winces. "Damn these sore ribs."

"I don't get it, either. I explained everything in the letter I gave Bubba, and Daddy said..."

The men stare at each other as realization soaks in. Clint stands and slaps the top of the dresser with open hands. "I should never have trusted the old man! I never dreamed he'd drop this low." He lets loose a string of cuss words, picks up his wallet and throws it on the floor. "Ah, dammit! How could he be so dead set against me marrying Angelina that he'd dive into the gutter… lying at every turn?"

"Marry Angelina?"

"Oh, come on, Cruz. That's no surprise. You know how I've always felt about her. I miss her every single day. Been worried sick. She's the only woman I ever wanted. Daddy figured that out and went to every length to betray us to the end. I'll tell you, it's damned hard for me to retain even the slightest good memory of him when I find out he's the lowest form of a-a—"

"What do you mean keep a good memory of him?"

"Oh, uh, Daddy died, Cruz. Last winter. As soon as the war ended, he left Mr. Brenshaw and our attorney in charge of Coyote Oil until I could get my walking papers out of the service, finish up my medicals, tie up loose ends. I had a load of surgeries to go through, and I… I was kind of messed up in the head for a little while. Saw a lot of my buddies die in the war. It, uh, gets to you pretty bad." He sighs. "It ruffled my feathers he couldn't be a little more patient and wait for me to come home, but he had the worst case of rambling fever I've ever seen. He restarted his galivanting with a vengeance. Right quick, he picked up some kind of disease in the tropics. They told me his liver was pretty much shot with all that drinking he's been doing since Mama died. He wasn't strong enough to recover."

"*Señor* Sutton gone? Only fifty-six? It doesn't seem possible, Clint."

"Yeah, but don't ask me to feel bad about it now. *Dios,* I didn't know he was so conniving. Cruz, I'm sorry. I'm as sorry as all hell for you and Lina and me, too. I give him credit for one thing. He turned to and ran the company with all his former grandeur until the war was over. At least he did that. I miss the way he was when we were kids, but I swear, if he walked through that door right now, you'd have to beat me off him with a horse whip."

The ticking clock is the only sound in the room the next few minutes. Clint shakes his head, smiles at Cruz. "Anyway, life goes on, doesn't it? How's my beautiful girl? God, how I've missed her. She isn't married, is she?"

"No."

"Hot damn! And she's okay, right?"

"Um… uh, what time is it?"

"Huh? Oh…" Clint picks up his watch from the nightstand. "Almost five. Yvonne will be down there rustling up some coffee any time now. She rises before sunup every day. She's part Cheyenne. Says you got to get up before the sun does or you don't count, or something like that. She's my cook nowadays, and I got another couple hired for everything else. Juanita and José. Hard workers. Good folks. Kind of night owls, though. I don't mind when they do their work, day or night, as long as all the animals are tended to on time. None of this means a thing without Angelina. Where is she, Cruz?"

"Nuevo Laredo."

"Still there, huh? What was all that talk about me not saying her name and beating the steaming *caca* out of me? You go *loco* for a minute?"

"Let's go downstairs and have some coffee. Do we need to get you to a hospital... *mi hermano?*"

"Aw, it'll wait." He untucks his shirt, raises it up to inspect the bandages over his abdomen. "Look, no fresh blood coming through right now. But, anyways, she's all right, isn't she?"

"Yes."

They both limp and hobble from the room and down the stairs.

"Let's go figure how to bring Lina back here as soon as possible. No more house duties for her. All she has to do is be my wife and help me spend all this money my crazy daddy left me. Hey, whatever happened to that poor little baby we found in the road? What was it Lina was going to call her?"

"Pinkie."

38
Saddle Up

San Antonio, Texas
1946

Yvonne appears as soon as Clint steps into the kitchen. *"Buenos diás, Señor* Clint. *¿Quieres que cocine tocino con huevos?*

"No, gracias. El café está bien."

He turns to Cruz. "You want some breakfast? Yvonne makes a good plate of bacon and eggs."

"No, no, I'm fine."

He couldn't swallow food with a shovel with what he hasn't yet told Clint playing on his mind. They sit at the kitchen table and add large servings of sugar and cream to their mugs of coffee Yvonne sets in front of them. She slips a plate of sliced melon in the middle of the table and busies herself at the sink.

Clint stares at the tilework above the stove and on the nearby wall. "If I'd known my girl was coming home this soon, I'd have waited to let José and Juanita do this new tile. Guess they were up late working on it. Kind of pretty, isn't it? Hope Lina likes it. You know, I think we need a little time here at the house getting reacquainted, but I sure as heck want us to tie the knot as soon as it's reasonable. Times a' wasting, as far as I see it. It feels like I've waited too long as it is. I'll take her anywhere in the world she wants to go for our honeymoon. You think she'll forgive me when she finds out the truth and knows I've been trying to find her, Cruz?"

Cruz glances anxiously at Yvonne's back as she stands at the sink. His eyes flick back at Clint and again at the woman. Clint, understanding, says, *"Yvonne, por favor, ayude a José afuera por un rato. Mi amigo Cruz y yo tenemos asuntos por resolver."*

Si, señor."

She dries her hands on her apron and leaves through the kitchen door to grant the requested privacy. Clint leans forward with a worried expression. Cruz shuffles his boots into a different position, then again. Takes a sip of coffee, rearranges the spoon beside his mug. Twice.

"What's wrong, little brother? Is it about her?"

"Clint, five years is a long time."

"Dang right it is. Too long, and—"

Cruz's raised hand silences Clint. "I-I was gone, too. I joined the *Bracero* program in '42. That was quite a deal. Worked just right for a lot of those fellas, but it wasn't for me. Tried working the California vineyards, but you know I'm no sod buster. I hired out to work on the railroads. Hated it, but it was better than working in the dirt. I kept my head down and my mouth shut. I thought we were wanted for murdering that fool, Raphael. *Dios,* if I had known…"

"I really tried to—"

"I got so antsy, I started hiring out on ranches. First, Montana. Then, one in Northern California. Finally landed on the Shiloh Valley Ranch up in Wyoming and stayed there. Ranchers don't ask questions of cowboys, just tell them where to drop their gear and wait and see if they're all hat and no cattle. If you got what it takes, they leave you be. You know me and ranching, so no one gave me any trouble. Just right for me, but now I could kick my own butt. I failed my sister."

"Ah, you never failed Lina. Y'all are two peas in a pod. Well, two *fighting peas* in a pod. We both got a lot to make up to her, sounds like."

"The *Bracero* contracts were six months long back then, so I made it back to Nuevo Laredo to see Lina a couple of times. And the little girl… she was so sweet."

"She kept her?"

"What else could she do, Clint? You didn't come back for her, and the little thing had no *familia* we knew of. They were so close. So close." Cruz puts his elbows on the table and rubs his face with both hands.

Clint's gut tightens. "What the hell happened?"

"She-she, uh, was taken. Kidnapped."

"Lina kidnapped?" Clint shoots up, knocking his chair over.

"Not Lina… Pinkie. Some crazy woman took her, and they never found out who it was or what happened to her. Damndest thing you ever heard of."

Clint's breath is uneven. "And Lina?"

Cruz shakes his head, looks down. "It broke her, Clint. Tore her up. Listen, I didn't see her since '44. Time got away from me. Didn't even know about Pinkie disappearing. A few days ago, I went there to see them, take them some gifts, money… and afterward, uh… afterward, I came here to avenge my sister's fate. Now I find out the one to blame is dead already."

"Her fate?" Clint moves closer to Cruz, his breathing erratic, fists clenched. "Tell me what's happened."

Cruz's eyes are bloodshot when he looks at his friend. "It's tough. You better sit back down."

"I'll stand."

"Please."

Clint picks his chair off the floor, sits, leans forward with trepidation hopscotching around his face.

"Mainly, she, uh, she's the local police captain's woman. He was married when they first got together."

Clint licks his lips. "All right, I-I can see where that might happen. She's alone. Thinks I don't care anymore. Scared and heartbroken. The little girl she loves meets a tragic fate. We can get her out of that one, Cruz. I'll help her forget all about him, take her somewhere exotic. She'll forget—"

"Clint, please… listen." His tone sends a cold wind through Clint's heart.

"I got to town and, of course, went first to the *casita* I rented for her and Pinkie before I left Mexico for California. Their little landlady was old… kind… not like that Madam Rosie woman at the boarding house where we first stayed.

"Strangers were living in Angelina's place. They told me the story of how the old woman died and the young woman's little girl disappeared that same night. They had no idea what happened to the little girl's mama.

"I was worried to death. I went to the cantina club where Angelina used to sing. What's the name? Oh, yeah, *Club de Fantasía.* I thought someone there might know where to find her. Um, hey, can I have a little more *café*, brother?"

Clint, eyes glazed, brings the coffee pot from the stove and refills Cruz's mug. Takes it back, then sits down waiting for the facts he's sure he doesn't want to hear.

"I-I didn't find her there, but I found out more than I ever wanted to know."

"What does that mean?"

Cruz adds sugar and cream, stirs, noisily sips. He wipes his mouth on the back of his hand. This is the part he hates to say aloud, let alone watch what it'll do to Clint. "She, uh, goes there to the club almost every night. She sings a little, drinks a lot, laughs with everyone, gets drunk most of the time. They gave her a little private room upstairs. They all seem protective of her, but not enough."

"Not enough?"

"I-I think, if I understand right, she sometimes, uh, entertains men? Or else they go in to her when she's too boozed to care. Maybe when she's unconscious, but they pay her and bring her expensive gifts. She's, uh, popular, I hear. The police guy, Captain Ramirez, knows about it, but she threatens to tell everyone about their affair if he tries to stop her. He already left his wife for Lina long ago, and everyone knows it. Seems like she uses that threat as an excuse to live as she pleases. They say he has tried to marry her for the last few years, but she chooses that other life. All this I learned from having *una cerveza* at that club."

Clint's frozen face has taken on the pallor of a dead man. His lips seal, open, seal again.

"Clint, I'm-I'm sorry to bring you this terrible news. Can I get you more coffee, maybe a drink of water? How about whiskey?"

"I-I, God, I, uh, can't believe... I mean... did you, uh, oh hell, Cruz, what have we done to that little thing? You're right. We both deserted her. She was never cut out to be alone in this world, especially bearing a tragedy like that. She was always protected and safe with us, and then, all of a sudden, she had no one. Did you find her?"

"I did. She lives in the fancy hotel you told us about when we first went down there. That's where Ramirez pays for her to stay. She cried and cried when she opened the door and I was standing there. I begged her to come away with me, but she said she has nothing to go to and nothing to stay for. She looks so tired, Clint, so very tired. She's still beautiful, but her eyes are empty.

"My first reaction was, well... to beat up Ramirez. Then I did some thinking on it. I came to the conclusion that he's been protecting her, taking care of her. Without him, she might have been in the streets by now, or worse. Who knows what would have happened with no one to watch over her? He must be very in love to put up with it. Has to be."

Clint stands up in slow motion, walks to the sink to stare out the kitchen window. Cruz watches him. If broken hearts made noise, the room would be filled with clatter. As it is, the silence is deafening. "I thought I would come and take my mad out on you, Clint, but... damn, it isn't your fault. I'm not a violent man, but I wanted to beat someone to a pulp after leaving Angelina in that hotel room. I didn't dare go back to that cantina feeling like that, so I came here." He sighs loud and long. "Hell, no one is to blame but our own *Señor* Sutton... he and that devil woman who stole Pinkie from my sister's arms and made her lose her mind."

Clint is quiet for several more minutes, filling the air and Cruz with a big dose of uneasiness. When he speaks, he sounds faraway.

"A thousand men may have had her, but nothing can ever ruin her innocence in my eyes. I have loved only her with a fierce passion, and that will never change." He abruptly turns from the window. "I'm bringing her home, Cruz. Saddle up. We're leaving in thirty minutes."

39
Zorro

Nuevo Laredo, Mexico
1946

From what he makes out in the dim light, the room is small but expensively decorated with dramatically draped curtains on the solo window and fresh roses in several vases. Lina always loved roses and pretty things. An ornate dressing table, mirror, and chaise lounge are barely visible in the darkened room. The air is stale and smells of liquor exhalation, rose fragrance, and candle fumes. Clint closes the door quietly and props one of the two wooden chairs in the room against the wall away from the circle of candlelight flickering from inside lacy pottery stands near the bed.

His gut instinct is to run to the sleeping woman and scoop her up in his arms forever, but he knows better. Well-versed in combat psychology, not to mention sensible horse behavior, he knows you can lead a horse to water, but you danged sure can't make it drink. People are no different. If Angelina no longer loves or wants him, or if her resentment toward him runs too deep, he can't force himself on her no matter how much he wants to. If she is too rooted in this degraded lifestyle, he'll be going back to Texas without her. The thought of it is intolerable.

Outside the door, the sounds of a scuffle. He crosses the room, steps outside in time to see Cruz fist-a-cuffing a man to the floor. The man rises rubbing his jaw.

"Señor, I got no trouble with you. I came only to see the *la mujer bonita, Señorita* Angelina. She likes me… a lot." His lustful smirk hits Clint's gut like a fist. "Ask her. I come a long way to see her every two months, but, of course, you know, she is worth it, *si?"*

The muscle under Clint's eye begins to twitch.

"This time, I brought pretty combs for her hair." He starts to unfold a scarf he pulls from inside his jacket. "Want to see? She loves the sparking ones like these. *Muy bonita* for a…" He looks up, absorbs the expressions of the men facing him, falls silent.

Cruz 's chin drops. He growls a low, throaty sound not unlike a cougar's warning rumble. Clint touches his arm, *"Cálmate, hermano.* I'll handle it." He steps in front of Cruz.

"Señor, allow me to introduce to you the beautiful *señorita's* brother. Only hours ago, he was released from the deadliest prison in Mexico to come here and check on his sister. I must confess for your sake… he enjoys watching the men he attacks suffer. M*uy malo.* He hates everyone, even his mother, but he loves his only sister—the beautiful *señorita* you are discussing so freely in front of him."

The man vigorously shakes his head. "I assure you, *señor,* I come only to be friendly."

"Por supuesto. You are lucky I can control him. He trusts me. So, if you already had an appointment with the *señorita,* then you should keep it."

"Really? I will be only an hour."

Clint dips his head agreeably and steps aside pulling a severely scowling Cruz with him. The man's eyes are glued to the men as he takes hesitant steps past them. He touches the door handle, asking for "permission to enter" with eyes dilated with uncertainty.

"Un momento, señor. Before you enter, I feel I should tell you something else," Clint says. "For your own good."

"Q-Que?" the man stutters.

"It's just a little thing… but sometimes, this brother of the beautiful *señorita* goes *loco.* It comes out of nowhere… like a streak of lightning." Clint shakes his head as though remembering past terrible experiences. "When that happens, we chain him up. Big, thick chains. Can you guess what he does?"

The man shakes his head.

"He chews through the metal."

The man's terrified eyes roll back and forth between Clint and Cruz. The latter glares fiercely, moans deep in his throat. Clint assumes a concerned look. *"Es mejor que te vayas. ¿Entiendes?"*

The man backs away, his body trembling. He takes a few backward steps, turns and gallops down the hallway with his boots clunking on the boarded stairs as he rapidly descends to the floor below. Clint and Cruz laugh heartily for only a moment before the criticality of their present undertaking returns.

"Okay, that should keep him and anybody else out of our way until I can talk to Lina." He lets out a burdened sigh. "She's still asleep." They exchange worried looks as Clint slips into her room. Cruz sits down on the hallway bench, grinds his boot heel impatiently on the floor. Everything in him wants to beat the hell out of someone, or maybe a whole room full of somebodies.

Clint resumes his vigil in the chair and waits for almost an hour. Angelina's sleeping form in the bed bathed by candlelight and mixed with the scent of roses gives him the eerie sense of attending a funeral. Angelina moans, changes position, says something indecipherable. In a few moments, she sits up rubbing her forehead. She's wearing a silky nightgown with her breasts mounding over the top. Her thick hair spreads over her shoulders.

Her hair is shorter is all he allows himself to think.

"Who-who's there?" she says, noticing Clint's boots and legs inside the circle of candlelight.

"A friend," he says in a voice he hopes won't reveal his identity.

She laughs, an ironic, humorless sound. "Of course… *un amigo.* I seem to collect more friends every day." She adjusts the pillows behind her to sit straighter in the bed. She picks up an etched glass and partly fills it from a half-empty bottle of Tanqueray gin sitting on the bedside table. "You want a drink? Clean glasses are in the cabinet above your head. Crystal glasses from Italy, no less. Only the very best from my… friends."

Clint ignores the stab in his heart. *"No hace falta bebida.* Liquor is unnecessary when someone is already intoxicated by your presence."

"Oh, naturally. What good is a drink and conversation between… friends?" She takes a long swallow of gin, draws her legs up, and rests her wrists on her knees. "And which of my good friends is here tonight? Are you *Alexander* or *The Great? Pancho* or *Villa?* She laughs again, a sound duller than the last time.

"Who do you wish me to be, pretty *señorita?* I am at your service."

"Who do *I* wish you to be?" She snorts, stares in his direction. "Very well, since you give me a choice, I wish you to be, hmm… Zorro."

"Zorro it shall be, but I must know more. Tell me, is it his sword, his cape, or his daring rescues you admire the most? Perhaps it is his magnificent physique?"

Angelina, surprised by the man's unusual responses, says, "I-I think I love his horse the most."

"Tornado?"

"Si."

"You are fond of horses, *señorita?*

"I was. A very long time ago."

"Zorro has many horses. He shall give you any horse you desire. Thoroughbreds, Arabians, Friesians. Your heart's desire, my fair lady. Now that you may have a hundred horses, what more do you wish your Zorro to do? Shall he rescue you, beautiful damsel?"

Angelina takes another sip of gin, then drains the glass and sets it down. "You're different, aren't you?" No answer. She rests a finger on her chin, looks thoughtful. "Well, Zorro, you chose the wrong, what did you call me… damsel? I'm afraid you've made a mistake. You see, I cannot be rescued, my mysterious hero, but… *gracias."*

He laughs lightly, careful to disguise his voice. "Oh, I must disagree. All women may be rescued if they want to be with all their hearts."

"Not all women, Zorro."

"Merely tell me—whisper it or shout it—what dangerous adversaries and dragons must I slay to earn your freedom and take you from this dreary fortress?"

She scoffs. "Now you sound like a fairytale prince rescuing a princess."

"I am. I have come from my castle to rescue Princess Angelina. So… whom shall I fight to win your love, *mi bella doncella?*"

Silence, followed by a weary sigh. She turns her head to stare at the wall. "I am the villain of my own life. You would have to fight me… to save me. I am the dragon. I am the enemy. You see, Zorro? It is hopeless."

"I cannot agree. When there is a brave Zorro who adores you, nothing is hopeless."

"Adore?" She scoffs. "Men admire me for my beauty, but no one can…or should adore me."

"I do."

Tears spring into her eyes. "It isn't kind to say things like that, *señor.* You-you don't know me."

"I understand you, *preciosa.*"

"I-I…" She buries her face in her hands. Her shoulders shake. Not looking up, she says, "Please, don't say any more, *mi amigo.* I am not good company tonight. I am sorry. Come back another time… Zorro."

"Unless she weeps for his touch, Zorro never leaves a lady in tears. I have offered you a stable of fine horses. I am ready to fight a legion of soldiers and commoners to win your freedom. Perhaps one kiss from Zorro before he departs might dry your tears, *mi belleza?*"

She looks up, reaches for a handkerchief to blot her eyes and nose. "I don't know who you are, but I pray you return one day. I get so-so lonely for good conversation. Yes, I think a goodbye kiss from Zorro is fine."

Clint stands, careful his face cannot be seen in the dark.

"You're tall."

"Por supuesto, I am Zorro." He takes off his hat, covers his face with it as he walks into the light. He crouches beside Angelina. "You must first close your eyes to experience the magic of our kiss."

She smiles and closes her eyes. Clint leans in and kisses her with all the tenderness and love he has felt for her for so long. She draws back in surprise, sees his face for the first time, gasps. She struggles to get out of the bed, frees a hand, and slaps his face.

"You-you abandoned me! You never came back for us! Why did you leave us? I loved you so much. You were my heart, my life, and you—"

She's all legs and arms coming at him with angry, tear-filled eyes. He catches her flailing hands and tucks them underneath his sore torso as he leans his body weight over her. She screams for help.

"Listen to me, Lina! I was drafted by the army. I had to leave the next day after I left you to fight the damned war."

"I don't care what you say! You should have told us! You should have written!"

"I did. So many times. Stop squirming, honey, and let me explain. It's Daddy who messed us up. Please stop fighting me."

"You're blaming *Señor* Sutton for what you did? Ay-yi—"

"Hush, Lina! Yes, I do blame him. He lied about everything to keep us apart. I sent you a letter the next day after I left you and Cruz. He told me Bubba gave it to you. Everything he said was a big, stupid lie. He cheated us all, Lina." Clint speaks quickly to get it all said. The wiggling underneath him subsides. "Me abandon you? I can barely breathe without you. I'll never love any woman but my Angelina. Ever."

"But-but where have you been since the war stopped?"

"I was injured. Pretty bad. I got out of the hospital and back to Texas only recently. Had to have one more operation after that. I was coming to find you, my love. I can't… I won't live without you, baby." He pulls her face to his and kisses her as passionately as he feels inside, draws back, blows a whisper of air on her face. "Don't you see… nothing matters but us. There is no history, only what is right now. Our future. Together. Always."

She stares into his face, drops her head. "No, Clint. I-I am not-not good now. Nothing is the same. *Cometió demasiados errores.* I am not your innocent Angelina anymore." A sob escapes her throat. "I'm-I'm ruined."

"Shh," he whispers, clamping his arms tightly around her. "Listen only with your heart. Are you listening, *mi amor?*"

She nods.

"You are my Angelina, my angel, my gift. Nothing on this earth, above it, or below it can ever ruin you in my eyes. Do you understand?"

"That can't be true, Clint. I—"

"Lina, it's *our* truth. I love only you, and I might as well die if I can't have you by my side."

"Dios mío, Clint… I, uh…" Her voice trails off.

He loosens his embrace, gazes tenderly in her eyes. "Let's go home, *mi corazón."*

40
Little Girl in an Ugly Wig

Buenos Aires, Argentina
1947

Pinkie

The first time Vincent Bonzini sees her, she is placing one foot in front of the other on a short wall, arms extended on each side, eyes straight ahead as if she were balancing on a high wire. The wall is a short distance from a tired-looking cottage painted a god-awful patchy blue with peeling mustard-yellow shutters. On the ground is a hinged A-board sign barely painted over in white. Uneven black letters spell out *Readings, 20-Centavos.* A coat is flung over part of the last word.

The girl looked delicate and out of place inside loose clothing, worn brown shoes, no socks, and a dreadful wig—yes, a dark, ugly wig of short, black curls pulled down on her head like a swimming cap. It didn't fit properly. Tight blond coils poked from the lower right-hand side of the wig.

The circumstance placing Bonzini in that particular area was an earlier appointment he had to view a juggling act. *Roma*—the gypsies—are excellent circus people. He often drives to their camps or certain parts of town after being alerted to a possible exceptional act for his minor, but exquisitely manned, Buenos Aires circus.

He is always interested in acrobatic acts. Perhaps the little girl has an acrobatic father? He parks his car, motor idling, across the road and watches her climb on the wall again and again. He admires her balance as she hops along the top with one leg straight out in front. The next time, she's holding one foot behind her with one arm high in the air. She does several strings of pinwheels on the wall, and when she executes a perfect air-somersault off the end, Bonzini cuts the motor.

The girl looks up as he crosses the road and quickly dons the discarded coat, buttoning it all the way to the top. He is surprised the coat is quite expensive, not at all like her other garments. Indian in design, it has elaborate brocade and embroidery. She pulls her ill-fitting wig further down on her head as he nears. He is startled by the hollow expression in the child's beautiful blue eyes. What had he expected? Not that. Not at all.

"*Buenas tardes!* And what, may I ask, is your name?" he says.

"Elena Banović."

"It's nice to meet you, Elena. You may call me Bonzini. What kind of readings are you selling?"

Like a *Princess Doraldina* machine springing to life to give one's fortune at the click of a coin, the girl lights up on cue. He, Bonzini, is the cue—a customer. It's fake, the excitement and pleasantness, but it's well done.

"Oh, mister, uh, sir, how nice of you to inquire! My aunt, the famous Madam Rosie, said a distinguished man in a…" she squints at the car across the road, "… a man in a red car would inquire of her services today. A man of great standing, of fine form, of impocca… uh, impacca… I mean, impeccable character." She breathes a sigh of relief. "And here you are. Madam Rosie is always right!"

"Your aunt, this Madam Rosie, tells fortunes?"

"Oh, no sir, not fortunes. Readings. The circum…" she swallows hard… "the circumstances of your life before and after this very moment! The ups. The downs. The romances and the tragedies. All the pieces of your human, uh… humanity is what she can share with you today, sir."

Great lines. Difficult lines. Bonzini is impressed with the young girl's ability to deliver them with such passion. *She should give lessons to Fernando. Ticket sales would soar!* While she recited her script, her eyes expressed the most charming counterfeit sincerity.

Her eyes… crystal clear and blue-bright with youthfulness.

What is she, maybe seven or eight years old? Her salesmanship is rather fantastical, but why the wig? Is she Romani? Why is she hawking for a fortune-teller in this downtrodden section of town? What's behind her façade?

The girl is a puzzle with odd-fitting parts, and isn't he the Great Bonzini… the discoverer of mystique and adventure wherever it can be found?

And so, their acquaintance begins… Bonzini, the circus entrepreneur, animal trainer, man of wealth, and Elena Banović, the trained puppet-child peddling fortune readings for an opportunistic *gitana* like a cheap carnival barker. Their relationship of trust builds slowly, most of it being conducted in the presence of Madam Rosie. Years of employing and dealing with people of every type and age from all over the world have given Bonzini *a second sense* in evaluating character. He notes the *gitana's* greed at their first encounter.

It is obvious the child has been warned or threatened to keep her mouth shut concerning their private lives. In two months, he knows only a pittance of why the eight-year-old, when not faking exuberance, possesses the most tragic eyes he has ever come across, let alone, in a child. What he knows as fact is that she speaks perfect Spanish and English and seems to have no relatives other than Madam Rosie. Her coloring and features are nothing like the *gitana.* She has shared one thing, and he takes that as a start to solving the mystery of her. She recently told him she prefers to be called Pinkie, not Elena, but she warned Bonzini never to call her that in front of Madam Rosie.

He asked her about the wig a few days ago out by the A-sign. She didn't answer at first, then, as if searching for the exact cataloged answer, she said, "Um, I-I wear it because I'm not always nice. It helps me remember to… to guard my words before speaking them." Then, she smiled a phony smile beneath sad eyes. That was the moment Bonzini, a rescuer of hapless folks and animals whenever possible, decides to rescue this girl no matter the cost. He suspects it will be a tremendous cost to pry her away from a leech such as Madam Rosie.

As his paternal concern for Pinkie grows, he makes time once a week to visit her and sits through tiresome fortune-telling sessions by putting his mind on his burgeoning circus business. Madam Rosie's style is passé, certainly not up to his high standards should he be looking for another fortune-telling act, which he is not. Let the carnivals have them. By dropping money into her coffers and faking his need for her staccato rhetoric, he engages with Pinkie as he arrives and departs.

He notes that Madam Rosie, though somewhat still attractive for her age, is on the downside, and this he judges by the worsening sallowness of her skin and her limp, which has grown noticeably worse in the last weeks. Resourceful almost to a fault, Bonzini portends the woman's deterioration may work in the child's favor.

Gina—Bonzini's star trapeze artist and girlfriend—presses him to invite Pinkie to the circus. "Bonzi, you must! Why must a little girl stand on the street all day in the heat and cold advertising a silly fortune teller? *Senza scrupoli!* It might even be dangerous. She should be playing and having fun."

"This I know, Gina, but her guardian is hard-hearted. Persuasion will take money and trickery for that one. I'm thinking of ways to outsmart her."

"Please hurry, Bonzi. I must see the beautiful child in the ugly wig for myself."

The next day, he invites Madam Rosie and Pinkie to the forthcoming Saturday afternoon show at the Bonzini Circus. Using his most charming ringmaster style, he proclaims, "I insist you be my guests. Lions, tigers, elephants, monkeys! The best high-wire act in South America you shall see, featuring the stunning Gina Ferrari. Our clowns will make you double over with laughter, and my new big tent is magnificent. We have gauchos, tumblers, jugglers, dancers, and even a camel. The foods you will taste! All as my special guests."

He ends his presentation with his face slanted upward, one arm extended high as though holding a baton. The reaction from the two females in the room is dull, but he didn't miss the flash of excitement that flickered in Pinkie's eyes for a brief moment. Not allowing Madam Rosie a chance to decline, he says, "I must tell you my other good news. I was given approval by the Buenos Aires City Council to continue my circus. They said the entertainment of my shows is good for the war-weary people arriving daily in Argentina. So, you see, it is a matter of civil importance that you attend."

He finishes his sales pitch with a broad smile. What he doesn't say is the City Council is politically placating all the Germans finding consolation and refuge within their borders and that those Germans are particularly fond of *der Zirkus*. Yes, that is the real truth of the matter.

He also doesn't mention that the Council lusts for the percentages they skim from his ticket sales, which, thankfully, grow each week. Bonzini is used to the necessity of bribing authorities and paying under the table to this official or the next one for the privilege of entertaining people within the city, or even when he takes his troupes on the road. Such is the normal corruption of life and business in the circus and carnival worlds.

41
The Negotiation

Buenos Aires, Argentina
1947

Madam Rosie opens the door a few inches to Bonzini's knock on Saturday morning. "I fell," she says, opening the door only enough for him to see her cast. It stretches from her foot into the layers of her long dress. "We cannot go with you today. Perhaps another time." She would have closed the door, but Bonzini puts his foot in the gap. Today, he has come to make a deal, and he has no intention of being put off.

"Madam, may I at least take Elena? Though I am deeply saddened by your accident, I will take full responsibility for her so that she may attend the circus today. In fact, I have a special surprise for her."

Madam Rosie's brow furrows. "If I cannot go, she cannot go. How can you run a circus and watch a child at the same time? No, she stays home. She needs no surprises, this one. Do you think I want her more spoiled than she is already? Perhaps today she will earn her keep for a change. Bring good business to me."

Bonzini swallows hard, forces a smile. "Allow me to assist in such an unfortunate circumstance, dear woman." Still uninvited inside the house, he reaches into his jacket pocket and pulls out a bag, shakes it, waits for the magic to take effect. It doesn't take long. Madam Rosie scrutinizes his face, drops her gaze to the bag, back to his face. She backs up slowly opening the door. Stepping inside, he notices Pinkie slumped on an ottoman in the corner of the room. Her clothes, as usual, do not fit well, but they seem a degree higher caliber than usual. The ugly wig sits off-center on her head with several short curls escaping at the bottom. Her face shows no emotion.

"Sit down," Madam Rosie says, pointing to the chair beside the table containing her crystal ball covered by a large square of purple velvet. Bonzini remains standing. Madam Rosie drops into one of the two chairs at the table, grunts with pain. She uses both hands to lift and place her casted leg to the side. "I, uh, didn't fall. My leg gave way and broke on its own. They say I have no calcium, that my bones are weak. What do they know?"

Aha! The gypsy has osteoporosis.

He invokes a look of sympathy and remains standing. When he has Madam Rosie's full attention, he empties the coins from the bag onto the table. Her eyes widen, then narrow from the unbridled greed abounding in her heart. Bonzini is familiar with that kind of look.

Very well. She will get more, and so shall I, he thinks.

He reaches into his pants pocket, retrieves ten coins, and drops them beside the other coins. "Spanish coins, madam. Quite rare. They will fetch a good price… a very good price. The other coins I gave you are worth three-hundred pesos."

A quick hand reaches for the coins, but Bonzini's hand is quicker. He places it over the money, fingers spread apart. "Naturally, you will need extra help while your leg heals. I suggest hiring a servant. In the meantime, I shall pick up Elena every morning and have her back by five for when your, uh, *business,* picks up. I'm sure your funds shall need replenishing often, yes? Do you think three-hundred pesos will help for now?"

Madam Rosie is inwardly licking her lips. He reads it in her eyes, and something else.

"Perhaps we can work something out," she mumbles. He takes his hand off the money. Quick as a snake strike, she slides it toward her with a possessive hand. "I don't understand why you want the child to go with you every day? It's senseless." she says, her eyes devouring the coins.

"Alas, there are many challenges when managing a circus. To my disdain, my horse trainer's daughter has decided to become a ballerina and doesn't care to work with the horses anymore. I need Elena to help me tame and train my new performance pony. It's a small horse requiring someone her size. She will learn trick riding, as well. I already know she is athletic enough to learn these things." Most of what he is telling the woman is true.

An ugly shadow invades the woman's face. "She knows nothing of horses."

"All the better. Now, she is free to learn the proper way."

Madam Rosie snorts. "Ha! She does not deserve—"

"A delivery of delicacies and wine shall be delivered to you this afternoon, madam. Will you be home to receive it? And may I take it upon myself to call a woman I know—Concie Perez—to assist you today, and perhaps longer, to lighten your burdens at home? All at my expense, of course."

Madam Rosie drops her shoulders in defeat. She stares at the money and knows she cannot, will not, refuse this man's bribes. It's impossible. Her fortune has dwindled pitifully since she was shunned by her own people and her only brother. Three years later, her monies are low, and her health is failing. How long can she exist on scarce fortune-telling customers, especially if she needs more medicines and care in the future?

She stands awkwardly, hobbles to a built-in cupboard, retrieves a bag with a drawstring. She puts all the coins inside the bag, pulls the strings tight, and sits down clutching it tightly in her lap. She feels a trickle of relief but also a flood of resentment. She stares at Pinkie. Why does everyone care about this stray? The same mysterious attachment happened to her nephew Luka. She was forced to have him detained because of it, but is it her fault he never returned to Argentina? She paid the men to hold him captive for ten days, not forever.

She calculated getting the girl to Argentina and feathering the circumstances about the fake dead couple who were her parents before Luka returned. The journey was so extreme and lasted so long, she was afraid Luka would beat her home. He didn't, and three years later, he is still missing.

The next day after arriving at her brother's abode, Madam Rosie was exhausted and slept in. The wine she imbibed the night before caused even deeper sleep. Five-year-old Pinkie awoke and wandered into the kitchen where Madam Rosie's brother was making coffee. She had not yet coached her ward of what she was allowed to say to Ivan and what would happen to her if she said more.

Pinkie told Ivan her version of Luka disappearing with two men putting a bag over his head and that Madam Rosie would not stop the wagon to help him. She told him Madam Rosie told her he would be at every port waiting for them, but he was never there.

If only the girl had not told the truth, Madam Rosie could have concocted an exquisite deception to satisfy her brother and the rest of her tribe. As it was, her brother was furious, and he, and everyone else, shunned her—all because of this waif's big mouth! This girl! Always bringing bad luck to her door. Stubborn with a wicked tongue when provoked. Now this rich circus man wants to help her, too? Why should she deserve these opportunities?

On the other hand, perhaps she, Madam Rosie, can milk this man for a portion of his wealth as long as he is interested in the girl. If Pinkie learns well, she can hire her out to work in the carnivals by day and direct more business to her in the evenings. It's no doubt her beauty will draw people when she is older. Perhaps she can harness the girl's newly learned talents with her strange charisma to use as bait for snagging rich suitors when she turns fourteen.

Is fortune at last smiling on me?

She would smile if she were not in the throes of a tough negotiation. She fixes Bonzini with a severe look. "She can go today. As far as your other proposition, she can train with you and your horse two times a week."

"Oh, no, no, that's not often enough. Seven times a week."

Madam Rosie scowls, shakes her head. "That is unreasonable."

"Okay, six days. Very necessary for intense training of this kind."

Madam Rosie shakes her head.

Bonzini sighs wearily, looks thoughtful. "You drive a hard bargain, Madam Rosie. I suppose we can attempt to do our training in five days a week if that is the best you can do." Inwardly, he laughs at getting the exact number of days he had wanted.

"I want her home every day at four, not five."

"Hmm, I suppose I can make that work."

"One other thing, she is never to eat sweets."

"No sweets, madam?"

"No, she, uh, she gets rashes. Not a single sweet delicacy. Do you understand?"

Bonzini glances at Pinkie. Her face is completely blank.

42
Let There Be Sweets

Buenos Aires, Argentina
1947

Gina pushes aside the burgundy velvet curtain separating her bedroom and lavatory from the kitchen in the Spartan Manor trailer Bonzini bought for her this year. The trailer stands as a sparkling jewel among the numerous humble trailers and makeshift tent houses behind the main circus tent. Gina is Bonzini's woman, the members of the circus rattle out in their gossip, so, naturally, she has the trailer of a queen. They tease her that if she weren't always baking, cooking, and sharing treats with them, they might get jealous of her good fortune. She waves their comments off good-naturedly and passes another tray or bowl or pan of delicacies she has prepared for them to sample.

Dressed in a pink angora sweater and dark slacks, Gina at last gets to meet the little girl her Bonzi is so fond of. She is, as he told her, a strikingly attractive child. Yet, she is dressed worse than a street urchin in her ill-fitting, tattered wig, sloppy old clothes, and worn boy shoes.

Pinkie waits timidly on the sofa twisting the tassels of a pillow. Gina is the first woman who compares in beauty to what she remembers of her mama's appearance. She finds the young woman's accent enticing, but her focused attentiveness on her makes her uneasy.

"Do you like my *arancini, bella* Pinkie? The *focaccia* with the olives and tomatoes on top is almost ready to come from the oven. Do you smell it yet? I made the *cannoli* for you this morning, too. You know *cannoli?"* Pinkie shakes her head. "It is from my Sicilian culture. Little rolled pastries with sweet insides. I know you will love it."

"I'm not allowed to eat sweets."

"Yes, Bonzi told me of this. He says you are allergic?"

"I guess so."

"What happens when you eat the sweets? A rash, or…?"

"I don't know."

Gina sits down on the opposite end of the sofa facing Pinkie. "I don't understand. Why you don't know what happens when you eat sweets? Do you go unconscious or have a fit?"

"Madam Rosie never lets me eat them, so I don't know what happens."

"I see. When did you eat a sweet the last time?"

Pinkie shrugs her shoulders.

"Perhaps a churro or a little sucker?"

"No."

"Do you wish to eat sweet things, Pinkie?"

"When Madam Rosie eats *pionono*, I wish I could taste it. She buys the kind with strawberry jam inside. She eats it while I watch. She smacks her lips."

"You can't have any?"

"No."

"Not one bite?"

"No."

"Does she say why?"

"She says if I were a good girl, I could have some."

"Oh, dio, cos'e' sta infanzia pazzesca?"

She silently answers her own question a second later. *I'll tell you what kind of childhood it is—a bad one!*

A tap on the door prevents Pinkie from asking Gina what language she is speaking. Some of her words are similar to Spanish, but not exactly.

"Come in," Gina says, then continues mumbling to herself in

Italian.

"Am I interrupting?" a smiling Bonzini asks.

Gina launches into a non-stop tirade in Italian. A far-away memory tries to form in Pinkie's conscious recollections but dissolves before she can grasp it. Bonzini looks from Gina to Pinkie, then grins.

"Well, *signorina* Pinkie, Gina wants to spoil you. She says after we eat lunch and you taste her *cannoli,* she is going to purchase you a cotton candy, a cinnamon candy apple, and the biggest lollipop we sell at our circus, all before the performances this afternoon. She wants you to watch her on the trapeze surrounded by every sweet thing we sell here, but..." he glances at Gina, "... I think it is better if Pinkie eats one sweet at a time, yes? We don't want her sick on her first day with us."

Gina and Bonzini smile at one another. Pinkie is quiet. There has been no teasing, laughing, or smiles these past three years. She understands how to be mechanically friendly when enticing customers for Madam Rosie, and her smiles are only for the same reason. The behavior of this couple is confusing, even frightening. She swallows hard, steps inside her safe, pretty place she has built over time, and manages a weak smile. Her eyes bear the distant look of one greatly disappointed by life's twists and turns. She corrects herself, produces a wide grin.

Fake, all fake, Bonzini notes. What will it take to reach this little girl's heart?

43
Bathing with Nisha

Bonzini Circus Grounds, Argentina
1947

Pinkie is soaked head to toe, laughing almost hysterically. Nisha draws another trunkful of water from the tub and sprays her again. Pinkie collapses on the ground giggling. She puts her palms up to Nisha. "Let me get my breath, *Señorita elefante loco!*"

Her black wig is drenched and falls drastically sideways. Gina has never heard Pinkie laugh until Nisha *adopted* her today on her fifth visit to the circus grounds. Later, Gina will swear Nisha was laughing right along with Pinkie during their romp. She watches from the sidelines, delighted to see the youngster so happy. She checks her watch. "Come along, Pinkie. It is time to get cleaned up," she says, holding a towel.

"May I stay here and play with Nisha? Bonzini said I am to be fitted in my riding clothes."

"That is the next time you come see us. We won't be gone long today."

"Why must I go?"

"For the shopping."

"Shopping? For what?"

"Clothes, of course. All women shop for clothes and shoes. It's part of our lives."

Pinkie looks down at her dull, too-large dress with the long waist.

The hemline almost touches the top of her lace-up boy boots, her only footwear except for a pair of scuffed brown shoes. "These are fine when they dry. Will they be dry before I go home?"

Gina sighs. "I'll make sure of it. Let's go now to my trailer so you can have the lovely bath I planned for you. I also have a surprise for you, *mia piccola angelo.*"

"A surprise?"

"Yes! You are going to meet your little horse after we shop."

"Why can't we do it now?"

"Because."

Do I have to go?"

Gina nods.

Pinkie lays her head against Nisha's trunk. The quickly-formed affection between the young elephant and the eight-year-old is profound. Nisha was rescued a year ago from a cruel elephant handler working for the Badawi Brothers Traveling Circus. Bonzini heard of her plight and traveled seventy-five miles with a trailer to get her before asking if she was for sale. In his pocket was more money than the Badawi Brothers, or anyone else, could think of resisting.

It was *Senor* Martinelli, the Bonzini Circus manager and head clown, who told Bonzini about Nisha, an Indian elephant pulled from her mother's side at an early age and currently being trained harshly with only profits in mind. Word of cruelty to humans or animals has a way of spreading like a summer wildfire in the backlots, trailers, trains, and tents of circus people, especially flowing from the mouths of the grinders and day workers. Anything less than humane in his own circus is not tolerated by Bonzini. His is not a widespread attitude, but in the Bonzini Circus, it is absolute law.

The word is always out that trainers with troubles they assuage by doling out cruelty are advised to walk quickly past the Bonzini Circus, never stopping and never bothering to ask for employment. Further, a fired trainer or handler is advised by the other employees to pack and depart in all haste before Bonzini's anger is fully released, something that has happened more than once. A fist through a door. A mangled water trough. A ladder smashed into splinters. Sometimes, when there is resistance, a punch or two. No, Bonzini is not one to make angry when it comes to matters of brutality.

"I wish I never had to leave you, Miss Crazy Elephant," Pinkie whispers. Nisha listens intently, stands perfectly still.

"Nisha will wait for you. Come, we must prepare you for your first shopping trip."

"It's not my first one, Gina," Pinkie says softly, still gazing up at Nisha's eyes.

"No? You mean Madam Rosie takes you to stores to buy those rags, um… I'm sorry, I mean, clothes?"

"No, not to stores. She takes me downtown to the *Sociedad Argentina Para Los Pobres.* She says it's so much trouble for her, but I can't run around naked. She tells the people at the Society I am an orphan in sad circumstances. I'm not an orphan. What are circumstances, Gina? I say it to customers for Madam Rosie, but I don't know what it is."

Gina tries unsuccessfully to quell her anger. *"Quella donna terribile!"* she blurts.

"What?" Pinkie asks.

"Terrible! A terrible woman!"

"Who?"

"That, uh… oh, the-the woman who came last night and-and argued with the ticket clerk." She manages a weak smile.

Pinkie hugs Nisha's trunk and lays her head against it. She suddenly wants to break Madam Rosie's rules and talk about her mama, a forbidden subject. "I-I used to go shopping for clothes in Nuevo Laredo. With my mama."

"Nuevo Laredo?"

"Uh-huh. In Mexico where I lived with my mama before she didn't want me anymore."

"Who said your mama didn't want you?"

"Madam Rosie told me. Mama was supposed to meet me here in Argentina. I had to come here with Madam Rosie because Mama came here first."

"Madam Rosie is the sister of your mama?"

"No, Mama doesn't have sisters. I never saw Madam Rosie except when she came to the hospital the night *Señora* Lupe died. My mama was at her work singing. I don't know why she made me go with Madam Rosie when I didn't even know her. Madam Rosie said my relative was sick, but Mama told me I have only one relative, an uncle in California."

"Did your mama come here?

Pinkie shakes her head. "Madam Rosie got a letter saying Mama changed her mind and left because she didn't want me anymore. She got another letter saying my mama died." Pinkie buries her face in Nisha's trunk.

Astonished, Gina turns away. She composes herself and turns back around. Pinkie—wide-eyed, sad, beautiful little Pinkie—is standing barely a foot away watching Gina closely. Her face is so pure, yet so ravaged with sorrow. Nisha is standing only inches behind the child.

"Oh, my sweet little babies! Come with me, Pinkie. Nisha, you may come, too."

Gina opens the window in the small lavatory of the trailer and pulls the curtains partly aside. Nisha stands outside the window looking in. Pinkie puts her hands flat against the glass. "There, see? Your Nisha is not far away. It is like you are bathing with Nisha!" Gina laughs and places a folded towel by the small, filled tub. "Here is a pretty-smelling bar of soap to use. I want you to scrub every inch of yourself, yes? I will go outside to give you the privacy and guard that no one but Nisha may come near the window. No monkeys. No horses. Of course, none of Priscilla's fancy dogs."

Pinkie half smiles.

"Hurry now. We must finish our shopping before it is time for me to practice for the evening show."

"I wish I could see it. It's the biggest show, isn't it? Madam Rosie makes me come home by four every time."

"We shall work on that, Pinkie, Bonzi and me. Before I go outside, will you remove your wig so you can also wash your hair? I have shampoo for you. The bottle by the soap. I will take your wig outside and, um, you know… shake it and air it for you."

"No thank you.

"No thank you?"

I don't want to take it off."

"Why?"

"My hair is ugly underneath."

"Oh no, I see pretty hair. Curly. Very light blond."

"It's not pretty. Madam Rosie cuts it crooked on the top with a big scissors. It looks like I have bald places."

Gina gasps. "Why does she do that, honey?"

"Because I'm bad."

"No, you are not bad. Why does she say that?"

Pinkie twists the material of her wet dress and stares at the floor.

"Tell me, *mia cara,"* Gina says. "You can trust me."

Pinkie licks her lips, looks down. "I-I always want to talk about my mama or my Uncle Cruz or about Mexico, but she slaps me or makes fun of me if I do it." A pink tinge spreads across Pinkie's cheeks. She looks up with blazing eyes. "It makes me so mad! She won't let me talk about Luka, either, so I tell her she's ugly, and she stinks, and I hate her! I say she's growing warts on her face, and I see them growing, and they are sickening just like her! I tell her one day she will have the face of an old frog, and one day when she can't walk because her bones hurt, she will sit like a warty old frog on a boiling hot rock and nobody will come to have their fortunes read!"

Gina stares open-mouthed.

Pinkie turns her gaze on Nisha outside the window. In a soft voice, she says, "She won't let me eat for a whole day and night when I say things like that. She gets out the scissors and cuts more of my hair. She says nice little girls have pretty hair, but I'm not a nice little girl, so my hair is ugly like me."

Gina steadies herself, takes a deep breath, places a hand on the credenza. "Let me see your hair, *mia piccola bambina."*

"What does that mean?"

"What?"

"What you said in the foreign language."

"*Mia piccola bambina?*"

"Uh-huh."

"I called you 'my little baby.'"

Pinkie wipes her eyes on her sleeve. She slides the wig off slowly, keeping her gaze on the floor.

"No, it is not so terrible. It will grow. There's the beautiful yellow hair I love." Pinkie looks up. Gina beams her a radiant smile before turning around and placing both her palms on the credenza. Her fervent stream of barely audible words in her native language stirs a faraway memory that finally hits the mark.

Her mama used to talk like that, didn't she?

44
Not Disappointed

Bangor, Maine
1958

Charlotte

Five in the morning, and I'm wide-awake casing the room. Through this long night, I have come to the conclusion that being humbled is the best way to stay in tune with what matters. What difference will the small glitches in life make in the scheme of things? How does torn hosiery in public, for example, compare to what happened to Pinkie in Los Angeles, or to Babe in China?

I'm realizing that sleep is secondary to me now, but as a child, I slept long hours to escape my life. It was my deepest need to prove my merit to my father, and I failed. Though Miss Wraith constantly sabotaged my relationship with him, his lack of perception to my plight was bewildering. Her words and his actions had demoralized me by the time I was graduating high school. My desire to do anything to escape was inevitable. I ran away from home a few months after I heard Mr. Wáng's speech. Father, of course, was out of town and missed another landmark of my life, that is—my high school graduation night.

I retired to my bedroom after the graduation ceremony, slipped out of the window, and walked to the end of my street where a dark car waited for me. My lying to the driver that I was already nineteen when I had turned eighteen only a few months previously was the first thing I was reprimanded for, and the last. *ROSE* management already knew my age and nearly everything else about me. They let me know in no uncertain terms that honesty with them at all times was an incontrovertible requirement if I were to be accepted. Why I did such a childish thing is still a mystery to me. Looking back, I think my newfound freedom caused me to behave foolishly, much as a young person might smoke cigarettes or down alcoholic drinks to prove he or she is suddenly mature or *grown up*. It was my first shot at being free from Miss Wraith, and I was definitely in new territory. Iron chains dropping off of me couldn't have felt more wonderful.

Of course, I didn't decide to join *ROSE* after that one brief speech delivered by Harry. I covertly met with agents who came to my high school under the guise of college representatives wishing to talk to me about my future. I spoke to several people via the pay phone by my school, and read the brief, coded messages that showed up almost daily in my hall locker—information I was instructed to flush down the toilet after reading.

It was mysterious and fascinating, and I wondered how I was so lucky to have captured their interest in me. I wasn't sure they would accept me since each person is screened methodically and meticulously before she or he finds out any deep and revealing details about *ROSE*. In fact, they are as secretive in their operations as Harry's intent was concealed in his words during his recitation. I think my grasping the true meaning of his vague speech so readily worked greatly in my favor.

Once they were ready to take me into the fold, I learned that they navigate across political, ethnic, religious, and geographical boundaries under the guise of horticulture, which, of course, is humorous. *ROSE International,* their public name, has nothing at all to do with gardening, but the initial gatekeepers one encounters on assignments think that it does. Those deeper in power understand what the agency truly is.

Did I join *ROSE* because I felt worthless and unloved? Partly, but my heart was always tender toward suffering of any kind. I suppose you might say I had an inborne altruistic side waiting to emerge. The opportunity to link with unsung, unheralded heroes who secretly did valiant, danger-packed deeds around the world was irresistible to me.

Taking part in dangerous missions to help others made me bloom like the proverbial rose in the agency's *non-existent garden.* Day after day, I faced me, myself, and I. Eventually, I found out what kind of person I really am when and where it matters most.

I am happy to say, and I mean no vanity by it… I was not disappointed.

45
Every Mile Closer

Mexico City, Mexico
1947

Luka

Luka walks out of the prison gates of *Palacio de Lecumberri* and into the plan that has consumed his mind for the bulk of three years. He is broke, but not broken. The terrible world war is over, but the war inside his soul rages hot. Each step away from the prison represents a step closer to redemption… and revenge. The plain, baggy clothes the prison provided for his release are preferable over the filthy rags he wore during his incarceration.

Freedom feels invigorating, and he lets it surge through him on his way to a new destiny. He puts on a feigned grin and sticks his thumb out, walks backward down the street. Several cars pass him by. An attractive gray car, new and obviously manufactured in *norteamerica,* slows and stops. A young woman, maybe twenty years old, wears glasses and a smile as she leans sideways and rolls down a window.

¿Adónde vas?"

"Nuevo Laredo."

"Ay, señor, sólo voy hasta Nicolás de Querétaro."

"Will *Nicolás de Querétaro* get me closer to, I mean, *eso me acercará más a* Nuevo Laredo?"

"Si, pero, esta mucho más lejos a Nuevo Laredo."

Every mile gets me closer to fulfilling my plan, he thinks.

Aloud, he says, "I am very grateful to ride as far as *Nicolás de Querétaro.*" He leans on the window frame looking at her. His odd clothes and shagged, prison-cut hair doesn't detract from his allure to the young woman. She nods. He opens the door and slides into the passenger seat. "*Bonito automóvil, señorita. ¿Ud. es rica?*" he asks, with a slight smile.

"*No, mi padre me lo compró. Sólo soy estudiante en la Universidad.*"

"You? In a… *I mean, en una universidad?*"

Her laugh is easy and fresh to Luka's spirit. Behind her studious, brown-rimmed glasses, he detects an interesting face. Quite a pretty one, he muses, but his current mission prevents his thinking any further about her looks or of the fact that he is male and she is female.

"I can speak English if you wish. You seem to favor it. I'm studying to be an architect." His surprised expression evicts another pleasant chortle from her. "Haven't you heard of Sophia Gray and the church designs she and her husband brought to South Africa, or Eugenie Dorothy Ullman of England and Kenya?"

"No."

She smiles. "I'm teasing you, of course. I love to see people's reaction when I ask them those topics. Very few people have heard of those ladies, especially here in Mexico. They are extraordinary women, *señor,* I assure you. By the way, my name is Victoria Cortez."

He clears his throat. "Luka."

"Where are you from, Luka? You do not look Mexican, I don't think."

He smiles pleasantly and lets his eyes stay on hers for a few seconds, a ploy always well received by the opposite sex. He has no intention of discussing himself. "You have piqued my interest, Victoria. You must tell me about the first lady architect. What was her name?"

"Sophia Gray. She made a remarkable difference to…"

Her voice fades as Luka reverts into his own thoughts. His plan going forward does not include women, even one as attractively intelligent as this one. The past three years may have destroyed his youthful exuberance toward life, but it has strengthened his capacity to focus on retaliation.

Unlike many of the prisoners in Mexico City's *Palacio de Lecumberri*'s history, Luka wasn't a political dissident or an opposing voice to a sensitive regime. He wasn't a rebel, a thief, or a murderer. He was an innocent man who was in the wrong place at the wrong time. The total blame lies on his aunt's shoulders. The two trivial crooks who nabbed him three years ago off the streets of Acapulco were abductors paid by her to restrain him for ten days, longer if he remained very angry. Because of her… because of them… he served an unjust prison term and fought daily to stay alive in the prison's formidable culture of torture, murder, sickness, and suicide.

The first year of his imprisonment at *Palacio de Lecumberri*, he vacillated between shock at the injustice of his captivity, blind fury toward his *tetka*, and a boyish faith that someone from his family, especially Papa, would come to save him. No one ever came, and, later, he learned that without bribery money, the guards threw the prisoners' letters in the trash. Now he understood why Papa didn't come. Did not Arturo or any of his family read of his arrest in the newspapers? Apparently not, and the cold isolation from all he had ever known was worse than the conditions inside the prison.

The next two years were bitter ones in which he fought to survive physically and emotionally while mentally conceiving a plan focused on saving Pinkie and paying back his evil aunt. Francisco "Pancho" Villa succeeded in escaping from *Palacio de Lecumberri* in 1912, but Luka never tried to escape. Being shot in the back during a failed prison break wasn't part of his plan.

"… and so, that is why I decided to be an architect, Luka. It's a profession that chose me, you know? What is your profession?" Victoria asks.

"Um, I-I am an artist."

"An artist? What kind?"

"I do it only for a hobby. I actually am a metal worker and glass cutter for the mosaics in Buenos Aires."

"Oh, so interesting! That, within itself, is art. Why are you here in Mexico?"

"Family. A holiday. Tell me of your family, Victoria," he says, redirecting her personal questions back at her.

Her conversation blurs once more as Luka fights off the pangs of anguish he feels every time he thinks of Pinkie in his *tetka*'s hands. Esé, one of his kidnappers, told him they were informed by the woman who hired them that Luka must be restrained so she could *get the little orphan girl away from him and to safety.* Those lies started a slow burn in Luka's gut that never went away. He feels it even now as he drives down the road with the young woman. What a cruel joke *tetka* played on all of them.

He snorts.

"I beg your pardon?" Victoria says.

"Oh, uh, my nose itched. Please excuse me," Luka says with a smile.

She continues telling him of her family, and he, similar to a soldier involuntarily reliving the horrors of war, can't stop the memories that flood his mind at their own discretion.

At first, he earnestly explained the true facts to his kidnappers in the hope they would let him go. Esé, the more benign of the two low-level criminals, seemed genuinely remorseful when he heard the whole story. It was soon obvious, however, that Esé wasn't strong enough to stand up to his cohort.

Jorge, whom Luka silently called Goat—*Gabro*—was aware of Esé's weaknesses and told him to gag Luka every time he spouted off anything about the child or the injustices of his plight. "We were paid good *dinero.* It is none of our concern who is right and who is wrong. Shut his mouth when he tells you this trash, Esé. That's an order."

Luka was held captive in an Acapulco hotel room with his hands tied to a bedstead. When it was time for his daily meal, his feet were bound and his hands untied. He was allowed to sit at the small table and chair inside the room to eat. On the sixth day, police officers burst through the door and arrested Luka and Esé. Unfortunately, it was the first time Esé had allowed Luka to eat with no binding on his hands or his feet. That one kind act, in addition to *Cabro*'s lies, sealed Luka's fate.

Cabro had been arrested in the hotel lobby before the raid for suspicion of committing several local crimes, including involvement in a drug-smuggling case. Hoping for a reduced sentence, *Cabro* pointed the finger at Esé and Luka, telling the police chief that the foreign man, the Croatian, was the mastermind of their gang.

Not knowing Esé had untied both Luka's feet and hands that particular day, *Cabro* painted Luka as a madman who sometimes asked to be tied up to prevent his own violence. "*Ese es un hombre extraño allí arriba*," he told the police. He swore that he, Jorge Martínez, in fear of his life, had been forced against his will to assist in Luka's criminal schemes. Esé turned on Jorge and told the truth, but Luka was not let go as a result.

Not wishing to sully his bloated reputation after bragging excessively to the press about the capture in an Acapulco hotel of a young Croatian gang leader, the *jefe de policía* persuaded the judge, his own brother-in-law, to quietly lock Luka up for three or four years until the story faded away, and so it was done.

"Are you hungry, Luka?" Victoria asks.

Her voice startles him from the bitter reflections bruising his mind. He forces a small laugh. "No, my stomach growls to make sure I remember its importance." She smiles at his joke. He discretely pushes his stomach in with his hand to silence the groans resulting from eating nothing the last two days.

46
Breakdown

Nuevo Laredo, Mexico
1947

Hitchhiking through Mexico is easy. Luka rides in the back of old trucks with rusty parts and bolts threatening to fly asunder as the vehicles wheeze down the road. One stretch of road has him traveling in the back of an old flatbed with crates of chickens and turkeys stacked high and strapped to the trailer. He slips his hands underneath the belts on the crates whenever the driver invariably speeds up to cross rutted, barely discernable roads or careen around sharp curves.

He eats under the stars one evening with a group of men he meets in the mountains. As the sun sinks behind the hills, the men liberally drink home-brewed liquors. Eventually, fist fights erupt. Some of the younger men—boys, really—punch and mistreat their burros. Luka, shocked, slips silently from the campfire light and disappears into the night.

His clothing is dirty, his hair shaggy, and he needs water and a good meal by the time he arrives in Nuevo Laredo in the back of an old horse trailer alongside a swaybacked mare. The truck and trailer stop, the backend opens, and Luka expresses his thanks to the driver.

Where will he start his plan? It's dusk with cool, early-winter temperatures. The outside lights of the restaurants and cantinas are turning on, lively music fills the distant air. Couples walk arm-in-arm in a town square… laughing, flirting, making plans. Families hop out of wagons and junk pickups to go into cafés. He does not expect the pangs of loneliness that hit him. He is struck by how different he is from the excited young man he was three years ago—three years that feel like twenty. Three years that stole his youth, his dreams, his soul. Waves of bottled-up remorse and anger pump through his veins. Small whitecaps of emotion turn into tidal waves that bend him in two. He can't breathe. In a panic, he starts running.

He runs past shops and homes and hovels and children fighting over a bicycle on a side street. He runs past restaurants, taverns, a tiny library housed in a building consisting of broken oxblood plaster over mud adobe bricks. He collides with a man in a large coat selling novelties mounted on long sticks to tourists. He passes a small panel truck painted with balloons and ice cream cones, now partially covered with a tarp for the winter. A flower shop, a *zapatería,* and finally, a hospital.

The hospital. The place where this madness started. The place where his aunt made him wait in the car while she stole a little girl. What happened to Pinkie? Why did he fail her so badly? He crumbles to the sidewalk hitting his fists on the concrete. He sobs uncontrollably. People quickly cross the street to avoid him. He wants to stop, but he can't, not even when the *policia* handcuff him and throw him in the back of a car.

The hard bed in the city jail with its two-inch-high mattress feels like a bed for a king compared to the concrete slab Luka slept on in prison. He yawns and sits up as a uniformed young man unlocks the barred door. The man slides a tray of food onto a steel ledge built into the wall and goes out, locking the door behind him with a key from a large ring of keys. Luka almost drools eyeing the glass of white milk, the tortillas, beans, rice, and a raw jalapeño. He mumbles his thanks and downs the milk, wipes his mouth on his hand. He stands motionless, luxuriating in the physical and emotional relief of consuming nourishment for his weakened body.

How long since he ate anything… a week? He remembers drinking from a water pump two days ago, eating a plate of *cabra asada* in the mountains. He sits down on the edge of the bed with the empty glass in his hand.

"Señor, ¿quiere más leche?" the young officer asks.

"Si, por favor."

The young man unlocks the door and hands Luka a half-filled pitcher of milk. Luka nods his thanks, lifts it, gulps down the contents, says breathlessly, "I need to talk to someone," he says breathlessly.

"Su familia?"

"No, someone in charge here."

"Señor, everyone is gone this late except for a few officers patrolling in their cars. Captain Ramirez came to get the keys for the new police station we are building. I'll go see if he left already." He partially walks from the room, sticks his head back in. "You slept twenty-four hours. *¿Necesita el baño?*

"Si, after I speak to the captain. *Gracias."*

In a few minutes, a tall man with an officious bearing and an open face reflecting the shadow of long-lost joy stands outside his cell. "Are you sober now, *amigo?*"

"Sober?"

"You don't remember all the trouble you gave us? You got hold of some bad *licor* or some *loco* weed, *compadre.* We got a nurse over here to give you a shot, a sedative, to quiet you down. Sorry, but you weren't reasonable. What happened?"

How can Luka explain what he himself doesn't understand? He shakes his head. "I apologize, sir, for my-my terrible behavior. I can only say that I had nothing to eat or drink for several days. I made a long journey, and I was, uh, exhausted. Not drunk. No, never that."

"I recognize your street clothing. How long were you in *Palacio?"*

"Three years."

"Didn't run away, did you?"

"Would I ask to see you if I had?"

Captain Ramirez studies the young man's face, clears his throat. "Manuel said you need to talk to someone?"

"Yes sir. I am looking for a person I do not know."

"How do you know you are looking for this person if you do not know them?"

Luka licks his cracked lips. "I am… well, I'm looking for someone I never met, but I know her daughter. Something very bad happened."

"Oh, young man…" the captain holds up his hands. "… do not confess to me. If you must find this young lady's mother, let it be between you and her and your priest."

"Que? Oh, no, that isn't the issue, sir. I am looking for a woman whose little girl was taken. Kidnapped three years ago. The little girl's name is Daniella Izabella Francisca Angelina Serrano."

The color drains from the officer's face. "And the, uh, did the little girl have another name?"

"Yes, Pinkie. She liked to be called Pinkie. Her mother is a singer, and they lived here in Nuevo Laredo before, well, before the girl was taken away. I know who did it and where she took her."

Captain Ramirez is already unlocking the cell door before Luka finishes speaking.

47
Why Didn't You?

Nuevo Laredo, Mexico
1947

The wooden table in Room 109 has a carving underneath Captain Ramirez's elbow—a heart with an initial A. The rest of the carved heart is unseeable. The young officer closes the door behind himself after bringing cups of stout coffee for the two men seated at the table. A tablet of paper in the middle of the table contains all the information Luka remembers about the day of, and those following, the kidnapping. The towns and places they went to, all the details in Acapulco, and the ship they were supposed to travel in to Argentina. He shared as much as he could remember of every aspect of his aunt's life—her looks, her mannerisms, where she will reside in Argentina, and, yes, even all the facts about Luka's own father.

When Captain Ramirez lifts his arm to pick up his coffee mug, Luka sees the other initial inside the heart, an S. The captain notices Luka looking at it, pulls a full ashtray over to cover it. "One thing keeps puzzling me," he says. "Tell me why you didn't bring *la niña* back after you realized the truth of her kidnapping?"

Any other question under the sun would have been less painful than this one. Luka closes his eyes and absorbs the inner pain that always comes when he asks himself the same question. Why *didn't* he take her away in the car and leave the old crone sleeping off her tequila?

Why didn't he sneak her away a hundred different times when he had the opportunity? He had possession of the car keys, he hated what his aunt was doing, and he came to care deeply for the welfare of the child. Why didn't he do something before it was too late?

He had been young and stupid, yes, and what about the other thing… that he was a coward? Had he really been afraid of his papa's wrath, or was it his papa's disappointment? Had he been secretly afraid of his *tetka?* He covers his face with his hands and sighs in what sounds like a moan.

Captain Ramirez watches him. He has a son only a few years younger than this young man. What if it were he sitting in this interrogation room losing his mind with guilt? He leans forward. "Listen, *mi hijo*, you have a criminal aunt, that's indisputable, but you don't need to carry the responsibility of her crimes."

Luka looks up with a flicker of redemption in his bloodshot eyes. "But… I-I should have—"

"Our lives are full of should-haves. We live, and we learn. She got you sent to prison, for God's sake. At least you are doing what's right now." With his pen, he spins the tablet of paper in a circle. "I'll file all your statements and contact the child's mother."

"She still lives here?"

Captain Ramirez clears his throat. "No, uh, she's been gone a year."

"She died?"

"She went back to Texas. San Antonio."

"Is she all right?"

"What mother is all right when she loses her child?" He sighs, sits up straight from his hunched posture, stares at something in his own mind.

"If you don't mind my asking, *señor,* what is her mother's name?" Luka says.

"Angelina. Angelina Serrano."

They are quiet a few minutes. Luka rest his arms on the table. "She didn't deserve this, the poor woman. I'm going back to Argentina as soon as I work long enough to pay for my travels. I'll do everything I can to find Pinkie and return her to her mama."

The captain's gaze is glued to the tile floor.

"Did her mother's brother go back to Texas, too? Pinkie said she had a *tio* living in California."

Captain Ramirez lights a cigarette, inhales, blows out streams of smoke from both nostrils. "She left here with her brother and, uh… a rich Texas oilman." He takes another long draw. Exhales. "The man… she loves."

Was it his dry tone, or something else? Call it a second sense, but Luka instantly knows the captain is desperately in love with Pinkie's mother, even to the point of, as would a lovesick schoolboy, carving her initials with a heart in the table in Interrogation Room 109.

48
Circo Shangri Lá-Sarrasani

Buenos Aires, Argentina
1948

Bonzini takes a swallow of tea, sets the cup down on a saucer. "I can't compete with the Sarrasani circus, Gina. They are the best funded and most influentially backed circus people in the world. They go down to ashes, then they rise again in full plumage like the Phoenix bird. Now they are coming here to Buenos Aires. They have been here before, but this time it will spell the end of the Bonzini Circus. Word has it they are joining Ismael Pace and José Lectoure."

"The men who own the amusement park*, Circo Shangri Lá* in Buenos Aires's *Parque de la Ciudad?"*

"Yes, that's them. They used to work with the Sarrasani's when they were in Argentina before. The rumor is they offered an engagement to Trude Sarrasani and Gabor Nemedi and have even agreed to reorganize their enterprise and name it *Circo Shangri Lá-Sarrasani."*

"But, can we not all co-exist in the same town?"

"Afraid not. The Sarrasani's have the backing of German industrials and the good will from many military connections. Money and more money will pour into their coffers. Our circus will be a single light bulb hanging in a field of bright lights. I am trying to get as many of my crew hired by them as I can, but only certain, uh… types qualify, of course."

"I am confused. What are you talking about, Bonzi?"

"Gina, you are adorable but naïve. Perhaps you do not know our president, Juan Perón, has, in the past, professed his admiration for the achievements of Mussolini and Hitler. I suppose it is to be expected of someone such as he who served as a military attaché in Italy during the early years of the big war. I know you are aware of how many Germans have come here to live during and since that war, my dear. Hundreds, maybe thousands, of them were Nazi officers and party members, though we must never say that aloud. Rumor has it that some escaped to Chile and Brazil, but most came to our country." He adds more sugar to his cup and stirs it. "Rumors. So many rumors I hear. More each day."

"Are they dangerous rumors?"

"Yes, I believe them to be dangerous, even though they are mostly history now. What my father taught me is truer than ever."

"What did he teach you?"

"To never forget that history repeats itself. It is foolish to think otherwise." He sighs. "It is whispered that Perón secretly ordered his intelligence officers to establish ratlines through Spain and Italy to smuggle thousands of former SS officers and Nazis out of Germany."

"What is that… a ratline?"

"An escape route."

Gina traces the rim of her teacup with a finger. "I do not know so much of this. All I know is concentrating my best performances on the wires to make the people clap and be happy to see me."

He pats her hand. "I do want you to stay innocent, my sweet Gina. You must keep a free mind when you fly through the air, yes?" He smiles, and she returns it. "The reason I tell you these disturbing details is that I want you to understand my motives. You see, it's only a matter of time before the political regime here in Argentina becomes so influenced they would, if I did nothing, destroy my little circus as if it were dangerous *bacteria* in a petri dish."

"What do you mean?"

"I mean the close ties our president and his military maintain with the Nazis shall eventually influence everything. We already feel the effect of it in his dictatorial style of governing. What do you suppose they would see if they looked closely at my little band of entertainers and crew?"

Gina shrugs. "Delightful people, of course."

He smiles at her. "Yes, the most talented, hardest working people in the world, but they wouldn't care about that. They would give me no choice but to *purge* my circus of its incorrigibles or risk bringing *inferno* down on my head."

"But why? What you are saying makes no sense."

"Gina, more than half of my circus is *gitano.* Talented show people who work so hard I have to make them stop and rest. Many Jews work for me, too, as well as many who are of mixed races. There are also my midgets who participate in all the circus arts. My main piano player during the performances is Blind Bert. Teddy, our tent-raising boss, was born with only one arm. And you know I never fire anyone if they must resort to using a cane or a wheelchair."

"Bonzi, what difference is it? I don't understand."

"No reasonable person does. The whole Nazi regime labeled itself as the only pure race on earth. Every other race or anyone with physical or mental inconsistencies, people of darker skin, *Roma* from all parts of the world… all classified as inferior and tagged to be sterilized or eliminated. If they had won the war… well, I refuse to think of it."

"That is… it's unbelievable. Our circus family is perfect!"

He squeezes her hand. "Yes, to us."

"What can we do, Bonzi?"

"I have already contacted show people in *norteamerica* about most of my acts and about buying my animals. Naturally, I am very particular about the conditions for all of them. Our trainers, if they desire, may go with their animals as a package deal."

"Dio mio! You have been very busy, and I knew nothing of it."

"I saw the signs some time ago."

"I am so sad! We have been happy here, and I love our circus family."

"It's heartbreaking."

"All of the animals must go? What of Nisha and Pinkie? They cannot be separated, Bonzi! Pinkie will recover from losing her pony if she must, but her elephant… their friendship is too big to lose!"

Bonzini smiles. "I know, Gina. Nisha and many other animals will go with us. I'm taking the pony, too. Pinkie is turning into a natural trick rider, and she needs that pony until she is ready for larger horses. Here's what else I have on my mind… I believe if I take enough money to the *gitana* woman, she will let us have Pinkie."

"You mean *buy* her?"

Bonzini nods.

"But that is so-so—"

"Repulsive? Yes, I agree, but money is the only language that hag understands. She is bedridden now, you know, and she looks pale and unhealthy. I think I can work out a deal with her."

"Oh, I pray so, Bonzi. Pinkie is already my own child in my heart."

"In mine, as well."

Gina drops her head. "And what of me… shall I never perform again?"

"I would never do that to you."

"But you are putting an end to our circus life."

"You know of the Ringling Brothers Barnum and Bailey Circus."

"Who does not?"

He smiles. I have surprises for you."

"Please tell me!"

"I am working on buying a *rancho* in California big enough for Nisha, several horses and dogs, and a monkey or two. Then, you, my sweet, are auditioning for Ringling Brothers whenever you are ready. They have already heard of your talents."

Gina leaps from the upholstered bench seat surrounding the small table in her trailer to hug Bonzini's neck. She kisses his face repeatedly. "I love you, I love you, I love you! You are always my wonderful Bonzini! And what of our Pinkie? This *rancho* is big enough for her to grow into a young lady?"

"Of course, and for other *bambini* when you tire of the wires."

"Oh, Bonzi, you mean…?"

"Marry me, Gina?"

Again, his face is covered in kisses.

"Let me breathe so I can tell you the last part of my surprise."

Gina gazes lovingly into his face.

"The *rancho?* Well, I'm considering making it into a winter training facility for circus people with cottages and winter housing for my friends and former crew. I shall build you a stupendous building with all the wires and ropes and everything you need to train and prepare. When you retire, you can train others or do something else," he says.

"What do you mean *something else?*"

"Why, raise our twenty *bimbi,* of course."

49
Empty Windows

Buenos Aires, Argentina
1948

Madam Rosie sits in a wheelchair with a blanket over her legs and a newly framed, worn picture of Jesus and the Sacred Heart on her lap. She peers from the doorway into the house she has occupied for more than three years. She never made it any more attractive than it was the day she rented it already furnished with humble necessities, though she did decorate the front room to receive customers wishing to have their fortunes told. The sparse bedrooms and kitchen were utilitarian—nothing more.

The windows have been open for ventilation during the packing, and the thin, full-length curtains in the front room now bulge tiredly outward from the open air circulating from the other end of the house. It's midnight, and the only light outside is from the first of many hired driver's headlights. Wide, flat boards have been placed from the doorway to the car for the wheelchair wheels. The car trunk is open awaiting the tubular steel wheelchair when the driver folds it after he carries Madam Rosie to the passenger seat up front.

Maneuvering the wheels with her hands, the woman backs the chair out of the doorway and rotates until she is facing the car. "Stop sniveling, Elena," she says. "Young man, take this picture and put it in the back seat for me. Be careful. It's fragile. Hold it by its new frame."

The driver takes it from her and slides it in the floorboard in the back. "No, place it in the seat beside where Elena will sit."

"Please let me say goodbye to Bonzini and Gina," Pinkie pleads for the hundredth time. "I promise I'll never be bad again if you let me. Please, please Madam Rosie." A sob escapes her as she furiously swipes away tears. The thought of leaving the couple behind is horrible, but leaving Nisha is more than her young heart can bear. She never mentioned the elephant to Madam Rosie. Instinct told her the woman would find a way to end their alliance if she knew how much Nisha meant to her.

Madam Rosie frowns at her, scoffs. "You never be bad? Of course, and the moon will never shine after tonight. Stop whining. The circus people are not your family. They don't deserve to know our business. The *Great Bonzini* is so smart, he'll understand who he was dealing with when he finds us gone." She chuckles in delight at the thought. "Now get in the car."

"But I promise. I really do," Pinkie whimpers, twisting the end of her sleeve.

"Do I have to slap your face? Get in the car!"

Sobbing bitterly, Pinkie trudges toward the car. She can't see for the flood of tears drowning her eyes. She stops to wipe her face on her sleeve, feels a surge of heat rising in her chest. She turns and points at Madam Rosie.

"You are the one who is not my family! Your real family hates you as much as I do! Snakes and spiders scream and run when they see your ugly face. It's uglier than the baboon's red bottom at the circus! You could win the contest for the ugliest woman in the whole wide world, but you'd never get a prize because everyone would run from a stinky monster who only tells lies!"

Madam Rosie spins the wheels so quickly, she arrives just short of Pinkie in seconds. She reaches to slap her face. Pinkie dodges. Each time she tries to hit her, Pinkie bends, hops, and ducks to miss the blows.

Her time at the circus has made her more agile and precocious than ever, Madam Rosie thinks with a mixture of anger and realization. She will have to switch tactics to get the girl out of town. She doesn't need her raising a commotion in the middle of the night. Their departure must remain a quiet secret. She sits for a moment with her hands folded over the blanket in her lap.

"Elena, um, Pinkie, I have been saving a surprise for you. The truth is that Luka is finally on his way back from Mexico. He is going to my brother's house in São Paulo," she says.

"You're lying. You said Luka would be lots of places, but he never was."

"This time is different. His papa said so."

Pinkie's hands are clenched, her face is swollen from crying. Her spirit is crushed from knowing what she wants or needs has never mattered to this mean woman. She snuffs, her head quivering as she does so. "Luka's papa never writes you letters or sends you money. How do you know Luka is coming home?"

"I already told you about it. Don't you remember?"

Pinkie's mind races through this past afternoon and evening. She was ten minutes late getting home today from her training session at the circus. Madam Rosie didn't yell or mention it, which was strange. Over their supper of *lepinja* bread and boiled beans, Madam Rosie told her that Ivan her brother, and most of the people in her tribe, had moved to Brazil because they felt safer there."

"Why do they feel safer?"

"Because they are *gitanos*, and because many have Jewish roots."

It was the first time Pinkie had heard this, but it made no impression one way or the other. "What do I care where Luka's papa lives or if he has roots. Trees have roots. Is he a tree?" she'd said, not looking up from her bowl. She expected a thump on top of her head for her sarcasm. When nothing happened, she looked up at Madam Rosie and was surprised at her unusual expression.

"You should care because he has come to his senses at last. Concie has been calling him to keep him informed of my condition. He said since I am crippled and infirm, we can come to Brazil. It's a long way. Go pack your suitcase. We leave later tonight. Don't take anything extra."

"I don't have anything extra."

"Well, don't take anything extra like your bed or-or..." She frowned and waved Pinkie away.

Pinkie went to the tiny room with the tiny bed and a chest with one drawer for her clothes. She threw part of her paltry belongings in the suitcase and hauled it to the front room, sat on top of it and waited.

"Did you pack everything?"

"Not everything."

"Go pack it all."

"Why, are we staying forever?" She meant that as another impertinent comment, but Madam Rosie didn't take the bait. Something different was in the air. It made her uneasy.

"Finish packing and go to bed. I'll wake you when the driver comes."

Upon awakening, she found that Concie had come and packed all of Madam Rosie's adornments from her fortune-telling room and all of her clothes and had sent everything ahead in a small truck. Walking through a house empty of all their personal belongings, Pinkie asked with dread in her heart if they were going to live in São Paulo. Madam Rosie nodded. It instantly reduced her to a whimpering crybaby. She begged Madam Rosie to allow her to tell her friends goodbye. Leaving them and Nisha forever was worse than being dead.

Now Madam Rosie is telling her Luka is coming to Brazil also? She warms at the memory of his kindness, how safe she felt when he was near. Luka would never stop caring about her like her mama did. Bonzini and Gina are almost like a real mama and a papa, and there's her beloved Nisha. Would Luka bring her back to them if she begged him? Would he rescue her from the hours of standing alone on the street to summon customers for Madam Rosie's business?

What if Madam Rosie is lying and Luka is dead?

When they first arrived at Ivan's house after the awful journey from Mexico, Madam Rosie and he had a terrible fight. Pinkie couldn't make out all their words from the other room through a closed door, but she heard her name and Luka's name shouted several times. Afterward, he sent Madam Rosie away. He offered to keep "the little girl," but Madam Rosie spat curses at him for such *a vulgar attempt to leave her penniless in her old age.*

Madam Rosie's voice breaks into her reflections. "Pinkie, get in the car so we can leave. What will Luka think of this impetuous attitude of yours?"

Pinkie entwines her fingers. Her eyes dart from the hired driver, who is leaning against the car with folded arms and an irritated expression, to the woman she despises. Another thought comes to her. She has been riding a horse and doing exercises to build up her muscles for trick riding for five months. She is strong and fast. What if she runs away from them? No one could catch her. She could disappear like a shadow into the darkness and find her way to the Bonzini Circus grounds.

The darkness.

She thinks of the stranger who has been driving by when she is outside with his window down two or three times a day this past week. Something in his leering gaze always filled her with unease. What if he found her walking down the dark road alone?

What monsters lie in wait for nine-year-old girls with no one to save them?

Without a word, Pinkie slips into the backseat through the open car door. She peels off the ugly wig, rolls down the window, and tosses it roughly to the ground. Her final act of treason is sticking her thumb through the weak texture of the Jesus and His Sacred Heart painting. She does it again. Now, the eyes of Madam Rosie's Jesus are vacant holes.

Bonzini feels it first in his belly as he parks along the street—an odd wave of desolation. *Pinkie must be inside,* he thinks, but she is always outside this time of day. He has come at an odd time for him, a Saturday, to bargain with the *gitana* for Pinkie's welfare and future. He has brought more money than the opportunistic crone can possibly resist.

When he brought Pinkie home yesterday afternoon, he was bubbling with secret excitement at his and Gina's plan to extract her from her current life. It was all he could do not to mention it to the child. Better to strike the bargain first, he decided.

The wide planks running from the street to the doorway hit him as peculiar. Obviously, they are for Madam Rosie's wheelchair, but Pinkie says she hasn't left the house for several months. The open windows with the cheap curtains hanging limply along the sides look like open mouths mocking him as he nears the peeling, mustard-yellow door. So great does his anxiety grow with each step, he doesn't bother to knock but simply turns the knob and pushes the door open with a hard thrust.

Empty!

The sheer fabric swaths hung with purple and blue lights to enhance the mysterious ambience of the entry room are gone, as are the footstools, the floor pillows, the floor carpet, the ottoman, and the crystal ball covered over by purple velvet when not in use. The table that held the crystal ball and the two straight-backed chairs sit alone by the built-in cupboard. The astrological and moon-phase posters are gone. The tattered picture of Jesus and the Sacred Heart is no longer hung on a wall, and Bonzini takes that as the period at the end of the sentence. The crafty woman has taken Pinkie and slipped quietly into the night. His boiling anger collides with his sense of loss.

How did she know he and Gina wanted Pinkie for their own child? Somehow, she did, and he is certain the one thing she never wanted for Pinkie was happiness of any kind. Of course, he will spend as much money as it takes trying to locate them, but he suspects the decaying woman is too clever to have left tracks.

A cold bitterness enters his heart, and he knows he will have to go to confession many times for the thoughts he is having toward Pinkie's abductor. He walks away from the house and stops abruptly at the sight of a dark object lying in the dirt. It's Pinkie's ugly black wig.

50
A Business Card

San Antonio, Texas
1948

Hereford cattle meander lazily around the pecan and mesquite trees in a distant green pasture. The blue-gray tint of water in the cattle tank presents a pleasing contrast to the greenery and the plump rusty red and white cows. Clint and Angeline watch the serene scene through their bedroom window as they lounge in matching chairs.

Angelina yawns. "All I do is sleep since we got home yesterday. I just got out of bed, and I feel sleepy again." She takes a sip of iced tea.

"It'll take us a few days, hon. We've been in so many different time zones these past months, it's bound to mess up our timers." He yawns big, finishes it with a chuckle. "See, I'm a dead horse myself." His eyes land on a maroon leather-bound book lying on the foot of the bed. It's gratifying to him that Angelina has been keeping a journal. It has helped her work through the chaos in her head after he brought her home from Nuevo Laredo. "Do you need to ask me any more names of all the trains and ships we were on… for your notes?"

"I did forget some of the names, *mi amor*. I remember your favorite ship, though, the RMS Queen Mary."

"You betcha. What an experience! I couldn't help thinking of all the thousands of soldiers that ship carried for hundreds of thousands of miles in the war, and there we were on its refitted deck eating fancy hors d'oeuvres and sipping champagne. Dang! Brought up lots of war memories, not all of them good, but mostly, *mi pequeña esposa,* it made me feel mighty proud.

She smiles. "You're so dramatic."

"I'm your Zorro. I have to be dramatic."

"You're my everything," she says.

"And you are mine."

They gaze and smile at one another like the newlyweds they are. For Clint, the best part of their travels to Europe and Africa was watching Angelina returning more to her normal personality. He stands and stretches. "I think I better go talk to our hired folk and see if anything big came up on the home front. I didn't get but three business wires a week, so I'm thinking everything's running pretty smooth with Canyon Coyote Oil. Tomorrow, I'll get slicked up and go see for myself. Probably need to dive into those company books with a vengeance."

"With a vengeance?"

"Well, maybe with a pea-shooter."

They both laugh. Angelina picks the business card off the table beside her chair and studies it. "Do you think the man serving drinks in the fancy bar in New York knew what he was talking about?"

"What? That he knows of an organization that helps look for lost loved ones? Well, honey, I don't know. I do know we both wish there was a magical business like that somewhere out there, but, hey… um, would you do me a favor?"

"Of course. What is it?"

"I don't want you getting your hopes up for nothing, and—"

"Don't worry. I have put my sweet Pinkie baby in God's hands, but I shall never lose hope we will find her, you know?"

He kisses the top of her head, squats down in front of her. "I would expect nothing less of my Lina. Truthfully, though, I am a little surprised you told that guy in the bar so much about it. A complete stranger."

"*Ay, caramba,* Clint. I don't know why I did it, either. He paid us so much attention, and the way he made those fancy drinks like it was the easiest thing in the world. He would go and serve them to other people sitting at the bar, then he came back to us and our sad story every time. Didn't he seem wise when he listened to our story, Clint, like he had some kind of… of intuition?" She gazes out the window "It's strange, what I did. I guess I was excited to be back in our own country and happy we were having a big night in New York. Maybe I felt like throwing out all my old problems. Maybe it was a Spring cleaning like your mama taught me how to do."

He looks in her eyes, leans in and kisses her. Then, again. "Hmm, I'd better stop that or I won't get any further than this room today." He stands. "I'm headed downstairs to check the telephone messages. Juanita and Yvonne said they left some on my desk in the library. Be back. Just rest, honey."

When he leaves, she runs her finger over the embossed gold rose on the front of the black business card. On the back, a solitary phone number and no address. She presses it against her cheek before placing it back on the table.

Clint returns to find Angelina dozing in her chair. He never gets over how angelic she appears to him. He sits down in the matching chair and listens to her even breathing. It took months to ease the effects of the hellish life she fell into and thought she deserved. Riding her new horse, a spirited white Arabian, spending quiet hours walking in the trees and along the river in town, baking breads together, reading… slowly allowing him to love her completely, eventually brought her back. As soon as the international travel restrictions eased, he took her everywhere it was allowed so as to harvest different memories for the two of them.

He leans his head back. Does he want to risk starting up all her pain again? What if he doesn't tell her about the seven urgent phone calls from the police captain in Nuevo Laredo over the past months? He's known about them, but he didn't tell Angelina. Still, he's home now, and it doesn't seem right to ignore them.

He slips from the room, goes to the library to call Cruz.

51
The File

Nuevo Laredo, Mexico
1948

Cruz takes the proffered manilla folder from the young officer. "I'm not sure the captain would approve of this, but…" the young man says.

"Trust me, he would approve. You have somewhere I can sit and look it over? Better yet, why not let me keep it overnight in my hotel room. I'll have it back here first thing in the morning."

"No, I think we should keep it here, *Señor* Serrano. Room 109 has a nice table you can sit at. You want some coffee?"

Seated at the table with a cup of bitter coffee, Cruz reads the firsthand testimony given six months ago by a man named Luka Banović. He is flabbergasted to learn the child his sister loves so deeply was stolen by a *gitana* and most likely taken to Argentina. It seems absurd, like a fantasy, but the nephew of the kidnapper gave too many details for it not to be true.

Captain Ramirez's notes on the piece of paper clipped to the inside of the file say that Luka is a *Machwaya* of Croatian descent who speaks many languages and seems sincere and remorseful for any part he played in the kidnapping. He writes details of Luka also being a victim of his aunt, Ivana Rosario Banović, and that he spent three years in a Mexico City prison because of her devious dishonesty.

She had him stolen by paid abductors? Cruz muses, sipping his coffee. How could a close relative be so evil? He snorts. Did he so soon forget? He and Angelina and Clint are all victims of the same kind of malicious behavior by Clint's own father, a man they had all once revered and respected.

He sighs noisily, feels sympathetic toward Luka. He finishes reading and taking notes on the small pad the young officer supplied him. He closes the file and traces with his finger a heart with the initials A.S. carved on the table's surface.

"I'm telling you, Clint, it's a long shot if ever there was one," Cruz says in the telephone receiver.

"I know, but we have to try. Argentina, huh? Damn, that's the craziest story I ever heard. No wonder they never found her. What about this Luka guy? Where is he now?"

"The officer at the police station said the last he knew about he was working at the Cadillac Bar. You know, that place you told us your mom and dad liked so much? I went over there. Beautiful place. I see why it's so popular with *turistas.* Anyhow, Luka was a bartender over there for several months. Seems he was well liked. Popular. All the women had a crush on him. They said he got enormous tips speaking so many languages and could charm your socks off. Oh, and with *that face,* they said he would write his own ticket in life.

"That face?"

"Their words, not mine. He worked at the bar and also in some kind of rock factory in his spare time."

"Umm, hard worker. Are you saying he's not there anymore?"

"He's gone, Clint. Left town about two weeks ago."

A big sigh on the other end of the phone. "Listen, I don't want Lina knowing any of this right now. It's been tough getting her back on her feet. I'll call the telephone number on the back of that business card I told you about—the one that bartender in New York gave us. I doubt it'll lead to anything, but it's worth a try. I'll hire a detective, too, but let's keep it between us. If we do find that little girl… what shape you think she'll be in?"

"Only *Dios* knows."

"She's how old now?"

"I think about nine. Been a long time since we found that little bump in the road, hasn't it, Clint?"

"Whew, you ain't just whistling Dixie. Poor kid's sure been through heck and high water. Lina, too."

"Yeah."

"How is, you know, the police chief doing?"

"Captain Ramirez? I went to see him in the hospital."

"Did you?"

"Yeah, pretty sad."

"That's too bad. You know any more details?"

"Just that he took on four bad *hombres* all by himself on a lonely road in the middle of the night. He got them, saved the American gal they were holding for some of her wealthy husband's money, then he got her back to town safe and sound with three bullets in him. Lost lots of blood. He's in a coma right now. They aren't sure he'll pull through."

"Damn. Sounds like he's quite the hero. You know, he did take care of our Lina when we weren't around. I owe him. We both do. Go ahead and find out what his hospital bill is and pay it, Cruz. Give them one of my private numbers to call if they need more cash for his medical care before it's over. Find out if he needs to be transported somewhere else for better medical help. Dallas maybe? New York? It doesn't matter where. If he's got any kids, set up a fund for them, and make a hefty donation to that police station there for whatever they need. More *pistoles,* vehicles, a better kitchen or jail facilities—that kind of thing. Keep it quiet. I don't want any thanks. Don't deserve it."

"I'll take care of it, Clint."

52
Lucinda Love-Sickness

Buenos Aires, Argentina
1948

Luka

A small square tent with a raised striped top has three of its sides rolled up allowing bright sunlight to reflect off the mirror attached to a lone dressing table inside the tent. The table top is cluttered with jars and tubes of face paint and makeup. The table and a brown stool are all that's inside the tent other than a man in a clown suit removing his clown paraphernalia. The floor is a canvas tarp anchored into place with two-way hooks run through grommets and attached to metal spikes around the border of the tent.

The clown pulls off a bulbous red ball from his nose, then removes two fake ears and a skull cap with coils of red and yellow yarn hair attached. Above the line where the skull cap fits on his head is tan skin and wavy black hair. He picks up a towel and swipes it down his cheek, removing a strip of white paint and the side of a huge painted red mouth. He squints in the mirror, moves his head to see past the glare of the sunshine, turns around and faces the young man standing just outside the tent.

"If you're looking for Bonzini, you'll find him over at that trailer," he says, pointing. "Yeah, that's right. That big shiny job over there. Fancy, huh? Him and Gina live in style."

"I'm looking for someone," Luka says. "Is Bonzini the right person to inquire of her whereabouts?"

The man's eyes narrow. "Hey, you looking for Lucinda, the belly-dancing wonder of the five continents? Or is it six continents? Anyways, she already took off for California with Hiram. Rest of us are headed over soon's we get the last of the trailers and tents sold. Guess you saw all the hubbub out there. A big mess. Most of the animals are gone. Shipped or sold."

He waves a hand. "This here tent is all that's left of my *clown alley*. I'm the manager of this outfit, just under Bonzini, so I leave last." He scrubs the paint on his face, chuckles, "Did a sendoff thing for the kids at the orphanage today. Gonna miss that little bunch of ragamuffins. Sure as hell, um, s'cuse me… sure as heck am."

He stands up and sticks out a hand. "Name's Martinelli." He looks down at his hand and notices the white makeup on it, smiles, sits back down.

Luka remains silent, his mind only partially registering what Martinelli is saying. He is weary beyond words. No, he is not looking for Lucinda or anyone else but one nine-year-old girl he is desperate to find. He worked rigorously for the past months in Nuevo Laredo to earn his way back to Argentina, only to find his papa and all the members of his close tribe had vanished.

When he questioned the neighbors where his tribe formerly resided, they said they woke up one morning to find all of them gone—no word as to where they were going, no goodbyes, *nada.* All their rented houses in the area, all twelve, were clean and empty. Yes, that is a normal *Machwaya* thing to do—take off for new horizons and leave no clues behind—but why now? He remembered an old German woman, a widow who married a Croatian member of the tribe, always saying, "*Romano Drom!* Never abandon *the Roma Road.* It is our future and our souls."

She was right, this long-gone lady, but why did Papa leave behind all they had established since coming from Croatia and Spain? Is it tied to the current political regime of Argentina? The worse part was Papa left no word for Luka, and he found no clues with the neighbors… except for one. A woman wearing a long skirt and a *peineta* underneath a lace head covering walked across the street as he conversed with a small group of neighbors. She beckoned Luka away from the others to speak to him privately.

"*Señor* Banović and I were close friends, she said, momentarily dropping her eyes. When she looked up, Luka instinctively knew his papa was still managing to acquire lady friends, and he was looking at one. The woman was not too young, but certainly much younger than his father.

"My name is Catalina."

Luka dipped his head politely. "*Mucho gusto.*"

"He didn't tell me he was leaving," she says, momentarily pooching her lips into a pout.

"Excuse me, *señora,* did you—"

"Recently, he said he wished to live out his life with his granddaughter, but I didn't know he meant—."

"Oh, no, you are mistaken, *señora.* I am *Señor* Banović's only child, and I have been away for more than three years. I have no children."

"*Y qué?* That is what he said, and his eyes were full of joy when he said it. He said *la niña pequeña* had been training on a horse at that Bonzini circus, but she was coming home at last. He said he needed the pleasure of watching his granddaughter grow up in his last years."

"Did *la niña pequeña,* the little girl, have yellow hair and blue eyes?"

The woman shrugged. "How should I know? I never saw her."

"She wasn't living with him already? What about my papa's sister, Rosario Ivana?"

"*No se, señor. Señor* Banović lived alone since I knew him. Two years I lived in this neighborhood since my husband died. Your father should have told me he was going away like this. Maybe I would have gone with him. If you find him…" Her voice trailed as Luka pivoted and hurried away.

At least I know Pinkie is alive. Training on a horse at a circus? She is too young and small, isn't she? Luka's mind was filled with thoughts as he rode through town in the taxi. In his memories, Pinkie is still the delicate five-year-old child with the beautiful sad eyes. Where is she? For all these years, he dreamed of making amends. First, his plan sent him to Nuevo Laredo to be sure her mother still lived there. She wasn't there, but the police chief assured him he knew how to find her and tell her all that Luka shared with him. Number two of his plan was rescuing Pinkie and taking her home. If he can't find her, what then?

When he stepped from the taxi, he observed the Bonzini Circus was three-fourths torn down with wagons, tents, and trailers in every phase of disarrayed, move-out status. Everyone seemed too busy for him to bother. Spotting an open tent with a clown sitting inside, he had wandered toward it and found Martinelli.

He watches now as a midget with a cap pulled low on his forehead and wearing work clothes covered in hay brings a bucket of water to place by Martinelli. *"Gracias,* Levine," Martinelli says. "Leaving tonight?"

"S'posed to. Can't get out of here soon enough, Nelli. Just got back from town to buy that special grain the boss gives Nisha. Only the best for the boss's bull, right? Damned nuisance having most of our roustabouts gone. Anyways, that German who owns the joint where we buy feed? He fills my order, takes my money. I'm walking out and he says, 'See you around, shyster.' Shyster! You know what that means. Man, I about lit into him."

"But you didn't?"

"Nah, I didn't smash his face up, but I wanted to."

"That's good, Levine. We don't need any spotlight on us before we leave. Say, you about to crate up Nisha?"

"Boss wants to wait 'til morning. Right before they bon voyage."

Martinelli laughs. "He's got a soft spot for that bull like I never saw before. Who but the boss takes his elephant on the ship with him?" He smiles. "I think him and Gina got Nisha mixed up with the kid. Maybe they'll let her stay inside the house in California. Anyways, check on those last loads of riggings for me, Levine. Boss wants it all shipped at the same time so's it's set up good and safe for Gina when she gets to California."

Levine nods and walks off. Martinelli dips his rag in the water, wrings it out, rubs it over his face. He glances at Luka, mistakes the young man's lingering as *Lucinda love-sickness.*

"Look, kid, I know how you feel. Hate to admit it, but I got stuck in Lucinda's web one time myself. Strangest thing, that gal. Almost casts a spell over a man. We've all had a taste of her magic. One day, out of the blue, her and Hiram go getting thick as flies on a carcass. Lovie-dovie all the way. Boss sends them off early so's we don't have to watch them canoodling every minute. Hiram, he's a lion handler and her newest fly in the ointment. Boss sold both of them to Big Bertha. For keeps—not for the season like some of us. I say good riddance. She's trouble, she is."

Despite his own reflections and downcast mood, Luka's curiosity gets the best of him, "Big Bertha?"

"Ringling Brothers. You know, Barnum and Bailey. They bought a lot of Bonzini's acts. Me? I'll stick with Bonzini all the way. We go way back."

"What happened, not enough business?"

"Oh, we had business out our noses till that Sarrasani dame brought her fancy show here from Europe. She's dripping with money. Lots of German backers. Germans love the circus, they do. Now, the *Circo Shangri La-Sarrasani* is pulling the crowds in like salt on popcorn. Town isn't big enough for an outfit like that and a small circus like ours. Didn't break our hearts. Nah, too much Germany here in Argentina these days, if you get what I mean. Not safe for some of us. Levine, for example."

Hearing the jingle of harnesses, Luka turns and sees a team of horses being led somewhere. He smells meat smoking, hears orders barked from the loading chutes. A tractor puffs dark smoke into the air as it pulls a trailer stacked with tall containers and hay bales. Trucks drive in and out, a lion roars in the distance. He is mesmerized by the electric atmosphere all around him. Worry, work, and suffering through prison life had been his life for three years. Now he's conversing with a clown?

Martinelli, who now looks like a regular man in a clown suit, says, "Kid, forget that wench. If it isn't some clod from the stands, it's one of our own letting himself fall for her spiel. You're better off without that lady, and I say 'lady' only because I'm supposed to be funny." He chuckles. "Next month, maybe tomorrow, she'll move on to some other dummy in love with those woman curves she throws around like ham on a sandwich."

He stands, squints, yells, "Bally, what's that camel doing loose? Watch it, son… behind you!"

Luka turns. A camel is rapidly clomping toward him.

53
Number Three on the List

Buenos Aires, Argentina
1948

Luka dabs at the camel spittle on his shirt with the wet cloth Gina hands him.

"We can get that spot off like that," Bonzini says, snapping his fingers. "You sure you don't want to wear one of my shirts for an hour or two?"

Luka grins. "I will keep this shirt as a souvenir, *senor,"* he says. At Bonzini's puzzled expression, he adds, "The stain I don't mind, but his breath… now that was a sin!" He fans himself and makes a face. Both men laugh as Gina sets a plate of *biscotti quaresimali* on the trailer table.

"Those look nice, *signorina,"* Luka says.

"As of last month, it's *signora. Signora Bonzini,"* Gina says, wiggling her fingers to show off her wedding ring.

"Auguri!"

"Grazie mille! Please, won't you try the biscuits I make with almonds and cinnamon? This time, Bonzi, I used the pinch of nutmeg powder only for you." She smiles pleasantly at her new husband, then watches Luka take a bite.

"Buonissimo!" he says.

"You speak *Italiano!"* Gina says.

"Un po. I pick up languages very easily."

"That's a great talent, Luka. We could use someone like that. Ever think of joining the circus world?" Bonzini says.

"Not before today, but I cannot do anything until I, well, I have a list I made while I was, uh, well… a list I made recently. As I mentioned already, locating Pinkie is Number Two on my list."

Bonzini says, "Ah, well, that old hag, er, I mean, I'm sorry. Your aunt—"

"Do not worry," Luka interrupts, holding up a hand. "She *is* a hag and much worse."

Bonzini clears his throat. "She's crafty, that one, and she disappeared in the dead of night with Pinkie. We love that kid! Planned to adopt her as our own little girl, but somehow, your aunt guessed our intentions."

Luka nods, says, "May we sit down, please? I have very much to explain. That is, if you have time. When is your ship leaving for *norteamerica?"*

"Noon tomorrow. Come… sit," Bonzini says, indicating the benches surrounding the miniature trailer table.

The next hour, the couple is transfixed with the story of how Pinkie came to be in Madam Rosie's clutches and the story of their journey through Mexico. Sometimes, they laugh, especially hearing how Luka introduced Madam Rosie to José Cuervo tequila. They are incredulous when he tells them of his abduction from the streets of Acapulco and how it caused him to be sent to prison.

Bonzini and Gina tell stories of Pinkie and Nisha and of Pinkie's talent for riding the pony and learning tricks. "She is fearless," Bonzini says, pride in his voice.

"I remember when she mentioned your name, Luka. She said Madam Rosie did not let her talk about you or she would get slapped," Gina says.

Luka grits his teeth, clenches a fist in the air.

"She stood up for herself. She can take your skin off with her words if she is angry," Gina says, smiling. She told me what she used to yell at the *gitana.* What courage!"

Gina wipes away tears when she learns Pinkie has a mama who is alive and still searching for her. Suddenly, she slams a palm down on the table. "That shameful Madam Rosie! She tells Pinkie her mama left Argentina without her because she no longer wanted her and she didn't love her anymore. She also lied that her mama was dead! Who is so cruel like that?" Gina lets loose a flood of Italian, excuses herself from the table, goes outside the trailer and screams several times.

Alarmed, Luka asks, "Is she all right?"

"Oh, sure, sure. It's Gina's way of blowing off steam. If you look out the window, you'll see workers running to check on her. See that?" They watch out the window as Gina waves away a cadre of men and two women. "This is hard on her, Luka. She loved that girl as soon as she met her, maybe before, from hearing my stories of her. To find out Madam Rosie told her atrocious lies only to hurt her more than she already was… and, you know, finding out we can't have Pinkie for our own… it's a lot to take in. Gina's emotional. We're Italian, so…"

Bonzini sighs. Picks up a biscuit and takes a bite. "Concie was nowhere to be found after Pinkie and Madam Rosie left, and I have to guess she was bought off. I tried to find her immediately, but she was gone, moved out. But, there's hope. Yesterday, gossip has it that Concie's son Tomas has returned from *norteamerica.* Tomas used to work for me, still has some buddies here at the circus. See, he got crazy to see how the Americans lived. Chasing dreams. He was gone a few years, but it turns out he never ended his engagement to a local girl here in Buenos Aires. My guess is she gave him the big *either-or,* and he headed home. If anyone knows where Concie is, it'll be her son."

"Who is Concie?" Luka asks.

"A woman I hired to assist your aunt. She was unable to walk by the time she left here. Used a wheelchair. Osteoporosis. I used her failing health as a tool. I was able to persuade her to let Pinkie come here five days a week to spend time with us and Nisha. The crone was deteriorating before my eyes."

Luka now knows Number Three on his list may not be necessary.

God is punishing his *tetka* without any help from him.

54
Keys to the City

Buenos Aires, Argentina
1948

The spark of optimism Luka felt after talking to Bonzini dies like a flame in the wind the next morning when he talks to him again.

"Concie begged Tomas not to go to *norteamerica,"* he says. "We all did, but his pants were on fire. Young men and their foolishness. Looks like *mamacita* was angrier than he figured. Unusual, but I guess that's how Concie is. Tomas says his mother can hold lifelong grudges. Saw her do it with her older sister. He hasn't heard from her since he took off two years ago. Knew nothing about her leaving Buenos Aires. Her own son, and she takes off like that.

"Bad luck, Luka, for all of us. I was sure we'd figure out where Pinkie went from this angle. Don't lose hope, son. I have many contacts here in Argentina, and I will constantly remind them to watch and listen. And… Luka?"

"Yes?"

"You call me if that itch to join the circus gets too uncomfortable, all right?

With that, Bonzini and Gina drive off to their waiting passenger ship and a new life in California. Luka is shocked at the deep sense of loss he experiences as they depart, feelings of not belonging anywhere.

Something about the fatherly mantle Bonzini wears made him wish he could chase their car shouting for them to take him with them.

Yes, indeed, the foolishness of young men such as he.

He returns to his hotel in a state of restless yearning. In less than an hour, he leaves the hotel and starts walking with no plan or purpose. He watches young boys laugh and tease one another as they race miniature sailboats on the lakes at *Parque de Palermo.* He sits long hours throwing pebbles into the chocolate waters of *Rio de la Plata* and letting the four steps of his prison plan tumble through his mind… 1) go back to Nuevo Laredo, 2) find Pinkie in Buenos Aires and take her home, 3) take revenge on *tetka,* 4) move from Argentina to *norteamerica.*

How can he accomplish Number Two on the list if Pinkie has disappeared? How can he do Number Four, leave Argentina permanently, without knowing the truth about both his papa and Pinkie? He can't.

He rides a streetcar downtown and roams sidewalks lined with jacaranda trees in their second purple blush of the season. Darkness descends, and the lights of the city twinkle to life. He finds himself in front of *El Federal* bar at Peru and Carlos Calvo Streets. He glances inside, sees a long, narrow room—miniscule in comparison to the *Cantina de Cactus* in Toluca, Mexico. The striking stained-glass arch over the wooden bar seems to beckon him inside.

First quenching the heavy thirst he was surprised he had, he drinks a mug of *yerba mate* through a metal straw, then asks the bartender for a glass of the bar's least expensive wine, highlighting another worry—his rapidly dwindling funds. Should he again seek work in Buenos Aires, or…? He sighs heavily. His plans are thwarted. Not even in prison did he feel so confused, so defeated. His four-step plan sustained him in there. What will sustain him now?

"Your drink okay, sir?" the bartender asks.

Luka looks up, is surprised to see by the clock on the wall he has been sitting like a hunched-over statue for the better part of an hour. Chairs, not stools, at the bar make it easier to lean on his elbows. He takes a sip from the wine glass. "It's fine. *Gracias.*"

"You seem troubled, *señor.*"

Luka looks down, runs his finger across the base of the wine glass, exhales a noisy sigh. Lonely and distraught, he's surprised at the surge of sentiments the man's kind tone stirs in him. "I, uh, traveled from Mexico a few days ago to-to find someone, someone I care very much for, and she… she wasn't here. I-I don't know where to look for her, and… she may be in danger, and she's only a child, and…" He catches himself. Why is he telling a stranger, an outsider, his problems? That is not the way of the *Machwaya.* He manages a weak smile. "I'm sorry. I talk too much when I am tired. Do not concern yourself."

The bartender nods pleasantly, places a bowl of red pistachios beside Luka's glass. He goes through a door on the other side of the bar mirror. When he returns, Luka has drained his glass and orders more of the terrible wine. A woman plops noisily into the chair next to his. She places her shopping bags all around her chair, bumping Luka's leg and foot as she does so. He ignores it. She orders a glass of Malbec wine, nurses it, lights a cigarette, and sporadically calls out greetings by name to customers who come and go. She appears to be extremely popular. And loud.

A man leans down on her other side. He tells her something too low for Luka to hear. A joke, apparently, because she cackles with laughter, hits her flat hand on the bar counter. The man leaves. She rises to straighten the belt around her waist, *accidentally* moves her chair closer to his, smiles when her arm jostles his as she sits back down.

"Oh, lo siento, señor."

He momentarily glances at her, nods slightly to accept her apology.

"Have you come here before?" she asks.

He gives her a quick once-over, frowning as he does so. She is perhaps in her late thirties or early forties, he guesses, has a wide, pleasant face, red lips, dark hair pulled back, and a well-proportioned, full body. She is wearing an off-the-shoulder white blouse and a dark blue skirt, high heels, hosiery. Black-lined green eyes hold a mischievous glint harboring no fear. She is attractive and much too cheerful for his current mood.

"No, I don't believe you have been here before. I would have remembered you," she says, lighting another cigarette. She blows the smoke in front of his face and turns her chair to look full at him.

"I have never been here before," Luka says in monotone, hoping to discourage her attention.

"You look sad, *guapo*. Woman troubles?"

"No."

"Bad news?"

"You might say so."

"What can I do to help?"

He emits an irritated snort loud enough for her to hear. *"Señora,* there is nothing anyone can do. *No hay remedio, y—"*

"It's useless? Are you sure?"

"I am not in the mood for conversation. Please… before I say something I regret, leave me to drink alone."

To his surprise, she stands and extends her hand. It's a hand that knows hard work but is well tended to. "I am Carmen. *Mucho gusto, señor."*

He looks at her hand, reluctantly shakes it lightly.

"Nothing is hopeless when Carmen is here. Haven't you heard? I hold the keys to the city!" She puts her head back and laughs. "Tell me what—"

Luka's jaw clenches. "Excuse me, but—"

"Mi nuevo amigo, sometimes, all you must do is ask, and help will come your way."

Luka blows an angry gaff of air in her direction. *"Dios mío,* are you serious?" He shakes his head, looks down, feels her eyes boring into him. He decides to call her bluff. Maybe then she will get out of his hair. He faces her. "I need to find a child who was stolen four years ago from Mexico. Now, she is stolen again. She disappeared from Buenes Aires recently, and no one has any idea where she is. Tell me, Carmen, do you have a solution for that?" he asks angrily. Something in the woman's pleasant face makes him feel terrible about his outburst. "I'm-I'm sorry. I wish to remain a gentleman, so please…" He downs a bitter swallow of the cheap wine.

"Do you think the child has left Argentina?"

He stares at the ceiling. "Why are you asking? What difference is it to you?" He drains his glass. "She is with my aunt somewhere. All I found out is she was training to be a trick rider with the Bonzini circus, but now, most of the circus people have left for *norteamerica.*"

"And she is not with them?"

"No. She was taken in the night by my *gitana* aunt who happens to be worse than Hitler." His last word is breathed out like a snake's hiss. Carmen doesn't say anything. Wondering why the silence, he side-glances at her and is taken back by her face. It's different now. Gone is the flippant expression. It is replaced with the look of a knowing person who has lived life in its full depth and width.

She catches the surprise in his eyes. Her closed-mouth smile crinkles the edges of her eyes. "Bonzini, you say? I know him well. It's a fact of life that I know most everyone in this town. It's my talent. Trick riding. Horses. Trainers. *Gitanos.* Someone knows how this woman and the child you seek left Buenos Aires. Uh-huh. *El guapo,* you may be in luck."

She whistles ever so slightly, and the bartender, who was conversing with a couple at the end of the bar, excuses himself and stands in front of her. Luka doesn't miss the excited expression on the man's face as he looks from him to Carmen.

"Get Julio on the phone for me, please, Gilberto," she says, her tone serious. "And bring me a pack of those American cigarettes in the back room while you're at it. Please take away the mule urine this poor man is trying to consume and bring him a glass of Malbec."

An hour later, Luka exits *El Federal* bar and steps into the taxi Julio called for him. He gives instructions to the driver for his hotel and, slightly tipsy, sits pressed tightly into the backseat. His spilling out his heart to two strangers and what they hinted at when he finished is more than he can grasp all at once, let alone, hope for. Should he be embarrassed or filled with optimism?

Why did he do it, admit his part in the kidnapping of a child and tell them about the terrible prison he was in and how he now feels his life is useless? No answers come. Never has he shared so much private information with outsiders other than the friendly circus owner who had as much of a stake in finding Pinkie as he. His troubles flowed from his mouth and wouldn't stop.

He squeezes the card Carmen pressed into his hand outside the bar after she kissed both his cheeks and said, "When you find gold in your hand, *guapo,* do not let it slip away."

What did she mean? Does he dare place any faith in what either she or Julio implied?

"Do you have a flashlight?" he asks the driver.

"Oh, no, *señor,* I am sorry. I have a cigarette for you *si lo desea.* I can light your cigarette with a match and hand it to you."

"No gracias."

He holds the card Carmen gave him up to the window attempting to read the telephone number on one side by the light of the street lights along the road. He turns the card over, squints, and makes out a single gold rose embossed over a black background.

55
Are You a Ghost?

São Paulo, Brazil
1948

It's spellbinding—impossible not to watch. Luka peeks from behind a thick eucalyptus tree and sees his papa, aged into pure white hair and a slightly bowed back, sitting in a chair outside a corral watching a girl on a bay horse gallop the perimeter of the enclosure. Her left leg is in the stirrup; her left hand grips the saddle horn while her body and extended right leg are parallel to the horse's side. She pivots effortlessly back into the saddle, slips off the other side leaving one leg hooked over the saddle. She raises her free leg straight into the air, letting her arms nearly drag the ground.

Luka almost screams *be careful!* but refrains.

Papa stands up clapping. The girl rights herself and slips her feet into holders on the horse's shoulders. The horse gallops at full speed with the girl standing up with both arms held out to the side. Papa hoots and claps furiously. *¡Bien hecho,* Pinkie! *¡Fantástico!"* He does a little shaky dance with his limp more pronounced than before, hands on his hips. He turns and spots Luka. His eyes widen.

"L-Luka? My son? Are you a ghost?" he says, placing his hands over his heart. "I-we-we thought you-you died, Luka. Where have you been?"

Luka quickly closes the distance, and the two men embrace. When they break apart, both are crying. "No, Papa. Where have *you* been? I came home, and you were gone. Everyone was gone. Why didn't you leave word for me?"

Ivan shakes his head, searches for the right words. "My son, I did not know. You have been gone so long… so long." He sits in the chair and buries his face in his hands to weep. A horse snort and energetic hooves dancing close by make Luka look up and into the face of the girl everyone seems to want to either find or hide.

"Pinkie! You are so-so grown up. The way you ride horses… I am astonished! I-I am sorry, little one…" He turns his face to compose himself.

Pinkie nudges her horse. "Come, Pimiento. There is nothing here for us." They gallop furiously around the corral several times. She pulls the horse up in a cloud of dust, dismounts, leads him through a gate to another pen with a partial roof covering, water trough, and a flake of hay in a feeder. Luka stares at her. Only nine or ten is this older Pinkie, but she is strong and confident—no longer the little frightened girl he knew before. Beautiful and hurt. *Does she now hate me?* he wonders.

His father wipes his eyes on his sleeve, takes in the expression on Luka's face as he watches Pinkie unsaddle Pimiento. "She grieved for you, Luka. So very much, and for such a long time. Do not worry. She will forgive you when she believes you will not leave her again."

"I know I failed her, but I did not abandon her, Papa."

"Children blame the ones they love when they are disappointed, even if it is not their fault. Be patient." Thinking it best to change the subject, Papa says, "How do you like *esto rancho hermoso,* my son? How lucky we were to find work on *Señor* Morales' ranch. I take care of his animals, trim the bushes and trees, and help with the vegetable garden. We live in that big house over there with the porch. His son and his *familia* lived in that house, but no more. They didn't enjoy to be far from a city. *¡Gente loca! Señor* Morales' gives us food, wood for our fires, everything *muy bien.* I enjoy being settled down while Pinkie grows up. Jesus… He smiled on us. He knew our Pinkie needed a place for her special horse. *Señor* Morales says Pinkie is *muy, muy* talented. He wishes her to ride beside him in the parades for the festivals."

Luka is still staring at Pinkie brushing her horse. Absently, he says, "Yes, Papa, it is very lovely here. I am humbled and grateful the people at that agency found you and Pinkie for me. I think they traced her by that horse she's riding, but I'm not sure."

"People? Agency?"

"*No importante, Papa.* I'll explain it later."

"Luka, I am sorry to inform you of this, but I spent your money to buy the horse for Pinkie. She was so sad. So sad for many reasons, and you were gone—"

"You used my money?"

"*Si.*"

"All of it?"

"Most of it." Ivan looks at the ground and back up with a long face.

"Oh, Papa, that is the best thing I have heard in so long! My money bought Pinkie a horse? *Bravo,* Papa! Thank you!" He lifts his father out of the chair and hugs him, laughing at the same time.

"I am happy you are not angry with me, son. I wanted to do much for her. My sister kept her in hell."

At the mention of his aunt, a line of red crawls across Luka's cheeks. "She-she is *Sotona!*" he growls. "*Tetka* sent me to prison, Papa, for three years! Where is she? I have much to repay that evil woman!"

Papa touches Luka's arm. "*Si, si,* it is true she is one of the worst persons. I allowed Ivana to come with us when we left Argentina to help Pinkie. I hate to say this, my son, but my sister went back to fortune telling after I sent her away for what she did to you. Pinkie had to stand on the streets every day and sometimes in the nighttime for hours to get customers for Ivana's business. I heard of it from many people who saw it with their own eyes.

"When our people moved to Brazil, I couldn't bear leaving Pinkie to that life. I sent word for my sister to come here. Now, I question what I did. Pinkie loves her new horse and not standing on the street, but she grieves for the circus people who were kind to her. She thought of them as her parents. And she was attached to one of their circus animals—an elephant, Luka! So many heartaches for one so young. Did I do the right thing bringing her to me? I still do not know. Perhaps I should have left things alone."

Luka's fists are in knots. A low rumble emerges from his throat. "Where is she, Papa? Where is the monster who ruined all our lives with her greed and selfishness? I have dreamed of the moment when I take revenge!" He stares at the house, his feet stirring up dust as he nervously paces along the edge of the corral.

"Only *Dios* can give retribution, my son. He has already done so. Do not disrespect His ways."

"You don't know what—"

"She is dying. Only a brittle shell of a person confined to bed in the hacienda is my twin sister now."

"You drew these pictures, Pinkie? So many are of me," Luka says. She doesn't answer. "You are an excellent artist. Ah, here we have the Silver-Masked Saint. I remember when you drew him. Look, I recognize your elephant, too. I know her name."

"No, you don't."

He smiles. "Nisha. She is Nisha, and she is very beautiful." Seeing the pain come into her eyes, he turns back to the wall of drawings. "The sketch of Bonzini and Gina are so good, too. I met them when I was searching for you."

She grabs his arm. "Please, Luka, take me to them?"

Her tragic eyes and the desolation in her voice kill him inside. Papa told him how *tetka* cut her hair to the scalp as a punishment and made her wear an ugly black wig. Also, the way she dressed her like a beggar, never let her eat anything sweet, the face slaps and cruelties. Now her hair is growing out full of blond, springy curls, but he still sees the unevenness of it—a leftover remnant of what she endured. If his aunt were not near death and generally out of her mind, he would… what? How far would his bitterness take him, all the way to hell? He shakes his head, concentrates on the little face shining up at him with a radiance of hope.

"Pinkie, I have much to tell—"

"Luka, I will give you everything I have and everything I can earn trick riding. Please take me to Gina and Bonzini! Your papa told me he can get me a job performing my horse tricks, and *Señor* Morales knows of a man who owns a carnival in the city. I know I can make lots of money. Will you take me to them if I give you all that I earn?"

Luka sits down on the edge of Pinkie's small bed. "Honey, the Bonzini's left Argentina. They moved to California in *norteamerica.*"

Her devastated expression is another knife jab to his heart.

"They didn't wait for me?"

"They tried so hard to find you when you disappeared, and then I came back from Mexico, and we all searched for you. *Señor* Bonzini sent people all over Argentina to search. So many people love you, Pinkie! All of us… the Bonzini's, your mama, and—"

Her face is instantly scarlet. "My mama is dead! She didn't want me anymore, and then she died. Why are you saying stupid things? I thought you were smart, but you have the brain of a *churro!* Go away! I hate you, Luka!"

He looks with wet eyes at the little spitfire who has lived the life of an unprotected pebble rolling down a riverbed, one ripple or wave at a time—turning, roiling—her future always dependent on who or what stirs the waters around her. He has so much to explain to her before the woman from the agency comes next week to fly with her on the first part of the journey to San Francisco. The *ROSE* International agency in San Francisco was adamant that their rules be followed precisely and that Pinkie go there first. Poor little girl! Again, she will be leaving part of her heart behind—her new horse, and possibly someone else she has grown to care for… Papa.

56
What Happened to Pinkie?

Bangor, Maine
1958

Charlotte

The hours pass so slowly this morning. Right now, I'm staring at another poster on the wall with a sleek bus driving through downtown Los Angeles, palm trees lining the streets, a blue, cheerful sky above. Ah, yes, Los Angeles—where we found Pinkie after she was rescued in Brazil and flown to Los Angeles instead of to our headquarters in San Francisco.

Just thinking of that awful time still makes my cheeks burn. Mistakes were made, pure and simple. *ROSE* was still a new organization fresh in establishing its network around the world in late 1948 when Pinkie was discovered in Brazil. Training, timing, and screening weren't of the caliber they evolved into the next few years. The founders hired only the best of the best to make it happen as quickly as possible, but it didn't hit full stride until around 1951, seven years after origination.

Our international outreach efforts were often hindered, postponed, or upset in the years immediately following World War II. Successes depended on political factions, which puppet regime controlled a country at any given time, what the government back in the states allowed or turned a blind eye to, and who was being paid off or bribed. Yes, it is, and was, delicate and often obtuse in execution. Occasionally, in those earlier years especially, someone slipped through the cracks.

Pinkie is the most heartbreaking example of that. Two people had contacted *ROSE* about her, almost at the same time—Clint Sutton in Texas and Luka Banović in Argentina. Both of the contacting parties had been given one of our special black cards through our *Gold-BAR network* of *ROSE*-trained bartenders across the world.

Bartenders?

Who better to come in contact with tragic stories than they? A large part of belonging to *ROSE* is studying and analyzing human behavior, and it has been proven to a fault that humans have an instinctual tendency to either frequent a bar or fervently seek to improve their looks when nursing a shattered heart.

Our *Gold-BEAUTY* network of *ROSE*-trained beauty experts who beautify females the world over claim they may soon overtake the bartender network on the success chart, and that, of course, is merely friendly rivalry and remains to be seen. So far, the bartenders are the ones who hear the worst cases and are in a position to offer the most help.

Poor Pinkie had love coming at her from several angles, much more than many of our *assignments,* but, sadly, she was in no position at that time to realize it. That makes it doubly ironic that she was given into the care of a very rare person, an unscrupulous *ROSE* agent, when she changed handlers in Florida. The rogue agent took her to Los Angeles, and for money, literally sold her.

How did something so atrocious occur? It's complicated, but trust that it *did* happen. What Pinkie went through as a consequence of our growing pains and the corruption of one individual in our employ is unforgiveable. That agent, a woman who looked like a sweet Betty Crocker but was a monster in disguise, was shown the door immediately—her credentials short circuited, any tangible proof of her employment with *ROSE* obliterated, and any tales she wished to use as blackmail were mere smoke in her mouth from that time forward.

And… that wasn't all that befell her, but that's another story.

It was 1948 when this terrible thing happened, and I had been with the agency a little over a year. I was finishing up the first sector of my

B-training in northern California, still a fledgling, but I begged to be assigned in some small way to Pinkie's case when I heard she was on her way to San Francisco.

Hers was one of the most tragic stories I had ever heard of—a child with dead parents found on a dirt road, later stolen from the woman who adored her in Mexico by a dishonest *Romani,* secreted to Brazil from Argentina in the middle of the night to keep a kind circus owner and his wife from adopting her, a four-year search for her by people who loved her… it sounded more like a novel than real life.

I pleaded to accompany Harry to meet Pinkie's plane when it landed in San Francisco, and it didn't take much for him to agree. San Francisco, by the way, is where *The Gold Rose* originated. It's the main office, the largest facility we own, and yet, it remains hidden in plain sight in side-by-side Victorian homes lining a steep hill.

It is absolutely obligatory that the *assignments* we rescue come first to San Francisco for medical treatment, counseling, adaptation, and re-acclimation classes—all conducted by the most qualified personnel in the world. Carefully screened for expertise, these experts must also have the compassionate disposition Harry insists on.

While the *assignments* are undergoing their treatment and classes, and not all of them are children, our network is checking and double checking on legalities and making sure the right people are put back together. Sometimes, there is no one for them to go to. Harry has a whole branch of the organization devoted to finding a new life for those particular *assignments.*

We waited until the stewardesses came off the plane before inquiring of one if any other passengers were still onboard. Her answer sent Harry sprinting to a public phone to make several quick calls. He came back with furrowed brow and the truth. Pinkie had been "stolen" by the unscrupulous second matron agent who took over her care after the plane landed in Florida from Brazil. It was such a shocking jolt, I felt faint and had to sit down. How could so many similar tragedies happen to one poor child?

Because I was still an amateur agent with my troubled past not yet resolved, I had a hard time not feeling guilty when Pinkie slipped from our grasp into obscurity. The longer Harry and I waited for her in the San Francisco airport holding a small sign with her name on it, the more I felt personally responsible. Later, of course, I found out why she and the appointed matron agent were not on the plane, but I was young and still dealing with my own misplaced guilt.

Harry contacted Mr. Sutton in Texas and the Banović's, Luka and Ivan, who were in Brazil, and told them she was missing… again. Oh, the heartache for everyone! Mr. Sutton was extremely angry, and I don't blame him. He said many things Harry dismissed as anguish, but one saving grace was that he had not yet told his wife that Pinkie had been located and was coming home. He had wisely delayed in case of any missteps, and we, the agency, misstepped unbearably. The distrust it built in all their hearts and minds toward *The Gold Rose* took a long time to rebuild.

We searched ardently for Pinkie for more than a year, discovering only that the plane with our former *bad apple* and Pinkie had flown into Los Angeles, and that she had turned her over to a woman and a man using fake names. She said the payoff was in cash, and that was the end of all she knew.

The truth shocked all of us, and everyone vowed to never stop looking for a little girl who, on the brink of turning ten years old, had already survived more than most people in their eighties. Harry told me privately he was using methods I didn't even want to know about to find her. The determination in his eyes gave me the hope to believe all was not lost.

57
Weak in Mind and Character

Shí Niú, Shuāngfēng, Húnán Province, China
August 1948

Babe

The sound of the Chén's house door splintering below them reaches Jìnhǎi's and Babe's ears simultaneously with several Red Chinese Army soldiers swarming up the ladder and through the open door of their secret martial arts room. The humidity of late summer made the room stuffy, and Jìnhǎi left the door behind the stacked hay ajar as the two went through their daily execution of *Yǒng Chūn.*

The army commander takes in the scene, especially noting the *mù rén zhuāng,* the wooden dummy, and crosses the space between he and Jìnhǎi. "Criminal!" he shouts, striking the side of Jìnhǎi's head and knocking him to the floor.

Babe emits a cry and springs into action with slaps and punches to the commander's neck, chest, and stomach. Before he can react, she kicks his groin. He bends forward grabbing his crotch. A knee to his jaw sends him spinning backward. Her three years of intense daily *wǔshù* with her *shīfu* has given her advanced skills beyond her age.

"Bójǖn!" Jìnhǎi shouts from the floor.

Several soldiers rush toward her. She pivots right and left, full circle... knees, blocks, slaps away arms and hands grabbing for her. A soldier draws his pistol and points it at her.

"Bójūn, stop now!" comes her *shīfu*'s stern order.

Babe freezes, her breathing rapid, her hands in a *xiǎo niàn tóu* position. Her eyes cut away to glance at her *shīfu.* He vigorously shakes his head. Soldiers seize the unmoving young girl, whom they believe to be a boy.

The commander, assisted by two soldiers, stands to his feet and resettles his cap. He walks over to Babe and slaps her hard across the face, one direction, then the other. She glares with watery eyes and clenched teeth at her *shīfu.* Again, he shakes his head. The hatred in her eyes disarms the commander as he studies her face. He takes a step backward.

"*Tù zǎi zi!* Brat! I should beat you with a cane! You can thank your young age for saving you from a bloody back. I might still give you one!" He raises a hand in the air toward her. She doesn't flinch. "You risk your life for emotions? Are you a baby? Emotion of this degree is for lunatics. Think independently. Babies are of no benefit to the Party."

He points at Jìnhǎi, looks back at Babe. "This man has broken the Standards proclaiming the practice of *wǔshù* as vanity, merely a way to show off in front of peasants—a pastime of wealthy fools and religious zealots. There is no place for such foolishness in the Revolution. You are old. You should already know these practices are being declared unlawful."

Jìnhǎi nods, interlocks his two smallest fingers in a gesture of agreement. Babe almost screams seeing her *shīfu* humble himself in front of the commander, but her respect for her trainer overshadows her disappointment.

"Get up, criminal," the commander orders, lightly kicking Jìnhǎi's foot. Jìnhǎi scrambles to his feet with a penetrating look at Babe that says *do not even consider attacking anyone.*

The sound of breakage below them, along with DānDān's scream, is unnerving. At the commander's signal, the men file out of the room and down the stairs with the two offenders surrounded. In the barn, a soldier is teasing their horse and making him unsettled. Babe imagines slamming the outside of her hand into the soldier's throat. The commander barks an order, and the soldier takes hold of the bridle and walks the horse outside. He returns and leads the two cows out of the barn with ropes around their necks. The animals are led up a ramp and into a trailer attached to a small truck. The goat is carried from the shed bug-eyed and bleating.

Furniture and dishes are piling up outside the *fángzi*. Six men are loading them into the back of a larger truck with a tarp enclosure on the back. The soldiers have formed a semi-circle facing outward from the gardens, a gesture of protecting the front of the house while leaving a space for the movers to go back and forth. *"Jìnqù,"* the commander tells Babe and Jìnhǎi. They follow his orders and go inside.

Chén Lì and DānDān are sitting on the floor with their hands tied behind their backs. DānDān sobs silently. The commander nods for Jìnhǎi and Babe to sit beside them. Their hands are quickly tied. Babe closes her eyes and fights off the flashes of memories she has diligently hidden from herself the past three years—memories of Japanese soldiers slitting Zhēn Gāng's throat, of angry men in uniform kicking and slapping her *Bǎo Māma* before taking her away. Japanese, Communists… what difference is it? Cruel soldiers are all the same to her.

These brainless men will not steal my voice as did the Japanese soldiers, she thinks. Eyes closed, she rocks slightly back and forth clearing her mind. From the deepest regions of her psyche, a steely fortitude slips smoothly into her heart like a silent ship and drops anchor. The *ship's cargo* is an unwavering determination that she will never obey any law that forbids *wǔshù*. Contrariwise, she will perfect her *Yǒng Chūn* even if she must practice in darkness in the middle of the night… in caves, or hidden deep in the forest in inaccessible places where you die if you do not understand the exact way to ascend or descend.

Encouraged by her own resolve, she smiles at her foster family. It's a reassuring smile rimmed in confidence and radiant with a strange air of superiority. It surprises the husband and wife, but not her *shīfu*. His years of guiding this girl who must pretend to be a boy, as well as watching her *devour* her educational studies, have allowed him to know her well. He knows she is as resilient as the birch tree branches growing along the rivers in the north.

While the owners watch, their house is emptied of all furniture and finery, jewelry and clothing, everything but bare necessities. Only the built-in cook stove and a small bamboo chair remain where they are. The servants who work for the family were dismissed earlier after vowing loyalty to the Revolution and the Party.

It is because of one of the servants that this army is here right now, Babe thinks. She scoffs inwardly at such disloyalty.

She heard it discussed at school that Máo Zédōng's army has recently captured large *Guómíndǎng* units, providing heavy artillery and arms needed to execute offensive operations south of the Great Wall. This past April, the city of Luòyáng, China's ancient capital under several dynasties, fell, which cut the *Guómíndǎng* army off from Xī'ān. Her history professor told her the Red Army is moving closer to them into the Yúnnán and Sìchuān providences, fiercely fighting the last vestiges of the *Guómíndǎng* army.

Today, her professor's words take on a new reality.

Today, she and the Chéns are personally experiencing the truth of all the civil war rumors filtering into their area.

Not long ago, one of her friend's servants told her employers she was quitting their home because it was time for the lower classes to rise, for the wealthy landowners and merchants to be overthrown and cast into a pool of obscurity. The family was shocked. The woman had been with them more than twenty years. Her friend said Communist propaganda is being received openly in the small, uneducated villages making up most of China.

The army commander in the Chén home has a routine he follows after a family has been properly humbled and *relieved* of all their physical encumbrances. Because he is a Communist Party convert only since the Japanese were defeated three years ago, he dispatches a form of compassion by informing and lecturing citizens to help them better understand the true purpose of the Party and the wonders of a forthcoming

Máo Zédōng led Chinese Communist Party, the CCP. First, he sends the loaded trucks away with the family's luxuries, then he shouts orders that his troops line up and wait patiently for him. They are used to it and pretend to stay in full attention until he goes back inside.

Right now, he sits on the bamboo chair near the cooking area and stares pleasantly at the family for a long time. He takes off his cap and hits it against his leg, puts it back on, smiles broadly. "I know you do not yet comprehend the greatness we are achieving here today. At one time, I, too, was disillusioned. I fought with the KMT, the *Guómíndǎng,* against the Communists before we joined together and formed an alliance to defeat the Japanese invaders. We fought side by side until the end of the Sino-Japanese War. With such close affiliation, I learned and listened until I became enlightened to the truth of our future needs in China.

"Is it not true that we Chinese have always suffered and died because of vicious warlords and intruders who only desired personal power and wealth, who cared not the least for the common people? We have lost everything for centuries and hung our heads in disgrace. Let me ask all of you… are you not weary of the shame and brutality of this past century?"

The family nods vigorously, especially Chén Lì. Babe stares straight ahead with no expression. Isn't that what the commander wanted from her earlier, no emotion?

"When I was reeducated, I eagerly joined Máo Zédōng. I came to see Communism as the only logical answer for restoring power to the people. I am willing to die for this great liberation of my people. When you fully grasp the truth, you will be willing as well."

As the commander conducts these generous talks, he closely observes the faces of his listeners. Eyes that sparkle with new knowledge and with an enthusiasm to hear more spur him on and help him judge receptiveness. He leans forward in a friendly stance with one elbow resting on his leg, his chin in his hand. "Be honest with me now… are any of your relatives or friends in the *Guómíndǎng?*"

An energetic shaking of three heads.

"One of our sons was killed by the Japanese soldiers, sir," Chén Lì says. "Our oldest son fled to Hong Kong with his family. We do not know what happened to them. No word in these years. That is all we know of anything military or political, sir. We are good citizens and honest merchants of China."

The commander nods. "I sympathize that your son was killed by the oppressors. Perhaps your other son is dead, as well." He is silent a few moments, crosses his legs. He points at Chén Lì. "You allowed this man in your household to practice *wǔshù,* and your youngest son, too." He points at Babe. "That is not being a good citizen of the new and free China. A good citizen listens to his leaders and vows his loyalty to all their statutes and laws. Now, because of your foolishness, I am forced to take you and your father… or is it her father?" He points at DānDān. Chén Lì pats his chest to indicate Jìnhǎi is his father. The commander sighs.

"Both of you will be tried for this act. If you have no previous political blemishes on your records, you will be dealt with lightly and reeducated to the truth. In the future, learn every edict passed down by leadership. If you think something you hear is merely rumor, run quickly to find out the truth or the untruth of it. It is your duty to do this.

"Next, I want to explain to you the special purpose of *Land Reform.* Have you heard of it? No?" He shakes his head. "Húnán Province is a stupid place, slow to learn, but it will change as our Party grows here. *Land Reform* is being implemented by our wise Party leaders all over China. You are fortunate to be participating in it even as we sit here! Isn't that exciting? It means *equality*—state-owned and state-dispersed equality. Wealthy landowners who see the truth willingly give up their lands and their possessions.

"All private properties will be nationalized soon, and the fat laziness of the bourgeois…" he smiles and extends his hand toward them, "… such as this rich merchant family only hours ago… will be ended. Do you wish to keep the disrespectful titles of *landlord* or *rich farmer?* Of course not, because the next terrible title after those titles will get you thrown into prison just like that!" He snaps his fingers.

"What, sir, is the next terrible title?" Chén Lì asks.

The commander leans forward staring at them with big eyes. "Counter-revolutionary."

Silence is heavy in the room.

58
Bourgeois Decadence

Shí Niú, Shuāngfēng, Húnán Province, China
August 1948

The commander's special speech to the ignorant mesmerizes all eyes of his captive audience except for the vacant two staring barely past his face in a manner in which he cannot tell where they are aimed. Babe perfects this new "art" as she sits motionless and plans her next *wŭshù* practice session in the forest.

"Now that you are becoming enlightened to the truth, you must see that practicing empty *wŭshù* instead of concerning one's self with day-to-day contributions to our new society is extravagant. What does it do but entertain the folly of the wealthy and the spoiled?" The commander holds their eyes for long moments. "Do you now understand what is wrong with the practice of *wŭshù*?"

Heads nod excitedly.

Naturally, the weak son of shīfu Jìnhǎi, who never wanted to learn nor had the ability to do Tàolù *or* Sànshŏu. *would agree*, Babe thinks. The commander knows nothing of *wŭshù,* that it is a sanctioned and secret art passed down and revealed only to the most trusted and capable family members. *Are the Communists afraid the people might rise up with their wŭshù skills and fight back?* She steals a look into *shīfu's* eyes. A split-second half-roll of his eyes in her direction and she knows they are in agreement that the the commander's speech is *fèihuà,* pure drivel.

She tunes back into the conversation as the commander says, "Yes, there is still hiding by *Guómíndǎng* in Húnán. Have no fear. It is temporary. The fighting is still fierce and dangerous in other places, but we will win. Do you wish to be on the wrong side when our final victory comes?"

"No *tóngzhì!* We wish to be on the right side," Chén Lì calls out cheerfully.

Babe imagines throwing both Chén Lì and the army commander to the floor, her hands tight around their throats. The commander nods his head. "Very good. All of us must understand it is important to abandon what our ancestors imprudently deemed as sacred. New China is no place for the ancient practices of *wǔshù*, religion, elder worship, temples, and shrines.

The Communist Army is slobbering over victories they have not yet won. Who says wǔshù *is illegal? Have we seen an official document proclaiming it?* Babe thinks.

"You are probably asking how to show your true devotion to this great cause. I will tell you. You begin by adopting a different attitude. It is normal to care about your family, but you must place the CCP before anyone or anything else. You become a good Communist by labor and hardship. By..." he pauses for effect, "...*drawing the line.* I see from your puzzled expressions that you are also ignorant of this important principle.

"*Drawing the line* is making hard decisions that build your character and make you worthy of Communism. Those decisions increase the gap between those who are 'in' and those who are 'out' of the Party. In the future, be quick to break all ties with anyone not a Communist. It makes no difference if it is your own mother, father, sister, or brother—any relative or friend. If they are rebels, they must no longer be part of your life. To do otherwise can bring severe consequences. Do you understand?"

"We understand very well, sir," Chén Lì says.

The skin inside Babe's jaw is sore from biting it.

"Let us now discuss the sad case of bourgeois decadence we found in this home. Do you not realize it is shameful to harbor excessive possessions far beyond your needs? We will share these belongings with many people. Is that not fair? Why should you have so much when so many have less? How can you understand the plight of the peasants if you live far above them? Are they supposed to respect people enjoying an easy life when they have never had one themselves?"

Babe wishes she could laugh aloud. She has already seen example after example of the opposite behavior from this army.

"Listen closely. Here is my advice to you. Give up the old-fashioned idea of your possessions as personal or private. Dress in only what you need. Eat only what you need, even less if you are very courageous. Do not avoid hardship. It is a sacrifice for the good of the Party. Do not be labeled as people from *the exploiting classes.*

"Everything personal, including your habits, are subject to being judged as *political.* Clinging to your wealthy possessions will now be considered an offense against our leader and the people of China. Have you heard this before?"

Head shakes from three listeners.

"Offending the state can send you to prison. It has to be this way to restore order after so much chaos. Even if you don't go to prison, you may be subject to a sentence of 'under surveillance.' Then you will be guarded and limited in everything you do for many years. No one wishes such a thing. Submit to those who know what is best for you. Am I being clear?"

DānDān sobs aloud. Chén Lì unleashes a flurry of low-volume reprimands in her direction. *A pitifully weak man,* Babe thinks. She wishes she could ask the commander in what manner the leaders live. She has heard whispered rumors at school of confiscated money, antiques, jewelry, and other expensive goods being stolen and redistributed to the families of political leaders or of being used in foreign bribes.

The commander smiles. Chén Lì's genuine, and Jìnhǎi's contrived yet ardent, responses assure him his kind and lavish lecture has hit the mark once again. He believes everyone deserves the chance to understand the superior qualities of Communism before they are judged too harshly, a carry-over from his other life. The weak wife will succumb to her husband's newfound knowledge, and once she is made to join the Women's Federation, she will respond properly or suffer the consequences.

"I sense you are going to be good Communists. Am I right?" he asks with gusto and a grin.

"Oh, yes sir, we are reforming immediately! If my father and I are sent away, my wife will seek out every condition and rule and live them correctly. We apologize for these transgressions, sir. When my father and I come home from receiving justice, we shall be respectful members of the Communist Party. No more laws will be broken. Be assured, *tóngzhì.*"

"Good! Then I shall personally put in a good word for you with the magistrate. Your rich farming lands connected to this estate are already the property of the state."

"Land Reform!" Chén Lì chirps.

The commander shoots him a huge grin. "Yes! And do not be astonished when your spacious home is confiscated for the housing of many others. This…" he rolls his eyes "… is extravagant for one family. Bourgeois. Bourgeois.

"One more point I wish to make." He flashes a stern look at Babe, "I want your promise the *háizi* will be taught respect for authority." DānDān frowns deeply at Babe and nods. The commander continues staring at Babe. "He will make a fine soldier in a few years when he places his loyalty to the Party… and when he puts some meat on those skinny bones. I think five his size can fit on the sleeping mat we are leaving for him!"

He puts his head back and laughs heartily at both his joke and the victory of teaching this uninformed family what they must know to appreciate their lives being ravaged along the righteous path of illumination.

Babe sees herself stuffing the commander's mouth with a rotten plum and hitting it with her fist. She looks past him through the open window and gasps. A soldier is holding a beautiful white ball of fluff upside down by his feet. Next, the soldier sets the rooster on his shoulder, stretches out both arms, turns in a circle as if he is an animal trainer *extraordinaire*. He turns Noodle upside down again and swings him back and forth, up and down, laughing and babbling as several soldiers gather around him, amused at his antics.

Behind her back, Babe struggles against the cords on her wrists. Her face nearly contorts with anger, but she manages to hide it. Noodle is placed on the man's shoulder for a third time. Without warning, he attacks. He jumps onto the soldier's head, digging his claws into his scalp. Wings flapping furiously for a few seconds, he bends and pecks the man's face, aiming directly for the eyes. The soldier yells and runs with a white blizzard jabbing and beating his head.

Babe licks her lips and laughs inside. Noodle and she are exactly alike. They will allow abuse only a short time before striking back. When they do, it is fierce.

59
Not Chinese

Shí Niú, Shuāngfēng, Húnán Province, China
1949

DānDān's contemptuous attitude toward Babe has become routine for nearly a year, ever since the invasion of their home by the Liberation Army. The lady of the house has changed so greatly, Babe no longer sees her as the subdued, slightly kind woman she knew before the takeover. She steadily attends People's Party education classes and joined the Women's Federation—an obligatory, Party-controlled group that supervises constructive things such as the freeing of concubines, closing brothels, and mobilizing women to make cotton shoes for the army. The *underbelly* character of the Federation operates as a strict military organization, rudely concerning itself with every miniscule aspect of a woman's life—what she says, thinks, and does.

Babe is maturing early, both physically and emotionally, and has grown increasingly uneasy in the Chén household while Chén Lì and *shīfu* Jìnhăi have been away paying for the crime of she and Jìnhăi practicing *wŭshù*. The men are scheduled to return in a few months after serving light sentences of easy labor for a little more than a year, and this light sentence is thanks to the commander's enthusiastic recommendation regarding the family's *transformation of thought*.

It is DānDān's growing hostility toward her that unsettles Babe and sends her running into the forest in what meager free time she has. Because soldiers from both the *Guómíndǎng* and the CCP hide in the forest from time to time, she goes alone to her most secluded and secret places to use tree branches for practicing *Yǒng Chūn* with only Noodle to testify of her *crimes against the state.* Sometimes, she straps Noodle to her back in a sling to access the places that require climbing up or down on narrow strips of rock too small for an adult foot.

"Nothing is working!" DānDān cries, exhaling loudly and looping the strips of material once more around her bent arm. She again takes the end of the thin material and tries wrapping it around Babe's chest. Lately, double undershirts are not enough to keep Babe's secret identity safe.

"Let me hold my chest flat while you come from the back of me pressing the binding tightly into my skin. I will slowly turn to let you wrap me like a mummy," Babe says. After two more failed attempts, DānDān throws the material on the floor.

"It is time to admit the truth! You are almost a woman, and you look like one already. Too tall now, and those *xiōngbù*… disgraceful for a girl so young. Why are you concerned to admit you are a girl? We don't worry anymore about the Japanese or Soviets raping us. You will be safe if you confess the truth and begin your journey as a happy member of the People's Party. They will understand why you were afraid before. Many women were afraid."

Babe tries to look pleasant, or at last compliant, but the truth is she has an almost violent aversion to giving her heart to the Communist Party. She doesn't know why exactly, but it's as true and embedded as the blood running through her veins. So far, she has avoided a showdown of either submission or admission at home or at the textile factory where she is responsible, with several other young *boys,* to dangerously dart in to oil or unstick the machines, sweep and mop the floors, wash the high windows, and fetch all needed supplies, including lunch every day for the supervisors and foremen.

The factory presents its own challenges. She licks hard-to-come-by or stolen salt and holds her urine all day so she does not have to urinate with the other boys on the bushes outside the factory yard. If the urge is unbearable, she slips away to the outhouse to squat over the stinky hole while praying none of the boys peek through the wall boards as she is supposedly relieving herself of more than urine. Lately, they tease her because they never see her urinate, though sometimes she is in excruciating pain from waiting so long. They laugh and hoot as they aim their streams at bugs, rocks, and trees. Babe finds their behavior severely immature and stupid, but she smiles along with them.

Last week, Lóngfēng suddenly knocked her down and straddled her outside during their twenty-minute lunch break. She restrained herself from responding to his attack, though it was difficult. He felt superior thinking he had pinned her to the ground. He looked around at the other boys to see if he had their full attention and cried out, "Let's see Bójūn's *xiǎo jījī* hiding in his pants. I bet it's so small he has to squat like a girl to pee!"

The other boys snickered and elbowed one another, each vying for a better view. Lóngfēng dramatically raised his hand in the air, wiggled his fingers, then dove for Babe's groin. Before his hand touched her pant material, he sailed over the boys and landed in a crooked pile of his own limbs. Every face looked in shock from Lóngfēng to Babe, who had scuttled up and was already standing over him. "Wha-what did you—?" he stuttered breathlessly.

"Don't ever touch me again, *húndàn,*" she said in a low voice curdled with threat. She stared at the other youths with an expression that dropped their chins to their chests.

"Hey! Back to work!" a foreman called.

The boys disbanded and hurried toward the factory door. Lóngfēng didn't miss the expression of cold triumph on Babe's face as she bumped into his shoulder on the way inside.

DānDān impatiently pats her foot. "Are you daydreaming? What are we to do with this material and your breasts that are already larger than mine? Whoever saw such a chest on a girl so young?"

"Oh, I am sorry, *DānDān Māma.* Please, do not trouble yourself any longer. I will practice wrapping myself in my room. I have an idea that may work."

"What about what I told you? Will you go and confess?"

"I promise to think about all your wise words."

DānDān's face turns red from not receiving the answer she wants. She puts her hands on her hips and takes in a breath of air that raises her chest high. She lets it out noisily to show her irritation.

"They missed how opulent my empty house is for almost a year. No more. Next week, the Federation is sending builders to rearrange this house and make it ready to house ten or more women. Part of where we are standing will be a sewing room to make more shoes for the soldiers. When Chén Lì returns, they are allowing us to share your bedroom. It is very generous! Our big bedroom we used before is being divided into partitions. You will use your mat and sleep out here with the other women workers. How will your lies hide your secrets then?"

DānDān's callous tone is shocking to Babe, but DānDān isn't finished yet.

"We have told lies for you. Do you not remember your previous life, or are you too simple minded? You didn't speak for almost a year when you first came to our home. Did your brain dry up? Why haven't you asked us who you are? We lied to our neighbors that you are the illegitimate, mixed-race child of my husband, but how long must we uphold these fantasies? It is a crime to lie to the Federation or the Party. I may miss my opportunity to become a full member of the Party next month because of you. I am doing what the Commander said we must do… *drawing the line.* You are becoming trouble to this household. Have you forgotten you are not Chinese?"

Babe gasps. Yes, she actually had forgotten, that is, if she ever knew. She also had no idea of the illegitimate, mixed-race-child fabrication of the Chén's.

"*DānDān Māma*, you-you are confusing me. Please promise you will not tell the Federation these awful things." DānDān's smug look closes the door to any of Babe's former feelings for the woman. She is a stranger to her now and someone not to be trusted.

"If you work hard to sacrifice for the Party and stop running off to the trees all the time, I may keep some of your secrets. Don't expect me to save that stupid chicken from the cooking pot when all the new tenants come. No one keeps a pet chicken. Bourgeois nonsense! Chickens are for eggs or food. We will go early tomorrow to tell the Federation you are not a boy and throw ourselves on their mercy. Perhaps, if you change your attitude… I shall also forget about telling them you are a child of *xī rén* missionaries."

60
Dire Circumstances

Shí Niú, Shuāngfēng, Húnán Province, China
1949

Babe flees from DānDān's cynicism, her harsh revelations, and the terrifying threat about Noodle. She will destroy anyone who hurts her rooster, but she cannot protect him the long hours she's away working at the factory. Inside her bedroom, the picture in her mind of people eating Noodle throws her into intricate *Yǒng Chūn* maneuvers fighting an invisible enemy who changes from DānDān to the army commander to some unknown person with no face.

If her real parents are Western missionaries, why is she only now finding out? Is she supposed to remember her life before *Bǎo Māma*? She doesn't. She was told by *Bǎo Māma* that her other parents had to leave her but would return one day. Nothing more, and it hadn't mattered. Her life was happy in those years with Bǎoyīn, Zhēn Gāng, and, sometimes LíngLíng. The years with the Chéns have been tolerable, even exciting because of *shīfu* Jìnhǎi, her passionate devotion to *Yǒng Chūn,* her enjoyable schooling, and her beloved rooster. She needed nothing else before the army took her *shīfu* away.

She stops hand fighting the air and stands perfectly still, her breath coming in shallow loops. Beads of perspiration cover her forehead. Chén Lì and DānDān lied that she is the illegitimate child of Chén Lì. Is it true she is not Chinese, not even partially? She snorts sarcastically into the air. Who is she then—a jumbled lie of pieces rammed together in no logical order?

She retrieves the beat-up wooden box and sits with it on the floor next to her state-issued sleeping mat. She removes the few undergarments folded inside it. The box has been with her as long as she can recall. It is shabby and of no value, and now she understands why. Someone, such as the soldiers who ransacked the Chén home, would have stolen it by now had it been otherwise. She turns it upside down. Hundreds of times she has inspected the faded abacus paintings on the bottom and knows by heart the words and numbers the beads spell out. The other painting on the box also contains hidden messages. Instructions from LíngLíng are burned into her memory—secret messages for her protection to use in case of *dire circumstances.*

She takes Noodle out of his pen and lets him strut around the room looking for ants in the floor cracks under the room's solitary window. From her pocket she brings out the wilted bean sprouts confiscated from the table this morning. Noodle quickly pecks them into flat, limp stems before swallowing them. She lies on her back staring at the ceiling. She will not pander to the Federation no matter what DānDān says. She shivers in repulsion at being told what to do every hour of every day, of becoming a puppet to their every whim… of truly giving up her beloved *Yǒng Chūn.*

DānDān said they will go in the morning to confess. What will the Federation do when they find out her secrets? Perhaps she will be thrown into prison. Noodle's future would then be the cooking pot. What if DānDān blurts out Babe has been lying about her gender *and* she is not Chinese *and* she is the daughter of Bible missionaries—Westerners—the ones the Communists most detest?

Unbidden, the memory of *Bǎo Māma* floods her mind. The kindness she masked with annoyance by calling her a *tiáopí* child—an insolent child—an expression of endearment. Her gentle eyes, her soft touch when she combed Babe's short hair or cleaned her face.

In the year since the men of the Chén household were arrested and sent away, Babe has allowed herself to recall what she witnessed that unbearable day long ago. She allows it only when she is deep in the forest in her special places, or in the small hidden cave with the water trickling through it. She falls to the mossy ground or against the cold wall of the cave and sobs until the crushing pain passes.

Noodle has been the only observer of these memories playing out a fragment at a time. Right now, he senses Babe's mood on this day of bleak revelation and gives up his search for ants to crouch beside her. She strokes his fluffy feathers until he closes his eyes.

She pulls off the undershirt she wore for DānDān to work on concealing her bosom and slips on one of the three plain shirts she is used to wearing every day. What she sees in the mirror is upsetting. Are those things on her chest growing by the hour? It seems so. She sighs aloud. At least, it will no longer be necessary to conceal them if DānDān forces her to stand before the stern, judgmental women tomorrow and beg their forgiveness for being a girl.

A suffocating resentment chokes her. She stares at the ugly wooden box. Her memory has not faded of what LíngLíng fed into her mind the months before she left Babe with the Chéns. Though she refused to react at the time, she heard and memorized every word.

Hours pass. Babe lies on her thin sleeping mat beside Noodle and the upturned box. Her body is still, but her mind churns with forced recollections of everything she has heard at home, the factory, or at school about the ongoing civil war and where it might be most dangerous or safe to travel. The morning passes into afternoon with no summons to eat or have afternoon tea, and it's just as well. Babe no longer feels any connection to DānDān and Chén Lì of the Chén household.

Shīfu Jìnhǎi, always a visionary, took her with him as he buried several silver coins in a wooden box beneath the damp ground in the forest a few years ago. He told her it was assurance for them in case of misfortune. What foresight! Those coins are her salvation now, and she will leave some for him, along with a letter, inside the box. She'll share the secret messages on the bottom of her box in case he also wishes to flee.

But… what if he has been tortured and brainwashed into becoming a real Communist? What if he tells the authorities what she has done and gives them the secret messages? They would find and imprison her or worse. Being young won't make a difference. She and the other students at school have been forced to watch soldiers beat and shoot people. Once, they cut hunks of skin from a fourteen-year-old schoolmate, finally killing her, for the innocent accident of meandering into a secret cave used by the army. They said it proved she was a *Guómíndǎng* spy. No emotions are allowed when watching these atrocities without incurring serious, painful consequences.

If the Federation learns of her connection to the hated missionaries... She grimaces and decides she will write Jìnhǎi a letter but it shall explain only how DānDān mistreated her these last months, making her feel unwanted to the point that she ran away. She will express her deep respect and gratitude for what he taught her as her honorable *shīfu.* Yes, this letter will also get her in trouble if it is shared, but at least it will not reveal the box's secrets. As another precaution, she will lie in the letter to *shīfu* about her proposed destination.

She lifts her rooster onto her lap. "I believe we are in dire circumstances, Noodle. Are you ready for a dangerous journey?"

61
I, Bójūn

Southwest China
1949

Noodle is a calm traveling companion. He is easily fed with Babe's leftovers, bugs, and the dried grains she stole from the Chén's kitchen, as well as other morsels she finds along the way. After finishing her *Yǒng Chūn* routine in the dead of night, she lights a few of the precious matchsticks from the stash Chén Lì kept hidden from the servants inside a loose stone in the side of the wall. She scooped up all the matches for her journey and now lights them to let Noodle walk around for exercise, though he prefers to be lazy and sleep all night.

Last year, *shīfu* made a collar to put around Noodle's neck to stop him from crowing at odd times and disturbing the Chén household. He doesn't crow often, but, in certain times, as when Babe hides a breath away from either Chiang Kaishek's or Máo Zédōng's soldiers in the forest, it is deadly crucial that both she and Noodle are silent. After explaining the dangers to Noodle, he doesn't mind the collar. She removes it in safe times, for which he is always grateful.

Fortunately, Babe is educated about forests from her years of living almost inside one and from all the questions she asked Jìnhǎi when they walked in the woods. She hides all day and travels only when darkness is first descending, making her progress slow. As a survival tactic, she becomes adroit at stealing food from camps, settlements, and small villages, even picking up a few extra shirts and a pair of boots not as worn out as hers.

Some of the mountains appear impossible to cross and bring tears as she stands looking up at them. She lets *shīfu's* wise words that *good medicine often tastes bitter* burn inside her as she struggles through steep passes and makes her way along rocky ridges high above deep gorges. *When bitterness ends, sweetness begins, shīfu* drilled into her when some of the *Yǒng Chūn* movements were especially difficult to master. He was always right. After conquering her hardest obstacles, she experienced the jubilation of victory and the glow of self-confidence. This impossible journey is to be her greatest challenge, and she will not back down.

After months of soul-crushing, solitary travel, Babe breaks from the trees onto a road busy with people passing by on foot, in handbarrows, in makeshift rickshaws, in old greying wagons, and on top of broken-down animals with ribs pushing hard against their skin. Thick sunshine pours down from an open sky with no trees to steal its light and lands warmly on her hair and eyelashes. Her eyes absorb the humans on the road with a primal hunger for companionship.

She drops her meager bundle of possessions to the ground. She gently places Noodle's enclosed wicker basket beside it and eases down onto the flat wooden top. The emptiness in the eyes of the passersby is frightening, almost making her want to run back into the forest. Questions tiptoe as shy shadows through her mind. *Where do I belong? Who am I? What is my future?* She allows herself time for a transition back into humanity before rising with her belongings and stepping into the traffic on the road.

"What direction is Guǎngzhōu in Guǎngdōng Province?" she asks a woman carrying a long bundle of tightly packed rags on her back. The woman stares at her, doesn't stop. She asks the same question of another woman limping her way slowly down the road. The woman points, and Babe resumes her journey to the waterways feeding into the estuaries of the Pearl River. In that river, she must travel southward by boat, then eastward, partly in the China Sea, eventually arriving in Hong

Kong. She hopes her remembrances of her geography and history studies are correct. Her escape plan is predicated upon them being so.

She falls into step beside an elderly man who considers her with hooded, yellow eyes. She walks with him for a time, then asks, "*Yěyè*, can you tell me how to cash a coin that my grandfather, a senior official in the Communist Party, instructed me to cash for him?"

The man stops, takes in her rough shirt and trousers, the enclosed basket with a chicken inside, the simple, tatty boots. He points down the road. "In the next village is a shop selling dried ducks, rice, cinnamon sticks, and red beans. They will cash your coin if you mention your grandfather. They will take one-fourth in interest for themselves. Take care no one sees you pocket your money or you will soon be parted from it." With that, the old man walks on leaving Babe standing in the road considering her vulnerability.

I appear to be a tall youth in my teens. I am capable of protecting myself. Anyway, most people are honest. By the end of the day, she has witnessed several cases of pickpocketing and stealing and is quickly educated into knowing impoverished people will do about anything for the smallest amount of money or food. The suffering and scarcity all around is shocking. For the first time, it becomes clear how protected the people of the Húnán Province were, until recently, from the ravages of war.

In no time, she learns how to finagle the best prices for food and the methods for bargaining a ride in a wagon, on a horse, in a man-drawn cart or handbarrow, or simply how to employ the art of seemingly walking with others without actually being part of their group. She proclaims often and loudly she is on a mission to earn membership in Máo Zédōng's Liberation Party by completing a long journey on foot while taking a rooster to her grandfather—a rooster he requires for his stock of high-bred chickens laying eggs for many officers' meals. He, a senior official in the Communist Party, wouldn't think of showing nepotism, so he has demanded his grandson Bójūn struggle alone from the Húnán Province to Nánjīng. The harder the journey, the more he will be proud of his grandson's indomitable spirit and durability.

Babe tells the story so often and so convincingly she half believes it herself. She also quotes what DānDān told her repeatedly over the last months; that is, *anyone who takes part in the revolution must give up his or her soft life and become hardened by hardship.* She follows it by saying, "I, Bójūn, will be a proper revolutionary and make my Communist grandfather proud!" garnering looks of respect or alarm from listeners depending on their loyalties or their losses. Regardless of the mixture of looks she receives, she experiences a certain degree of protection because of her so-called kinship to a high Communist official.

Though nearly fourteen, she claims to be on the edge of sixteen, and her height, education, maturity, and quick mind easily back up her lie. She is keenly aware of growing taller since she left home more than three months ago because the hem of her two pairs of trousers have shortened from her ankles into the rise of her calf muscles. And… those terrible breasts! The work she puts into concealing them and finding the privacy to do so is the hardest part of her journey since she left the forest.

It is always problematic keeping Noodle safe and dry while crossing the tributaries and rivers, but the river she is facing today is wider and faster flowing than any of the previous ones. She studies it for a long time and watches others either make it or fall into the water. If they are not fished out by companions, do they drown? She doesn't know. She puts Noodle's basket on the ground with the bundle of her belongings on top of it. She hoists them onto her head and steps into the water. The rocks are slick. The waist-high water and the necessity of using both her arms to balance her load make it treacherous to stay upright. She grows more tense each time she loses her footing. Noodle flaps against the basket sides as it tips right and left. He crows discontentedly when water wets the bottom of his basket.

"Be strong, Noodle," she says with a trembling voice. The water gets deeper at the half-way mark. She slips, bobs side to side, is going down when strong arms grab her from behind. Someone carries her to the other shore and places her feet on dry land. She turns to see a tall man who looks unlike anyone she has ever seen before. He beams at her with a luxurious smile that makes her insides jump.

He is so open… so friendly and kind.

An attractive woman runs and jumps into his arms. He swings her around. They laugh, kiss, and hug. Babe has never seen a public display of affection, or even a private one. It is considered disgraceful to touch or show feelings in public. A large group of smiling people surrounds the couple. Somehow, they look different than the people Babe has always known. Men slap the tall man on the back. Others come forward with hugs, kisses on both cheeks, laughter, and more pats on the back.

Tears spring into Babe's eyes, and she doesn't understand why. She quickly wipes them away before she is accused of acting like *a precious person of the exploiting classes.* Too late. The woman who jumped into the tall man's arms saw her tears.

"Do not worry, young man. It's all right. We laugh! We cry! No one can stop tender feelings from a big heart. I am Jasmine, the wife of Abbas." She nods toward the tall man, then touches Babe's hand.

"I-I am Bójūn."

The woman smiles. "Our Abbas has been away for a long time. We worried and prayed for him, but see? He has come back to us. Will you share food with us tonight as we welcome him home?"

Babe, still surprised at the unusual emotions she experienced, accepts the invitation.

62
The Lúolì

Southwest China
1949

Throughout the day, Babe notices this group's ease in traveling in many small, seemingly disconnected clusters and how they blend into whatever environment or people they are around. Jasmine enjoys talking, and Babe learns from her that the group, who refers to themselves as a tribe, is departing for another country after living in China for many generations. Though she says they are departing by sea, no other details of their plans are mentioned. When Babe tells Jasmine her destination is the Pearl River Delta, Jasmine invites her to join them on that piece of their shared journey.

Babe agrees, thinking, *I can learn from these unusual people, and my tired feet will thank me that I may sometimes ride in one of the wagons hiding their provisions behind hay.*

As soon as Babe agrees to go with them to the Delta, Jasmine fetches Abbas. He is followed by several men. "My wife tells me you will travel with us for a time. You are welcome, Bójǖn! One provision," he says, his look turning solemn. "You must swear you will say nothing of our private ways or of anything you may learn while you are with us."

Uncertain, Babe is silent.

"To seal your promise, we will have a spit-swear ceremony."

"I-I don't know what that is."

"It is your public pledge that you agree to our serious provision. Me and you will spit in our hands and then shake hands in front of all the tribe. Do you agree?"

Babe looks around at the faces staring at her. They don't look angry or unfriendly, but she has never heard of anything such as this. She swallows hard, can't seem to find her tongue.

"I see you are unsure. Don't worry! This kind of promise no longer needs a blood oath as it did with our ancestors. Spit is good enough for us now," Abbas booms, breaking into a hearty laugh.

His merriment is contagious. Babe smiles along with everyone else, thinking, *Am I not a fake boy with fake stories? Why not concede?* She nods her assent, and the ceremony is performed. The cheers during the handshake make her feel joyful, a foreign but pleasant feeling.

The seemingly disconnected bands of people come together as darkness descends. Babe helps Jasmine and some of the younger children gather wood and make fires when they stop for the night. While the evening food is cooking over the fires, she allows Noodle to wander inside a barrier she creates from her basket, her bundle, and a small wall constructed from sticks. An older boy squats beside her, tears off the end of a loaf of bread for himself, hands the rest to her.

"Sweet bread fills your belly and makes you content. I'm Barde."

"I'm Bójǖn."

"How old are you, Bójǖn?"

"Almost sixteen."

"I'm nineteen. You're tall for your age. Tall men have to eat more so they aren't so skinny as you." She glances at him to see if he is criticizing her. His face is pleasant, and his handsome grin makes her insides churn. "I've never traveled alone, Bójǖn. My tribe… we're always together in some way. Why are you and your rooster traveling alone?"

"Perhaps I can explain tomorrow when I am not so tired," she says, wondering what he will say when she recites her made-up story.

Barde nods and shifts position. "It's admirable… you going on a difficult journey by yourself so young. Are you sure you are not part *Lúolì?*"

"What is *Lúolì?*"

"Our tribe, and others like us, are called *Lúolì* by the Chinese. Have you never heard of us?" She shakes her head. He leans back on his elbows. "Good. That is how we like it, Bójǖn. We are a people of an ancient culture who hides inside other cultures. We dress and speak and eat as the people we are around, sometimes marry into them, but we never put aside our own traditions and beliefs, even when we have to conceal them for centuries. It is impossible for us to deny our roots, no matter what our circumstances are."

"Where are your roots?"

"It might be hard for you to understand, but our roots are not a place. They are a spirit of adventure living inside us. Our *Romani* roots urge us to go where our hearts lead."

His words stir a strange longing, almost a loneliness, inside her. It's surprising, but what he says resonates as if she has heard it before in her own spirit.

"Tomorrow night, far from outsiders, we celebrate the return of our leader Abbas. You will know our tribe better afterward. Goodnight, Skinny Traveller. Get some rest."

Babe touches her unusually warm cheeks as he walks away.

As light diffuses into dusk the next evening, assigned men depart into the outer edges of an isolated bamboo forest to watch for trespassers. After making camp, many of the tribe members disappear into the tall canes. Off come the ugly, plain shirts, trousers, and dull shoes. The women reappear from their makeshift dressing rooms wearing colorful blouses revealing bare shoulders covered in glistening, loosened hair. Full skirts make circles as they twirl. Fancy shoes grace feet at the end of shapely, bare legs. Fingers covered in rings make rhythmic clicking sounds with castanets. Looped earrings sparkle from the reflection of the large fire in the middle of camp.

The men undergo a transformation into tight breeches and blousy sleeved shirts open at the throat. Firelight bounces off the gold-coin necklaces around their necks. Unusual stringed-instrument music fills the air as dancers joyfully dance in the firelight. From the sidelines,

Babe is mesmerized. Barde drops beside her on the ground.

"Are you in a trance, Bójūn?"

"Wha-what? No, I never, uh… She takes a calming breath. "I have not seen such a ceremony as this before. Or clothing. It represents, um, such an expression of freedom."

"Do you like it?"

"Very much."

He laughs. "I thought you would. You may not be *Luoli,* but I sense you are in your spirit. You don't look Chinese. Are you of different nationalities?"

Her heart jumps into her throat. "I-I am mixed blood, but still Chinese." He studies her face until she thinks she might run into the tall canes and hide. He hands her a bowl and spoon. "What is it?" she asks, sniffing above the bowl.

"Ash Reshteh."

"I do not know of this food."

He laughs and leans back on his elbows. "Of course not. It is a Persian soup made with greens, noodles, and beans."

A new song begins with a baritone voice singing emotionally about love.

"His singing is beautiful. What are those musical instruments the men are playing, Barde?"

"The drum my uncle and several other men are playing is called a *tombak*. It's made from goatskin stretched over wooden cylinders. The *cimbalom* is the stringed instrument my grandfather is playing."

"I-I don't understand how your, uh… your tribe stays out of trouble. Aren't you afraid the Communists will throw you into prison for being bourgeois, or for not pledging loyalty to their Party?"

"We are experts of camouflage, Bójūn. We couldn't leave during the occupation or many other hard times, but we are taking this opportunity to do it now. We no longer wish to tolerate the restrictions of China when so many other countries permit freedom."

"What country is so free?"

His closed-mouth smile lets her know she is trespassing in restricted territory. He abruptly sits up, draws his knees under his chin. "Oh, my soul… look at Galina dance! She makes me weak with desire. Is she not the ripest peach ever waiting to be plucked, Bójǖn?"

"Who?"

"That vision dancing in the red shoes. Look at her! How I wish I could kiss those lips, those shoulders…"

Babe fidgets. "She-she is very pretty."

"She is a goddess. Hands off, Bójǖn!" he says, smiling and glancing at the side of Babe's face.

"I-I don't, I mean, I am in no way trying to-to, uh… if, um—"

Barde laughs. "Such blushing! I see you are still a pup. I don't think a boy still suckling his mama's teats will steal my Galina."

Babe's face burns hot with anger or embarrassment, she isn't sure which. She wishes she could tell Barde she is a female and that he might try looking at her the way he looks at Galina, but she remains frozen in place and completely uncomfortable with her new feelings.

"Eat your soup, Skinny Traveller. I'm only teasing you."

Babe puts the spoon into the bowl, remains motionless.

"I hope I didn't insult you, my friend. You're a braver man than I to travel so far alone."

Babe manages a small smile in his direction.

"Bójǖn, if you like, I'll tell you some of my people's history while you eat your soup."

"I would, uh, like that," she says softly, bringing the spoon to her lips.

"It is said we migrated to China from Persia and Russia centuries ago. History tells us our ancestors settled in the Shǎnxī and Gānsù Provinces, and then around Dàlǐ in Yúnnán. They mingled with the Hàn culture of the region, learned their languages and customs. Our musicians wrote more than a hundred songs while living in Dàlǐ during the Qīng Dynasty. The outsiders loved those songs and came from everywhere to hear them performed. I am named after a balladeer who wrote many of those songs. That's what my name means in Chinese, *someone who sings ballads*. What do you think of my history?"

"I-I think it is one of the most interesting stories I have ever heard."

"Last night, you said you would tell me why you are traveling alone, Bójūn."

"It's not very interesting. Not like the story of your people, I mean, your tribe."

"I still want to hear it."

She takes a resigned breath and tells him her made-up story, wondering constantly how he will receive it. From his expression, it is obvious he doesn't like or trust the Communists. Will he tell Abbas? Will they rescind their offer? She desperately wishes she could tell Barde the truth, that she would never be a Communist, that her aversion to the Party is why she is running away. She bites the inside of her jaw and stares into the fire. *Being strong often means being silent,* her *shīfu* said many times. Not then, but now, she finally understands the wisdom of those words.

"You won't inform on us, will you, to your grandfather the Communist? We should be gone from China by the time you reach your faraway destination, so what good would it serve to tell him about us?"

"Barde, I am… um, you are right… I will not see my grandfather for many months. I-I promise never to speak to him of your tribe. I took a spit oath, remember? Besides, I do not plan to be a Communist."

Did I really say that?

"What? How can you avoid it?"

"By remaining faithful to what I believe and nothing else."

He studies her with admiring eyes. "I must ask you again… are you positive you are not *Luoli?"*

The firelight reflecting in Barde's eyes makes her want to confess all the truths of her life, including her odd feelings toward him.

Being strong often means being silent.

She smiles. "Do you sing, Barde?"

"Of course! Do you wish to hear me?"

Babe is sorry she nodded *yes* because watching and listening to Barde, she knows she will hereafter struggle to hide her feelings for him. Never has she been so attracted to anyone, and why does his love and passion for Galina feel like glass shards ripping apart her heart?

63
Smuggling Isn't What It Used to Be

Pearl River, China
1949

"Are you sure you will not join us, Bójūn? We consider you part of us now. We are going somewhere very beautiful. Much better than here, I promise! I can't tell you where it is unless you agree to come with us," Jasmine says, holding both of Babe's hands as they stand on the dock beside the Pearl River. Jasmine has asked her many times to come with them. Now she pleads for the last time.

Babe is torn between staying with these people she has come to love, especially Barde, or continuing to seek her true identity and solve the riddle from the box Bǎoyīn gave her. In any case, what would Barde do when he discovered she was female? What if he laughed at her or stopped being her friend? The thought of it almost makes her sick.

Babe shakes her head. "I am sorry, but I must continue my journey. I shall never forget any of you." She fights back tears as several women step forward to hug her and give her good luck tokens and baked delicacies. Last night, Barde gave her a knife to carry *in case you need to protect yourself.* How she had yearned with all her heart to show him how she really protects herself, but she merely smiled.

Abbas grins and shakes her hand with gusto, a strange custom to Babe. "We will miss you, young man. Take good care of yourself and your wise white rooster!" He laughs that rich laugh of his and puts his arm around Jasmine. He was the one who cajoled the boat captain into letting her travel on his boat to Lantau Island. Babe starts her walk up the boat ramp when she feels a hand on her back. She turns. Jasmine steps close to whisper in her ear that the boat captain is obviously a smuggler.

"It is good because he will keep you safe from water pirates and other criminals until you reach Lantau Island, but keep one eye open all the time, my young friend. *Be-Salāmat*, Bójū̄n. I pray we meet again someday."

Babe nods with a heavy heart. She continues waving from the deck of the boat with Noodle tucked under one arm. Her eyes seek out Barde in the crowd. He kisses his fingers and throws them into the air as a farewell salute.

"Goodbye, Skinny Traveller! I wish you and Noodle safe travels! Watch out for the beautiful women you meet, you handsome tiger!"

His teasing grin breaks her innocent heart.

As her new friends grow smaller in the distance and the waves slap erratically against the side of the boat, a deep loneliness settles into her soul. Cháoxiáng, the plump owner and captain of the boat, comes to stand beside her. He rocks back and forth on his heels.

"So, you made friends with some of the *Lúolì*?" He chuckles. "Well, you are young with no good sense yet. I admit, they have the most beautiful women. Oh, the one who stood beside you with the big, soft lips? What a tasty plum… umm. The jewel with the long hair and chocolate eyes who whispered in your ear… she made me ache. If you think it was the tall man who made up my mind to let you come aboard, you are wrong. I wanted to look important in the eyes of those luscious women. Did you know many of their women used to be concubines for important Asian men?"

Babe gives him a hard look, remembers she needs to stay on his good side, changes her expression to what she hopes is that of one learning new information. Mentally, she dismisses him as ignorant.

"The legend says there was a Mongolian general, I think his name was Uriyanghatai, who had eight concubines. The favored of them were his three *Lúolì* women. Lady Lotus, the daughter of her former tribe's leader, was his most favorite. When he died, Lady Lotus honored him at his tomb on Tomb-Sweeping Day for thirty years. Ah, yes, they are delectable as concubines, but never trust people who dance by the light of the fire. Ugh, they will steal all you own when you are not looking." He puffs blue-tinged pipe smoke into the air.

"Concubines are illegal in the new People's Party," Babe says, carefully scrutinizing his reaction. His look of alarm shows her how to manipulate him in the future.

Now Cháoxiáng knows he is going down the river with someone attuned to the Communist Party dogma. He wasn't told Bójūn is supposedly the grandson of an important Communist official, something which would have canceled the deal of hiring him to come aboard. He feels anxious now that the Party has been mentioned.

These are treacherous times for merchants such as he, considering that Máo Zédōng proclaimed the founding of the People's Republic from the top of the Gate of Heavenly Peace in Peking only weeks ago. He didn't hear the broadcast himself, but it was all the talk at the Inn of the Lost Fisherman in Kowloon, his favored place to buy fiery shots of *báijiǔ,* delicious pickled duck necks, and, of course, loose women. One thing is certain, smuggling isn't what it used to be, and it becomes more hazardous by the hour.

From her slumber, Babe feels her shirt collar tightening around her neck. She springs to her feet blocking Cháoxiáng's hand with a move that throws him off balance. He stumbles backward and falls onto his backside, feet in the air. Her body smooths into a natural *xiǎo niàn tóu* position in perfect alignment over the surprised assailant. Cháoxiáng growls in protest. "What's the matter with you? I was waking you up, you idle boy! I am the captain of this boat. Respect me, or I'll throw you in the river for the fish to eat!"

Babe relaxes her hand position and tries to smile, manages to look apologetic. Lately, she has to wake in the deepest part of night and steal onto the deck to practice *wǔshù.* Only old Song is awake up there at that hour, usually drunk and partly snoozing. If he wakes up, she tells him she is emptying her pee can from the cabin, and she is. She goes to the stern behind the hanging nets and performs her movements. Twice now, she has fallen asleep topside during the day listening to the old motor whine as the boat rocks and chugs with the motion of the water.

She steps away to allow Cháoxiáng to stand up. "Forgive me, Cháoxiáng. I thought you were the authorities trying to strangle me and steal our salt and the, uh, other necessities you are so bravely taking to Kowloon from Macau and Burma."

"Humph," he says, disturbed by her words. He is, after all, not only genuinely fishing but also smuggling precious salt to Hong Kong. They are desperate for it, making it a smuggler's dream. Their vast supply was depleted during and after the big war ended. The opium, which this boy discovered only because Song's drinking loosened his tongue the other night, is marked for delivery to the prosperous peasant owners of the opium dens still operating in Kowloon. This trip marks the last time Cháoxiáng will risk smuggling a commodity as dangerous as opium because of tightened surveillance and rumors of recent swift punishment for *opium pirates.*

The Communists are a dangerous concern. Smugglers are shaking in their boots over the new regime taking control of lands, the government, and the sea. Salt and other common product smuggling is not so serious and are often winked at by the authorities when their pockets are lined with bribery money. Drugs? Too risky.

Now, this skinny branch of a willow tree dares to pretend he understands the whole of my business? Brazen lout! "Get busy with your duties, Bójūn! Earn your travel on this vessel. I was trying to wake you, that is all," he croaks.

"By choking me?"

Cháoxiáng's foot attempts making contact with her rear end to heighten his show of exasperation. Anticipating the move, Babe quickly sidesteps. Cháoxiáng misses his target and kicks the mast, bellowing out in pain. Babe grabs her basket with Noodle inside and scurries into the hull to clean Cháoxiáng's cabin and collect guts from the smaller fish in the hold to use as more fish bait. The fish meat will be set aside for her to cook for Cháoxiáng and the four other fishermen onboard.

The smile on her face as she descends the steps is her secret, and nearly constant, companion these days. She is, quite simply, feeling proud of herself. She can't believe she did what she did, but she did do it, and the freedom it is bringing her fills her with joy.

She *did* dig up the little chest of silver coins in the forest that *shīfu* Jìnhǎi left for her. She *did* sew several coins into hidden pockets in her trousers by candlelight while DānDān slept. She *did* leave in the middle of the night with only Noodle, her secret money, and the messages from her wooden box burned into her memory. She *did* make the unbelievably long and dangerous journey through the mountains and trees. She *did* make up a series of believable stories to keep her safe in her travels to Hong Kong.

She also lied to Cháoxiáng that she could cook, and so far, she has copied everything she has ever seen prepared in a kitchen or has eaten, and neither he nor the other men have complained. Perhaps it is because they have no idea what good food is, she muses as she prepares rice, shoots, fish, baked sweet potatoes, and other commodities brought onboard from the villages or caught from the water.

Traveling down the Pearl River estuary to the island of Lantau wouldn't take so long if Cháoxiáng was not obsessed with giving the appearance of operating an important fishing vessel. Every few days, the boat docks to unload its catch. Today, while cooking in the galley, Babe recalls the secrets on the bottom of her box at the Chéns. One abacus spells a telephone number; the other one has hidden instructions if she is in Hong Kong. She smiles. LíngLíng would be proud of her traveling alone for so many months. How extraordinary that she will actually be in Hong Kong soon to send… what is it called? A telegram?

At Lantau Island, she will cash another silver coin and solicit the help of someone who understands what a telegram is and how to send one to a faraway place called San Francisco, California.

Who will receive the telegram in San Francisco?

What will happen afterward?

What if nothing happens?

64
I Lied… So What?

Victoria Harbour, Hong Kong
1949

Babe scowls at Cháoxiáng's shiny eyes and the sun reflecting off his bald head. She desperately wants to throw him onto the deck and make him sorry. He lied to her, and he doesn't care. In fact, he's smiling and rubbing the mustache hair that feeds into his short beard.

"What difference is it, Bójǖn? I have many fish to be delivered at Victoria Harbour."

"You have opium to be delivered in Kowloon, you mean. What about your salt, are you taking it to the prostitutes in Kowloon, too?"

"Quiet! I don't know what you are talking about. Do you want me to throw you in the water?"

"Try it," she says, glaring at him.

Cháoxiáng stares in her eyes, doesn't like what he sees, throws his hands up as a signal he is finished with their discussion. "I lied… so what? Lantau, Kowloon, no difference to you, foolish boy."

She turns her gaze out to sea, and it does what it always does… calms her down.

Why do I care where we dock? All the islands will lead me to Hong Kong. Maybe I am ready to fight for no reason. Maybe I am tired, she thinks.

She finishes mopping the deck, wrings the head over the railing, and escapes to her tiny sleeping quarters to be alone with Noodle. She is still nursing the surprise she had last night. She knew what it was from her health classes and from the giggles of the older girls talking about it at school.

She aches down low below her stomach. Of course… *lái yuèjīngle*—another female problem she must now hide in her life as a male. At least it had the good manners to show up later than it does for some of the girls, but how difficult it will be to keep it a secret!

How much longer must I tolerate this deception?

She buries her face in her makeshift pillow and sobs herself to sleep. She wakes with a start. Noodle is pecking at a mole on her arm. "What are you doing, crazy rooster?" She sits up. "Oh, I'm sorry. You want your food, don't you?" She takes the lid off a small pan and lets Noodle peck the shrimp pieces inside.

How long was I asleep? From the gyrations of the boat and the sounds on deck, they are preparing to dock. She is instantly wide awake, rubs her face.

"We have come to the end of our journey, Noodle! We must remember all that we were told by LíngLíng. Because we shall be in Hong Kong, we use the second instructions *Bǎo Māma* gave us for that city, yes? Do you remember the painting of the rose on the bottom of the box? The stem contained a name, and the address was hidden in the lines of the leaves. We must find a place where they understand telegrams. We are supposed to tell the telegram person the secret message and the name and address from the rose. They will know what to do, won't they? Of course, they will. What do we do after that, Noodle? Do you remember?"

He cocks an eye and looks at her.

"I knew you would remember! What we do is wait."

She gathers her few things into a cloth bundle and puts Noodle in his wicker basket. She sets them aside, turns and folds her blanket. She places it into the suspended net that served as her bed aboard the smuggler's boat, looks around the tiny space, and walks into the narrow hallway abutting the stairs leading to the deck.

65
One Rare Jewel

Kowloon, Hong Kong
1949

Edgar takes a white handkerchief from the inside pocket of his suit jacket, removes his glasses, and proceeds to clean the lenses while staring out the window of the Royal Air Force Kai Tak Airport terminal. His blue pinstriped suit hangs in loose folds. His hair, prematurely gray, is cut short and combed neatly to the side. A young man in a uniform approaches him.

"Sir, are you Mr. Edgar Wayne?"

"I am."

"We received a wire in the back office addressed to you from the Governor's office. Well, it's actually from the Lieutenant Governor himself."

The young man refuses the coins Edgar tries to give him and recedes to his place behind the counter. Edgar struggles to hide a fresh gush of tears. The tears come much too often these days, and they are indicative of the man he has become. Experiencing his wife declining daily in mind and body—not to mention, witnessing her death—severe prison conditions with his son for two years, and the futility of searching for his daughter in a country besieged by war and turmoil have taken a bitter toll on the once robust, enthusiastic Edgar Wayne.

He has flown from the states to China three times in the years since the big war ended to fulfill the promise he made to Olivia as she lay dying in the road. The deadly civil war raging between the Nationalists and the Communists following the end of the Japanese occupation has greatly complicated, and now perhaps halted, his quest.

Everything was drastically different when the war first ended and the Japanese invaders were driven from China. For the first three years, parts of China literally glowed with revival and hope. Missionaries traveled freely to and fro, some calling it "the golden gospel age of China, the halcyon period of open doors and open hearts."

Edgar, caught up in the excitement, entertained the idea of coming back to continue his work with the Mission once he found his daughter. He soon changed his mind. The thought of losing his children again was too raw, too horrible.

The golden age vanished, not only for the missionaries, but also for the hundreds of thousands of Chinese who resisted Máo Zédōng's Communist revolution. In 1948, a female missionary from Sweden was tried by a People's Tribunal and executed. Such a thing had never happened before, an execution "by the will of the people," *the people* meaning *the state.* A shockwave ran through the missionary community, the ripples of which changed localities, directions, and lifestyles for thousands of people.

More gruesome reports from various parts of China flooded in, and by late in that same year, the Nationalists were in full retreat. It seemed nothing could stop the flow of arms and aid from the Soviet Union to support the CCP. Edgar was beyond thankful he had already covered so much ground in his search for Babe, traveling in the back of wagons, in carts, in cars, on trains, and in old fishing boats and ferries in his search. Fortunately, he previously paid a visit to Hiroshi and Ena in the Shāndōng Province before they moved from China to Tokyo, a city quickly filling with Westerners and Japanese businessmen.

Due to the slower takeover of Máo's armies in the southwest regions of China, Edgar has traveled quite freely and extensively through Yúnnán Province, the area his family was living before the Japanese bombed Pearl Harbor. Sìchuān, Húnán, and Guìzhōu Provinces were scoured. Notices were posted, rewards offered, peasant and farmer "grapevines" utilized for any information about a girl named Bernadette Beatrice Wayne, also known as *Babe*.

Traveling to Bǎoyīn's home in Zhījiāng, Húnán Province, in 1947, was the most heart-wrenching part of his pursuit. He had held onto hope he would find Bǎoyīn, her family, and Babe surviving and in good health. Instead, as the villagers told him, the family had been accused of treason and were overtaken, their dwelling torn apart. Any of their belongings that could be stolen, utilized, or sold were gone. His heart was heavy to the point of bursting as he followed their directions through the village to Bǎoyīn's house.

A ransacked mess of what had been a well-tended, modest home and courtyard greeted him. The whitewashed walls had gaping holes, and the roof tiles were ripped away. The hidden tunnels underneath the property now lay exposed, crumbling, serving only as a thoroughfare for burrowing animals residing in holes dug from the main alleys. The channels formed a spider-web network from every part of the house and courtyard and led into the forest and toward the mountains. He shook his head in wonderment, amazed that in his lifetime, he had rubbed shoulders with a saint such as Bǎoyīn.

Yet, where was his daughter?

Was my child fortunate enough to use this tunnel system to escape? he pondered, heart throbbing, as he squatted beside a dirt hole dropping from the floor in a corner of the main room of the house. Villagers told him Bǎoyīn's husband Zhēn Gāng was murdered that fateful day, Bǎoyīn was taken prisoner by the soldiers, and the little girl who had lived with them for three years vanished without a trace.

The unknowing of it is the worst part. Always wondering whether his daughter is alive or dead, and if she is dead, what she might have endured before the end. If alive, what is happening to her?

After seeing Bǎoyīn's ruined home, Edgar traveled to a nearby settlement where the townspeople said Bǎoyīn's daughter, LíngLíng, and her in-laws lived. The house had been taken over by three families who said they knew nothing of the former family nor anyone named LíngLíng, Bǎoyīn, or Babe.

From the missionary office in Shānghǎi, all the way to far southwest China, Edgar has searched for Babe. One incident early this year stands out and still causes an odd sense of *deja vu* each time he recalls it. He was accompanying an undercover KMT official through Shí Niú, Shuāngfēng, in Húnán Province and caught a glimpse of a boy sitting on a large concrete pipe along with three or four other lads. They were talking and eating lunch outside a textile factory. Something about the boy felt hauntingly familiar. As if by signal, the boys jumped off the pipe and hurried into the factory.

"Can we stop, please?" Edgar had asked.

The official shook his head. "I regret that we cannot. We must go quickly past the factories and through town. The Communists are in control of nearly everything here now. We must never pause or cause suspicion. In fact, this is a great risk already, me driving you to the villages. If they find out I am KMT, I will be dead. My family, too."

"But, I… I don't know. That boy back there, he—"

"A boy?"

"He, uh, seemed… oh, dear God, I don't know anymore." Edgar rolled down the window and turned his head to gaze at the factory yard until it was out of sight. He cried bitterly that evening in his hotel room, which he attributed to exhaustion and frustration.

This last trip to Hong Kong is to throw himself on the mercy of the British governor to aid in his search for his daughter. A kind secretary in that office, Mrs. Clarke, upon hearing Edgar's tragic story, promised she herself would put his plea in front of the Governor and would make sure Edgar received an answer by the next day.

Too pent up to wait around the hotel, he called Mrs. Clarke this morning and said he would be spending the morning visiting the Kowloon Union Church. Since she was interested, he explained, "The Union Church is rebuilding after being desecrated and looted during the invasion. Many of my former missionary associates are volunteering to teach and preach at the church until they find a permanent pastor. I thought it might be nice to stop by and pay my respects."

"That sounds like a brilliant idea, Mr. Wayne. Shall I send the Governor's wired response to your hotel later today?"

"If you don't mind, and if it comes before evening, would you be so kind as to send it to the Royal Air Force Kai Tak Airport terminal in Kowloon? I have permission from an old friend to visit there this afternoon and watch the Spitfires take off and land. I hear they conduct two patrols each hour, and it might be, well, gratifying to see." He sighed. "I must keep myself busy, you understand. With things as uncertain as they are, it very well may be midnight before I arrive back at my hotel. It would be so very helpful to learn what my next steps are, Mrs. Clarke, and, naturally, everything depends on what your governor replies."

"Everything, sir?"

"I'm afraid so."

"I see." After a brief silence, "Mr. Wayne?"

"Yes?"

"I'm so awfully sorry about your family."

Her sympathy delivered in her lovely English accent brought tears to Edgar's eyes.

He has been at the airport only a short while, having gotten permission to stay in the main lobby, when the wire comes through. When he steps close to the window to read it, the color drains from his face. The governor's office offers no hope, and, to the contraire, suggests he accept the fact that, regrettably, thousands of people go unaccounted for in wartime, most especially in foreign countries such as China, a country experiencing continual civil wars. The last paragraph rips the heart from his chest.

"Of course, the Office of the Governor is always attuned and diligent to the task of finding missing family members. Take heart that we shall notify you of any new developments when and if they arise. The Governor and I are dreadfully sorry for your loss and wish you Godspeed on your journey back home."

Because he has pestered the officials of Hong Kong, the United States Government, his own missionary offices, and any official office still under the control of the Nationalists countless times over the past four years, Edgar knows this is it—the end of the line.

He takes a chair, never breaking his stare at the paper containing the polite but cold words. *It's as if I have been searching for one rare jewel buried somewhere in the sandy bottoms of the vast oceans of the world. It's all futility.*

Hopeless. I've been dismissed, he thinks. He blots the tears dripping onto his trousers, folds the telegram, and gently places it in his jacket pocket. His sigh bespeaks hurtful surrender. When he recovers enough to stand up without sobbing, he asks the young man at the counter to make a call for him for transportation back to his hotel.

At that exact moment, immediately south of the Kai Tak airport, a slender lad carrying a wicker basket and a small cloth bundle disembarks from a fishing vessel moored in Victoria Harbour.

66
Of Mice and Men

Bangor, Maine
1958

Charlotte

People are waking up and wandering around the bus station like sleepyheads on a holiday. At seven this morning, a different security guard came on duty and stirred the tangle of street people. They gathered their odd assortment of belongings and left. Before the door closed behind them, I noticed the snow and sleet had ended, leaving only a thick, gray sky behind. What a night this has been—tiring and introspective with an overabundance of memories traipsing through my mind.

The rumble of a loud motor from the street provokes cheers from the sparce crowd. That means the buses are starting to run again. I get a quick flutter of butterflies in my stomach. What will it be like to come face to face with Daddy after all these years? What a shock it must have been to receive my telegram last week, the first direct communication from me in more than ten years.

I lean back into the bench that has served as my bed all night and blow out a loud gaff of air. I don't recall ever having this much time to plunder through my life experiences as this night of isolation has provided. Was it the cold grip of the storm bearing down on us, or the act of spending a whole night watching people publicly perform the private act of sleeping that caused the relentless winds of recollection to suck me inside?

A middle-aged man I saw come into the station not long ago walks by, circles around and comes back. He leans in close and stares deeply into my eyes. "Excuse me, Miss, do you know the time?"

Oh, for heaven's sake. How dumb does he think I am?

I glance at my watch and tell him the time as if he can't see the big clock on the wall behind him. He grins and rubs the front of his thigh. "You look like you could use some real man company. Mind if I sit down, honey?"

"No, I don't mind at all. That is, if you don't mind having your nose relocated to the centerline of your buttocks."

"Huh?"

I lean toward him with narrowed eyes. "You heard me."

The look on his face gives me deep satisfaction. I feel so liberated, so much like Pinkie in the old days! Of course, I'll have to work on becoming as skilled as she at slicing a menace into slivers, but it's a start.

The truth is, armed as I am, I really have no desire to turn into pitiful characters such as in *Of Mice and Men* by letting my sad childhood drive me to *seek and destroy* simply because I can. Not at all. I strive to use my protective abilities only when *apropos.*

I spy through the station's glass door a small, white panel truck driving along the sloshy road. It parks by the snow-capped curb. Painted on the side of the truck is a smiling doughnut, a steaming cup of coffee, and *Mr. Happy Donut!* A man dressed in a white coverall and a red cap opens the two swinging doors in the back of the truck. He props the front door to the bus station open with a brick and brings in three stacked white boxes. He places them by the coffee urns, flips open the top one, and leaves.

The loud speaker crackles as a man's voice says, "Folks, it sure was a long night, but we made it. For your pleasure, we have fresh doughnuts over on our courtesy table. Please help yourselves. No charge. Coffee urns were just refilled. I'm pleased to announce the roads are clearing and buses are beginning to roll. Mr. Eisley is at the ticket counter waiting to assist you in continuing or starting your journey. Better finish that Christmas shopping. 'Ol Santa is coming in a week! Have a good day."

It's amazing how fast I overcome my southern-girl decorum to rush across the lobby to get to those fresh doughnuts—holey hose, stockinged feet, and all. I help myself to two doughnuts and a cup of coffee and return to my bench feeling quite refreshed for someone who hasn't slept all night. I find out the bus taking me to Boston, the first leg of my trip, will arrive in about an hour. I freshen up in the ladies' room and try to occupy myself with people watching.

The subject of heroes crosses my mind. The only one I have from my childhood, since Daddy failed the test, is Mrs. Cudahy. I didn't get to tell her goodbye when I packed my suitcase and climbed out my bedroom window to meet my *ROSE* handler a decade ago. I wouldn't have known she was fired as Daddy's cook if not for my best friend and co-conspirator in high school, Flora Belle Watson.

Flora and I are still in contact, albeit, surreptitiously, and she keeps me updated about my father's life. We speak on the telephone every New Year's Day, but she never knows where I am. That's the way it is when you work for a private underground group. She says Daddy mourns for me and wants desperately to share himself and his wealth with his only child.

That tells me he still knows nothing of what Miss Wraith, my childhood nanny, did to my mind regarding *affluency,* how shameful she made me feel for being born into a monied family. Of course, I've outgrown such nonsense, and I think I'll be shocking Daddy all the way to his socks when I tell him how much money I would like him to give me for a special project. He'll have to understand that letting him finance a project in no way constitutes a mending of our relationship.

67
Mrs. Cudahy and a Revelation

Bangor, Maine
1958

Heroes in one's life are rare. The people I work with are all heroes to me, but only Mrs. Cudahy was my hero on the home front. She was an Irish widow with one grown son and two younger children. She proudly told us during her interview she originally came from County Kilkenny in Ireland. Not familiar with Irish counties, or of their significance to their inhabitants, we nodded and smiled politely.

Our other cook, Esmeralda, had also been Mother's nanny, and she grew too sad to stay in our employ after Mother passed. With Daddy's help, she bought an alligator farm and tourist attraction in Florida and drove off in the car Daddy bought her, a two-tone green 1941 Pontiac Streamliner Torpedo Eight coupe, a beauty of a car. I still see her white-glove wave out the car window as she drove away, her pill-box hat covered in purple petunias tilted to the side on her curly gray hair.

Come to think of it, Daddy generously invested in a whole new life for Esmeralda. I wonder how many employers would go so far as that?

He hired Mrs. Cudahy knowing of her hardships and that she, being an immigrant with no other family living stateside, had no financial means other than what she was able to earn. He insisted one requirement of her employment was that she prepare abundantly more food than we could eat so the leftover food could go home to her family. She got tears in her eyes when Daddy said that. She became fiercely loyal to my father, and who can blame her?

Her distaste for Miss Wraith, who was hired a week after Mrs. Cudahy became our cook, was carefully concealed, but I felt it when the two were in the same room. Often, I sensed her feelings of sympathy coming toward me, though it never showed in her neutral expressions. She needed her job, and she couldn't afford to cross the woman who utterly hoodwinked and charmed my father in an outrageously short time.

Miss Wraith was fiendishly meticulous in concealing her dark side to everyone but me, but I know Mrs. Cudahy suspected the woman had two personalities. Often, Mrs. Cudahy brought me something to eat when I was not allowed to eat supper and after being forced to tell her I wasn't hungry because of a bad headache. Mrs. Cudahy would go upstairs to use the maid's bathroom and then dart across the hall to my room.

Without a word, she brought me food wrapped in waxed paper or aluminum foil. Fried chicken legs, strips of roast beef, a chop, cake—a sundry of items depending on the day's menu. She also brought a clean sheet of white butcher paper with the food so I could disguise the empty pieces of waxed paper or foil inside it after I drew a few art scribbles or mathematical scratches on the outside. That way, it passed as regular trash in my bedroom waste receptacle until the maid emptied it that day or the morning after. It was a clever ploy to keep Miss Wraith from finding out our secret. We never discussed it except the first time when Mrs. Cudahy instructed me how to dispose of my wrappers.

I would never have known the appalling way Mrs. Cudahy left our home if not for Flora returning the ostrich feather shoulder cape Daddy brought me from Europe the year before. I had carefully hidden that beautiful cape for more than a year under the false bottom of a bin built in my closet that even the ever-prying Miss Wraith knew nothing of. I lent it to Flora for a fancy high school graduation party her parents hosted in her honor at the Colonial Country Club. The Watson's devotion to their two daughters was a matter of both awe and pain to me. I had no such public gilding of my life from my father.

On the way to her summer job as a procurer's assistant in the *After-Five Cocktail Dresses* department of Leonard's Department Store in downtown Fort Worth—a posh and coveted summer position—Flora drove by my house to return the cape. It was disguised craftily inside a box of artist supplies as I had directed.

I had told no one of my plans to leave, and I earnestly hated that I couldn't confide at least in my best friend. Of course, being unaware, Flora expected me to be at home as usual. Ronald, our butler, left her waiting in the foyer while he went to find Miss Wraith, and that act alone should prove to anyone the power that woman wielded over every employee and every action in our household. Flora noticed my father's travel valise sitting inside the door as though he had returned only a short while before or was preparing to leave. She was startled a few minutes later to hear loud female voices coming from the library.

The doors opened, and Mrs. Cudahy emerged with a flushed face and her purse in hand. She swiftly passed by Flora on her way to the front door. Miss Wraith stepped from the library looking haughtily triumphant, her hands on her hips, and Daddy—poor Daddy—dumbfoundedly stood in the doorway behind Miss Wraith.

"It'll be a hot potato down my shirt, Mr. Basse, before I work again with a woman such as herself. I have never taken one thing what you didn't give me, sir, and I would gladly go to Judgment Day this instant for the truth of what I tell you! I knew it was fortune smiling on me when you hired me, sir, and I will not be forgetting that Godly act, no, I will not."

She pointed at Miss Wrath. "That woman standing there is Hell's own daughter, I tell you, and look no farther than herself to figure why your fair babe flew the nest. She's been a torturing the poor child long enough, and I don't blame her for leaving this house. I would have done the same and long before! I pray she won't be a'foolin' you much longer, sir. Now I've said my piece, and I stand by it. Great is my gratitude for all you done for me and mine. I'll be forever remembering you, Mr. Basse, in my mind and in my prayers. R*ath Dé ort.* Good day to you, sir."

Mrs. Cudahy's accent was so thick in her anger, Flora said she barely made out all the words, but her intent was as clear as a brand-new mirror. As soon as the door closed behind her, Daddy slowly walked toward the staircase looking as if he had just lost the Battle of Waterloo. Miss Wraith said, "Flora, please forgive this ridiculous display of foolishness from our hired help. Some things are simply out of our control, and rude employees do tend to forget their places, don't they?"

Poor Flora! She almost swooned but collected herself enough to say, "Oh, um, yes ma'am. I came by to, uh, Charlotte ordered art supplies before school dismissed for the summer, and they were delivered to the school yesterday. Mr. Peterson asked me to bring them to her if I didn't mind, and, of course, I didn't." She said her mouth was as dry as a cactus from spouting those lies, but she managed to ask, "Is she, uh… is she in?"

"No, I'm afraid she has left us."

"Left us?"

"Indeed, she has, like a thief in the night. How is that for gratitude?" Miss Wraith took the box from Flora and placed it on the antique hall credenza. "I tried to warn him, told him she should be, well… she should be put where she couldn't harm herself or anyone else. Do you think he could see it? Ha! Blind as a bat when it comes to his own flesh and blood."

"Wha-what happened to her?"

"It seems our little Miss Fancy-Pants has run away, Flora. Climbed out her bedroom window like a bird escaping a golden cage. Left a note on her pillow with a mere two words. Two words!"

"What did they say?"

"Goodbye, Daddy."

"That's all?"

"Indeed! Let's see how she does out there in the cruel world without her daddy's money. Spoiled rotten. We'll get word, never doubt it, from the authorities somewhere. Wait and see."

Flora said Miss Wraith practically spat in disgust as she spoke, her face as hard as frozen steel, and with that one evil left eyebrow in the severe arc that used to send shivers up my spine. She turned to my friend and said, "Is there anything else I can help you with, Flora?"

Flora mumbled a few words of required protocol—after all, the Watsons are a well-turned-out family—and left as quickly as her legs would carry her. Later, through the grapevine, she learned Miss Wraith had accused Mrs. Cudahy of stealing a pair of diamond earrings and an emerald ring from my mother's jewelry box. The grapevine, which included the housekeeper's daughter, a friend of Flora's cousin, also gossiped that Miss Wraith framed Mrs. Cudahy, and they, the other employees, knew it and would quit in protest if they didn't need the wages, which they all desperately did.

The other part of the rumor was that Miss Wraith wanted Mrs. Cudahy gone simply because my father held her in such high esteem. Apparently, only she, Miss Wraith, was allowed to be the apple of his eye.

That… I knew firsthand.

Suddenly, I am aware of feeling hot and uncomfortable. Something is slowly forming in the back of my mind, and I can't face it head on. It may cut too deep. It started when I thought about how Daddy expelled Miss Wraith from our home with only her clothes and personal effects less than a month after she fired Mrs. Cudahy. The jewelry she accused Mrs. Cudahy of stealing was recovered six months later when Miss Wraith attempted to sell it to the Houston Jewelry store in Tyler, Texas.

The owner of the store knew my father personally. Of course, he did. Daddy purchased many expensive pieces of jewelry from him for Mother over the years. In fact, the ring Miss Wraith stole was designed by those same jewelers and was engraved with my mother's name inside. To be on the safe side, the owner telephoned my father, who, astonishingly, was home and not traveling. After the telephone call, the owner called the police, and Miss Wraith was arrested. Flora doesn't know what became of her after that.

I take several deep breaths as our psychology instructors advise before delving into intensely emotional subjects. Preparing to let the new revelation that has been building all night come forward, I intentionally relax all my muscles, one at a time. The truth that is threatening to hit me in the face is about Daddy. When I put all the pieces together, his big crime of my childhood was his ignorance of my predicament, his blind eye. He believed a stranger's word over his own daughter, and shame on him for that. Of course, Miss Wraith's womanly wiles and skillful cunning played into his male vulnerability in the wake of losing my mother.

How can I ignore the generous way he helped Esmeralda start a new life in Florida, all at his expense? What of Mrs. Cudahy and Daddy's insistence that she feed her family right along with cooking for us? How do I block out his many benevolences to members of the community when he heard of ill fortune befalling them, his anonymous checks to their families, the many secret college funds he set up? What of the beautiful presents he brought me from around the world and his tears when he thought his little girl was emotionally troubled?

The truth before me is no less dramatic than a mountain intombing me under a landslide. Without looking down, I retrieve my handkerchief from my purse and let the tears flow, all ten-years' worth of them… southern protocol and *certain public behavior* be hanged. Who could have guessed I feel grateful to Dolion for his untoward behavior last night? His terrible conduct placed me all night alone in a bus station—a situation that forced me to slow down and think.

What have I been doing all these other years… *not thinking?*

Perhaps certain painful emotions place us in a proverbial water-filled tunnel in which we stay afloat but never dive or sink deeper. We ride along the top of the current not looking down, right, or left… merely floating through to the next thing, the next year, the next carefully supervised thought.

That's the best way I can describe why I'm only now realizing my father is absolutely a good man, and that I can easily forgive him for anything and everything from the past.

68
Remembering the Telegram of 1949

The Road to Texas
1958

Charlotte

Comfortably seated at last in bus seats, we carefully drive on snow-cleared roads through Bangor. The bus driver announces over the speaker we may be in Boston for a late lunch if the roads stay clear. I put my head back and close my eyes.

We never gave up searching for Pinkie, of course, but life moved on. One day in 1949, an important telegram from Hong Kong was delivered to our door in San Francisco. I was sitting on the sofa with my Italian language instructor going over complex verb forms when the doorbell rang. Harry rose from his desk in the corner of the room and called out, "I'll get it," loud enough for the rest of the employees and visiting agents in the two-story Victorian house to hear him. In moments, I heard him shout something in Mandarin Chinese that sounded like "tee-en-nah." Later, I found out he said, *tiān na!* which was "Oh, my God!"

Heads appeared above the staircase railing. Bodies came from different rooms into the entry and library. "Is everything all right, Harry?" Annika, one of our agents from South Africa, asked. Harry stared at the telegram, looked up shaking his head. He repeated that two or three more times, apparently in a state of shock. To our surprise, he slung an arm over his eyes and broke into loud sobs.

We never witnessed Harry breaking down before, he being the iron platform in our undercover organization. Sent at age seventeen by his wealthy family from China to San Francisco shortly after the Japanese invasion of China's mainland in 1937, he and two other altruistic people, they also having apparently unlimited funds, established the home office in San Francisco in 1944. They set up an annex in South Africa in 1948, and they had plans to open another one in Hong Kong in late 1950. The *Three Arteries of the World*, they would refer to it, and San Francisco would remain the heartbeat of it all.

Now, here was our leader, overwrought and overcome with emotion. A strange silence filled the house. I gently took the telegram from his hand and read it aloud, softly, out of respect for Harry's present condition.

"It's addressed to, uh, let's see, Wáng Hālǐ, but I'm not sure I'm saying it right, from someone named Chén Bójǖn, Babe. Good heavens, I don't understand how to pronounce Chinese names at all, do I? Anyway, she, or he, is in Hong Kong. Let me look at the time and date. Okay, this wire was sent two days ago. Here's the whole message, *'Tomorrow will be a joyful day. Please hurry, Wáng Hālǐ. I am at the Castle Peak Hotel in Hong Kong. Not safe'*. The message, time, and date are repeated in Chinese after the English version."

Several of the long-term internal staff clapped quietly and slapped each other on the back. Harry recovered enough to smile at them with watery eyes.

"Isn't the Castle Peak that hotel they were putting the finishing touches to when we traveled to Hong Kong six months ago, Harry, that lovely place on the bay?" John Alderman, a financial contributor and ground-floor patron of *ROSE,* asked. Harry nodded.

"What does he mean by *tomorrow will be a joyful day?"* asked Boris.

"Who's Chén Bójǖn, Babe?" I asked, knowing full well I was butchering the pronunciation of the Asian name. Harry stepped quietly to his now cold cup of tea, sipped, turned back to all of us. He accepted the tissue from his secretary and blew his nose.

'Tomorrow will be a joyful day is a secret-code message created by my Aunt Bǎoyīn and me when *The Gold Rose* was first conceived. My aunt was my idol, my mentor. She is the true spirit behind our whole operation, the ultimate rescuer." He closed his eyes, took a deep breath. "Aunt Bǎoyīn is… was… a fearless woman of great faith who risked her life for others for many years, even when I was a boy. She took under her wing hundreds of people escaping tyranny, but the one who held her heart most captive was a little girl named Babe, the daughter of a missionary couple who went into hiding after the Japanese bombed Pearl Harbor in 1941."

The ticking of the grandfather clock by the bookshelves was the only sound in the room.

"Neither my family here in California nor I have heard from my aunt for more than four years. I do not know…" His ragged breath came out with a sigh. "I do not know if she is alive or dead. Because the person named Babe has contacted me by wire using our secret-code message but does not mention Aunt Bǎoyīn, I assume my aunt has encountered tragedy." He bowed his head. "These are the dire circumstances we dreaded but meticulously planned for."

Harry's personal pain was contagious in a room full of people who dedicated their whole lives to helping others escape painful situations. A heavy silence fell over us.

"Harry, shall I make plane reservations for you?" Susie Chin, his secretary, asked in almost a whisper.

He was silent a few more minutes. When he looked up, the fire was back in his eyes. "Yes, Susie, for two. I'll take the trolly to the Western Union office right now. Babe needs to know we heard her message loud and clear. We'll have some paperwork to do, probably have to get some inoculations. See about those, Susie. Maybe we can get out of here in a few days if I pull some strings."

He looked at me. "Are you ready for your first international assignment, CeeCee?"

I was, and I've been ready ever since to go any place, anywhere, and under any circumstances.

69
Hong Kong

Hong Kong
1949

Babe

Babe has no choice but to lie to the clerk in the telegram office, else he won't give her the wire from Wáng Hālǐ. It arrived earlier today, the fourth day after her wire was sent to San Francisco. She inquired of it several times each day, growing more anxious each time she was informed there was no reply.

She added the words, "Not safe," to the wire to add an air of urgency. In truth, with her *wǔshù* skills, she has felt safe ever since she left Húnán Province, even though she recognizes unsavory characters and pickpockets abound in Hong Kong as much as in any other city she has traveled through. The true urgency she feels is over the depletion of her coins and the uncertainty of how her life unfolds from this point.

The excitement of Hong Kong—the freedom, the colors, the bustling activity, the immigrants from all over the world, the refugees from mainline China—is both terrifying and fascinating. If only she were confident of receiving word from the man *Bǎo Māma* trusted to rescue her in case of dire circumstances, she would be dimwittedly happy mingling with all strata of people when she leaves her hotel room to buy food or wander the busy streets and shops of the city with an assumed air of confidence.

She never tires of watching the two-decker buses loaded with too many passengers, the rickshaws pulled by skinny-legged men dashing through the streets like energetic sand pipers carrying Westerners and Chinese people wearing nice clothes and self-assured expressions. It is almost impossible to believe Hong Kong is truly free of both the Japanese invaders and the tyranny of the Communist Party, but one has only to inhale the air of jubilation and watch the vendors and immigrants go about their daily activities to catch the spirit of hope that trumps everyday worries. Everything seems possible in Hong Kong.

How can this kind of freedom be next door to suffocating oppression? she wonders as she absorbs the sights, sounds, and smells of a place and people under a different set of rules than the ones she has known for so long. The insecure worries that began the day DānDān told her she was not Chinese, along with the other shocking revelations the woman threw at her, lessen in this magical kingdom of eclectic people.

This morning, she timidly dressed in the first female clothes she ever remembers wearing—a dress, elegant in design, a beautiful pale-blue silk with embroidered white blossoms surrounding tangerine-colored centers and hanging from delicate green-thread branches. Dressed as Bójǖn yesterday, she told the lady in the store she was buying a dress for her "sister," who was her exact size but had more up here, and she pointed to her own chest currently bound flat under a colorless, loose shirt. The clerk smiled and assured her the dress would fit. It did, and so did the slippers she purchased at the same store.

Her hair has grown a few inches longer than shoulder-length. On the last part of her journey, she wore it twirled tightly under caps or pulled back in a braided pigtail. Today, she brushed it and left it loose. She gasped when she stood in front of the mirror and beheld a young lady whose early maturation gives her the look of someone three or four years older than her true age. The strangeness of the feminine emotions her image conjured sent her into a controlled-breathing respite for a few minutes. *I am a girl!* she declared to herself, over and over, and, finally, she left her hotel room dressed as one.

As usual, before seeking nourishment, she stopped by the telegraph office to inquire of the expected wire from San Francisco. The clerk rifled through a small stack of papers and lifted one into the air. "Yes, here is a wire from Wáng Hālǐ in San Francisco, California, for Chén Bójǖn," he says.

Her spirit leaps at the good news. "Thank you. May I have it, please?"

"No, sorry. The wire is for someone else."

"What are you saying? It is a wire for Chén Bójǖn."

He smiled a patronizing smile.

"I am Chén Bójǖn!"

His eyes drop down and back up inspecting her. He lets them rest on her bosom, breaks out in laughter."

Babe's hands and body go rigid, a side effect of her trained fighting instinct. Her face burns hot, but, thankfully, she realizes her mistake. She forces herself to chuckle, nods her head. "I am sorry. Yes, I understand your confusion. I am Babe. My brother, Bójǖn, sent me to pick up this wire for him."

His eyes, squinting through black-rimmed glasses, reflect skepticism.

"Read it again. My name Babe is also on the telegram. It says Chén Bójǖn, Babe."

"Do you have identification?"

He asks for identification because I am a girl?

She imagines shaking him by his collar until his teeth rattle, but she smiles sweetly. "I have this," she says, bringing out enough money from her new pocketbook to make his eyes bulge. She hands him the money, snatches the wire from his hand, exits quickly before he has time to protest. Her heart pounds in her chest as she maintains a fast pace back to her hotel and up the stairs to her room.

She lets Noodle out of his basket, sprinkles a handful of dried grain and bean sprouts in his bowl, and attempts dropping cross legged to the floor. For the first time in her life, she is aware that movements in *female* clothing aren't the same as movements in *male* clothing. She hurriedly disrobes and redresses in her formless gray clothing. She drops to the floor beside her rooster and reads…

Your message is clear. Take heart; we are coming for you as quickly as possible. Check hotel desk often for messages from me or CeeCee Davis. Use caution. – Wáng Hālǐ, Harry

70
Catch My Rooster!

Hong Kong
1949

After five long days, news arrives at the hotel front desk from the manager's office that Wáng Hālǐ, also known as Harry, and his assistant CeeCee Davis have received British military permission to fly into the Royal Air Force Kai Tak Airport in Kowloon and will meet Babe at the Castle Peak Hotel sometime late this afternoon or evening, the time depending on local transportation conditions and customs entanglements.

Young and restless, Babe doesn't know how to wait from morning until evening for something so uniquely frightening and exciting. What secrets of her life will be revealed through this man so trusted by her first foster family?

As usual, she practices *Yǒng Chūn* long and leisurely in the privacy of her hotel room. That part of her Hong Kong stay has been particularly satisfying, as has her acceptance of her true gender and how it makes men of all ages open doors for her, smile at her, send admiring looks in her direction. What she doesn't like is how some, such as the clerk in the telegram office, treat her more suspiciously or lower in class than they do males.

The day rolls by slowly, endlessly. As Bójūn, she kills time by visiting a pottery store, an art studio, and picks out another dress and a pair of combs at a dress shop *for her sister.* She sits at an outside counter in a small eatery over a bowl of steamed rice and fish and listens to the local residents gossip and complain about the one-hundred thousand immigrants fleeing the People's Republic of China every month and swarming into Hong Kong, some of them former rich land owners, many others farmers and peasants resisting oppression.

Where will they all live? How can the government support its own residents if they support all these migrants? Why isn't the government doing something about the thousands of Triad criminals coming here? Soon, it will be too dangerous for us if this continues. Has anyone seen one of the new Cantonese operas? The more people immigrate here from Shanghai, the more of those operas will open. That is good, isn't it?

Such is the chatter she hears and that which she can understand throughout the day. Many dialects abound in Hong Kong, most too difficult for her to decipher other than the highlights of the conversation. She returns to the hotel and dresses as Babe in her new dress. Undresses. Dresses as Bójǖn. Undresses. As the afternoon drags on, she thinks Noodle and she must have some fresh air or perish. She again dresses as Babe and goes to the hotel lobby carrying her rooster basket and her pocketbook.

"I am expecting important people from San Francisco to arrive at this hotel. They will ask for my brother, Chén Bójǖn, or for me, Chén Babe. Very important. If they come before I return, please tell them we, um, my brother and I, are taking a walk on the hill along the bay and shall return before dark." She hands the elderly man behind the counter a few coins for his trouble and also as a safeguard for his taking her request to heart.

He smiles at her, revealing four missing teeth. "Be most careful, please, by water. Dark time most danger. Beautiful hotel ground danger for pretty girl," he tells her.

She smirks inwardly, smiles politely. "I will be vigilant. Thank you, *yěyè.*

"Please, before I go, will you cash two special silver coins for me?" She hands the manager the expensive silver pieces, bends to readjust the cloth over Noodle's basket lest he be discovered, and misses the wily look a young woman standing nearby directs toward a young porter with unruly hair. The porter is resting with his elbow on the counter after carrying a large load of luggage into the lobby. Both he and the young woman watch Babe as she leaves the hotel.

The late afternoon shadows filter through the branches of the willow trees lining the hillock's pebbled path. The path winds gently, sometimes steeply, above the bay feeding into the South China Sea. Babe allows Noodle to amble beside her pecking and scratching at anything that catches his attention. Her gentle tugs on the soft string around his neck encourages him to continue moving when he tarries too long.

She resists the constant urge to run back down the path to the hotel to check if her mystery guests have arrived. The lapping of the water below and the dancing sway of the trees are relaxing, but not enough to quell her intense anticipation. The sun lowers in the west as she waits. She sits down on a marble bench under an expansive willow and teases her rooster to make him peck at an imaginary bug on a string.

"Why not crow when you have the opportunity, Noodle? No one will care up here. Maybe I will learn to crow with you if Wáng Hālǐ finds us a good life." Noodle squats down. She studies him. "Listen closely, Noodle. I know it has been a long journey, but you must not grow weary. Or old. I won't permit it." She pulls his string to encourage him to come nearer her feet. He looks up at her, cocks his head. They share a smile before his eyelids close.

The sound of a motor on the water pulls her attention toward the bay. A small dinghy filled with four people putts closer. Dark smoke rises from the motor. A man throws an anchor onto the wooden piling along the edge of the water. Hand over hand along the chain, they pull the boat closer to shore. She watches as all four figures, which she now sees are male, step from the boat shading their eyes and staring up at her. Her heart beats a little faster when they ignore the pathway and climb straight up the rocky side of the hillock, rapidly closing the distance between them and her.

By instinct, she throws her pocketbook into the basket and scoops Noodle into her arms. She stands up with a stern expression on her face. The young men plant themselves in a half circle in front of her. She takes note of their dirty clothes reeking with the smell of fish guts.

"Are you Babe?" a man with pockmarks asks.

"Who is asking?"

"Where is your brother?" the one with disheveled hair says. She recognizes him as one of the porters from the hotel lobby.

"My brother Bójǖn will be here in a few minutes. Why do you ask?"

"Give us your money!" demands Pockmark.

"What money? I have no money."

"You lie! You cashed expensive silver at the hotel," the porter says.

She chuckles. "Oh that? My brother went to spend it already on… on his own rickshaw. He is going into business." She flicks a dismissive hand at them. "You can leave now."

Pockmark takes a step closer to her. She takes one toward him—a move that surprises him.

"Babe!" someone calls in the distance, or is it the crooning of a colony of seagulls suddenly floating down from the sky? She thinks she hears her name again, but nothing is sure with the squawking and cooing of the birds covering the sand below them. *The birds smell the fish on these simpletons,* she thinks. She tilts her head to glance between the space of Pockmark's body and the two men standing beside him. She sees a woman and a man coming up the path from the hotel. Are they Wáng Hālǐ and CeeCee Davis?

Whoever they are, their arrival will surprise these thieves.

Her trained mind quickly sizes up the situation, considers solutions, seeks a way out. *Shīfu* taught her in times when she is outnumbered, all style and form is forfeited to execute a brutal self-defense, but first… try to avoid. Tricks and surprise may be needed to even the odds. Her mind flashes through several scenarios and actions. Number one, Noodle cannot be harmed. Number two, her female dress is a hindrance. Can it also aid her in this predicament?

She smiles. "I perceive I am facing strong men who will not leave until they get what they want. Am I correct?" Heads nod. Their uncertain glances at each other further prove to her they are dumb and easily fooled.

"Since I have no choice, I will give you what you ask for. Tell me, will you handsome men be leaving me all alone up here after you relieve me of my money?" she asks demurely, scanning their faces. The tilt of her head, the batting of her eyelashes, and the poutiness of her lips comes from a buried instinct, she knows not from where. It surprises her how quickly their adversarial expressions change to salty grins exposing neglected teeth. The men elbow each other, snickering.

These imbeciles will gobble up any grain I throw them, she thinks. *I am in control. I will always be in control.*

Pockmark smiles crookedly. "Maybe we will go, or maybe we shall stay and have some fun. Are you a fun girl?"

She dips her head, half-closes her eyes. "Oh, yes," she answers softly. The space between the men's bodies reveals the man and woman are coming nearer. She sets her rooster on the ground.

"What if I remove this dress so you see how fun I can be?"

The unsure looks in their widened eyes dissolve into more than the desire to separate her from her currency. With deliberate movements, she is quickly standing in her shoes and underclothing, her new dress cast aside. Noodle is lifted into the crook of her arm. The gasps and low whistles from the men do not embarrass her. She has lived as a fake boy for so long, her femininity is a tool to be used as a distraction today, nothing more. The art of *Yǒng Chūn* heralds using all of a person's wiles in an emergency.

The man and woman are now standing behind the thieves. The man is Chinese, the woman is not. Are they her saviors from San Francisco? It's a gamble, but she has to assume they are, else why are they standing so close to all of them?

"Are you ready to see more?" she teases.

"More!" the ruffians chant in unison.

She turns in a circle to distract them, turns back the other way, smiling, teasing. She steps just outside of their half-ring enclosure, and shouts in Mandarin, "CeeCee Jones, catch my rooster!" She hurls Noodle to the young woman who, hearing the girl shout in a foreign language and seeing a white ball of feathers coming at her, awkwardly throws her arms up. Incredibly, she catches Noodle, then struggles to subdue his flapping wings and pecking beak. The men, caught off guard, turn to look behind them.

"Wáng Hālǐ, these men are thieves! Fight with me!" Babe shouts. She steps closer to Pockmark, her weight on one leg, her feet positioned. She says in a loud voice, "I am not giving you my money, you ugly boy! If you are fortunate, you will escape alive."

It takes a few moments for the new truth of the situation to soak in. The louts shuffle, look confused. Henry has thrown off his hat and assumed a posture that lets Babe know he is familiar with *wǔshù*. She presents flat hands toward the group. "Just go," she says gently but firmly, looking each one in the face. "It will not go well for you if you stay."

The paradox of this situation is bordering on ridiculous. A half-naked young teen with a voluptuous body is standing in wǔshù readiness in front of four unsavory characters. I'm about to jump into a fight, and Charlotte is holding a protesting Silkie rooster, Harry thinks as he prepares for action.

Pockmark growls and draws back a hand to slap Babe. She blocks him with *Tan shǒu* and *Pak shǒu* movements so easy and beautiful they draw admiration from Harry even as he begins fighting his own opponent. The hotel porter and the man who has remained silent during the encounter watch Babe's expert moves and Harry's ease of handling their cohort and take off in a fast run along the path where Charlotte is trying to restrain Noodle. They briskly clip her in their haste. She stumbles backward, loses her balance, and screams as she falls over the short rail into the water below.

Harry and Babe momentarily freeze as they realize Charlotte has fallen into the bay. The brief interlude allows Pockmark and Harry's adversary to race down the side of the hillock on the rocky side. They sprint to their boat, hoist anchor, start the motor, and chug—black smoke and all—toward the open sea.

"You are Babe?" Harry asks, rapidly retrieving his hat off the ground.

"I am, and you are Wáng Hālǐ?" she asks, turning to wiggle into her dress. When she turns around, Harry is half way down the hill. Babe glances over the railing. The young woman appears to be losing her battle with her one-handed dog paddle, fighting the current, and keeping Noodle's head out of the deep water. She scoops up Noodle's basket holding her funds in a disguised compartment on the side and runs down the pathway.

A junket boat on its way to the harbor skims by, spots Charlotte's desperate splashes. A man dives off the boat and reaches her as she is about to go under. He pulls her through the water by her shirt collar. Noodle solemnly rides on Charlotte's chest all the way to the boat.

Harry and Babe meet on the shore and watch as Charlotte and Noodle are hoisted from the water by a woman and another man on the boat. Charlotte's water rescuer climbs aboard, and all three people huddle around her. Harry and Babe exchange worried looks. Charlotte sits up. The woman puts a blanket around Charlotte's shoulders. In a few moments, Charlotte waves at them, then raises Noodle in the air with both hands.

"She is pretty, your companion. American?"

"Yes, American," Henry says, staring at the boat. "She's been with my agency less than two years. Only twenty years old." He shakes his head and mumbles, "She will be taking serious swimming lessons when we return home."

71
Urine-Soaked Carpets

Los Angeles, California
1950

Charlotte and Pinkie
Two years after Pinkie's disappearance…

You have to give Snake Eyes credit. He really does slither into the smallest cracks of life's trashiest habitations, taxing his yellowed eyes to the limit to see through the dirt, flicking his forked tongue in and out to gather information that could never be gathered but by a miscreant such as he who fits in with the sordid, the wretched, the most dismal characters populating the seedy side of Los Angeles.

It's a stroke of genius that Harry solicited such a character as Snake Eyes to help us search for Pinkie in Los Angeles. What caused him to do it? Call it instinct, insight, or divine revelation. The fact is, in the two years since Pinkie went missing, our hopes of finding her dimmed considerably. Our spirits were renewed two days ago when Snake Eyes called Harry with the most unusual news. He said he saw a "yellow-haired" girl dressed in a black cloak slinking… is that what he called it, *slinking?* in the hallways of a tenement apartment building. Snake Eyes was there with other distasteful characters working on God knows what kind of an illicit proposition when he witnessed the strange sight.

"She ain't human, Mr. Dang…" that's the false name Harry gave to the rogue "… no, she ain't. She disappears in thin air, she does. All crazy in the eyes. Blue eyes, some of the bluest out there, I'm thinkin'. Ghost skin so white you see right through it. Curly yellow hair is springy like that Medoozal woman with them snakes on her head. Might be kin to her, I'm thinkin'. Not human. No, she shore ain't," Snake Eyes relayed to Harry in a coffee shop in downtown Los Angeles yesterday morning before receiving his payment.

"You're referring to a child and not an adult woman, correct?" Harry asked.

"Yeah. A girl. A ghost girl with yellow snake hair. Good luck getting in that place to gawk at her. It ain't easy. Got it guarded real hard. Locked down. Miz Chestney's real mad at that ghost girl 'cause she can't catch her. Nobody can. See what I told you, Mr. Dang? She ain't real."

Our quickly assembled Los Angeles team includes Harry, Bill Spruce, and another intern from Switzerland who joined us to observe and run errands. Still in my third year of training, I am also considered an intern, so I was surprised I was allowed to come along as a full member of the team.

Our strategy meeting went long this evening, and Harry took it to heart what Snake Eyes said about the building. Apparently, it's almost hidden between an old, dusty grocery store with a peeling sign and a deserted theatre. Because it's safeguarded—which gives us another shudder about what goes on inside there—we'll be bribing whoever's controlling access.

I was thrilled to be the one chosen to go inside the apartment building tomorrow to check out this phenomenon and see if it's Pinkie. I think I was picked because I was the one most upset by Pinkie's disappearance two years ago. Bill Spruce, one of our many muscle men, and Harry will wait down the street in what looks like an old Ford four-door sedan, and it is, but it's also souped-up and can go as fast as needed when needed. Of course, they'll be dressed shabbily so as not to attract attention in the slum district.

I'm wearing a two-way wristwatch. I'm supposed to give two presses to a button on the side of it if I need to be rescued from the building. It's a modern test device, not entirely reliable, and it won't work at all if I get too far away from the car with Harry and Bill inside. I kidded with Harry that the watch makes me feel like that comic book detective, Dick Tracy.

Snake Eyes said his pal told him the ghost girl *belongs* to Miz Chestney, a retired madam who uses attractive adolescent girls, teens, and women for the hustle she runs out of her apartment in that building. That alone sent icy daggers down our spines, and we prayed ardently that Pinkie had not been victimized by that woman's revolting business ventures.

I'm fluttering my eyelashes and flashing my most alluring southern-girl smiles at the one-eyed man in the hotel lobby. I lean my elbows on the counter and say, "Yes, that's right. I represent a foreign client who shall, of course, remain anonymous. He's willing to pay big-time cash for a special girl—one who's young, fair-haired, and hopefully, a bit on the wild side."

The man grins, adjusts the elastic band holding his black eye patch, runs a hand through his hair. "Uh-huh. Well, you sure are a sweet thing yourself, aren't you? I'll tell you this, they talk about a girl like that running crazy somewhere in this building. I haven't seen her so maybe it's just a load of bull.

I run my hand like a caress along the top of the counter. "Oh, you know Miz Chestney. She can fill any order, especially an audacious one like mine," I say in my heaviest Texas accent.

"Who did you say sent you?"

"Big Al. He's very good friends with my foreign client."

"Don't know him."

"'Course you do. He heads up some of those big operations on the east side. He knows all about you, handsome. Said you ought to mosey over sometime and talk to him about a better job."

"Wait a minute… is he the big shot behind the Shuester heist, Al

Cappini?"

I smile demurely and trace a finger along my lower lip. "Aren't you the clever one! Know what? He sent you a little gift." I pull a bottle of Jack Daniels and a fifty-dollar bill from an attractive cloth sack. The man's one eye widens.

"Al Cappini knows me? I never did any real big jobs. How did he, I mean, I didn't think he knew me from squat."

"Oh, my goodness. He has eyes everywhere, and he wants to see… you," I say breathlessly, pointing a manicured finger at his chest.

The glint I never fail to induce with my *siren act* now gleams from the man's eye. He licks his lips. "Listen, honey, you go on up to the third floor and get your business done. Room 319. Soon's you get done, come on back here and have a little celebration drink with me. I got me a cozy little leisure room in the back where we can have some privacy. We'll toast to, uh… Big Al. What do you say?"

I give him a promising smile and, because I know he's watching, add a wiggle as I climb the stairs. Out of sight, I quickly ascend to the third floor.

The hallway reeks of urine-soaked carpet, almost making me gag. The scent-ghosts of smoke and a thousand spilled liquors haunt the soured corridors. Examining the numbers on the doors, I nibble with no appetite the dry tuna sandwich I pull from my purse. It's a prop, that sandwich, to give me the air of nonchalance Harry wanted for me as I bargain with the ill-reputed Miz Chestney.

I can't stem the disgust I feel spying a door with number 319 barely visible through the milky film of nicotine clinging to it. Of course, *her* door, Miz Chestney's, would be the most revolting one in this scabby tenement, that is, if one were to imagine her door as a symbol of the wretched woman behind it. It gives me great satisfaction knowing Harry will immediately blow the whistle on her and her operation after our rescue operation is completed whether or not we find Pinkie.

Feeling queasy, I wrap what's left of the sandwich, which is all of it except for two nibbles, into its waxy wrapper and take a few steps back down the corridor to dispose of it in a pedestal ashtray overflowing with stobbed-out cigarette butts. I glance back at the door I dread to knock on, let alone enter. Flaxen ringlets spark across my peripheral vision—quickly, furtively, as a creature materializing only from the stains on the walls. A lump of dark cloak appears with hair springing haphazardly from underneath the hooded head covering. A small hand with fingernails crowned in black half-moons juts from the cloak and wraps around the sandwich.

A dirty face stares at me with narrowed scavenger eyes that beg and threaten at the same time. Her movements are animalistic, much like those of a squirrel dashing up a tree an inch ahead of a feral cat. The cloaked apparition turns and floats rapidly down the hallway, my discarded sandwich in her hand.

"Pinkie!" I call. The glob of black material and matted hair halts. "Pinkie, wait! I'm here to help you!"

After the brief hesitation, the girl is on the move again, swiftly, an animal with one arrow in its side desperately trying to escape the next one. As Snake Eyes reported, she appears to vanish into the wall. Where she went, I have no idea. She was there, and then she wasn't.

Unexpected tears and shakes overtake me. I know with all my heart this wild little person is our Pinkie. I also know I'll die before I leave her in this hell-on-earth place. I run to where she *disappeared* and slap the wall with the palm of my hand. Again. A hollow sound? I turn so I can keep my eye on Apartment 319. My shoulder touching the wall, my head leaning sideways, I attempt communicating with Pinkie.

"I'm so terribly sorry, Pinkie, for everything. I promise we will save you. No more lies. No more bad people. We'll never let anyone hurt you again. Are you hearing me?" Several doors in close range crack open. I stand up straight and pretend to search inside my purse, humming quite loudly. The apartment doors close.

"Please, sweetheart, many people love you. Your mama, Luka, Ivan, Bonzini, and Gina."

The rancid smell of the carpet drifting upward literally stings my eyes. I ignore it. I know without a doubt I am fighting for Pinkie's life. Everything we stand for at the agency comes down to moments like these, moments in which *ROSE* agents take a stand for the innocents in this world—the victims of the evil monsters who walk among us.

If we can't save this one little girl, what's the use of anything?

Far down the hallway, a thick woman with messy hair steps outside Apartment 319. Two men step out and stand behind her. They don't know me, so I wonder what they are thinking of a well-dressed young woman standing almost at the other end of the hallway animatedly digging in her purse. The woman goes back inside; the men don't. I'm not sure what to do, but my sorrow for the child and the tears I swipe away are making my nose run. I pull out a handkerchief and allow myself the luxury of sobbing briefly into the white linen.

A light touch on my hand, almost like a breath, and I open my eyes to peer into the bluest, saddest eyes I've ever seen. Floating inside the pain is a spark of trust so earnest it ignites my spirit like an Olympic torch. For one blink of time, Pinkie is in my arms, and then she is pulling me down the hallway as we run from the two men starting to gallop toward us.

We race to the very end of the hall and down a flight of stairs. Behind the stairway on the second floor, Pinkie jerks off a panel and pushes me inside a dark void, a space behind the walls. The short sleeve of my blouse catches on a nail. I pull loose, hearing the material rip. Pinkie is trying to replace the panel when the tip of a shoe pokes through the hole. With no time to conceal her secret place, she grabs my hand and drags me left through a narrow passage. At a dead end, we turn right.

We clip off another set of downward steps, pivot left, turn again into darkness, finding ourselves in a dim room with exposed beams. I gasp at the grotesque laughing masks, plumes, cloaks, and a jester costume hanging from hooks fastened into the wall. A black electrical wire looping through metal clips runs along a thick beam, then drops downward with a single lit bulb on its end. Cans of food, I assume foraged from the grocery store next door, are neatly arranged on a long wall shelf. I stare at a sword painted with red streaks on the blade leaning against the shelves.

"Props from the theatre," Pinkie whispers in a raspy voice. She leads us through a maze of passages, and I, quivering from being in the bowels of a slum apartment, as well as from the spider webs dropping into my hair, follow a heartbeat behind her. Our run ends in front of a heavy double door with a metal bar crossing in front of it. Pinkie throws herself against it.

"Help me! It's rusted. Stuck! I never can make it work," she cries. "It's the only way out."

The man behind us noisily crashes into dead ends and corners, signifying no one knew of this maze, at least lately, except for Pinkie. The moment it took to get my blouse unstuck from the nail was the moment Pinkie had needed to keep her secret safe. She pushes against the metal bar, beseeching me with terrified eyes to do something. For half an instant, I consider pushing the button on the two-way watch, but I doubt Harry could locate us in time to save us.

I throw my entire weight against the bar. Hit it, squeeze it, pound it with my fists. It doesn't move. We shove and grunt with all our might. My face burns from exertion. A click, similar to an ancient groan, and the bar pushes down slightly.

"Harder! Push harder!" I shout as the footsteps draw nearer.

We both scream and push. The bar gives, the door swings open onto a sidewalk. The outward thrust nearly throws both of us onto the concrete. One of the two men spies us from his lookout post at the building's front entrance. He starts running. Our other pursuer crashes through the open door right behind us, his eyes shiny with victory.

"Hurry!" I shriek, grabbing Pinkie's hand and sprinting toward the car parked down the street. Harry jumps from the car and flings open the rear door closest to the sidewalk. Bill draws his pistol and steadies his lower arm on top of the open driver's door. Seeing the gun aimed at them, our chasers halt in their tracks.

Harry, Pinkie, and I furiously leap into the car. Doors slam. Bill slides underneath the steering wheel, shifts the car into gear, peels out with tires screeching. Hearts pounding in our chests, we drive away from the long nightmare of Pinkie's life.

72
Babe Unleashed

Rome, Italy
1959

The Trevi Fountain in Rome seemed the perfect place for a reunion. The ladies felt the fountain exemplified the elements of their lives—earth, water, and fire. Would it not be fitting, even a bit ironic, to indulge their personal victories in the sunlight reflecting off a world-famous *morceau d'antiquité* in a place where civilization seems not only to have sprung, but also to celebrate itself like a drunken god languishing through the pages of art and history?

The first to arrive at the fountain is Babe. She fights for a position to better see the authoritarian Oceanus sculpture standing under a triumphal arch. She studies his face, decides it looks arrogant, and considers giving him a certain rude gesture she learned stateside a few years ago.

Now, now, that's the old Babe fighting to survive. What you really need is to peel off these irritating false eyelashes, roll up your slacks, and dip your freshly painted toes in the…

A heavy shove cancels her reveries. She stumbles, steps forward to re-balance. The tourists cloistering forward to photograph and witness the famous fountain threaten to flatten her to the ground. An arm spins her partly around like a dizzy bowling pin. A quick hand grabs at her midriff, reaching for the strap of the purse crisscrossed over her shoulder and lodges below her ample bosom. The hand pauses on her breast, then resumes tugging at her purse.

A familiar gear turns in Babe's head, something akin to hands ticking off the last seconds before a bomb explodes. She digs her fingernails into the invading hand, latches on with an iron grip. She swivels, steps close, smoothly brings a knee into the attacker's crotch. He grabs himself. She slams her other knee into his stomach, then issues a spray of hand chops to his back as he leans forward.

Am I really fighting a thief in the city of Rome? I thought my street scuffles only happened in Hong Kong.

The man falls sideways onto a woman. She screams. He cascades into the spray of onlookers' feet. Babe straddles him, her hands slapping his chest and face.

"Aiutatemi! Portatela via da me!" he shrieks.

Arms lift a resisting Babe to a standing position. The purse snatcher flips onto his side with knees drawn up. Babe places her foot on the side of his face, holding it against the concrete. A *poliziotto* pushes through the crowd and stares back and forth at the two of them. He fixes his eyes on Babe.

"Cosa é successo, signora?"

"I assume you want to know what's going on? This insect under my shoe assaulted me. Tried to steal my purse and feel my, um, my bosom at the same time."

"The *poliziotto* frowns, then blows a whistle—a high-pitched, irritating sound. Two more *poliziotti* push through the circle of onlookers. The policemen handcuff the hapless man, the effort made easier by his willing assistance. He furiously stares at *the crazy woman with the strange accent* as they lead him away.

"Mi scusi, signora, lei e' Americana o…?"

"I am an American citizen, if that's what you are asking. I also live in Hong Kong, and just so you understand, I don't put up with street crooks trying to rob me or touch me."

"No, no, of course not. *Come hai imparato a combattere in quell modo?"* The look in his eyes is admiration, which calms Babe down a few notches.

"Uh, I'm not fluent in Italian, but, listen, my friends are meeting me here any time now. One speaks all the Spanish languages and dialects, and the other speaks Italian, French, and German. I speak only English and Mandarin. That's it. Oh, a little French. If you wait a few minutes, my friend CeeCee can translate for us. Or, perhaps you know Mandarin?"

"Mandarin? *Lingua Cinese?* Oh, no, but I speak much of the English. I am curious, *signora.* I wonder how you learned to, uh, conduct yourself in such a... such an advantageous manner against this offender."

"Oh, that. It's a long story. I'm sure you can tell by my accent I grew up in the Orient. You, um, well, you just pick it up sometimes."

All these years later, Babe remains secretive, even protective, about outsiders knowing of her *wǔshù* training. She glances at her watch. "Sir... I'm meeting my friends on the other side of the fountain in a few minutes. Do you mind if I leave now?"

"Of course not, *signora.*"

"Signora? That's what you've been calling me? It means a married woman, doesn't it? I'm not married."

His brown eyes are warmer when he smiles, she thinks.

"I merely need your name before *prima di partire la nostra bella I'talia*... oh, *scusi,* I mean to say... before you depart our beautiful Italy, we will require a formal statement to press the charges against this... this terrible man who dared to assault you. Are you staying locally at this time?"

"The Inn at the Roman Forum."

"I see. May I ask how long you plan to stay at the inn, *signorina?"*

"Three days. Then we're driving to a private villa with vineyards for a week, and... hmm, I'll have to ask my friend the other places we're scheduled to visit."

"Very well. I shall be in contact with you before you leave Rome, *signorina...?"*

"Wayne. Bernadette Beatrice Wayne. That's what it says on my passport, but my friends call me Babe. I actually prefer *Wěi Bèibèi."*

"Mi scusi, I don't—"

She shakes her head. "Never mind. The Mandarin language confuses most people.

"Sono l'agente Lombardi al tuo servizio."

"Um…"

He smiles. "Officer Lombardi at your service." He touches his cap and walks away with military preciseness and a lingering smile.

Babe defiantly glares at any eyes still watching her, hand brushes her now wrinkled linen slacks, and walks through a path of people that parts as she goes forward. She spies the exact step on the side of the fountain the women agreed was perfect for their reunion. *It really needs to be vacant,* she thinks, feeling ridiculously playful. *Here's a chance to practice the few Italian words I've learned.* She checks her watch. She has time, so why not?

She runs toward the group flailing her arms yelling, *"Merda di piccione! Merda di piccione!"* She scowls toward the sky, flicks imaginary bird droppings off her shoulders. *"Merda di piccione!"* She shakes a fist at the made-up birds.

It seems no one wants to be showered with pigeon poop, or, perhaps they think she's touched in the head. In any case, the almost-private step is now empty. She stretches her legs out to redeem the whole space. A young man holding a camera bends and speaks to her in Italian. She gathers he wants to sit down. She groans, rubs her foot, smiles mischievously as he leaves.

73
Three Women in a Fountain

Rome, Italy
1959

Charlotte, Babe, and Pinkie

"Babe?"

"CeeCee!"

The women run to hug one another. Charlotte holds Babe at arms' length, smiling. "You look wonderful, Babe! Just grand! I forgot you're so tall now, like a fashion model. You must tell me what you use on your hair to make it so shiny and… wait, false eyelashes? You?"

"I have to keep up with you and our glamour-pot Pinkie, don't I?"

"Oh, my stars, never worry about that. We may need to run to catch up with you! I see Hong Kong is the perfect place for you. You simply glow."

"Any place with danger and *Bǎo Māma* is the perfect place for me, CeeCee. I love my work with *ROSE* in Hong Kong, especially fighting my way out of trouble. Bullies and criminals beware!"

They laugh together, a sound they both cherish. They sit on the steps feasting their eyes on one other.

"What a perfect fit it is, you and the *Angel of Mercy* working together to save the world. Did you ever track down anyone from that other family you stayed with?"

"The Chéns? Only enough to find out my *shīfu* Jìnhǎi escaped from China after he was released from prison. I love that because it tells me he didn't buy into the lies of the Communists. As far as the other Chéns, I don't care, I mean… they never felt like my family. I carry my *shīfu* and my dear Noodle, rest his brave little soul, right here," she says, touching her heart."

Tender subjects. Charlotte switches the conversation. "You know, I still remember the day Bǎoyīn contacted the agency. It was 1949, about a year after we rescued you in Hong Kong."

"Sounds about right. I had already been reacclimated and united with my dad and brother in Texas for a few months."

Charlotte takes Babe's hand. "I'm so sorry about your father, Babe."

"Well, he lived out his last years with his two children near, CeeCee, and that was his greatest desire. Eddie and I did everything we could to bring him joy, and I spent every other six months back in the states with him. He had an emotional breakdown, you know, after his return from China the last time. He cried so much, but we always managed to cheer him up and make him laugh. He was in awe of *The Gold Rose* and all its connections to Bǎoyīn. She was a real angel on earth in his eyes."

"She's a living legend to all of us at *ROSE*. Imagine losing your memory for almost five years and then, one day, it comes back, just like that. What a miracle!"

"Yeah, she went through so much. Seeing poor Zhēn Gāng's throat sliced open was horrible enough, but the torture she endured in prison before the invaders were completely run out of China was… unmentionable."

They are silent for a few minutes. Charlotte says, "And losing you was another blow at the same time. You and Harry were always her special lights."

Babe looks down. "I wish we could find LíngLíng for her. No trace of her, her in-laws or *Bǎo Māma*'s grandson. LíngLíng was so kind to me. I was a mixed-up kid back then. I wish things had been different."

"I know." She pats Babe's hand. "Have you been here long?"

"Long enough to beat the tar out of someone grabbing my bosom and trying to steal my purse. I'd have folded him into a Chinese dumpling if that policeman hadn't shown up. The only good thing was the policeman who came to check out the situation was good looking. Not wearing a wedding band, either."

Charlotte laughs, glad the subject has shifted to lighter subjects. "I'll bet your unusual accent charmed him all the way to his fancy Italian shoes. And that poor thief! He had no idea he was about to tangle with a Chinese-Texas tornado, did he? Nobody gets away with anything when you're around. What on earth are Pinkie and I to do with you?"

Charlotte's smile still lights the universe for Babe. With LíngLíng gone, she's the big sister she cherishes. She wets the ends of her fingers and proceeds to scrub a dirty spot on her white pants leg.

"Oh, I don't know. Maybe you should keep me around to protect you two flowers from the savage world?" Babe looks up. Both women burst out laughing.

"The day you have to protect Pinkie…"

Babe smiles sheepishly. "Yeah, well, you have to admit I'm pretty good at what I do."

"To say the least. I'm so grateful for the *Yǒng Chūn* moves you taught me. It changed my life, and that's for sure. Now… our Pinkie, she takes them down, hog ties them, and chops off their calf fries with one swipe aimed at their egos."

"She does, the little rascal! So, how is your Nantucket project coming along, CeeCee? You and your dad still doing all right?"

"Better than I ever dreamed. We're making up for lost time. I'm so excited for us—you, Pinkie, and me, and even some of our weary fellow agents—to have a peaceful place by the sea to stay when our lives need rejuvenation. Our builders are putting the finishing touches on the guest bungalows in the next few months. Don't you find the ocean wonderfully refreshing, Babe? I know I do."

"As long as you're not drowning to save a rooster at the same time, right?"

Both women laugh.

"Now… *that* was an experience. Harry made me take swimming and diving lessons from a pro for a whole year afterward. Talk about overkill, and why the diving? I think he tried to turn me into Esther Williams, but that's Harry for you."

"Yes, that's Harry."

"Babe, I have a bit of remarkable news to share with you and Pinkie."

"Really? How about telling me now, and we tell her later?"

"You don't want to wait?"

"I don't mind hearing it twice."

"Well, as it turns out, I was a rescue *assignment* of *The Gold Rose*. I found out only a few months ago. Harry told me right after Christmas this past year."

"What? How is that possible?"

"It isn't. That's why I have to write my book on the probability of the impossible becoming possible. Don't look so confused. When you think about it, all three of our lives border on the impossible. I mean, how did you cross a whole mountain range by yourself as a young teen-ager?"

"Noodle led the way."

"Sure he did, and he got you safely to Hong Kong traveling with a tribe of Persian gypsies too. He kept you from harm on a smuggler's boat and taught you martial arts in his spare time, right?"

"Of course."

"Your whole life is one big impossibility, Babe."

"I suppose you're right, but tell me how this impossible thing happened to you."

"It's crazy. See, we had a cook while I was growing up, Mrs. Cudahy, and she had two young children and one older son who had already enlisted in the U.S. Army at the time she took the job. That young man, Patrick, whom I never met, was given one of our *business cards* one evening in a bar in Dallas."

"You're kidding!"

"I'm not. Apparently, if I understand it correctly, Mrs. Cudahy told him all about me and my predicament. It seems she knew a lot more than she let on about Miss Wraith's cruel treatment toward me, but she desperately needed to keep her job. She knew Daddy was blind to any of Miss Wraith's faults, so she was afraid to go to him. Bless her heart, she poured out all her grief to her son when he came home on leave.

"Later that evening, he went bar hopping with a couple of his army buddies. When he, as Shakespeare would put it, was *deep into his cups,* he relayed the whole story to an attentive, sympathetic bartender. Of course, that bartender happened to be one of us."

"That's… unbelievable."

"And impossible, right? Well, Patrick called the number on the back the next day, told the person on the phone the details, and returned to his army life. That's all he knew of it, but the wheels were put into motion. The case was secretly investigated, and Harry finagled his way into recruiting me through that Civics class townhall meeting.

"I knew nothing of this, and the way Harry worked it due to my tender age of barely eighteen, and because the one reporting my situation was not family, nor did I have a family member he could trust, I was led to believe I was being recruited to work with them. That became a reality very quickly after Harry saw my eagerness to serve and… his words, not mine… *my reckless abandon in rescuing the helpless and lost.*"

"I don't even know what to say, CeeCee."

"Believe me, I understand. I was an *assignment* who became an international rescuer. Not unlike you, though. You, too, were an *assignment* who now works for *ROSE.* Yes, I really must write that book one of these days. I only wish I had known my story sooner, but Harry was adamant that it had to remain an internal agency secret until recently."

"Why?"

"Hon, if I understood how that man's mind works, I'd be running the world. My suspicion is that he was waiting for a reconcilement to happen between Daddy and me, which finally happened right before Christmas last year. I had to spend one lonely night in a bus station in Bangor, Maine, last December to see the truth of my life."

"One lonely night in a bus station? You're so philosophical, CeeCee. Okay, that's a story we'll hear sipping wine over dinner tonight."

"I agree… oh, wait a minute. Looks like someone's creating quite a stir walking through the crowd." She squints. "Um-huh, it's our Pinkie. There's a train of men following her."

Pinkie spies Charlotte and Babe, breaks into a run. All three women hug, jump up and down, squeal, hug again.

'Mi scusi, signorina, may I have your autograph? I know I see you somewhere. Are you Brigette Bardot's sister or…?" says a middle-aged man ogling Pinkie and falling all over himself to intrude in the space surrounding the steps.

"Aw, scoozi-baloozie! Get out of here!" Babe says, waving her arms and shooing the man and several staring males away. "Pinkie, will you please get a little *uglier* so I don't have to beat up so many men everywhere we go? They fall stupidly in love with you at first sight."

"Well, we are in Rome, the city of love…" Charlotte teases, grinning. "Pinkie, my little Pinkie, all grown up and the star of the Bonzini American-European Circus Tour. What is it on the posters… *Pinkie, the Most Beautiful, the Most Courageous, the Most Talented Elephant Performer in the World!*

Pinkie rolls her eyes. "Oh, that Martinelli. He's the greatest hype-artist in the world. Nisha and I ignore all the fuss and just have fun wowing the crowds." She looks down, then into the faces of her friends. "You know, I'm right where I want to be, and I'm doing exactly what I love. I'm even happier when we go on the road every year. It satisfies the restlessness I deal with sometimes. You know… a carry-over from my first twelve years."

"Understandable, hon. So, how are the Bonzini's?" Charlotte asks.

"Gina stopped performing a few years ago. She trains, oversees everything to do with the air performers, rigging, the high wires. She and Bonzini take all four of their kids on the road when we go. Luka, you know who he is, of course, I mean, what female doesn't? Anyway, he's now in charge of all the circus dancers, their choreography, themes, costumes, show sets. You remember I taught him trick riding last year, don't you? Turns out, with all his dancing talent, he's a natural on horseback."

"At his age?" Babe asks.

"He's only thirty-five."

"Mm-mm, he is one handsome man," Charlotte says.

"Almost makes me want to settle down," Babe says.

"Sorry, girls, he's getting married to someone he met a long time ago."

"What?" Babe says.

"Uh-huh. Her name is Victoria. She's an architect from Mexico, really nice. Smart, too. One afternoon after a performance, she came right up to him and told him who she was and said she gave him a ride in her car in Mexico City a long time ago."

Babe pouts her lips.

"Oh, stop it, Babe. You know you still carry a torch for that *Romani* guy from long ago. What was his name?" Pinkie says.

"Barde, and yes, if I could find him, I'd marry him on the spot. I had the biggest crush on him. My first one. He'd die, wouldn't he, finding out the truth? Especially since Dad confessed to Eddie and me his mother, our grandmother, was French *Gitan.* Imagine it... I'm a gypsy and a Texan and an almost-Chinese international rescuer."

"We won't hold it against you, though," Pinkie teases.

"Say, how are Clint and Angelina, Pinkie?" Charlotte asks.

"They're fun. They still act like newlyweds. I spend a month or two with them every winter, you know, depending on everyone's schedules. Their two kids always called me Auntie Pinkie, what with the age difference between us, and now, well... now, it's a fact."

No one says anything for a minute or two until her words soak in.

"What do you mean, *it's a fact?* Babe asks.

"Oh, nothing."

"You can't keep secrets from us." Charlotte says.

"I'll tell you if you promise to jump in the fountain with me right afterward."

"What? It's against the law."

"And, so...?" Pinkie says, shrugging her shoulders.

"I'll do it. Who cares? Now, confess, Pink." Babe says.

"I don't know... what about my hosiery?" Charlotte says, frowning. After the looks she receives from her companions, she says, "Oh, all right, I'm in, but plan on spending the night in a foreign jail. Don't say I didn't warn you."

"Okay, tell us," Babe says.

Pinkie taps her finger on her forehead. "I think I forgot what I was going to tell you." Babe glares at her. "My goodness, such impatience, Babe, and you being culturally Oriental and all. What is it they say in China about patience, *The fretting bird will—"*

"Pinkie!" both women yell in unison.

"Okay, okay, hold your horses. You see, my Texas parents, Mama-Lina and Papa-Clint, felt obligated to put together the pieces of my past. Mama-Lina knew from the beginning I didn't have any other family."

"How?" Charlotte asks.

"Her intuition. Listen, I don't get it, but it's real. Almost spooky. I've seen it in operation so many times. Anyway, everything was a dead end. That is, until they found Pete." She sighs and stares at the fountain. "You know, Oceanus looks bored, doesn't he? I wonder if—"

"You're killing us. Who's Pete?" Babe says.

"The new detective working on the case found him. He's my real mother's distant cousin once removed or something like that. Used to live in the little town I'm originally from. These days, he lives in a little cabin on the Brazos River—a piece of land his grandfather homesteaded a long time ago. He's old and grizzled, Papa-Clint said, but he still has a good mind. He made Papa-Clint go fishing with him before he'd tell him anything. So, there they are with their poles in the water catching bigmouth bass, an old hound dog lying by their feet, and Pete tells him the story of the baby girl who went missing so many years ago."

Babe rubs her hands together. "Now we're getting somewhere."

"It seems Grant Sutton, Clint's daddy, was what we call in Texas *a dirt-road sport,* if you know what I mean."

Charlotte nods. Babe says, "What is that?"

"Sometimes it means a country guy who dresses fancy, but in this case, it means a philanderer, a man who loves the ladies and has scads of them. That's the best way to describe Grant Sutton. Y'all know the story of the night they found me in the road?"

Nods from both women.

"Yeah, but why the biography about Clint's dad?" Babe says.

"You'll see. Oh, wait, I forgot to tell you some movie people from Hollywood are filming a John Wayne movie on Uncle Cruz's ranch in Wyoming. Not the whole picture, but several scenes."

Babe growls. "Pinkie… that's lovely, but will you please…"

"But it's so much fun making you twitchy, Babe. Oh, all right, you want to know why my no-good daddy killed my no-good mama?"

"That's so harsh, hon." Charlotte says.

"Yeah, sorry. I have a few rough edges. Circus life, you know. I suppose you can't blame my poor mama for, shall we say… seeking comfort outside of a marriage full of her husband's insane jealousy. Really, I don't. Poor thing. She married an insecure man who constantly accused her of what she eventually did. I see it as his fault.

"Anyway, my mama worked in a restaurant in the little town I'm from. Attached to the restaurant was an interesting old bar with several pieces of Texas history in locked glass cases or hanging on the walls. Pete told Papa-Clint that my mama was the best-looking woman in South Texas back then, and men always came by to gawk at her. Said she was really good for business in both the restaurant and bar."

"Gee, I don't think I've ever experienced a phenomenon like that," Babe says, rolling her eyes.

"One time, a wealthy man from San Antonio stopped at the tavern. When he went to use the bathroom in the restaurant, he met my mama, and they, uh, obviously hit it off. Long story short, it turns out that I'm the child of that woman and…" she pauses. "Clint's daddy. Grant Sutton is my daddy, too."

"What?" Charlotte says, jumping up.

"Oh, come on, Pinkie! That's impossible." Babe says.

"I know, but it's the truth. Clint Sutton, whom I consider one of my papas—Bonzini being the other one—and I are… siblings. We even have written proof from the hospital where I was born.

"My Lord in Heaven," Charlotte says, clamping a hand over her mouth.

"Mama-Lina says God put us all together that night on the dirt road when they found me, and, actually, I find it strangely coincidental myself—almost like it was preordained."

"Another impossibility…" Charlotte says in a faraway voice.

"She said Papa-Clint whooped and waltzed across the entire house when he heard of our connection."

Babe jumps up thrashing the air for several seconds, stops, grins. "The way I see it, this is the perfect icing on the cake of our peculiar lives. And now, you're a double millionaire, Pinkie."

"My, my, my," Charlotte says.

They sit in contemplative silence watching the fountain.

"Hey, how about that swim? Remember, you promised." Pinkie peels off her shoes and dashes toward the statues and writhing horses.

Lost in the weight of Pinkie's news, Charlotte and Babe slip out of their shoes and follow Pinkie into the fountain. In minutes, the sound of shrill police whistles permeates the air from every direction. The women look at one another and break out laughing.

– The End –

Acknowledgements

English poet John Donne postulated in the seventeenth century that *no man is an island.* That concept was never truer than now. *The Gold Rose* has an international setting originating in Texas and spreading into Mexico, China, Argentina, Hong Kong, and Italy, thus obliging me to consult with five language advisors, three *specific-content* experts, and an ink and brush artist specializing in Asian art. Ergo, you will find Spanish, Chinese, Italian, Croatian, and a splash of Irish words and phrases sprinkled throughout this novel. Do I personally speak those languages? No, not at all. My specialty is storytelling. Though I am an eager fan of foreign languages, I, unfortunately, am not a linguist.

Why add foreign words and phrases into one's novels?

Such a question begs to be answered with more questions. Why does one add spices when cooking? Why does an artist sign his or her name in artful swirls or in block letters signifying the type of art they represent or love? Why does a poet prefer the use of certain stanzas? Why do we choose different colors of clothing? The answer to all those questions is the same. We do it for *flavor,* for *originality*, to be *deliciously unique.*

Indeed, no man—or woman, or author—is an island.

My heartfelt thanks to…

Spanish Language Advisor, Stephanie DeSonier

Stephanie hails from Texas and lived abroad in Spain for several years. In the largest city in Southern Spain, a city famous for its flamenco dancing and architectural designs, she met a man who not only stole her heart, but also was *the one* destined to become her husband. They now reside with their two children in Fort Worth, Texas, where Stephanie works as a Spanish Medical Interpreter. She adores traveling, books, and, of course, the Spanish language.

Chinese Language and Protocol Advisor, Cyndie Panzera

When Cyndie first traveled to China in 1999, the country was still in the early stages of reengaging the world after closing its doors decades before. There were no "comforts of home" that first year while living in a classroom building of a private school next door to third grade, but the opportunities to learn the language and culture were immense. Cyndie returned to China for a second teaching experience in 2005 knowing enough Chinese language to get tasked with translating for other American teachers. That led to many amusing conversations with street vendors ending in hand gestures and laughter. Her desire to go deeper in conversations with Chinese friends led her to take two years of formal Chinese language school.

Her experiences in China, including teaching, spanned a period of twelve years—long enough, she is happy to report, for China to develop almost all of the "comforts of home." Having made herself a valuable resource for the Chinese language and culture, she moved back to the USA and began working on her PhD in Curriculum, Instruction, and Assessment. Presently, Cyndie, who happens to be Jodi Lea Stewart's daughter-in-law, lives in Arizona with her husband and their two orange-tabby rescue cats. They enjoy welcoming Airbnb guests from all over the world into their home, as well as exploring the dirt roads of the Sonoran Desert.

Chinese Language and Protocol Advisor, Wei Wei, aka Vivi Wei

Vivi was born in a small town in south China and was blessed to be raised in a traditional family rich with historical stories. To this day, she loves hearing stories from her 90+-year-old grandfather. He is a rare university graduate and high school history teacher who survived the chaos, changes, and persecutions of China in the twentieth and first part of the twenty-first centuries. Vivi, who loves to learn languages, graduated with a Master's Degree in Linguistics in 2007 and began teaching at a university. In 2012, she went to Shanghai to pursue her PhD in Linguistics, focusing on the contrastive comparison of English and Chinese Syntactic Structures.

She had a chance to be an academic visitor at the University of Manchester in England in 2016 and, while there, fell in love with freedoms she hadn't experienced in China. She and her husband immigrated to Canada the next year, adopted their poodle, Heyhey, in 2018, and now delight in their young son. Vivi is patiently awaiting travel opportunities to open up again so she can satisfy her love of exploring and learning about different cultures.

Croatian Language Advisor, Filip Stojkovski

Filip is from Skopje, North Macedonia. He and his wife currently reside in Washington D.C. where he works as a political intelligence analyst while pursuing his PhD in Political Science. Previously he worked as an advisor to the Minister of Defense of Macedonia assisting in the process of NATO accession. He enjoys spending time with his family, his rabbit Trixie, his Siberian Husky Lucy, as well as playing tennis and traveling across Europe.

Italian Language Advisor, Stacey Taylor

Stacey lived in Italy for seven years as a teacher and translator gaining experience in many diversified positions – positions that included teaching everything from second graders to business professionals to women's groups. She was blessed to have Italian ladies, Nonna Chicca and her daughter Anna, share with her their language and adoration of Italy's colorful culture. They became her Italian *family* as she absorbed knowledge of the country, its exquisite cuisine, and a genuine love of the people from every part of Italy.

A highlight of her experiences in Italy was assisting the mayor of her adopted Italian *hometown* win his bid for a seat on the Johannesburg, South African, Council by serving as his English advisor on his written Proposal. Stacey now lives in Texas with her son, loves to cook Italian food, might be defined by many as a social icon, and creates outstanding Limoncello every year in her own kitchen.

Communication Professional, Wayne Edgin

To tread through the waters of communication in the 1940s, I called upon twentieth and twenty-first century communication researcher and professional Wayne Edgin. Wayne was formerly a radioman in the United States Navy. He became my advisor for how a main character might communicate from Hong Kong to San Francisco in 1949. I had it all wrong twice, but Wayne patiently steered me back onto the right path. Wayne is currently an action-shooting competitor, an extra-avid reader, and publicly performs with a *bodhran*, a classic Irish frame drum. If that isn't enough, he is also an amateur geologist, lapidarist, silversmith, and a self-proclaimed bourbon/scotch enthusiast.

Irish Culture and Hong Kong Advisor, John Flynn

To understand the spirit of Hong Kong, as well as gain insight into the Irish culture (yes, I realize both subjects are quite different from one another), I contacted multi-faceted John Flynn, a proud Irish-American who has a wide travel history. John, a retired member of the San Francisco police, educated me that the Irish people in Ireland put a lot of stock into the county they are from as it literally defines them within their culture. He was a rich source for understanding Irish names, their meanings, and in what manner an Irish immigrant woman in the United States would speak in the era in which I was writing.

Working in the travel world before settling into law enforcement, John has a wide knowledge of Hong Kong and the electrified current of life he personally experienced there. His enthusiasm inspired me to dig deep into my writing skills to capture the pulsebeat he described. He also shared his knowledge of smugglers' boats and facts about the Islands of Hong Kong.

Martial Arts Professional, Terry Sanders

One of *The Gold Rose* main characters, Babe, becomes proficient in *wǔshù*, mainly in the art of *Yǒng Chūn,* widely known today as *Wing Chun.* Who better to consult about her *wǔshù* moves than martial-arts expert Terry Sanders? Terry studied Medieval Weapons Arts in Japan for two years, but his martial-arts career began much earlier. He served as an apprentice learning and teaching *Shorei-ryu* karate during high school. He has been the Mensa Martial Arts Moderator since 1988, which led to his being awarded a lifetime appointment as *Style Head* for *Shorei-ryu* karate.

Working in the public school system, Terry was a teacher, rifle-team coach, and once served as an administrator and teacher in the Chinle Public Schools on the Navajo Reservation. He finished his educational career as a counselor and teacher of Special Education in southern New Mexico, where he also ran a public karate school for twenty-six years. Currently, he has a private karate school at his home in New Mexico where his Pitweiler, Clint, and his Queensland Red Heeler, Aka—which means "Red" in Japanese—assist in, as well as evaluate, all of his diversified, numerous activities.

Asian Ink and Brush Artist, Bob Schmitt

Displaying a brush-art rose in the Asian style in the front pages of *The Gold Rose* seemed artfully appropriate, and luckily, one of my Chinese language experts, Cyndie Panzera, knew of a talented artist of that caliber. Bob Schmitt of Laughing Waters Studio in Minnesota created the beautiful brush-art rose for *The Gold Rose.* Bob is a brush painter and teacher extraordinaire who has been using ink and brush in the manner of Asian brush painters for more than six decades.

Bob also created the Chinese characters beside the ink and brush-art rose in the front pages. The words basically translate to *danger is right around the corner,* referring to the pages that follow. Mysterious, yes?

In his traditional Asian art, he uses ink, brushes, and Xuan paper. He also works with gold leaf and various digital creations. He bills himself as "a Chinese brush with a Minnesota Spirit." His workplace, Laughing Waters Studio, is located "a stone's throw from Minnehaha Falls in Minneapolis." He also performs as a brush artist with Taiko drummers, jazz combos, improv artists, and in multi-modal performance pieces. These amazing performances are captivatingly artistic and unique and can be viewed on his website: laughingwatersstudio.com.

Mr. Schmitt shares his multi-artistic talents via in-person classes and in on-line training. His book, *One Stroke Makes a Painting: Enso &*

Other Zen Paintings is available on his website.

Thanks to each and every one of these talented professionals. You are awesome!

About The Author

Jodi Lea Stewart is a fiction author who believes in and writes about the triumph of the human spirit through overcoming adversity of all kinds. Her writing reflects her life beginning in Texas, relocating as a youngster to an Arizona cattle ranch next door to the Navajo and Apache Nations, and, as a young adult, resuming in her native Texas. Growing up, she climbed petroglyph-etched boulders, bounced two feet in the air in the backend of pickups wrestling through washed-out terra-cotta roads, and rode horseback on the winds of her imagination through the arroyos and mountains of the Arizona high country.

At age seventeen, she left her studies at the University of Arizona to move to San Francisco, where she learned about peace, love, and exactly what she didn't want to do with her life. Since then, Jodi graduated *summa cum laude* with a BS in Business Management, raised three children, worked as an electro-mechanical drafter, penned humor columns for a college periodical, wrote regional Western articles, and served as managing editor of a Fortune 500 corporate newsletter. Her lifetime friendship with an eclectic mix of all races, seasoned cow punchers, country folks, and intellectuals, as well as the southern gentry, inspires Jodi to write historical and contemporary novels set in the South, the Southwest, and beyond.

Affiliations:
Historical Novel Society of North America
Southwest Writers
Arizona Professional Writers
Writers Guild of Texas
New Mexico/Arizona Book Co-Op

For more information about the author, visit her website at **https://jodileastewart.com/**, or visit these other sites:

Facebook Profile:

https://www.facebook.com/jodi.lea.stewart

Facebook Page:

https://www.facebook.com/AuthorJodiLeaStewart/

YouTube:

https://www.youtube.com/@jodileastewart

About Me:

https://about.me/jodileastewart

Amazon:

https://www.amazon.com/Jodi-Lea-Stewart/e/B0085YFWZ6

LinkedIn:

https://www.linkedin.com/in/jodileastewart/

Instagram:

https://www.instagram.com/jodileastewart/

Twitter:

https://twitter.com/JodiLeaStewart

Progressive Rising Phoenix Press is an independent publisher. We offer wholesale pricing and multiple binding options with no minimum purchases for schools, libraries, book clubs, and retail vendors. We offer substantial discounts on bulk orders and discounts on individual sales through our online store. Please visit our website at:

www.ProgressiveRisingPhoenix.com

If you enjoyed reading this book, please review it on Amazon, B & N, or Goodreads. Thank you in advance!

ormation can be obtained
Gtesting.com
e USA
7280223
00004B/121